D1099513

CITY OF THE SUN

SARAH BRYANT

snowbooks

LONDON

Proudly published by

Snowbooks Ltd.

120 Pentonville Road

London

N1 9JN

Tel: 0207 837 6482

Fax: 0207 837 6348

email: info@snowbooks.com

www.snowbooks.com

British Library Cataloguing in Publication Data

A catalogue record for this book is available from the British Library.

ISBN 1-905005-14-8

Printed and bound in Great Britain by Bookmarque Ltd

To Colin

Acknowledgements

Any book, but particularly one written over so many years, owes its existence to many people. I'd like to specifically thank a few of them for their efforts. First, Phil Whitbeck and Jerry Murphy, for their high-school electives on the Soviet Union and Political Science, respectively. I owe many of the central ideas in this book to them. Ted Mulkerin—who would have excelled at Institute 1—also stoked the fire early on with his interest and advice.

Colin Caughie, Sophie Smout, Ali Nimmo, Elaine Thompson, Mara Lang and Bar Purser all bravely read the 900+ page original draft, and still enthused. Heartfelt gratitude to them all! More thanks to Colin for his support, technical knowledge, plotting prowess, and willingness to talk about imaginary people at the dinner table for months on end. Mara also deserves thanks for being my advisor on all things Jewish, and, along with Colin Miller, for providing excellent information about late-stage syphilis.

Thanks to Anastasia Karpushko Cardownie for teaching me the rudiments of her language, and Anastasia again, plus Stas Kouprianov and Rabea Klatt, for supplying me with Russian words and names in a pinch. Any mistakes are mine, not theirs.

And of course, a million thanks to Gilly Barnard, Emma Cahill, and everyone at Snowbooks—the nicest people in the business!

CITY OF THE SUN

An ordinary city, is in fact two cities, one the city of the poor, the other of the rich, each at war with the other, and in either domain there are smaller ones... you would make a great mistake if you treated them as single states.

Plato— "The Republic"

PROLOGUE

Sasha looked up through the shattered ceiling. Across the square, a rim of crumbling walls still bore traces of green paint and gold leaf, and the limbs of trees in the courtyard gardens reached up like the hands of famine victims. From the violet billows of evening sky, the angel of the Aleksander Column met her look with one of mild retribution.

"It's too quiet," Sasha told the angel, drifting in a haze of blood loss and hunger and fever. It wasn't delirium. There ought to have been women calling between their cooking fires, dogs fighting for food scraps, children's whoops and shrieks as they paddled in the Moyka in the summer dusk, but there was only a recondite silence. Sasha hadn't heard anything to indicate a raid, but Dvortsovaya Square had been oddly still now for almost a day. Moreover, the midwife, who had promised to come in the morning, had never showed.

Olga had told her several days before that somebody had talked. The officials knew that she was in the city, and worse, they knew about the baby. If the delivery hadn't been so difficult, she would have been far away from Myortvograd by now. She was still too weak to travel, though, still dangerously reliant on her friends; she could only hide and hope the officials didn't come looking.

It was a faint hope at best. The Pomoshchniki—the Auxiliaries of Solntse's Platonic state—had been searching for her since Stepan had been arrested, and given the child, the Opyekuni might well be involved, too. The thought of the Opyekuni, the Guardians, filled Sasha with cold, creeping panic. She clutched the baby, who opened her eyes. They weren't the pale blue of most babies' eyes, but deep hazel, both luminous and dark. They were her father's eyes. Her fuzzy white hair stuck up from her head, giving her a comically wild appearance, like her father had looked in the morning, thought Sasha, choking over something between a laugh and a sob.

The baby blinked. The next moment Sasha heard the footsteps, the thought of which had haunted the seven nights and days since her daughter's birth. They ricocheted off the ruined walls, echoed through bereft streets. The first face appeared in the hole in the roof, flat and slick as the painted face of a mummy. The face of an Opyekun. Fear closed over Sasha like ice over a winter river. With the remnants of her own Opyekun training, she had tried to distance herself from the child, to prepare herself for this moment, but she could never have imagined the anguish of its reality. Her resolution to stay calm evaporated into wild panic.

"Please," she cried in a shredded voice, "don't take her!"

There were three of them, two men and one woman in gray uniforms with Solntse's golden sun on the sleeve. The men climbed down into the basement room, and one held Sasha's arms while the other took the wailing child. Sasha tore free, flung herself at his feet.

"Kill us both!"

The official said nothing, just handed the child up to the one waiting outside. When Sasha tried to follow, a knee flattened her and a rough hand covered her mouth. She tried to scream, and the hand clamped down harder, cutting her lips on her teeth. The woman Opyekun had opened a syringe, and the baby's wail echoed Sasha's as the needle punctured her skin. Sasha tried to tell herself that to pass this test was her daughter's only chance of surviving childhood, that she would be well taken care of, and if she made it through the training she would live free of the guilt that tormented Sasha. But the raw place left when they had torn the child from her superceded everything but the need to keep her baby from them, at any cost.

The Opyekun had taken the blood sample, and the machine was analyzing it. "Gold," she said, finally. Yet despite the rarity of such an assessment, and Solntse's greed for gifted babies, her look was equivocal.

Sasha lurched against the body holding her down, and this time she broke free. She hiked herself up and out of the room, and screamed, "Wait!" at the Opyekun who was already retreating with her child. The Guardian didn't stop. Infuriated, Sasha stumbled after the woman, ignoring the sharp pain in her abdomen. She dodged the reaching arms of the others, and caught the sleeve of the stone-faced woman holding her baby. The Opyekun turned and looked at Sasha with eyes like arrowheads. Sasha clenched her teeth and closed her fingers around the bone handle of the knife she had kept in her pocket since her brother gave it to her, when she joined the Soviet. She saw the Opyekun register the movement and willed her hand still.

"Her name is Sifte," she said softly, looking into the other woman's eyes, ignoring the man who once again held her arms. A pair of handcuffs dangled like sickles from the hands of the other. For a moment, Sasha thought the Opyekun would answer her. Then she turned and began to walk away.

Sasha took a pitching step toward her. "Her name is Sifte!" she cried, rage surging. Now she grasped the knife handle with resolve. The woman continued to walk away from her, the other officials to wait for a decisive movement. Sasha pulled the knife from her pocket, and with an animal's snarl she pounced on the retreating Opyekun, wrenched the child from her.

The baby screamed, but Sasha didn't heed it. She tore the blanket away from the small body, tilted the chin upward, poised the knife to end the tiny, hapless life—and found that she couldn't do it. Her eyes blurred with tears, she let go of the baby's chin and turned her frail forearm outward. She managed to scratch a recognizable Cyrillic "C," the symbol for the Soviet, into the vulnerable flesh before the Opyekun tore the child from her again, knocked her to the ground. With what she suspected would be her final gesture of defiance, Sasha drove the knife into the arm of the man who reached for her, and smiled grimly at the thought that now, whatever Solntse made of the child, there would always be one part of her that was beyond his reach.

PART 1

OUT OF THE SHADOWS

"Imagine an underground chamber like a cave, with a long entrance open to the daylight and as wide as the cave. In this chamber are men who have been prisoners since they were children, their legs and necks being so fastened that they can only look straight ahead of them and cannot turn their heads... behind and higher up a fire is burning, and behind the fire and the prisoners and above them runs a road, in front of which a curtain-wall has been built...do you think our prisoners could see anything of themselves or their fellows except the shadows thrown by the fire on the wall of the cave?"

Socrates to Galaucon
On the Simile of the Cave
"The Republic"

1

The April morning that Isaak 1 Dmitriev was scheduled to die was chilly and bright. He awakened at dawn in his solitary confinement cell in the Trubetskoy Bastion to the sound of the old-fashioned lock sliding out of its socket. For the first time in sixteen months, he was taken outside. His glasses had been broken long ago, so the world around him appeared only as indistinct blotches of color. Still, he blessed the light. He knew that darkness awaited him somewhere in this cheerful morning, but he had stopped fearing death. His only fear now was that he would be forced to return to the fraudulent life he had lived before his confinement.

Isaak 1 was an anomaly of the Fortress prison. Most of its inmates were Soviets or other dissidents, people who flaunted their blasphemous patronymics and family surnames as fiercely as Isaak clung to his numeric—the Institute number that proved his rank—and the surname passed to him by a teacher he'd hated. They were people who had acted openly against Solntse, doomed to the humiliations of his mock-trials and martyrs' deaths by the Kronstadt guns. They would live on in the memories of friends and comrades and feed the fire of a new generation of rebels, while Isaak would pass into the anonymity of his own making. He envied them.

Isaak's parents had been high-ranking Pomoshchniki, but his mother had also belonged to a small group of Jews who had kept their faith when Solntse declared himself Russia's secular deity, and continued to practice it secretly. Acting against all of Solntse's laws on the education of Opyekuni, Isaak's mother had sought him out when he graduated from Institute 1, in order to pass her faith on to him.

In those days, Isaak 1 had been heralded as the most brilliant political theorist to emerge since the holocaust. He had studied the war in depth, and as a boy it had been the basis for a fervid nationalism. By the age of nineteen, he had published three acclaimed treatises on Solntse's New Platonism, and he was slotted for the advisory circle. Yet a good portion of Isaak's brilliance was the openness of his mind, and he was already beginning to question some of Solntse's practices when his mother came to him with the story of her faith and the terrible persecutions of its past and present.

Perhaps if she had had more time, she would have convinced him to make a stand for what she believed in. But not long after she spoke to him she was executed for blasphemy, and Isaak toppled into a solitary limbo. His faith in Solntse was gone, but he had found no other to take its place. His theories were erased with his certainty, leaving only questions.

He landed in a tedious teaching job at Siberia's Institute 29, the smallest and remotest of the Pomoshchnik training schools. For thirty years he watched as children were fed to the Institute, chewed up and spat back out as slaves to Solntse's tyranny, all in the name of a philosophy that had never been intended as anything but an allegory for justice. Then, one cold black morning, he shot the head teacher. He pleaded guilty without explanation. He knew that no jury would ever understand what he had done.

Isaak sighed. The young Pomoshchnik who was leading him stopped by the ponderous, neo-classical façade of the Neva Gate. In the city's early days, prisoners had been picked up at the gate to be taken to the penal colonies of Siberia, or the dreaded Schlüsselburg Fortress for execution. In his fascination with Peter's Golden Age, Solntse had reinstated this use of the gate, but he no longer bothered with the labor camps, as the sub-race now carried out what had been prisoners' work. These days, a walk through Neva Gate ended in the Kronstadt quadrangle.

Isaak closed his eyes, shivered in the wind that came off the Gulf with its last rime of ice, rifling what was left of his gray hair. He addressed the silent Pomoshchnik beside him. "Gospazha, might I trouble you for some water?"

She started at the sound of his voice, and for a moment her eyes focused on his face. Then, without answering, she turned away again. Isaak sighed: a thin, almost superfluous sound that was quickly incorporated by the wind. Of course his thirst wouldn't matter much longer, but at the same time, even the simple pleasure of filling a need was now precious to him.

A moment later he forgot about his thirst and the cold as the sound of a boat's engine approached, and the metal reinforcement gates within the granite archway slid back. A small, open motorboat drew up at the quay. The Pomoshchnik pushed Isaak down the steps to the water, took the bow line from the boat's pilot, but didn't bother to tie it off, nor to help the frail man onto the pitching deck.

She merely spat the order, "Get in," and then, as soon as he was seated, threw the bowline into the boat and turned her back on it. Isaak watched her stand like that, her shoulders too high and still, under the anchor spreading like a sinister bird across the gate's gray pediment, until she was lost from his sight. Then he looked at his companions.

Three of them were men—two old and wasted, one young, with a head of thick black hair. The other was a woman; a girl really, with long, dark hair that whipped out behind her like a pirate's flag. Isaak could not make out the features of her face, but her hunched posture and drooping head told him that she was afraid.

Isaak closed his eyes, touched her shoulder and said, *"Shema yisrael adonai eloheinu adonai echad."* Though she could not have understood the Hebrew words, the girl raised her head and looked up at him with what could only be gratitude.

Hear, O Israel: The Lord our God, the Lord is One. It was the only prayer Isaak knew, but it seemed appropriate when he thought of the people who had spoken it before him, during the darkest hours of the Jews' collective history, and of the fundamental belief they maintained: that there was but one true God. He was awed, as he had been awed every day since his mother told him of a culture and religion as old as history, by the exactitude with which he believed this.

Before the girl could answer, the boat's driver, a middle-aged, low-ranking Pomoshchnik, barked, "Silence!"

Isaak smiled, for the rest of the prayer was indeed meant to be said silently. He thought it to himself: *Baruch shaem kevod malchuto leiolam va-ed. Praise be His glorious sovereignty throughout all time.*

For the rest of the journey to Kronstadt, the five prisoners stared in five different directions, but Isaak suspected that

23

they were thinking nearly the same things. He wondered how the order ran in each mind. Was fear foremost, or regret, or sadness to be leaving even as cruel a world as theirs was? Fear was the most likely for those who had not been trained to control it, and this seemed to him a pity, because it was so often misconstrued. The girl probably thought she was afraid to die, yet what she really feared was the unknown. She would no doubt choose her present miserable existence over that unknown.

The boat's engine choked to a lower gear, jolting Isaak from his reverie. It seemed only minutes since they had pulled away from the Fortress gate, yet now the turgid granite block of Kronstadt prison loomed before them, apparently suspended on the bright water. No adornment cluttered its outer walls, which pitched straight into the sea. It was this perfect connection that gave the impression that the building was floating. There was only one gate, as symmetrically clinical as the rest of the prison, and only one landing dock, which sloped down from this to the waiting water.

Four more armed Pomoshchniki stood at the end of the dock. One of them ushered the prisoners off the boat and towards the gate in the wall that seemed impossibly high when they finally stood underneath it. They were led through the gate, then a series of inner corridors, and finally out again into a quadrangle surrounded by more armed Pomoshchniki.

Nothing moved in the quadrangle, and Isaak watched as the sun rose in the white sky, topped the prison wall, and then closeted itself behind the cloud that had rolled in from the west. The cloud turned the sun's light a dirty copper color, like water tinged with blood. Isaak heard a choked sob. The dark-haired girl had begun to cry. Not knowing

24

any other words of comfort, he said, *"Shalom alechem." Peace be with you.* Not a prayer, exactly, but the only other Hebrew words he knew. This time, nobody silenced him.

A few minutes later another ragged string of prisoners filed into the courtyard through a smaller gate. One of the Pomoshchniki ordered them all against the north wall of the enclosure. Some of the prisoners moved into position on command; others merely looked up and around with the slow disorientation of the recently wakened. Only a few cried or begged. Though Isaak believed that it was best to die bravely, he found it disturbing that so few pleaded for their lives.

"Might as well try to pave the Neva with gold," he muttered to himself, "as try to rebuild Russia on a foundation of terror and apathy."

Isaak was irritated that his last thoughts should focus on Solntse's fallacies, yet he couldn't think what ought to have filled them. Perhaps this is as much as can be expected of life, he thought, wishing that he had had the idea when he still had time to write it down: a brief struggle against hopeless odds, and a ridiculous death colored by petty regrets. Now he was inches from the wall he would die against, but rather than fear he felt only further irritation at the fact that it was not smooth, as it appeared from a distance, but stained and pockmarked with the hieroglyphs of thousands of pointless deaths.

Suddenly glad that he was about to dispense with disappointment forever, he turned to face the guns. Behind its cloud, the sun hovered above the south wall. On an order from the commander, the firing squad raised their weapons, aimed, and released their safety catches with a sound like a handful of dropped coins. Isaak raised his eyes past the shrouded sun to a patch of empty sky, where a flock of gulls dipped and screamed. Finally, blissfully, he let go of words and thoughts, focused only on the birds. He waited for the crack of the guns, the reverberant thud of metal into flesh, but it didn't come. It took him a moment to draw himself back from the boundless sky, to realize that something was wrong. The firing squad had lowered their weapons, were standing in disarray as their commander argued with an Opyekun who was brandishing a piece of paper. Finally, the latter appeared to have made her point, and strode towards the line of prisoners. She stopped before Isaak.

"Isaak 1 Dmitriev?" she demanded.

"Yes," the prisoner replied, wondering if he had lost his mind or was tangled in a particularly lucid nightmare, and would soon wake in his isolation cell. This last thought was almost unbearable.

"Come with me, please."

Isaak shook his head. "But what—"

"I'll ask you one more time, and then I'll tell them to fire!"

"All right."

Isaak followed the woman as she strode back toward the firing line. As they passed through its ranks, they raised their guns again. Isaak heard the sickening reports, the screams of those who had not been killed cleanly. By the time the Opyekun shut the gate behind them, though, the courtyard was silent.

Isaak tried not to think of the dark-haired girl as he followed the Opyekun through endless, austere corridors, and finally into an office deep in the guts of the prison. The Opyekun reached into her pocket and handed something to

Isaak. It was a pair of glasses. Isaak put them on, and the room resolved into the kind of detail he had almost forgotten.

If he had not known the Opyekuni to be immune to aesthetic pride, Isaak would have suspected that this one had withheld the glasses to compound his awe. Compared with the prison's stark corridors, this room was a shock of color and texture. The walls' mahogany veneer glowed in the subtle light, picking up the wine tones in the silk carpet which had probably cost the lives, or at least the legs, of several Turkmenistani children. A row of delicate palms lined the back wall, and carefully-spaced paintings hung on the others. Isaak recognized a lesser-known Rubens, a Titian, and two Chinese scrolls which appeared to belong to a pre-Christian dynasty.

Despite the profuse opulence, something seemed to be wrong with the room, and after a few moments Isaak realized what it was: there were no windows. He didn't have long to think about this, though. The Opyekun had sat down behind a desk and a nameplate reading "Apraksina" and was looking at Isaak intently, with gray eyes that might have been beautiful if they hadn't been so cold.

"You are a lucky man," Apraksina said grimly. "The Sun has seen fit to spare you."

"Why?" Isaak asked, without apparent emotion.

"Why indeed," Apraksina said, then paused contemplatively before she continued with her answer. "I can tell you that I was against the idea, as were the rest of the advisors. However, even we do not question Solntse when he has made a decision, and he has decided that you may yet serve a purpose."

Foreboding clutched at Isaak's chest. "What purpose?"

Apraksina smiled a tight, unpleasant smile. "One you are well suited for. He wants you to teach again." Isaak shook his head. "Institute 1," Apraksina elaborated, "your own alma mater. It seems Solntse finds himself burdened with a difficult and delicate situation—a child, you must have realized, whose present instructor is not fit to handle her."

"Sub-race or super-race?"

Apraksina watched him for another moment with her predator's eyes, then said, "She's something entirely different."

"I'm afraid I don't understand. If the child is super-race, why not demote her to a Pomoshchnik school? Or if she's sub-race, do what you do with the other sub-race children who don't pan out."

Apraksina seemed amused. "It's not so simple. Like you, she is valuable to Solntse. And though she came to us from the gutter, she is not actually *of* the gutter. Besides, she herself is not causing the problems; in fact, she is unaware of them. Tell me, have you ever heard of Aleksandra Kirillovna Umanskaya? Sasha to her friends."

"She was with the socialists, wasn't she? I thought she was in prison."

Apraksina answered with another question. "How about Stepan Pierson?"

"Who hasn't heard of him?"

"The child concerned is their daughter."

Isaak blinked, drew a breath, then burst out: "But they're two of the most notorious criminals in Russia!"

"Your point?"

Isaak considered what his point actually was, then said, "I've always thought Solntse was pushing his luck to educate the sub-race behind his people's back—never mind

28

dissidents. Surely if Institute 1 knew who this child's parents were, they'd refuse to educate her." Apraksina looked at him calmly and said nothing. For the first time in a long time, Isaak felt true incredulity. "They don't know?"

Apraksina shook her head. "Only a handful of people know. Ten years ago, Umanskaya was arrested for her work with the Noviy Soviet, but she was Opyekun by birth and educated at Institute 1—until she was found unfit at the age of fifteen. After that she was sent to her mother in Solntsegrad for a short time, to wait for her reassignment. Before she received it, she ran away to her brother, who had joined the Soviet not long after he graduated as an Opyekun, and so began her illustrious career. When Solntse learned that she'd had a child, and who its father was—well, how could he ignore such a challenge? The mother was mad, tried to kill the baby when the Opyekuni came to take her. I suppose she might as well have succeeded. It would have saved a lot of argument, and some Opyekun lives as well."

"I wouldn't have thought Solntse would sacrifice Opyekuni for the sake of a child, however promising…or perverse," Isaak observed.

"She isn't just promising," Apraksina answered. "She is the most promising child we've ever come across."

"In what?"

"In everything. How well do you remember your Plato?" Isaak shrugged. Apraksina quoted, "'Readiness to learn and remember, quickness and keenness of mind and the qualities that go with them, and enterprise and breadth of vision… steady, consistent characters on whom you can rely, and who are unmoved by fear in war …'"

"So, she has the qualities of the philosopher-ruler. Others do, too."

"Mmm, yes, but she also has an interest in political history, and a flare for the kind of synthesis Solntse likes. Of course, we didn't know that at first. At first, she was only promising—but promising enough that Solntse wanted to have her trained as an Opyekun. He knew she would be easy enough to dispose of if she turned out to be useless or too much of a liability, because he packed her in with the sub-race babies. The teachers, even the venerable Alla, would never know the difference." Apraksina was watching Isaak cannily again. "To be frank, when he told the advisors of his plans, half of us wanted her dead then and there. But not all. There was a stand-off. I don't need to tell you the outcome." She looked at Isaak, as if waiting for an affirmation, but Isaak said nothing.

"The trouble is," Apraksina continued, pushing a pile of papers across her desk and leaning back in her chair, "the girl's become more valuable than Solntse could have hoped, or any of the opposition feared. She's the crux of his plans for the future."

"Which are... ?"

Apraksina was suddenly cagey again. "Not your concern. But I can tell you that as a first step, he intends for her to mastermind the purge."

"He actually means to go through with that?"

"He wants to clear the city of opposition once and for all."

"Don't you think the sub-race will fight back? There are still more of them than his hybrids."

Apraksina shrugged again. "There are four generations of their genes in our ranks now, and the sub-race is of course operating at a great disadvantage. That will be more than enough to ensure that it all goes smoothly."

"Why now?" Isaak asked tiredly.

"Solntse is old. He knows that his son might succeed him very young. He wants to clear the way for him, so to speak. Give him the best possible chance of success."

"I see." Isaak knew that this explanation was far too simple to be worthy of Solntse, but he also realized that he would never learn the truth from Apraksina.

They were both silent for a time, then Apraksina said, "Do you accept?"

"You want me to train this girl to eradicate the sub-race?"

"Solntse wants you to train her to be his right hand, and later, his son's."

"What makes you think I'm the right person to do this?"

"I don't. But Solntse seems to think you haven't yet lived up to your potential."

Isaak sighed, and for a moment wished that Apraksina had not caught the firing squad in time. Then he said, "If I refuse?"

"You'll be shot tomorrow morning."

"And if I agree?"

"You will serve your term at Institute 1—then, we'll see."

All at once, Isaak did see—that there was still a way to die as something more than an equivocal coward. He fixed his haggard eyes on the official's and said, "When will I start?"

2

At the same time that Isaak 1 was leaving Kronstadt for Institute 1, Ivan 15 Kiriyenko was walking down one of the prison's inner corridors. Painfully aware of the surveillance system, Ivan willed his steps to sound slow and casual. Finally, he reached the door to the maximum security wing, looked into the retinal scanner, and then stepped inside as the door opened for him.

At the same unhurried pace, he made his way to the surveillance station. These localized, manned stations were stopgaps for the main automated one, which was controlled from the Fortress. Gostyukin would be at the end of a five-hour shift, more than ready for a break. When Ivan entered the station, the junior guard was dozing. Ivan shook Gostyukin, and the man leapt to his feet, a look of horror on his face.

"Sir, allow me to apologize—" he began, but Ivan cut him off.

"Take a break," he said, then smiled at the younger Auxiliary. "I know; it's a boring job. Sometimes I wonder why The Sun bothers with human monitors when his automated system is perfect. Go on, I'll take your watch until Simonov comes."

"Thank you, sir."

When he was gone, Ivan left the monitor station, as certain as he could be that he was unwatched. He had studied the rotation of the automated surveillance carefully. It was supposed to operate randomly, but weeks of laborious sorting through footage had showed him that it did not. Aside from a few deviations, it tended to follow the same pattern over a period of about thirty-four hours. He didn't know for certain why this was, but his theory was that Solntse's paranoia was so great that he himself watched his high-security prisons, and that his observation followed a compulsively habitual path.

Stepan scrambled to his feet as the cell door slid back. Standing, he looked down at Ivan, who was not a short man. The thinness and poor muscle tone symptomatic of years of prison rations and inactivity made him appear awkward and unstable, but it was clear that his had once been a powerful body.

"Well?" Stepan asked, in Russian so perfect that it still amazed Ivan. Stepan's anxiety was clear in his hazel eyes and the tightness of the muscles around his jaw.

"Everything looks good," Ivan replied, unfastening the knee-locks imposed on all Kronstadt prisoners. He handed Stepan a set of metal key-cards, a visitor's pass, and the gray uniform of a prison doctor. "The monitor station is empty. I'll short out the main security system once you're out of the wing, and the key-cards will override the auto-lock. I couldn't test them, but I trust Petya to have made good copies." His briskness couldn't hide his own anxiety. "You'll have less than twenty minutes."

Stepan smiled austerely in response. He was already changing into the uniform.

"I suppose I don't need to tell you that." Ivan tried to smile, but it faltered. Stepan watched with a twinge of regret. Despite all the ways they had devised to cover their tracks, there was no doubt in his mind that Apraksina would discover Ivan's betrayal, and there could be none in Ivan's.

"Come with me," Stepan said as he buttoned the smock-like coat over the white shirt and gray trousers. "Your knowledge of the prisons would be invaluable to the Soviet."

Ivan smiled his sad half-smile, shaking his head. "I don't have the stomach for intrigue. Helping you is the greatest thing I have ever done, but I don't think I could do it again. Now, you must go." He held out his hand, in the Western fashion. Stepan shook it, then followed him out of the cell which had been his home for the past nine years, disguising his limp as best he could. It was the result of a break that hadn't healed properly, and it would be the giveaway if anything would.

They passed down the aisle of cells to the door through which Ivan had entered the wing. Ivan put his eye to the scanner, and the door opened onto another corridor. Stepan passed through without looking at Ivan again.

He kept to his measured pace, but with difficulty. Ten feet, then twenty, then thirty passed and nothing happened. At forty, he began to worry. The override which he had devised from Ivan's descriptions of the security system should have worked by now. He wondered whether Ivan had done something wrong, whether there was a safeguard in the system that he hadn't anticipated. But that couldn't be. The program was American, and he himself had helped to design an early version of it. Underneath his fleeting conjectures

34

was another, like an ugly secret: that Ivan had set him up, that behind one of these doors was a carefully-set trap.

On the heels of this thought, the lights cut out. As the system failure alarms began to sound and the stark, white emergency lights came on, he ran as best he could to the end of the hallway, then turned away from the elevator doors toward the smaller door that led to the stairs. He shuffled the metal cards, located the right one, and slid it into the lock. The door opened with a faint suck of air onto the dimly-lit stairway beyond.

Stepan crept up the first staircase to the ground floor and passed silently into the main corridor. This was also deserted, but somewhere on this floor other guards would be patrolling. He had almost reached the exit to the courtyard when he heard the precise, unmistakable click of Pomoshchnik boots heading in his direction. He considered running, but he knew that he wouldn't be fast enough, and that the limp showed more plainly when he ran. So he composed his face and turned, presenting the two Pomoshchniki with a calm smile.

"Problem with the security system?" he asked them.

"Looks that way, doctor," the younger one answered. She had round, gray eyes and red hair, a face that looked ready to smile. She wasn't cut out for the job, Stepan thought. Solntse was scraping the barrel.

The other Pomoshchnik was older, more obvious in his vocation. "I'll need to see your I.D.," he said.

Stepan handed him the pass that Ivan had forged, which made him a visiting prison doctor from Arkangelsk. The man squinted at it for a few minutes, then he said, "I'm going to have to ask you to come with me. There's a routine check when the system goes down."

35

"I'm late," Stepan answered curtly. "My transport is probably already here."

"Procedure," the Pomoshchnik returned. The other one, the woman, gave her partner a questioning sideways glance. It was almost imperceptible, but it was enough.

"I'm afraid I don't have time for procedure," Stepan said, and pulling a gun with a silencer from his pocket, he shot both officials before they could think to react.

He ran the rest of the way to the courtyard door without looking back. Its smooth metal surface was forbidding, but he willed himself calm as he slipped the key-card into the slot in the wall below the disabled scanner. Nothing happened.

With growing apprehension, he tried all of the cards in the slot, but none of them opened the door. Now he could hear more footsteps approaching. He saw that there was a small crack where the two sides of the door met: it hadn't closed properly. He slotted his fingertips into the gap, and pulled. The sides inched apart. The footsteps sounded louder, and beneath them, in his mind, the voice of his first firearms trainer played a paranoid loop: bullets fired from an automatic weapon carry one mile in full…forty yards with accuracy…and with one monumental shove, the door was open.

Once through, Stepan slipped the card into the slot on the opposite side. The door shut, and there was a nearly-inaudible click as the bolts slid into place. He ran across the courtyard. Heavily-armed Pomoshchniki stood at attention every ten feet along the wall. None had noticed him yet. As Stepan watched, the shock field came on, forming a nebulous ring outside the ring of Pomoshchniki. The eerie blue glow extended six feet above the top of the wall; typical overkill,

Stepan thought with a mixture of disgust and professional admiration.

Composing his face once more, he strode purposefully toward the gate. There were guard houses on either side of it, each with two guards standing outside of them. They watched his approach, not yet with suspicion but without welcome. He saluted them. "Long live The Sun," he said, and they saluted him back. He handed the ranking official his visitor's pass and the forged orders to open the gates. The Pomoshchnik looked at them carefully; too carefully.

Finally, he said, "Order declined."

Struggling to keep the annoyance from his face, Stepan said, "On what grounds?"

"There's been an incident. No one is permitted to leave until the matter has been cleared up."

"But sir—" he persisted, with the beginnings of desperation.

The Pomoshchnik leaned towards him, and now there was distrust in his eyes. "Do I know you?" he asked.

"I don't think so," Stepan answered. "I'm here on a research project from Arkangelsk."

"Name?"

"Dr. Molokov," he answered. Molokov was indeed the name of an Arkangelsk prison doctor scheduled to be at Kronstadt on a research mission. He bore a striking resemblance to Stepan—or he had, before the Soviet had kidnapped and killed him. "I believe my transport is waiting. You'll find all my papers in order."

"I'm sorry, Dr. Molokov, but—" the guard began, raising his radio. Stepan shot him before he could finish the sentence. He killed two more as seamlessly as he had the ones inside, but the fourth managed a shot of his own before he fell. His bullet grazed Stepan's temple, and he felt the blood begin to course down the side of his face. He was furious at this, not because the man had come so close to killing him, but because the wound would make him much more noticeable. He relieved the dead guards of their extra ammunition, typed in the override code to open the gate, and was off into the night before half of the Kronstadt Pomoshchniki were aware that anything was wrong.

*

"How could you have let this happen, Kiriyenko?" demanded Apraksina. She was pacing the floor of her office, her pallid, predatory face contorted with anger. The sun insignia on her gray jacket gleamed garishly under the emergency lights.

"He slipped between the cracks," Ivan answered with admirable composure.

"There are no cracks in Kronstadt." Apraksina narrowed her eyes and scrutinized Ivan. "You were in the wing at the time. Gostyukin tells me you spoke to him in the monitor station. If this is true, then how did you fail to see Pierson leaving his cell?"

Ivan knew that the worst thing he could do was fail to answer promptly, but his mind was suddenly blank.

"You are withholding information, Kiriyenko," Apraksina said with sudden gentleness, though Ivan knew that somewhere in its layers, the anger was wadded like a knife in velvet.

Ivan looked straight ahead, his face unreadable. "Ma'am, by the time I was aware—"

"Yes, of course. While we're on the subject of awareness, I assume you are aware of the punishment for treason?"

"Of course." It came out in a ragged attempt at an even tone.

Apraksina's face twisted into a derisive smile. She looked at Ivan for a time with the same false gentleness before she asked, "Have you been to Schlüsselburg Fortress, Kiriyenko?"

Slowly, Ivan shook his head.

Apraksina's smiled widened. "Perhaps you'll learn something, then, before you die." She turned to the eight Pomoshchniki who stood waiting in two parallel lines along the side walls of her office, faces blank and rifles cocked. "Take him to Schlüsselburg to await his trial," she said to them, lingering over the last word as a snake might its trapped prey.

As the Pomoshchniki led him away, Ivan held his head defiantly high. Though he hid it well, his dread increased with every step, not so much because of the impending punishment as the fact that they had caught him so effortlessly. He felt as if he'd awakened from a long, pleasant dream to a horrifying reality. Stepan had been a fool to think that escape from Solntse was possible, and Ivan had been a fool to believe in him.

Yet if Ivan could have seen what happened in that office once Apraksina was alone again, he might have regarded his fate differently. For the first time since Solntse had put Stepan Pierson's daughter into Institute 1, Opyekun Apraksina indulged in a display of rage. She pounded her desk with both fists five times, and then sat still, glowering at the far wall. She thought of the years she and the others had spent tracking Stepan, and the elation they had felt when they finally captured him—an adversary truly worthy of an Opyekun. If Solntse hadn't so enjoyed the mind games of the trials to which he subjected his most notorious prisoners, the man would have been dead by now.

Instead he was free again. Apraksina had no doubt that she would bear the brunt of Solntse's anger, and if she was not sent to Schlüsselburg for it like that fool of a Pomoshchnik, then the responsibility of finding Stepan again would certainly fall to her. It had been hard enough the first time, when Stepan had been young and relatively naive. Now he knew too many of Solntse's secrets; he knew what he had to fear. He would be on guard, embittered, perhaps worse when he learned what had happened to his wife and child. Apraksina did not deceive herself into thinking that the task would be anything but onerous.

The rage rose again, threatened to master her. She couldn't breathe, the walls themselves seemed to be suffocating her. She shoved out of her office and into the corridors. Finally, she located a window. She opened it, leaned out into the cold night. The wind off the Gulf cleared her mind, and in the place of the haze of fury, a different kind of idea began to grow.

One of the newer Pomoshchniki found her there several minutes later, staring out into the dark night with a strange smile on her face. "Ma'am—" the boy began tentatively.

Apraksina left the window and regarded the young man in front of her. "Yes?"

"I only wondered…would you like help in calling a search?"

Apraksina smiled. "That won't be necessary."

"But the prisoner—"

"We will find him."

40

"But without a search—"

"There is more than one way to catch a rat."

Apraksina smiled indulgently at the young one's eagerness, elated by the brilliance of her own idea. Properly executed, it would not only eradicate Stepan Pierson, it would mean the end of the Soviet's plotting, and as an added bonus it would provide the perfect use for the socialist brat Solntse insisted on keeping at Institute 1. The Opyekun had forgotten the boy in front of her. Her mind was on Solntse, the awards she would no doubt receive for conceiving such an innovative idea—one which would play right into her leader's taste for perversity, as Dmitriev had so aptly and blasphemously described it. This would be far better than any twisted trial Solntse could have devised to break Stepan Pierson's mind. This plan would break his very soul. And then she could retire in style, perhaps in the south…

"Stepan Pierson won't go far," she finally said, remembering the young Pomoshchnik, who was still looking at her with apprehension. "In fact, I think he'll go no farther than Myortvograd."

"Should we move on the Soviet?"

"No."

"But surely with their help, he'll escape. If he goes back to America—"

"He doesn't want to escape, certainly not to America. Or he won't once he finds he has a debt to settle with Solntse." Her eyes gleamed like a gambler's who'd just been dealt a flush. "Stepan Pierson has a weak spot that even he isn't aware of—yet." Apraksina's smile blossomed, and for a moment, was almost benign.

3

The day that Isaak 1 Dmitriev came to Institute 1, Sifte
was last in line for the showers. Everyone was gone from her
dorm by the time she was finished, and then she found that
her screen was missing from her locker. She didn't actually
need the screen for class that day, but she had used it to write
out her latest punishment, a four-page essay on a quote from
The Republic:

*"We are left with the question whether it pays to act justly
and behave honorably and be just irrespective of appearances,
or to do wrong and be unjust provided you escape punishment
and consequent improvement."*

She had earned the punishment for being three minutes
late to her first class the previous morning. She looked for
the screen for a few halfhearted minutes, knowing that she
wouldn't find it. Sifte was always meticulously careful of her
things. Someone had taken it, and she had a good idea who
it had been.

The last bell was ringing by the time she left the dorm. Sifte
sprinted up the dark green line painted on the cement floor,
which designated the area as Level 5, the ten-year-olds'. It
was an uphill battle, as the central corridor was an elliptical

helix that climbed steadily around a core of elevator tubes from the bottom floor of the Institute to the top. Soon Sifte was breathless, and wondering why she bothered running. Long ago, Gospazha Maria had re-programmed the scanner on the classroom door to reject Sifte's scan if she was late. Her only hope now was that Aleksei had desensitized the lock so that she wouldn't miss the class itself. If she missed one more she would be back on probation; two more times on probation and she would be expelled from Institute 1.

For a moment, she entertained a fantasy: she would keep running right past her classroom, past the weapons practice console and the cafeteria with its terrible, tasteless food and all the other parts of the building she hated, until she reached the few feet of roof that weren't submerged in the freezing waters of the Gulf. She would wait there in the fresh air and the sun until the teachers came and expelled her. A few times she had even started to carry out this plan, but in the end she always thought of Mila and Aleksei, and turned back.

Yet when she arrived at the classroom she found that the door wasn't locked, or even closed. Gospazha Maria wasn't there. Sifte slipped into her seat between Mila and Aleksei, ignoring the smug smile Tanya cast at her from the front row. There was a screen-shaped bulge in the left breast pocket of Tanya's jumpsuit. Sifte decided to deal with it later; instead, she looked at her terminal. There was a message on it reading: Trigonometry Test Today.

"Did you know there was going to be a test?" Sifte asked her friends.

"Of course," Mila answered, her blue eyes sympathetic and mildly disbelieving behind her thick glasses. "Gospazha Maria told us at the beginning of class a few days ago. It was—oh, it was the day you were late. She never told you?"

Sifte glowered. She knew that she could do the work on the test even without having studied, but the fact that her teacher had purposely kept her ignorant infuriated her. Adult footsteps sounded in the corridor outside, and Sifte's stomach sank. It wasn't Gospazha Maria who entered, though, but Gospazha Alla, Institute 1's head teacher. She was a gaunt-faced, middle-aged Opyekun. Sifte was sent to her for discipline fairly regularly, but the headmistress had never come to their classroom before.

Gospazha Alla walked to the front of the room and looked out at the class, which had stilled in anticipation of something extraordinary. "Children," she said, in a shrill voice, "I am here to tell you that your teacher, Gospazha Maria, has had to leave Institute 1."

A wave of muttered surprise moved across the room. Neither Sifte nor her classmates had ever heard of a teacher leaving Institute 1. Teachers were specially-trained Pomoshchniki, or occasionally Opyekuni, required to sever all contact with their friends and to pledge not to take partners in order to devote themselves to training the next generation of officials. Most stayed at their schools until they died.

"Her skills were required elsewhere," Gospazha Alla continued. "It isn't common, but this type of thing does happen sometimes in a teacher's service to Solntse. We already have a new teacher for you, who I'm certain will live up to the standards set by your last." Let's hope not, Sifte thought. "He will be arriving this afternoon."

Sifte was suddenly elated. Her teacher had been the one person in her small world whom she truly hated. Worse, Institute teachers traveled with a class through the lower and middle academic levels, until the students branched into

44

individual concentrations in the upper level and the teachers started at the beginning again with a new group of six-year-olds. Sifte had often wondered how she would possibly make it through another four years with Gospazha Maria.

"You are to go to your dorms and study until lunchtime," Alla continued, already moving in the direction of the door again, as if the children made her uncomfortable, "after which you will return here, to meet your new teacher."

The class sat in stunned silence for a moment after Alla had gone, and then they all began moving at once, talking excitedly to one another. Sifte slipped out of her seat and into the corridor. In a moment, Mila and Aleksei caught up with her. They walked toward the dormitories together for a few silent moments, Mila on Sifte's left, Aleksei on her right. They made an odd group: Mila small and frail and soft-featured; Sifte tall and reed-thin and colorless, except for her hazel eyes; Aleksei taller still but dark as Sifte was light, with even Arabic features and the determined eyes of the persecuted. Finally, Mila broke the silence with Sifte's own thought:

"It feels like this isn't real. It's like a dream, and we're going to wake up any minute." Her heart-shaped face was troubled, and she was anxiously twisting the end of her dark-blond braid around her hand.

"It's the best dream I've ever had, then," said Aleksei, his own black eyes glowing with excitement.

"Lyosha!" Mila reprimanded.

"Don't 'Lyosha' me. Why should I be sorry? She was a bitch."

"She wasn't that bad," Mila said.

"Not to you."

Mila looked to Sifte for support, but Sifte shrugged. "Sorry, Milyonka, I have to agree with him on this one. She wouldn't have cared if one of us failed and got sent away, so why should we care when she does?"

"Do you really think she wouldn't have cared?" Mila asked.

"Well, maybe she would have missed you." Sifte squeezed her friend's hand. "But me and Lyosha—well, she never liked us. She gave us bad marks and punishments when we didn't deserve them, so why should I miss her?" Sifte paused, then added, "I guess I do feel sorry for her, though."

"Why?" asked Mila.

"Because when you do something nice for someone you feel happy, and when you're mean you don't. Gospazha Maria never did anything nice. She must have felt unhappy all the time."

"She deserved it," Aleksei grumbled, then his face brightened again with inspiration. "But if you don't know what it's like to be happy, do you even know that you're unhappy?"

This idea captured Sifte's imagination as well. She wondered how many good things she didn't know about because she had never had reason to try them. She wondered whether the way she felt right now was actually bad, but she didn't know it because she had never felt good. But then, she wondered, were bad and good only ever relative to something else?

"Do you think it's true?" Sifte asked, breaking her own reverie.

"What?" asked Aleksei.

"That she was needed somewhere else? Why couldn't they send a new teacher wherever she went?"

"Maybe it was something else," Mila said.

"What else could it be?"

"Maybe...maybe it was an emergency with an old friend. Maybe he was sick and he needed somebody to take care of him."

Sifte smiled at Mila's tenuous altruism. "Teachers don't have friends."

"Everyone has friends," Mila rejoined.

"Teachers have to give them up when they come here."

"Besides," said Aleksei, "why would they lie?"

"Maybe she did something they don't want us to know about," Sifte answered. "Maybe teachers can fail and get sent away like we can."

"But how could she have become a teacher in the first place if Solntse knew she might fail?" Mila persisted. "And we saw her every day. We never saw her fail."

Sifte didn't have the heart to answer as she had been thinking—that perhaps Gospazha Maria's disappearance had to do with her very mistreatment of them, and where it might have led. Despite her earlier fantasy, Sifte didn't really want to be expelled from Institute 1, and even her enemies would have admitted that she was far too gifted for such a disgrace. Yet Sifte knew that that was just what Gospazha Maria had intended.

Sifte sometimes wondered where her teacher's antipathy for her had originated. It seemed to go beyond ordinary annoyance at a student's faults, or even personal dislike. Besides, Gospazha Maria had had no legitimate reason to find fault with her. Sifte was always polite, always completed her work to the highest standard, and if she was sometimes late or forgetful, she wasn't more so than the others. In the end Sifte's conclusion was the same as always: there must be something wrong with Sifte herself that Gospazha Maria had felt her unfit to become an Opyekun.

"I don't know," Sifte finally answered. "Never mind." But she caught Aleksei's eye over Mila's head for a moment, and was disturbed to see that he looked worried, too.

"I wish we could leave," said Mila wistfully. "I know we're lucky to be here, and of course Solntse knows what's best for us...but it's so ugly." She looked despairingly at the green stripe on the cement floor. It screamed in protest to the dismal gray background.

"Not all of it's ugly," Sifte reminded her. "You like the greenhouses, and the art gallery, and anyway it's better than the land. At least here there are no diseases and radiation, or crazy sub-race gangs trying to kill us."

But Sifte's words weren't entirely sincere. She didn't remember a time when she hadn't seen the concrete walls of Institute 1 as a barrier, or the thick windows framing black water as sinister. Like Mila, she dreamed of the outside world. She longed to feel real sunshine, not the brash, unnatural light that came from the sunlamps in the greenhouses where they were sent to play every second afternoon. She dreamed of the limitless—trees that towered above her, expanses of grass or sand or water that stretched unbroken to the horizon, nights not made of uniform, institutional dimness, but true dark broken only by stars or moon.

"There aren't in Solntsegrad, either." Mila sighed. "I wish we were already there."

"We will be someday," replied Sifte.

"But it's so long to wait..." Nobody answered. They walked the rest of the way to the girls' dorm in silence.

Most of the ten other girls with whom they shared the room were huddled together talking with anxious faces. Sifte and Mila's bunk was on the right side of the dorm's window. Sifte jammed a pillow against the corner of the window the bunk overlapped, then flopped down on it and stared up at the wire mesh that supported Mila's mattress above.

Mila was Sifte's only girl friend. Sifte saw the other girls as silly and petty and not worth her time, or too hardened by the ostracism of their peers to respond to any overture. The teachers did nothing to stop the warfare of the cliques, even when they ganged up on solitary children. Everyone knew that these experiences were as much a part of their training as math or language.

Of all the cliques in the lower school, Tanya's was the most powerful. Now Tanya came over to Sifte's bed and stared down at her with contempt. She was the stereotype of childhood perfection, with bright blue eyes and hair the same silvery-blond color as Sifte's, though it was much thicker.

"Too sad to do anything but stare at pee-stains?" she asked with blatant sarcasm. "Don't you care that Gospazha Maria's gone?"

Sifte knew that anything she said would be wrong, so she kept her mouth shut.

"Sifte doesn't care," Tanya announced. "She probably wanted her to leave."

Sifte stared at the wire supports of the top bunk and willed Tanya to shut up.

"I bet Gospazha Maria knew a secret about Sifte so bad they would have put her in prison for it. Why else would Sifte have hated her so much?"

Sifte knew that Tanya didn't really care about Gospazha Maria, that she was probably only harping on about her now because she was worried that she wouldn't hold the same privileged position with their new teacher. However, this taunt touched too close to her deepest fear. She sat up and fixed Tanya with narrowed eyes.

"What did you say?" she asked.

Tanya seemed to hesitate for a moment, then she spat back, "It's obvious there's something wrong with you!"

"Only someone as mean and twisted as you would say something like that."

"I've heard you say worse about Gospazha Maria. Maybe you got them to take her away, you and your darkie boyfriend, izmyennitsa!"

Tanya turned to her subjects for affirmation, but they recoiled from her. *Izmyennitsa*, traitor, was the worst slur among Institute children. In fact, it was one of the few such transgressions that the teachers would punish. Opyekuni were meant to be communally minded, and the solidarity of their collective faith in The Sun was more important than anything else they would learn at the Institute. Though teachers were more than ready to listen to one student's private accusation of another, a public one was seen as detrimental to the collective faith, and so equally seditious.

Sifte's face set in a menacing calm. "What did you call me?"

Tanya's eyes flickered uncertainty, but she answered defiantly: "I said you're a traitor, the child of traitors!"

Sifte could almost respect the spirit, but she couldn't forgive the slight. "You don't know anything about my parents," she said with dangerous softness, surprising herself with her need to defend people she couldn't imagine and would never know.

"Only traitor parents give their children foreign names," Tanya said coldly, with an insidious softness of her own.

"Only traitor parents would have a child with a socialist brand on her arm for everyone to see."

Sifte wasn't sensitive about much in her appearance, but she hated the C-shaped scar on her arm. Though she would never have admitted it to anyone, she, too, had worried that it might refer to the Soviet. In the shocked silence of the room Sifte leapt up, reached out with a swiftness that caught even herself by surprise, and grabbed hold of Tanya's hair. She twisted it in her fingers and jerked it hard. When Tanya stumbled backwards, crying out in pain and surprise, Sifte grabbed her arm and twisted it behind her.

"Take it back," she commanded. The other girls watched with a mixture of horror and fascination.

"Let...me...GO, you little bitch!" Tanya shrieked, struggling, which only twisted her arm more violently.

"Not until you take it back!"

Tanya's disbanded followers avoided each other's eyes. Tanya had her own eyes closed and her teeth clenched against the pain as Sifte twisted her arm harder.

"Take it back!" Sifte snarled.

Tears began to form at the corners of Tanya's eyes; the children watched with unwavering attention, to see if she would fail herself by giving in to the urge to cry. To show such weakness was a terrible disgrace, a failure not only of oneself but also of Solntse.

"Please, let go," she said.

"Not until you take it back."

Tanya's silence meant that she was trying to hold onto some vestige of dignity, and again, Sifte saw something respectable in this. Yet she could also see that Tanya was rapidly losing self-control.

Finally, the pain was too much for her to bear. "Stop!" she sobbed, "Please, stop! I take it back!" Sifte let her go. Tanya stumbled back into her group of followers, who parted around her. She glared at Sifte, who noted with delight that there were ugly red blotches on her face. "You little bitch!"

"You started it," Mila retorted before Sifte could. "You called her—that."

"Shut up, Mila!" Tanya spat, like an angry kitten. "You won't even fight your own battles!"

"All of you, shut up! I've heard enough of your bitching to last a lifetime!" This came from a dark-haired, thin-faced girl called Anastasia. "Do you want me to get a teacher in here?" Tanya flashed her an icy look, but she finally kept her mouth shut. She lay down on her bunk facing the wall, and she wouldn't talk to any of the friends who timidly attempted to comfort her.

Sifte looked at Anastasia. She was of the tougher variety of children, shunned and tormented like Aleksei for her dark coloring. Her face was unremarkable, but her dark eyes were quick and sharp.

"I meant it," Anastasia said. "You're as bad as she is if you rise to her bait."

Sifte smiled at her, with the sudden brilliance of one who doesn't smile often. "You're right," she said. Anastasia shrugged, and resumed her reading. Sifte turned to Mila. "Library?" she asked. Mila nodded, and together they left the dorm.

4

There were three parts of Institute 1 where Sifte didn't feel like a prisoner. The first was the games room, or more accurately Cave, the only game that Sifte hadn't solved long ago. The second was the film room. Sifte was fascinated with the pre-war films, and would spend hours watching them over and over again. They were only short clips: pieces of television dramas, news reports, advertisements. Most were silent, and though she didn't know it they had all been carefully selected to cast pre-holocaust society in a sinister light. Nevertheless, Sifte would have given anything to spend a day in that world, to see what it had really been like.

During class time, both the games room and the film room were off limits, which was why she had suggested the library to Mila. At two levels high, the library was the largest of the common rooms. Most of the books were stored on hard drives or disks for hand-held screens, but there were also thousands of printed volumes. Sifte liked these tangible books best, particularly those on holocaust or pre-war history. It was rumored that the library even held some books printed before the war, which only the White Level students were allowed to use. Sifte didn't even dare to dream about these. The shelves were protected like the Institute's doorways and elevators with retinal scanners to check for access permission.

The library was nearly empty when Sifte and Mila arrived. There were a few upper-level students scattered around research tables, and a Red Level class with their teacher having a lesson in the far corner. A small, graying teacher hunched over one of the terminals. Sifte didn't recognize him, but she assumed that he was one of the reclusive specialists who taught the upper levels.

Mila went off to the science section, but Sifte wanted a history. She was half-heartedly surveying the bound books to which she had access, all of which she'd already read, when she noticed a slim, unfamiliar volume in the bottom corner of one shelf. All of the other books in the section had their titles stamped on their spines in clear block letters, but this one was blank. The cover was also blank.

The binding creaked when Sifte opened to the fly-leaf. She blinked at two blank pages, unheard of in Russian books printed after the holocaust, when paper became so scarce and expensive. The third page bore the title: nine letters of the Roman alphabet, printed not in the heavy, utilitarian font of the books Sifte was used to, but in a tall, artistic one.

Sifte spoke and read English fluently, but she was so surprised at finding such a book on shelves she thought she knew inside-out that she had to stare at the letters for a long time until they resolved into something meaningful. F-O-L-E-Y-S-W-A-R. Foley's War. Below the title were the name and address of a publisher in London. Sifte knew that she shouldn't even be holding the book, but her greed for knowledge outweighed her fear. She took it to a secluded table and began reading, not noticing that the unfamiliar teacher at the terminals was watching her intently.

It was a history of the political lead-up to the Third World War, but its similarity to the others she'd read on the subject ended there. It was presented from the Western point of view, specifically that of the U.S. president at the time of the war, Elisa Foley. Sifte didn't know much about President Foley. Like her peers, she had simply been told that the president had been the puppet of a corrupt alliance of Western nations that wished to destroy any foreign power that threatened to match its own.

Yet this book claimed that President Foley had done everything she could to prevent the war with Russia. In the end, of course, she had failed, through a web of circumstances too complex for Sifte to engage all at once. It was too different from what she had always been told, particularly the ending, which described the President's resignation the day before the bombings. Sifte had been taught that Foley had given the order to bomb Russia.

Sifte put the book down, deeply troubled. Though the war was many years distant, it was all too real to her. The Institute owned a few clips of the bombing of the old capitol. Upon entering the first academic level, every child was made to watch them. It was meant to cement their nationalistic spirit, but Sifte still had nightmares of the dark cloud blooming from the city on its stem of fire, curling under and spreading like a deadly lily that swallowed the sky. When the cloud dissipated there was nothing left. Where the city had sent its jagged teeth up from the earth, there was only a level plain of coagulated lava and glass, with a few tenuous ruins slanting from its surface. Then the fallout would begin, fine golden dust first, then darker particles and ash like negative snowflakes, and the film would flicker out.

Once, Sifte had played the clip in reverse, so the cloud funneled away like an evil genie and the city sprang up in its place, but this didn't erase the images of destruction, nor her fierce hatred of the country that had caused it. Now she was conflicted. She still thought of President Foley as a monster who had destroyed her country, but she found that she could not think of the book's main character as such. Most disturbing of all, Sifte found herself wondering what had happened to Elisa Foley, who had made the fatal decision in her place, and how she had faced its consequences.

Sifte stared at the title page as if the Roman letters could solve her dilemma. It was only then she realized that no author was credited. Among the small print of the publisher's information, Sifte found the word "anonymous." Without a name. Why, she wondered, would the author of so accomplished a book want to go unnamed? She closed her eyes, flipped through the pages in her mind. It was a trick she used during exams, which also sometimes helped to clarify difficult things she read. This time it didn't. She picked up the book again and thumbed through it. As she turned the last blank leaves a piece of old paper fell into her lap. It was folded into quarters and yellowed by time. She opened it carefully.

It was a drawing in black ink, except for a dark red sun rising or setting behind the buildings. Though they had not seen it in person, every child at Institute 1 knew the skyline of Solntsegrad from pictures. The drawing was accurate, showing the wall, the roofs and spires rising above it, and the Peter and Paul Fortress in the foreground. The spire of its Cathedral, the seat and symbol of Solntse's power, split the sun's red disk in half. An inscription in the lower right-hand corner read: "To Elisa, From Charlie."

Elisa had been married to a man named Charles. Sifte didn't know what the drawing meant, or even how Charles Foley, if he were Charlie, could have owned a picture of a city that didn't yet exist. She only knew she couldn't let some unknown teacher find it and file it away for study, or worse, burn it as blasphemy. Before she really thought, Sifte had slipped the paper into her pocket.

Only then did she sense that someone was watching her. Remembering the little man at the terminals she turned, expecting to see him approaching her with an accusatory look. However, all of the terminals were empty. She put the book back where she had found it, then went to the terminal the teacher had vacated. The screen still displayed a news report, a brief account of the escape of a political prisoner. He had been a Western spy, an American, but once in Russia he had joined the Noviy Soviet, bent on destroying as much of Solntse's political integrity as possible as quickly as possible. In a rare interview, Opyekun Apraksina of Kronstadt Prison assured everyone that the capture of this "scourge of their country and leader" was imminent.

Sifte breathed a sigh of relief. For a moment she had had the feeling that there would be something significant on that screen, something to hint that the teacher knew what she had done. Still buoyant with relief, she went to look for Mila and found her reading in the biology section.

"We should probably go," she said. "It's time for lunch."

"I didn't know it was so late," Mila replied. She put her own book away, and they started off toward the dining hall. Sifte glanced back once, but the room was empty except for one librarian behind the front desk, dwarfed by the looming black window behind her.

*

Alone in the dark observation booth, Isaak 1 Dmitriev watched the retreating girls with a mixture of exhilaration and turmoil. In this unlikeliest of places, he had found a purpose for his life at last. That the child had chosen and read the book he had planted showed that she was both brave and open-minded. That she had taken the priceless drawing he had planted within it showed that it had touched her. Yet more significant than either of these things was the fact that she had not confided in her friend. No doubt she was disturbed and probably frightened by what she had read and what it had made her do. Any child in her position would be longing for the comfort of confidence, and his single day of observation had convinced Isaak that if Sifte would confide in anyone, it would be Mila. The only conceivable reason why she hadn't done so was that she wanted to protect her friend from similar discomfort and potential danger.

But for this sensitivity, Sifte would have been Solntse's perfect servant. Because of it, she would never be. It was incredible to Isaak that the rest of the teachers didn't see this. Yet they couldn't have seen it, or she would have been destroyed long ago. His only fear now was that someone would realize how dangerous she was before she was ready to defend herself. She needed to learn the truth, and quickly. Breaking the scaffolding of thirty years' misery, Isaak smiled. For the first time in his unassailable regime, Solntse had made a fatal mistake.

5

Sasha was dozing fitfully when the door to her cell rattled open. She awakened with a start and sat up as a flood of light poured in from the corridor, casting a mercurous sheen on the slimy walls. The lights in the cell were weak at best, and they had stopped working altogether half a day before. Sasha's eyes had become accustomed to the darkness; now the light burned them, blurring her vision. Nina and Igor, asleep near the far wall, didn't stir.

Two figures were silhouetted against the brightness of the doorway. Both wore prison-guards' uniforms, but one supported the other, who seemed to be barely conscious. "Where's the light in here?" the first guard demanded. Sasha flinched. She had been tormented by Koffsky since her first day in prison, and he only became bolder with time. "Sashenka," he said with heavy-fisted sarcasm, "get up and get the lights! What are you doing in the dark, anyway?"

"I was sleeping," she answered coldly. "Or giving it my best try. And I can't 'get the lights,' because the lights haven't worked for hours."

His body stiffened. "I hope you know that I can make a lot of trouble for you if you keep taking that tone with me. You're within an inch of Kronstadt anyway."

"Better there than this bloody leaking dungeon."

"You of all people should know that prisoners only leave Kronstadt for a mass grave."

"I'd risk it," she spat back, "if it meant I'd never have to see you again."

"I'll see what I can do. Till then, you can figure out how to feed him on your rations." He jerked his head in the direction of the man who lolled in his grasp. "Don't worry. He shouldn't last long."

Laughing, he let go of the prisoner. The man's legs buckled. He hit the stone floor heavily and let out a low groan, then pressed his face to the floor as blood began to ooze, dark and sluggish, from his nose, mouth, and countless cuts on his face.

Sasha could see now that the new prisoner's uniform was that of a prison Pomoshchnik, outranking Koffsky by several degrees. She was surprised by this, but she wasn't shocked. She had learned long ago that both friends and enemies come in many kinds of package. She fastened Koffsky with a look as brutal as his own, and when she spoke her tone was chillingly authoritative.

"Laugh while you can," she said. "You'll pay for all of this one day."

Koffsky laughed again, but this time there was a shade of discomfiture in it. "You'll be lucky if you live long enough to face the guns, never mind make good on a pitiful threat."

He slammed the door and locked it with a clatter of keys that assured Sasha she had unnerved him. She smiled to herself, then turned to the man on the ground, untied his hands and examined him with her fingers. His face was battered and bleeding, and he had welts on his wrists and arms where he had been bound, probably by something harsher than the rags she had just dispensed with. His left thigh was broken, as were several ribs, and his nose. No doubt there would be injuries to the internal organs, but she couldn't diagnose these. At least his abdomen was soft. She tried not to hurt him, but he moaned pitifully as she shifted him to a more natural position.

"I'm going to set your leg, and splint it," she told him. "You must try not to scream, or Koffsky could come back, and then you'll know the real meaning of pain." He barely nodded. It occurred to her that if the uniform was genuine, then he wouldn't need such a warning.

With the deftness of years of practice in the worst conditions, Sasha tore strips of cloth from one of the rags that made up her bed, wrenched off two door panels which she had loosened gradually with just such a necessity in mind, and positioned one of them on top of the rags. She smoothed the man's hair back from his face. He was feverish beneath the clammy perspiration.

"You're going to have to help me," she said. "I'm not strong enough to lift you." He nodded faintly again, and on the count of three she half-dragged, half-guided him onto the bottom panel of the splint. She felt him stifle a scream as she pushed the two halves of the bone into place. She was impressed by his stoicism. This kind of pain was more than even an Opyekun would be expected to bear silently.

"That's the worst of it," she said, beginning to bind the two pieces of wood together with the rags. When she finished, she touched his hot face again. It was wet with silent tears. Despite the fact that he might still prove an adversary, her studied detachment foundered into pity. His suffering would certainly worsen before infection, or something less organic, killed him. She reached for the bottle she kept hidden in her bed-rags, unstopped it, and handed it to him. "Take as little as you can," she said. "The guard who used to smuggle it to us was sacked."

"What is it?"

"Vodka. And morphine."

He accepted the bottle, took a healthy swallow, and then handed it back to her. "What's your name?"

"Aleksandra Kirillovna," she answered, after only a slight pause to consider whether the Institute numermic would work more in her favor. It might, she thought, if the man really was a lapsed official; but it might also concede more than she was yet willing to. "Sasha," she added.

"Sasha," he repeated slowly. The name scrawled blazing letters across his pain-fogged mind. It meant something, but he couldn't think beyond the agony of his broken bones or the haze of the drug already beginning to work on his starved body.

"And yours?"

"Ivan 15 Kiriyenko." He paused, then asked her, "Why are you being kind to me? For all you know, we could be enemies."

"Down here, we are all on the same side," she said.

Ivan was silent so long that she thought he had finally passed out. Then, as she was crawling back to her pile of rags, his sickened, reedy voice challenged the blackness once more. "Where did you learn to repair bones in the dark?"

Sasha smiled to herself again, though her pity redoubled. A Soviet would not have asked such a question. The man must have been a real official, perhaps even a faithful one.

For that reason alone he would suffer more and sooner than she and the others who might still prove valuable as barter chips or informants. She was suddenly intrigued by him.

"I'm not at liberty to tell you that, tavarishch," she answered gently, knowing that the title would tell him just enough, and hopefully bolster his trust in her. She paused for a moment, deliberating whether it was worth trying to get information out of him in his present state. Finally, she asked, "What are you in for?"

He realized that despite her assertion of their equal footing, she was asking him whether or not he could be trusted. It seemed to him that he would do better here if he made this woman his friend. "They think I helped a prisoner to escape from Kronstadt," he answered. "Soviet, if that's what you wanted to know." Anticipating Sasha's surprise at his unguarded speech, he explained: "I am—was—a guard there. One of the first things you learn is that the cells in these outer prisons are never bugged. The technology is expensive, not to mention the labor required to monitor it. The Sun doesn't consider it worthwhile. You…we…aren't expected to live long enough to plot anything meaningful."

Sasha was silent for nearly a minute, digesting this. "Shit," she said. Then, "We've spent years trying to devise ways to communicate without being detected. We even have a rudimentary language of our own, passed along each time a prisoner is moved…well, hindsight is twenty-twenty."

Ivan heard rustling, then the scrape of a match on stone. A small, flickering light cracked the obdurate darkness. Sasha touched the match to a stub of candle, then blew it out.

"You think I'm cruel," she said, "because I didn't light it when it might have helped me set your leg less painfully." She looked at Ivan speculatively. He was in his early twenties, with what appeared to be a handsome face under the bruises and the crust of dried blood. His hair was red, like her own, but his eyes were a husky's blue-white.

"No," he said, examining her with equal care. She had keen, dark eyes, and a delicate face that might have been arresting for its beauty if its expression hadn't been more so. He had only ever seen such unremitting, crystalline hardness on the faces of the Opyekuni. Yet the Opyekuni looked soulless, and there was compassion in Sasha's face along with the austerity. Trying to resolve the two qualities into one countenance was like trying to align the two parts of a stereoscopic image without the stereoscope. He couldn't see one for the other, yet they clearly co-existed, formed some kind of whole. In the end he found it easier not to look at her at all. "Understandably...wary," he said with effort.

"Then you'll understand that I want to ask you a few questions."

He blinked at her as her image doubled, blurred. He was trying to remember what she had just said, to think of the right answer, and why he ought to know her. But her unnerving face was retreating, and blessedly, the pain was too.

Sasha saw his eyes losing their focus, sighed with weary patience and said, "All right then. Sleep first, talk later." She blew out the candle, pitching them again into the soupy, river-tinged darkness where prisoners had waited to die since the days before the city stood.

*

Ivan didn't know how long he slept before the pain awakened him again, but he knew that it had either been a very short time or a very long one, because the two people who had slept while he spoke to Sasha earlier were asleep now in the same corner. Sasha, likewise, was next to him, leaning against the wall with her arms circling her knees, face intractable and unblinking eyes fixed on his. The candle burned by her side, apparently no shorter than it had been before.

Ivan's first, simultaneous sensations were of extreme heat and cold. Sasha seemed to have receded and to be glowing from within like the angels in old Bible illustrations. Ivan realized that he was beginning to die. He didn't much care, but he did feel an inexplicable urgency in relation to her. He couldn't decide whether this was a result of the raging infection or of something more tangible, but either way he wasn't surprised when she said, "I've helped you as best I can. Now it's time for you to help me."

Her words were expressionless, her eyes artful. They reached into him, touching the surface of his secret like her cool fingers had touched his face, seducing him. Ivan looked away from her, at the first thing that came into view—his broken leg. Its throbbing pain had taken on an apparition's semi-form, rising from him with the color and heat of something freshly killed. This had nearly convinced him that he had little to lose in telling Sasha what she wanted to know, when it occurred to him that he also had something to gain.

"Give me…the rest of it," he said hoarsely.

She did not ask him what he meant, didn't even hesitate before picking up the bottle and dangling it just beyond his reach. "Tell me who escaped from Kronstadt, and I'll give you a sip of it. I know what you're thinking, Ivan 15, but there isn't enough here to kill you, and you'll thank me later for rationing what there is."

"How did you know—"

"You told me a lot of things while you slept," she interrupted. "But not everything. Who was it?"

Ivan wavered. If Sasha was truly of the Noviy Soviet, it might give her peace of mind to know that Stepan had escaped—he need not tell her that he had been captured again soon afterwards. She would probably never have the chance to find out anyway. However, he was not convinced that she was who she claimed to be. Her intensity worried him. A Soviet leader would be intense, but she wouldn't show such meticulous self-possession, such perfect, cold calculation. It didn't make sense that they would send a spy to make him repeat what they already knew, but then again they might be looking for something more. Perhaps something which would seal Stepan's fate, if it wasn't already sealed. He told himself that he could stand a few more hours of pain if it might buy Stepan time.

He said, "I can't tell you that."

Sasha was silent for a time, swinging the bottle slowly back and forth like the pendulum of a clock. Finally, she said, "He must have been quite a prisoner for them to put you in here on spec."

"Yes—he was quite famous."

Sasha's smile deepened. "He," she said. "That's a good beginning." She proffered the bottle. Ivan's eyes flickered away from her uneasily; he didn't accept it. Sasha sighed. "I'm not a spy, Ivan 15," she said. "Far from it. I have reason to believe I might know this man. It would put me at ease to know that he is free."

"What makes you think that he *is* free? Don't you think that they would have sent the Opyekuni after him?"

"If it's Stepan," she said, pinning him with her shrewd stare, "then they won't find him." Once again, Ivan's eyes recoiled from hers. Sasha's smile finally cracked the mask of reserve. "It's Stepan."

Ivan waited for her to begin castigating him. It took him some time to realize that the look on her face meant something quite different. "Then—then you really knew him?" he asked.

Long ago, she had convinced herself that Stepan was dead. She had wanted to spare herself the torture of wondering, but had come to believe her own fiction so completely that its sudden dissolution pitched her into sudden unreality. She looked at the unlikely courier of her world's unmaking, glowing in the light of her candle and the heat of his own battling blood. For a mad moment she wondered if he would burst into flames, or dissolve like so many previous dreams. But he only stared at her with what she gradually realized were fear and supplication.

"Yes," she finally answered, "I knew him. All these years, I thought that he had died. All these years…" Sasha's smile faded. "Did he make it? There's so much that depends on him. Much more than you could guess. Much more than *he* could guess." She dropped her head into her hands. "I should have thought of it before…" She turned to Ivan again. "Did he make it? Have they caught him?"

Ivan studied her face, the terrible, tortured hope struggling on it with despair. He realized that it might well crush her to know the truth, but in the end he didn't have the strength to lie to her with conviction.

"They caught him on the outskirts of Solntsegrad," he said, his eyes shying away from her shocked and uncomprehending face. "I'm sorry."

Sasha's eyes locked on the rough stones of the wall across from her, as the color that had risen in her pale face drained away again. When she looked back at Ivan, the blunt determination had returned. She reached slowly toward his broken leg and he watched, paralyzed by the anticipation of another explosion of pain. But she only touched the inflamed skin with the tips of her fingers. Their coldness matched the coldness in her eyes, driving a fear into Ivan that was worse than the image of pain. He saw that she would not hesitate to rip him to pieces if he proved false to her faith. Once again, he wondered how a Soviet could wear an Opyekun's mask.

"Do you swear to me that you are who you claim to be?" she asked softly, not moving her hand from his leg.

"Yes."

"All right, then—did you help Stepan Pierson to escape from Kronstadt Prison?"

"Yes."

"When?"

"Three days ago…I think."

"Where were you until they brought you here?"

"In questioning at Kronstadt."

"Who questioned you?"

"Apraksina, and several Pomoshchniki."

"When did you learn that Stepan had been caught?"

"Yesterday."

"The Pomoshchniki told you?"

"Yes. No."

"Which?"

He shook his head in confusion. "Neither. Apraksina came in to tell them, and I heard what she said."

Sasha watched him, her eyes glittering and merciless as a raptor's. "Did you see him at Kronstadt after they caught him?"

"No. They took him to the Fortress."

"Apraksina said this to the Pomoshchniki, with you in the room?"

"Yes."

"And is the Fortress still used exclusively for prisoners awaiting execution?"

"Yes—unless they've changed the laws since I was arrested."

She watched him for another moment and then, as suddenly as it had hardened, her face thawed. She retracted her hand and offered him the bottle again, smiling faintly. This time Ivan took it and drank. Only when he had given it back to her and she had hidden it again did he speak.

"I—I'm sorry—" he began.

Sasha looked up at him curiously. "For what?"

"For having to tell you—"

To his surprise, she laughed. "Forgive me for saying it, Ivan 15, but the most incredible part of this story is that Stepan would have trusted his life to as great a fool as you."

"What do you mean?" he cried.

"Stepan wasn't caught."

Ivan shook his swimming head. "But Apraksina…she didn't even say it to me…"

"Of course not. That would have been too obvious."

"But why would she care whether I thought that Stepan had been caught?"

Sasha shook her head. "Tell me—why do you think that they brought you here instead of keeping you at Kronstadt?"

Ivan sighed. "Apraksina said it would teach me something—but I suppose that they needed the space for more dangerous criminals than I am."

Sasha shrugged. "Quite likely, but that's not why you're here. Has it occurred to you as odd yet that they would imprison the man who helped Stepan Pierson escape with three Soviet leaders, one of whom, it appears, has some interest in his whereabouts?"

"Schlüsselburg is full of Soviet leaders, and no doubt you all have some stake in Stepan's life."

"Yes—but none of them like I do." Sasha smiled with the fondness of a reminiscing war hero. "You must know that this prison has had three major riots in the last five years. But you don't know that I helped organize all of them, and those two in the corner, Nina and Igor, helped with two. You couldn't know, because even the Opyekun doesn't know—if he did, we'd be dead by now. But he suspects, and he's worried. Last time, we nearly succeeded."

Ivan shook his head. "You could never take this prison."

Sasha tilted her head to the side. "Perhaps not. But the Opyekuni aren't convinced, and Schlüsselburg's strategic position makes it a disturbing uncertainty. That's why they made Stepan an example. He was one of the best. He inspired us to stand up to our oppressors in a way that only someone who's grown up in freedom could do. They must have hoped that once word of his failed escape reached us—through you—we'd lose the inspiration and the will for revolt."

"It's a clever theory," Ivan conceded, "but what makes you so sure they didn't catch him?"

"Well, first, they wouldn't have put him in the Fortress, because then they would have had to kill him."

"He was on death row in Kronstadt."

She shook her head. "It was to Solntse's advantage to let everyone believe that. But he won't kill Stepan Pierson until he doesn't have a choice. For one thing, Stepan's too complicated. Solntse doesn't know what he wants, why he stayed here, and The Sun needs to know everything. More than that, he's afraid that Stepan is still connected with the West. He's arrogant, but he's far from stupid.

"And then, Stepan's probably the best intelligence agent alive. He should be. The American government spent God knows how much money on his training." Sasha paused, her lips parted as if she couldn't decide whether to speak another thought.

"What else?" Ivan prompted.

Sasha shrugged. "I know him," she said simply. "He'd slit his own throat before he'd let them put him back in prison. Either he made it, or he's dead. And if he were dead, they'd be trumpeting it from one end of this country to the other."

Ivan was far from convinced, but he thought that it was wiser not to contradict the woman, given her volatile temper and proximity to his injured leg. Besides, the morphine was spindling into his veins again, draining him of the will to do anything but watch Sasha's beautiful face advance and retreat, like a gauze curtain in a window on a breezy day.

"Stay with me, Ivan 15," she said after a time. "Can you remember where he was going?"

"To the city," he heard himself say, in a voice that didn't sound solid enough to be his own.

"Andrei," she said. Ivan looked at her with half-lidded eyes. Sasha smiled at him. "You're wondering if I'm mad."

71

"No—"

"I am. We all are." She gestured to the sleepers at the other side of the cell. "You will be too, if you live."

"How do you know?"

"Only the mad ones live."

The words jerked him from his torpid reverie. "For fuck's sake!" he cried, but then found that he didn't have the will to stay angry. He fell back to studying her face. The duality of its expression had become much more difficult to see. Ivan wondered whether it had ever really existed or had merely been a product of his delirium. Delirious or not, though, he still had the feeling that there was something about Sasha which was more important than her fickle kindness or her beauty.

"Have I met you before?" he asked, and then was appalled at himself for asking.

She laughed again, softly. "No. But I'm certain that you have heard of me somewhere other than your schoolbooks, and as more than a famous criminal." She appraised the young man. He was as brave and as foolish as she had once been. Sweat had cleaned most of the dried blood from his face, showing the wounds more clearly. "I know you must be a friend of Stepan's," she said, "and more importantly of the Soviet, to have risked your life to help him escape. I'll tell you my story, but only if you promise to die with it."

"How can you be sure I will?"

"Because I have yours as collateral."

Ivan wondered whether she could really be as calculating as she was determined to appear. Her general demeanor was indeed that of a hardened criminal, but her eyes were clear and honest, with a suggestion that she was guarding something.

"All right," he replied. "I promise."

She sighed. "I was born in Solntsegrad," she began matter-of-factly. "My father was an Opyekun. My mother had failed Pomoshchnik training. She didn't support many of the government practices, but I didn't know that until after she died. My father and her parents adhered strictly to the breeding structures, so it was an arranged marriage. My father was twice her age, and chose her for her beauty and health. She had no choice." Sasha paused, frowned, and then continued brusquely:

"Andrei Umanskiy, as I'm sure you know, is my half-brother—our father's son from his first marriage. The name is our father's. We both took it when we left the ranks, as it were." For a second, a smile flickered across her lips. "We both went to Institute 1. He managed to graduate, but it didn't make him any more compliant than I was. When he got out and saw what was happening in Myortvograd, he left the Opyekuni and never went back. It didn't take me that long. I was sent home when I was fifteen, and that's when I met Andrei for the first time. It's odd, really; we aren't meant to have family, and he and I weren't friends at Institute 1, but when he came and told me that he was my brother, it wasn't a surprise. He said that I would make a good leader, and I was more than ready to go with him to Myortvograd before they could put me in another school, or marry me off.

"At that time Andrei was living in a community of Soviets in the Mihailovskiy Palace. Andrei had joined them not long after leaving the Opyekuni, and had since become a leader. Just as he had thought, I took to the Soviet right away. It all just seemed to click. Of course, I had a lot of learning to do before I could be a leader, but I knew that the Soviet's primary goal was to take back power from Solntse, to end his oppression. To build a society of equality. I was determined to be a part of it. I went with Andrei on his trips, and helped him with his teachings. I learned the horrors of Myortvograd, and of Solntsegrad itself—horrors that no Institute child knows exist. When I was seventeen, I became a Soviet leader. When I was eighteen, I met Stepan."

All at once, the haze in Ivan's mind cleared.

"He was twenty-one then," she said, "and he had been in the country six months. He had become acquainted with an up-and-coming Soviet leader, Olga, in his efforts to gain the support of Russian opposition groups. Olga brought him to a meeting that night. Stepan spoke, telling us that the Western Alliance knew about Solntse's corruption and that they wanted to help oust him. He said that many of their goals were the same as the Soviet's, and that they wanted some kind of treaty with us. He was so sure of himself—so stupid." She smiled, but it only flickered briefly before it died.

"Many of the Soviet did not trust him, including myself. We thought that if the Alliance took over, they would be just as bad as Solntse. They certainly didn't share our socialist principles, and even if we could have come to an ideological compromise, they wouldn't understand the Russian spirit, the Russian soul. We knew they would want to rebuild Russia in their own image, and we didn't want a Westernized Russia. I confronted Stepan about this after the meeting, and we ended up arguing all night. By the next morning I had pretty well turned him around to our point of view, which is a good thing, because I had also fallen in love with him." Sasha looked intently into the candle flame.

"Do I even need to tell you the rest?" she continued after a moment, sighing. "No doubt you've heard it. We were married the old fashioned way, sort of—by a self-ordained priest in what's left of St. Isaak's Cathedral. We lived together for about a year, but the Opyekuni traced Stepan to the Soviet, and he had to leave. He was meant to go to another Soviet enclave in Novosibirsk, but he never arrived. We feared that he had been captured, and in the end it was easier for me to believe that he was dead than to imagine him suffering in one of Solntse's prisons. I never knew what actually happened to him until tonight."

She paused again, then said with a bluntness that could only be meant to cover great pain, "Eight months after Stepan left, our daughter was born. He never knew about her, which is maybe just as well, because the Opyekuni took her. Then the Pomoshchniki took me…and here I am, ten years later."

Neither of them spoke for a time. Then Ivan said, "He talked about you." Sasha didn't look at him, but her nervous hand movements stilled. "I can't pretend that Stepan didn't have many reasons to want to escape, and many plans for what he would do if he could…but I know that you gave him the courage to go through with it."

"Yes," Sasha said bitterly, "and I was the reason he was locked up in the first place, just as he was the reason I stayed in the city long enough for myself and our child to be taken. Did you ever hear the story about the woman who cuts off her hair to buy a watch chain? No, you wouldn't have, not in an Institute. It goes like this. There was a young woman who had beautiful, long hair, but she was too poor to buy ornaments for it. Her husband had a lovely old pocket watch, but no chain to wear it with. So, on their first Christmas together, each wanting to give the other what they would most cherish, the woman cut off her hair and sold it to buy a watch chain, and the man sold his watch to buy her a pair of tortoiseshell combs. Two beautiful gestures which landed them exactly where they began—with nothing."

"Not nothing," Ivan answered softly, sadly. "They were both loved more than anything else in the world."

"That's right," Sasha answered after a pause, her tone faltering for the first time since she had begun speaking to him. "But sometimes it's hard to remember what that feels like."

Ivan sifted through his tangled mind for words of comfort; but in the end, he could only repeat her own. "You said yourself that Stepan made it. Surely the first thing he'll do is try to help you."

Sasha shook her head, smiled sadly. "I prefer to think he's wiser than that."

Ivan felt a twinge of anger through the alternate waves of heat and cold. "Do you mean you've given up?" he said.

"I told you, I'm crazy. I still have hope that something will change. But I'm not crazy enough to think that Stepan will come riding in here on a white horse to save me—or that if he tries, he'll live to tell the tale. Tell me," she said, before he could contradict her, "do you know what Stepan's plans were, if he reached the city?"

"He wouldn't tell me."

"But he'll go to Andrei, I'm sure of it. If he makes it there, they might do some good—if Andrei's Menshevik tendencies don't get in the way."

"They'll want to help you," Ivan repeated.

Sasha smiled with a pity that frightened him. He flinched when her fingers touched his forehead again: they seemed to be made of ice. Gradually, though, they absorbed the heat of his own skin, and he relaxed under their gentle pressure.

"Nobody escapes Schlüsselburg," she answered. "You know that."

"Nobody escapes Kronstadt, either," he rejoined blearily. "But Stepan did."

"Stepan had the help of a rather extraordinary man, who happened to be in the right place at the right time. That's what Stepan is like—he's always led a charmed life. Unfortunately, it doesn't work like that for most of us."

Ivan smiled weakly before he slipped back into unconsciousness, uncertain whether he said or only thought the reply: "He'll come for you."

6

The man who picked Stepan up from the Kronstadt dock took a roundabout route to the mainland, cutting north offshore almost as far as Zelenogorsk and then creeping southward again along the coast. Neither he nor Stepan spoke during the journey. Neither wanted to endanger the other by disclosing any more information than was necessary. They parted about twenty kilometers north of Sestroretsk, near the spot where a causeway had once joined Kronstadt to the mainland.

Stepan walked east, avoiding Solntsegrad's northern suburbs. No stranger to the country he walked would ever have guessed that it was early spring. The forests which had once covered the flatlands had all died during the first dark years after the holocaust, and none of the re-plantings near the city had survived. Between the trees' skeletal ruins grew stiff, brown grass and small white flowers with a sickly-sweet smell. In treeless patches they ran in parallel lines to the horizon, marking the furrows of derelict fields.

Stepan kept his bearings by the red glow of Solntsegrad on the right-hand horizon. He pressed onward in a half-stupor of hunger and cold and exhaustion until the red blotch was well behind him, then he turned south. His starved muscles had begun to protest along with the old injury. He took a short rest, and ate one of the two bananas Ivan had been able to steal for him, then pushed himself forward again.

For the first time in years, Stepan allowed himself to think of Sasha. He pictured her face rosy with firelight, as it had been on the last night they spent together. The memory of the way they had parted had in many ways been harder to bear than anything that happened to Stepan in prison. It would have been easier if he had left her angry. Sasha had not been able to understand the strength of Stepan's instinct for self-preservation, any more than he could empathize with her willingness to die for something as intangible as an ideology. Even so, she had let him go without protest. He wondered whether he would be able to do the same.

The next moment Stepan forgot the unanswered question, for the city had come into view. Beyond the Vyborgside shanty town and the sluggish Neva, the smoking hulk of Myortvograd glowed like a funeral pyre in its own dirty light. Myortvograd—the Dead City. It was a poetic name, but there was nothing poetic about it, even in the mild dawn light. It was a junk-heap of twisted stumps of palaces and cathedrals, grand hotels and museums that had made up one of the most splendorous cities ever to stand. What had been rebuilt was disfigured and warped, a better testament than any to the state of its affairs.

Technically, there was no Myortvograd—it was all Solntsegrad, the City of the Sun. Behind the walls that protected the little the bomb had not touched, the name was appropriate. There were still grand houses and gardens, clean water and food. What the new breed of sub-race serfs could not grow or produce with the limited local resources

79

was supplied by Asia and western Europe via a tortuous black market.

It had an air of invincibility as Stepan looked at it, like something very old and precious kept behind thick museum glass, yet it was no more than a lucky fluke. Only a sudden, heavy rain had stopped the fires that raged in the bomb's aftermath from crossing the river and destroying the islands. The people on the islands had quickly built walls against the influx of refugees from the scorched land to the south and east. When Solntse won his coup, the second since the holocaust, he made the islands his center of government. Now the walls meant to maintain the last vestige of order in a disintegrating country kept the sub-race away from the super-race's sterile hothouse.

It made Stepan sick to think about this integral hypocrisy of Solntse's regime. His propaganda machine instructed the upper classes to hate the lower, even as the lower class fed, clothed and sheltered them; even as he requisitioned their children to maintain his power. That the people of Solntsegrad and its counterparts didn't realize this seemed ludicrous to Stepan. But then, he had not been educated into Solntse's doctrine of fear.

As the sky brightened, Stepan tried to see the city as a whole, but the Neva bisected it too perfectly. Three of the old bridges had been destroyed in the war, two others later on by those who feared invasion of the islands. Only two bridges still joined Myortvograd to Solntsegrad proper: Dvortsoviy Most, which connected to Vasilevskiy Ostrov, and Troitskiy Most, which joined Petrogradskaya meters from the Fortress. Nobody used them, and they were heavily guarded at all times. The little official interaction between the islands and the slums was carried out by ferries. Any other kind went through the rotting flood and Metro tunnels. Stepan didn't know why the bridges remained, unless as some perversion of the dictator's mind—which, when he thought about it, was easy enough to believe.

The sun finally shook itself free of the horizon, and daylight unrolled sluggishly over the city. For a moment, it gave even Myortvograd a kind of beauty. Then it slipped behind a thin layer of cloud. The light muddied, and shadow reclaimed the Dead City. Stepan realized that he had been still too long.

Ivan had told Stepan that if he went to the junction with the river Okkervil, he would find a sympathetic boatman waiting to take him across. He moved into the shanty town as if into a nightmare. Clusters of people huddled in makeshift shelters, barely clothed, covered with the filth that lay stagnant in the gutters. Children and dogs picked through rotting heaps of refuse and fought over edible scraps. People and animals alike bore the welts of a leprosy-like disease, one of the many resistant strains of old diseases the bomb's destruction had bred. Some of their faces and bodies were so deteriorated by the illness that they barely looked human, and the smell that came from so many running sores was almost unbearable. They cried out to Stepan for food or money, but he had nothing to give.

But the children were the worst of the slums' horrors. Those left behind by the Opyekuni were generally sick or deformed. They paused in their garbage-sifting when they saw Stepan, reaching out with matchstick arms and wasted fingers, touching their mouths and their stomachs in a universal plea for food. Others were so starved and ill that they could not get up, just slumped in the shadows of crumbling walls. They all showed the signs of starvation;

some also had the lesions of the new leprosy, and most of the older ones bore scars left by the smallpox epidemic that had swept the city at about the time Stepan had been captured. Others had the purple bruises of leukemia, or the red and white blotches of the bizarre and untraceable sun sickness, which drained the skin's pigment and left its victims to die in the daylight.

Yet though many people were sick, many others weren't. What had always struck Stepan as odd about the so-called sub-race, and what struck him anew, was that so many of them were healthy. Starvation, radiation, resistant diseases and a hundred other assailants of the human immune system had fast-forwarded evolution at a rate he wouldn't have believed possible, if he hadn't lived with it for so many years. Though the motivation disgusted him, Stepan could understand why Solntse wanted the sub-race's healthy offspring.

When Stepan reached the Okkervil, he found the boatman waiting for him at its confluence with the Neva. After another silent journey, for which he paid the man the rest of the little money he had, he set off into Myortvograd proper. It had changed little. The only difference seemed to be in the population, apparently much smaller than when he had left.

Nevskiy was too exposed, so he wound his way to Karavannaya through side streets, and finally located the right building. It was a nondescript reconstruction, built on a pre-war foundation. Stepan pushed the single button on the door, and a buzz sounded somewhere. He waited, and after a few minutes the door opened a crack. A pair of eyes unnervingly like Sasha's peered out at him.

"Andrei?" asked Stepan. The man nodded curtly and opened the door wider. Stepan moved inside, and Andrei closed and bolted it.

Andrei's eyes were his only physical likeness to his half-sister. Sasha had been small and wiry, her pale skin and fervent eyes giving the impression that her driving passion was always close to consuming her. Andrei was more solidly built, with a countenance and bearing like a siege wall.

"Come," he said, and led Stepan up three flights of stairs to the top floor. Andrei turned again, and Stepan followed him down a dark, narrow hallway. Andrei stopped, unlocked a door, and pushed it open onto a small, dimly-lit, and sparsely furnished room. There was a table with two stools, a bed pushed into the corner, a few miscellaneous chairs, and a desk cluttered with papers. Once they were inside, Andrei visibly relaxed.

"Sit down, please, Stepan," he said. "I am sorry if I seemed abrupt, but anybody could be watching or listening, even here." He smiled a reticent, somewhat stilted, but genuine smile which Stepan knew would be rare, because it, too, was Sasha's. "I'm pleased to finally meet you."

Stepan caught the look of bewilderment on Andrei's face. He wondered if he had watched his smile a moment too long; he couldn't remember. He tried to make up for it now with a strong, steady tone as he answered, "Likewise. I was always sorry that your time in the south overlapped with my time in Myortvograd, and then or course—"

Andrei nodded, making it unnecessary for Stepan to continue, then moved towards a makeshift kitchen in the corner of the room and began taking things out of an icebox. "Tell me—did the escape go as planned?"

"More or less," Stepan answered, sighing as he stretched his throbbing leg out in front of him. "I had to kill six Pomoshchniki. Two of them inside."

"It won't matter," Andrei answered, returning with a tray of food and two unlabelled bottles. "You wouldn't have fooled them long, anyway."

As Stepan watched him, his similarity to Sasha seemed to lessen. Sasha had possessed the preternatural self-control of the trainee Opyekun, but even so, the expression in her eyes had always been at least two parts contempt and tenacity to one of anything else. Andrei's eyes showed nothing at all. It was as if the reticence of his smile concentrated in them.

He was saying, "Now, Stepan, you must be hungry. And yes," he smiled again, though it was clear to Stepan that it did not come easily, "it is beer in the bottles. It's not as hard to come by as it once was. I thought you might appreciate it after your time on prison rations."

"Thank you." Stepan accepted the bottle that Andrei proffered, and couldn't help a flinch of surprise when the liquid hit his tongue. The cold, the sharpness of the bubbles, the bittersweet taste were almost more than he could incorporate all at once. He had forgotten that food could be so varied in its properties.

"Tell me," Stepan said after a moment, "how is the Soviet's work going?"

Andrei seemed to be thinking carefully before he answered. "There is a substantial following in the city, now—far bigger than when you left. We do our best to keep the pockets small and scattered…still, we won't be able to keep our numbers a secret much longer."

"You don't seem pleased about the increase."

"One of our struggles has always been to maintain our numbers in accordance with our ability to use them. Otherwise enthusiasm sours, sometimes turns against us. We're in danger of exceeding our capacity for the first time since you were captured."

"How far are you from being able to act?"

Andrei looked up quickly, his eyes still unreadable. "You mean a coup?" He didn't wait for Stepan to answer. "Years. We have the numbers, but not the organization. We have leaders, but not the right kind. There's no solidarity among them, their ages and personalities and training—their whole experience, really—is too disparate for them to be able to form a cohesive army."

"They all want to be generals?"

"The opposite. No one wants the task of uniting such diverse forces. They are of course already united against Solntse. But even so, they each have a different idea of how to unseat him. If only we had a training ground half as effective as Solntse's Institutes. One of his eight-year-olds could probably organize us better than anyone we have now…"

Both men were silent for a time. Then Stepan said, "Perhaps it was only my youth, but it seemed when I left that we weren't so far away from having a group of leaders with the kind of unity you're talking about."

Andrei sighed. "We had many good men and women ten, even five years ago. But we've lost the best of them. You were captured, of course. Katya and Boris were shot at a demonstration a few years later. Igor and Nina and Maria all went to prison, though Olga managed to escape the trap that caught them. And then Sasha disappeared."

Andrei looked at Stepan. Stepan looked back with an intensity that made it clear to Andrei that he had been waiting for this all along. Drawing a deep breath, he said, "I don't know where she is. Nobody knows. There are rumors that the Pomoshchniki took her when they found out about…I mean when they realized that you and she…"

"I thought as much," Stepan sighed. "Do you know any more?"

"It's the same as always. All that we've been able to learn is that she 'disappeared mysteriously.' Of course, it doesn't help that I was in the south at the time. For me, it's all hearsay." Andrei wouldn't look at him.

"Still—that's all you've found out in all this time?"

"No…that isn't quite everything." He paused, then said, "Stepan—Sasha had a child after you left. I never saw the baby; it was taken when Sasha was."

Andrei paused again, watching Stepan, who was silent for a long time. Finally Stepan asked, "Is there more?"

"The child was a girl, and she was taken by the Opyekuni. Beyond that—well, you know the possibilities. I don't know whether Sasha named her."

None of this was of any consequence to Stepan. If the child was still alive, she was certainly Solntse's slave by now. He could only think of Sasha, and what had no doubt become of her. His composure must have slipped, he thought, because Andrei said, "You couldn't have done anything, Stepan. Even if you'd been there, you couldn't have stopped the Opyekuni from taking a child they wanted."

"I'm not thinking of the child," he answered, his voice flat with despair.

When Andrei spoke again, his tone had become persuasive. "But perhaps you ought to be thinking of her."

"Why?"

Andrei sighed again. "If the Opyekuni took this child, then she had to have been gifted. If she's alive, then she's at an Institute, and growing up at an Institute she is being educated against us."

Stepan looked up, suddenly angry at Andrei for continuing to force this unwanted eddy into the flow of his despair. "I don't want to know!" he said.

Andrei's eyes were like weights. "I can't forcibly change your mind, Stepan. Please, though, consider what I've said. If she has even half of your intelligence or Sasha's charisma and determination, that child is dangerous to her enemies, and in all likelihood she is being raised by yours."

"He wouldn't have taken a child of mine and Sasha's," Stepan said irritably. "Too many people would be against it."

"If Solntse will educate children of the sub-race as his own, then why not children of dissidents? Besides, only the Opyekuni know about the breeding schemes."

"We're not run-of-the-mill dissidents. Even the 'kuni would find that kind of child hard to swallow."

Andrei shook his head in exasperation. "I'm telling you, if he will go so far as to lie to his people about the sub-race babies he imports into super-race lives, he'll go one step further. As for the 'kuni swallowing it, how many of them actually have to know? Given one or two loyal confidantes, Solntse could lie to the rest as easily as he does everyone else. Stepan, irony is Solntse's vice. Wouldn't the ultimate irony be to train the child of dissidents to stamp them out?"

Stepan considered this, weighing the repugnance of the idea of trying to locate the child against his debt to Andrei, and his greater one to Sasha. He realized that he could not deny them this. So he said, "All right, then. Where should I begin?"

7

When Sifte's class gathered for the second time, an undercurrent of whispered speculation circled the room. Sifte, however, was silent, wondering whether the new teacher would be better than the last. That she couldn't imagine one much worse was little comfort.

When the door finally opened, an ambiguous silence fell over the children. The man who entered was frail and stooped, yet there was a subtle pride in his bearing which demanded their attention, and they found themselves sitting up straighter. With a shock, Sifte realized that this was the same man who had been reading the news in the library earlier. A twinge of fear and guilt went through her, and her hand went to the drawing in her jumpsuit pocket.

The new teacher proceeded to the front of the room, then turned and faced the class. His features were stark and eagle-like, his nose long and slightly crooked, as if it had been broken and healed without being properly set. He was short and stooped, his olive skin loose and papery, but his eyes, behind their thick glasses, were those of a man still in his prime.

The man cleared his throat. "My name is Gospadin Dmitri," he began, "and from now on I will be your teacher. I do not like to distance myself from my students, so please address me simply as 'Dmitri.'" He paused, scrutinized them again. The children watched him as intently. "I realize that this has been an unsettling day," said Dmitri, and his eyes rested for a moment on Sifte's before he continued. "I think we should take the afternoon off from lessons and spend the time getting to know each other. Why don't we begin with you telling me a few things about yourselves. You first, please, Gospazha—" He nodded at Tanya, who sat in the front, right-hand corner. His eyes fell on the rim of bruise her jumpsuit sleeve didn't cover, but he said nothing about it.

Tanya giggled at being called 'Miss,' but when she saw that he was serious she quickly answered, "Tanya. I, um… don't know what to say." Sifte rolled her eyes. "Um…I like reading, and being with my friends, and…"

"Perhaps you could tell us what you hope for your future post to be, Tanya," Dmitri said. "In fact, why don't you all do that?"

"Well," Tanya began again, "I'm interested in the philosophy of government, and I'd like to be one of Solntse's advisors."

"Quite ambitious," Dmitri replied neutrally, then moved on to the next student. Something flickered on Sifte's terminal screen. It was the letter box, which Aleksei had invented to help them pass the time during their redundant lessons.

Ass-kisser.

The letters walked around the perimeter of the box, settled at the top, exploded and fell to the bottom as a pile of ashes, which sprouted a row of daisies. Sifte smiled, but it was forced. She was worrying about what she would say when it was her turn to answer the teacher's question.

All too soon, Mila was saying, "I want to work in medical research, and find cures for resistant diseases."

For a moment Sifte's apprehension gave way to the squeeze of panic she always felt when Mila spoke about her ambition, knowing that it came from Mila's terrible predilection for illness. Mila had come to Institute 1 with a lung infection that turned into pneumonia. Illness wasn't uncommon in the chosen babies, who were taken from their mothers so young. However, Mila's infection didn't respond to treatment. The doctors had nearly given her up when she began to improve on her own, but the illness had weakened her, and she would be prone to recurring bouts of it throughout her childhood.

Dmitri was nodding when Sifte tuned back in. "A noble goal. Solntse certainly needs good minds on his research teams."

And then his eyes were resting on her. "My name is Sifte," she said, and met his eyes to see whether he disapproved. Gospazha Maria had constantly goaded her about her foreign name.

Dmitri only said, "A pretty name. Finnish, is it?"

"I don't know," Sifte replied.

Dmitri nodded, his expression neutral. "And your thoughts for the future?"

Sifte paused, still grasping for the right answer—the one that would make him forget about her. In the end, all she could manage was, "I don't know yet."

"Does the present give you no clue?" he persisted. She said nothing, and after a moment, Dmitri continued, "What do you like to do?"

Sifte let out a breath of relief she had not realized she was holding. "I like to play Cave. And read. And watch old films."

"You're interested in pre-holocaust history."

Sifte didn't manage to mask her surprise at his insight, or the nervous suspicion that followed on its heels. Dmitri clearly noticed it too, but apparently he misconstrued it. He smiled at her and said, "I haven't read your mind. I already know a bit about all of you."

"Then why are you asking us these things?" Tanya demanded.

Sifte exchanged looks with Mila. Tanya had gotten away with this kind of brazenness when Gospazha Maria was their teacher, but they could already see that Dmitri was cut from a different cloth.

Nonetheless, he remained unruffled. "Because I haven't heard the answers in your own words. It is your own ambitions in which I am interested, not others' ambitions for you. So, what is yours?"

It took Sifte a moment to realize that he wasn't asking this of Tanya, but of her. Sifte decided that she didn't trust him.

"To do the job for which I am best equipped, and for which our leader most needs me," she answered evenly. It was the right answer, the trained answer, and would serve the purpose of making her unremarkable. Yet as she spoke the lie an anger awakened in her that she hadn't realize she was suppressing.

She looked up at Dmitri's dark, taciturn eyes and said, "I don't know why you're asking us what we want. When it comes time to take up our posts, we'll be told, not asked."

Everyone was staring at her in shocked silence. What Sifte had said was close to blasphemous, and a part of her wished the words hadn't rung so true in her own ears. Slowly, Dmitri removed his glasses, wiped them, then replaced them. He studied Sifte in the lengthening silence, but it was Tanya who finally broke it.

"I told you she was an izmyennitsa," she said softly, poisonously.

Dmitri turned away from Sifte and looked at Tanya. She stared back at him, challenging him to punish her for speaking the words everyone was thinking. Finally Dmitri answered, but not as anyone had expected.

"You're wrong, Tanya. Sifte is not a traitor, and has in fact said something quite wise. When you leave here, you will not be asked what you want." Sifte felt the beginnings of a smug smile, along with a heady surge of elation at having her daring thought confirmed. Then Dmitri said, "But Sifte is also wrong. It's true, you will not be asked what you want…but you will not be told, either. If you make it through Institute 1, what you want to be will also be what you must." He looked once more at Sifte. "You—all of you—already know what you will be, whether or not you yet realize it. It is my job to make you realize it." He turned abruptly to Aleksei, and began questioning him.

Sifte's mind reeled with conflicting ideas. She couldn't listen to the rest of her classmates. She longed for the hour to be over, so that she could retreat to the quiet of the film room or the library and think. But when the class finally ended, before she could slip out of the classroom, Dmitri stopped her.

"Could I speak with you for a moment, Sifte?" he asked. She walked back to his desk, the guilty dread rising again.

He studied her for a long time before he said, "I'm interested in what you said earlier. You know that I could have you punished for it. On the basis of such an outburst, some teachers might even question your fitness to continue your study at Institute 1."

She looked squarely back at him. "Do you?"

He started, then smiled. "I think you know the answer to that, just like you know that I won't punish you for your words."

She didn't answer him, although he was right. She had known, though she couldn't say how, that he wouldn't punish her. Once again he was scrutinizing her, as though her face, already so carefully trained in blankness, would betray something for which he was searching.

"What made you say something like that to me in front of all your classmates and, if I am any judge of character, one significant enemy?"

"I don't know," she replied, but she felt herself flushing, hated her body for betraying her.

Dmitri raised his eyebrows and sighed. "Well, you'd best think carefully in the future about what you say before you say it."

Now it was Sifte's turn to scrutinize him. The words had been a typical teacher's platitude, yet she thought there had been a slight and unnecessary emphasis on the word 'say.' Dmitri held her eyes a moment too long. Now she was certain that he had intended the emphasis, but she had no idea what he had meant by it.

"I'll be careful," she answered, hoping that it would prompt him to say more.

"The things you say can be misconstrued," he continued, as though they were chatting about the selections at lunch. He picked up some papers and moved toward the door. "Not everyone will understand your meaning as I do."

Once again, his eyes caught hers and held them a moment too long. He was trying to tell her something, but she still had no idea what it was, or even whether it was intended as helpful or hostile. Just before they passed through the doorway, he said, "I noticed you in the library earlier. I'm glad to see you have an interest in history. A future Opyekun needs a solid understanding of the past in order to fully give herself to the future. Do you often spend your free periods in the library?"

"Or the film room," Sifte stumbled, wondering what to make of his questions, and how to safely answer them. "Or playing Cave."

"Cave?" Dmitri asked, raising his eyebrows again.

Sifte looked up at him, wondering how any Institute teacher could possibly not know about Cave. "It's a game," she said.

"I see," he said, in the absent tone he had used when questioning Tanya. "I imagine you plug into your neural jacks to play?" He didn't let her respond before continuing, "So it's a game about a cave."

"Well, no," Sifte answered. "Not exactly." In fact, this was a discrepancy she had considered before, but the game was engaging enough that she hadn't pursued it. "The settings change all the time—whenever we move up a level. But none of them have been a cave."

"Do all players change levels together?"

"No. You only get out of a level when you solve it—by yourself."

"Success is often a lonely predicament. Why not help each other?"

"Sometimes we do…but if we always helped each other, then no one would win."

94

Dmitri smiled faintly. "Dubious logic, but right on target, I suppose. Well then, how do you move up a level?"

Sifte shook her head. "It depends on the level. It's always different."

"What about the first level?" Dmitri prompted. "How did you progress from there?" Once again, Sifte had the uncomfortable sensation that he already knew what she was going to tell him, that he was really interested in the way she told it.

Sifte sighed. "Well," she began, "you're in a cinema. The old fashioned kind, with a stage and curtains and everything. You can't move from the chairs. You can't even move your head. You have to figure out how to get free."

"And in this cinema, are there films?"

"Of course."

"Good films?"

"Yes. Some are even from before the war."

"Forgive me," Dmitri said. "I'm an old man, so perhaps I no longer understand what appeals to a younger generation… but if you enjoy the movies, then what makes you want to move from the chairs?"

"Not everybody does—at least, not at first. But I thought there must be more of a point to the game than watching movies. Otherwise they'd just have showed us the movies in the film room."

"Indeed. So how did you free yourself from the chair?"

Sifte smiled to recall how simple it had been, and yet how difficult so many of her peers had found it. "You have to stop paying attention to the movies…except it's more than that. You have to stop thinking of them as what you're supposed to be thinking about. Once you realize that the movies have nothing to do with the game at all, your chair lets you go."

"And where do you go?"

"The projection room."

"What's in the projection room?"

"Soviet rebels. They're running the movies, but they don't want you to know that. When they realize you've found out, they try to kill you."

"Let me guess—you have to kill them to get to the next level?"

"Well, partly," Sifte answered. "You also have to figure out how they were working the projector, because the projector is the only light and it goes out when they die. If you can't see, you can't get out of the theater."

Dmitri sighed, and Sifte couldn't help thinking that the primary component of that sigh was disappointment. But he only asked, "What level are you working on now?"

"Twelve."

"And are your classmates also at this level?"

"Only three of us—me, Aleksei, and Anastasia. There's also one younger boy, Misha. The others are middle-level."

"Why isn't your friend Mila at your level? Don't you help her?"

"Mila won't play it. She doesn't like the killing."

Dmitri narrowed his eyes at her. "Do you?"

Sifte shrugged. "Not all the levels are about killing, and anyway, it isn't real."

"I suppose not. How many levels do you need to pass before you win? And for that matter, what is the object of winning?"

Sifte considered the question for a few moments before answering, "I don't know. Nobody does. But everybody also knows that you *can* win. I think," she continued slowly, "that part of the point is not knowing what the object is, and not knowing how to get there, at least not at first…you know, not seeing the answer until you see it. Like getting out of the seat at the beginning."

"Knowing and seeing are two different things," Dmitri suggested.

"Not in this game."

The answer seemed to surprise him. "Tell me…is there any way for people to watch without plugging in?"

"There's a screen in the games room that projects it all two-dimensionally," she said, "and you can also watch on any of the terminals. A teacher can watch any level. We can only watch the ones we've already passed."

"Perhaps," Dmitri suggested, after regarding her quizzically for several more seconds, "I could observe a session? Would you like to play now?"

Sifte didn't try to hide her surprise: teachers never involved themselves in the games. "I'm not signed in today, and the schedule's full."

Dmitri smiled. "I can take care of that. Shall we?"

"All right," Sifte said. "Only, I usually play with Aleksei. We've been working on this level together."

"Go get him, then. I'll have the room free in fifteen minutes." Dmitri left her standing in the empty classroom, staring after him.

8

"He wants to watch us play Cave?" Aleksei repeated incredulously, following Sifte down the corridor. "He's even crazier than Gospazha Maria."

"At least this is more fun."

Aleksei smiled. "Did he threaten to put you on garbage duty if you said no?"

"Just you. Come on."

Four disgruntled-looking Level 8 students, thugs who had always given Sifte and her friends a hard time, were leaving the games room as Aleksei and Sifte arrived. "Fantastic," Aleksei mumbled.

"Just keep walking," Sifte said.

Nevertheless, the boys blocked their path a few feet from the door. The biggest of them, a heavy-set boy called Rodya, said, "Got us kicked off, shitheads. Trying to up us a level while we aren't looking?"

Sifte stiffened in anticipation of a fight. "We're only doing what the new teacher told us to."

Rodya stepped toward her with menace. "Maybe you better explain the rules to the new teacher, since he doesn't seem to understand them very well."

"On the contrary," Dmitri answered, emerging from the games room door. "I understand them perfectly. You have one probation for disrespect of authority already. Open criticism of a teacher's decision is adequate grounds for another. I'm willing to overlook it if you go quietly. Now." Dmitri smiled frostily, and though the sneer twisted further into his face, Rodya went without another word.

When they were gone, Dmitri turned to Sifte and Aleksei. "I hope I haven't laid you open for trouble from them."

Sifte sighed. "No more than usual."

"Well then, are you ready?"

"We're always ready for Cave," Aleksei answered, pushing past them into the room.

Sifte and Aleksei chose jack points close together, sat down and leaned back, so that the interface plugs connected to their jacks. Their last game was already running. "Ready?" Aleksei asked.

"Wait a minute," she answered.

It had been a week since they had played together, and Sifte wanted to re-acquaint herself with the terrain. Level twelve was set in the ruins of a city. When the game was paused, the scenery shimmered slightly and its focus was indistinct, but it was realistic enough to remind Sifte how much she hated the level. The city was too much like the sub-race slums they had been taught to fear from their earliest childhood. It seemed to Sifte that the city itself was the level's most potent enemy, a semi-sentience luring them toward its dark heart, where some unimaginable danger waited.

The maze of rubble-strewn streets stretched as far as the eye could see, monotonously desolate. Nothing moved in them but enemies. No sound but Sifte's own deadened footsteps and heartbeat shifted the ominous silence. No sun or moon altered the darkness, and this was what Sifte hated most, because it meant that the level had to be played in the old-blood light of infrared goggles.

"Sifte?" Aleksei said.

"Sorry. Go ahead."

Aleksei unfroze the program. The infrared landscape resolved into distinct focus around them, losing its remoteness, though not its hallucinatory quality,. The game had dressed them in the gray woolen uniforms of the Opyekuni, with the goggles like bulbous insect eyes over their own. Each of them held an automatic pistol with one clip of bullets: barely enough for the number of enemies they would have to defeat to win the level.

"Left!" Aleksei yelled, and Sifte whirled in time to see an appalling distortion of a man lurching toward her, his form aswirl with the multicolored light of body heat. She reacted almost instantaneously, and the monster fell twitching only a few inches away from her.

"Thanks," she said to Aleksei shakily. "Owe you one."

They looked around, scanning for any other brightening of the sickly red, but all around them the coast was clear. "Together or alone?" Aleksei asked.

Splitting up might give them a better chance of discovering a way out, but the eerie desolation made Sifte reluctant to explore it by herself. "Together," she said.

They started off down one of the streets, clambering over piles of rubble or crumbling walls. They had learned through previous failed efforts to avoid stepping in the opaque liquid that pooled in crevices and potholes. It contained some corrosive which ate through their boots and then their skin, ultimately paralyzing them and sending them back to the beginning of the level. Likewise, they dodged the streams of mist which pulsed with dull heat—appropriately, since breathing it burned out their lungs. None of these ailments actually caused them physical pain, but the simulation of the topical symptoms was horrific on its own.

Several turnings in from their starting point, they encountered their first real challenge: an ambush by five heavily-armed Soviet soldiers. The Soviets cut off their escape routes deftly, as though they had been watching them for some time. With the instinct perfected by years of playing together, Sifte and Aleksei turned so that their backs were together.

"Ideas?" Aleksei asked.

Sifte looked at the enemy. None of the attempts they'd made to fight or escape these soldiers had ever worked. She was fairly certain that violence wasn't the answer, because the soldiers made no move to attack. Yet there seemed to be no way through the enemy ring.

"We can't kill them, and we can't get past them," Sifte said aloud. "Maybe we're meant to distract them."

"How?" Aleksei asked, with a shortness that told Sifte he was as uncomfortable as she was.

"Disarm them," she suggested, though she had only the prologue of an idea.

"If we could disarm them—" Aleksei began.

"Not like that," she said. "Psychologically. Make them think we're giving up. Get them to let their defenses down."

"And how are we supposed to do that?"

"Like this." Sifte laid down her gun.

"Are you crazy?"

"Has anything else worked?"

Reluctantly, Aleksei laid down his gun beside Sifte's. Sifte raised both hands in surrender, and Aleksei did the same.

They had never tried to surrender to enemy projections before. As far as she knew, no one had.

The Soviet kept their guns trained on Sifte and Aleksei, and their stances remained offensive. "I think...I think we have to say something," Sifte suggested.

"What are we supposed to say?"

"We give up," Sifte said, loudly enough that the Soviet would hear her if they were programmed to be able to.

The shimmering forms began to move. At first Sifte was transfixed by the flickering lights of their bodies, the shadows that slid and shifted within them as different muscles moved, like fish in a clear stream. It took her some moments to realize that they were lowering their weapons. One ragged man stepped forward. He was tall, with straggly, pale hair and eyes hidden in shadow.

"Do you wish to join us?" he asked, with a touch of an accent so faint that Sifte could not place it, or even be certain that she heard it.

For a moment Sifte was too stunned to answer. No character in Cave had ever tried to engage her in conversation. Some responded to specific words, and others spoke, but only to hurl threats or taunts. Yet this man had a pleasant, steady voice, one that sounded as reasonable to Sifte as those of her friends or teachers.

"Join you in what?" Aleksei asked him.

"Our mission," the man answered.

"What's your mission?" Sifte asked.

"We can't tell you that until we know that we can trust you."

"And how will you know?"

"You'll leave your weapons and come with us."

"But how can we know whether we can trust you?" Aleksei rejoined.

"Sometimes a leap of faith is the only way forward."

Sifte looked at Aleksei, but the goggles made it impossible to read his expression. He shrugged. "We don't have much to lose," he said.

Sifte didn't entirely agree with this—the stealthy paranoia of the city was beginning to grip her in earnest—but she couldn't think of any other way out of this trap. "Okay," she said.

"Good," the man answered in the same dispassionate tone. He turned, and gestured to the others to follow him. They surrounded Sifte and Aleksei, and moved off at a fast pace through narrow alleys and streets the Soviet man seemed to know well.

"Where do you think they're taking us?" Aleksei asked.

Sifte shook her head. The pace they were keeping was too fast to leave much breath for talking. Instead, she studied the terrain. The buildings seemed to be thinning out as they moved along, which was odd, because she and Aleksei had traveled at least as far into the city before without this happening. Also, the enemies seemed to have thinned with the buildings. Now and again they caught sight of figures in the shadows, but none approached them. The clouds of poisonous gas and the acidic pools had disappeared too.

Despite all of this, and the Soviet soldiers' apparent lack of hostility, Sifte's unease was mounting. Accepting the enemy's challenge had certainly gotten them further than they ever had been before, but there was no indication that it was where they wanted to be. Finally the buildings petered out, like trees on a mountain's summit. The tall man kept moving until the last building was out of sight, then he stopped.

"Look," he commanded. They stood on a smooth plane, cross-hatched with the deep cracks of a long drought. No light challenged the darkness but a dim red glow from the cracked earth; without the infrared goggles they would be entirely blind. This thought terrified Sifte, because the plane looked as infinite as the city once had, but its desolation was profoundly greater. It was more than the barrenness of the landscape. The parched ground seemed to have sucked the hope out of Sifte, leaving her as close to despair as she had ever been.

"Do you like this place?" the man asked.

Sifte shook her head. Aleksei said nothing at all. She reached for his hand and it was already open, seeking her own. The warmth of it made her feel a bit better, but she remained tense with foreboding.

"Of course not," the Soviet said. Now scorn tinged the neutrality of his tone. "Who could like the embodiment of loneliness? To be utterly alone is mankind's greatest fear… one which I imagine an orphan feels more acutely than most."

"We're not orphans," Aleksei said. "Solntse is father to us all."

Sifte gripped his hand more tightly. "And we're not alone."

The Soviet smiled a caricature of a smile which was visible even through the hazy refraction of the goggles. "Now you are." And suddenly, she was.

She looked at the hand Aleksei had held, watched the residual heat fading from it. "Lyosha!" she cried, with such heartbreaking despair that Dmitri, watching on the games room monitor, nearly stopped the program. However, he recognized how close Sifte was to beating this level, and whether or not she could do so would tell him a good deal of what he needed to know in order to progress with his plans. Reluctantly, he lowered the hand resting on the controls and resumed his scrutiny.

Sifte waited for a reply. "Lyosha?" she called again. "Aleksei, please don't leave me!" Sifte reached her arms around in every direction, but touched nothing. "Aleksei!" she cried again. Her eyes filled with tears of fear and frustration.

"End game," she commanded the computer, then stood staring at the blank horizon, waiting for it to dissolve into the familiar half-light of the games room, but nothing changed. "End game," she said again, and again the computer ignored her request. Sifte clung to her composure for one valiant moment, then she sank onto the ground, consumed by tears and blind panic.

For a few minutes she let herself cry, but then the tears began to cloud her goggles. She lifted them for a moment to dry her eyes, and at the shock of the total darkness beyond, she regained a bit of her self-control. The game had never presented her with a problem she didn't have the means to solve; she didn't dare consider that she might be caught in some kind of malfunction. She replaced the goggles, stood up shakily, and looked around. There was still nothing in the landscape to help her determine the next move, not even any indication of the direction of the city. For a few minutes she tried to dig , but the earth was as hard as cement.

She sat down again and considered the possibilities. She knew she couldn't leave the desert by physical means. She wouldn't need any tools but the ones she had with her, and all she had with her was her clothing, a clip of bullets, and a pair of infrared goggles. The bullets were useless without a gun, but even a gun would have been useless against this

105

wasteland, or her own panic. The goggles kept the darkness at bay, but they were otherwise meaningless when there was nothing to see.

Sifte thought back further. The early parts in the city with Aleksei hadn't covered any new ground: they had been a straightforward test of learned and instinctive reactions. The first deviation had been the Soviet leader's ability to converse with them. The solution must begin with this deviation—otherwise, why bother with it?

She tried to recall all that the projection had said. He had asked them to join him in his mission, and though he had never explained what it was, it seemed to Sifte now that it must be equivalent or at least related to solving the level. And when Aleksei had asked why they should trust him, he had answered that sometimes the only way forward is a leap of faith. But in this place, with nothing to touch or taste or hear, nothing now to love or fear losing, it seemed there was nowhere to leap.

Then, all at once, she knew. For a moment, she physically clung to the goggles, as if something might actually tear them from her. Gradually, though, she became convinced that to give them up was what the game intended, had even suggested to her with the Soviet's words.

Sifte realized that she was breathing in quick, shallow gasps, and the first thing she did was to take control of this, forcing herself to pace her breathing as they had been taught in their meditation lessons. Then, to ease herself into the reality of darkness, she closed her eyes. When she had sat for several minutes like this, concentrating on her breathing until it filled her mind and pushed out the panic, she pulled the goggles off and laid them on the ground in front of her. Immediately they disappeared. For a moment panic fought to surface again, but she pushed it back. When she was sure of herself, she opened her eyes.

They strained into the unremitting darkness. Sifte felt for the rough ground around her, but her hands met nothing. When she tried to touch her own arms and legs, she found that she could no longer feel them, either. She was a consciousness only, suspended in a void. Rather than succumb to fear this time, she concentrated on shutting out the false reality of the void, and searched for the self she had left behind in the games room.

That was when she realized that she was not alone. Other thoughts surrounded hers; another consciousness was listening to hers. *Who are you?* she asked it. There was no immediate reply, but after a few moments, an answer formed in her mind: *I am the source of truth.* She could not be certain whether they came from the other mind or her own, but then that mind opened its eyes.

Sifte found herself looking down at a city not unlike the one she and Aleksei had left behind. However, she no longer saw it through the ruddy haze, but in the clear light of day, with all its colors, lights, and shadows. One side of the city was a green Eden, the other a ruin. She could see into every corner of it, into the eyes and hearts of every being who walked its streets. The rush of omnipotence was the most intense feeling she had ever had. Then the vision and the feeling and the other mind were gone, leaving her in the void again.

Oddly, it was easier to concentrate than it had been before the strange vision. After a time she became aware of the weight to her body, then the solidity of the chair in the games room, and finally the sounds of machinery, its hot metal-plastic smell. When she was certain of all of these things, she opened her eyes.

Dmitri was standing in front of her, his face white and anxious. "Sifte," he said, "I tried to stop it, but—"

"Where's Lyosha?" she asked.

"Here," Aleksei answered. He was perched unsteadily on the edge of his chair. Fear edged his eyes like ice on an autumn pond.

Sifte managed a weak smile. "Don't tell me you beat me out."

Aleksei frowned. "I don't know how to explain it. I was with you until the Soviet guy disappeared, but then you were suddenly just...gone."

He shook his head. "I got out not long after that—there was this stupid plot with a rainstorm that uncovered some pieces of machinery I had to put together into these digging robots to tunnel my way out. Anyway, I watched the end of your game with Dmitri. We saw everything until you took off the goggles, then the screen just went blank. What happened?"

Sifte shook her head. She was suddenly exhausted; she could barely think to answer him, but she managed to say, "I'll try to explain it to you sometime, but right now I think I need to rest."

"Yes," Dmitri agreed, "and if I were you, I'd rest from the game for a while, too."

Sifte shook her head. "No," she answered, with vehemence she hadn't intended. "I need to go back."

Dmitri looked at her white, wide-eyed face, and sighed. "I might suggest that the library is a better place for a trainee Opyekun to spend her time, but of course it's up to you." This time, the stress on the word "library" was unmistakable. "I'll see you soon, Sifte, and in the meantime, be careful."

9

Andrei gave Stepan a few days to recover, but it was clear to Stepan that he was impatient to begin looking for the child. So, on Stepan's fourth day out of prison, he broached the topic himself.

"The first place we should look is the Institutes," Andrei said, as if there hadn't been an interruption in their initial conversation. "Solntse keeps students to their local schools, except of course for Institute 1, so you'll only have to check the two in the Solntsegrad vicinity. Well, three, including Institute 1. We'd better begin by calling up a list of ten-year-olds. That shouldn't be too highly-classified."

"You have access to a computer?" asked Stepan. Computers in Solntse's economically-depressed state were generally accessories of the elite.

"I was waiting to show you until you'd recovered," said Andrei. And until I knew I could trust you, Stepan finished for him, in his mind. The unspoken addendum didn't anger him. He would have done the same in Andrei's position.

Andrei walked over to a battered wooden cabinet at the far side of the room and opened its double doors. Inside was a clothes bar. A few shirts, a ragged coat and a string of sausages hung from it. Andrei pushed these aside, then slid his finger into a nearly-invisible hole in a knot in the wood of the cabinet's back. The panel pushed inward to reveal a small opening in the wall behind the cupboard, with a ladder stretching up out of sight. Stepan went up first, and Andrei followed him, closing both the cupboard doors and the inner one. They climbed a short way up through the darkness, and emerged onto a plank floor.

Andrei flicked a switch, and the little room filled with light. Stepan looked around in amazement. The room had obviously once been part of the building's attic, but had been partitioned off from the rest with cinder-block walls on three sides. The other wall was slanted, part of the roof. One wall was all shelves, stacked with canned food. There was a bed in one corner; in another was a desk with a network antenna and the computer. It was a hybrid of salvaged parts, mainly Chinese and Russian. Andrei's connections could no doubt have provided him with a new, black-market computer, but this reclaimed type worked almost as well and was safer contraband, as it could not be traced.

"We've been establishing bunkers all over Myortvograd," Andrei explained. "We're also working on a central control station and an underground bunker with the capacity to hold a good number of people, but we don't yet have the means to finish it. At any rate, the computer is a nice asset." He touched the power key, and the screen flickered to life. As the antenna had suggested, it was running through Glaza.

Glaza, 'Eyes,' was Solntse's wireless network, the computerized forum for all communication, business and media in Russia. It was also a filter, a mesh of watchful eyes through which all transactions passed, to ensure their purity before being released to the general public. Despite this, a constant trickle of illegal and distinctly factious traffic ran through Glaza, most of it Soviet. Sometimes these transmissions were detected and traced; more often they weren't. No one knew why so many transmissions slipped through the net, but then no one knew what the eyes consisted of in the first place.

Stepan picked up the transceiver unit next to the computer. It was American-made. "This is no salvage," he said.

Andrei smiled with paternal pride. "It's the most advanced piece of transmission technology ever produced. It hasn't even been released onto the world market yet."

"Which begs the question—"

"The Soviet waylaid a shipment. There were only five of them. No doubt some kind of bribe for Solntse."

"Where are the other four?"

"In good hands."

Stepan put the device down again. "Running through Glaza takes more than fancy technology. You need codes, identities, countless safeguards."

"We might not have leaders, but in the last few years we've taken on more than our fair share of hackers. All competent, some brilliant."

"Can't the officials trace you through your transmissions?"

Andrei shrugged. "Theoretically. But so far they haven't."

"So it's a gamble."

"Maybe. But personally, I think the eyes are only programs, written to look for keywords and their more common encryptions. Whatever they are, they fail with consoling regularity. Glaza's gotten too big. When there's too much traffic the programs can't check all of it, or at least not carefully."

"But if they know you stole transceivers—"

Andrei sighed. "Stepan, believe me, if this wasn't almost foolproof, I wouldn't be doing it." Andrei pulled the keyboard toward him, located a search engine, and typed in:

```
Institutes Solntsegrad
```

The screen displayed a number of matching files. Andrei chose one, then entered a search within it for a list of Level 5 female students. The screen blanked, and then displayed the message:

```
Please enter name, rank and code.
```

"So much for that idea," said Stepan dryly. "Unless you have Pomoshchnik clearance."

Andrei smiled, and typed in a long string of numbers and letters. A list of names appeared in its wake.

"How did you manage that?"

"Professional secret." Stepan raised his eyebrows, and Andrei relented. "Actually, it's one of our great success stories. It wasn't easy, and it took a lot of courage on the part of the woman who accomplished it. Vera is one of our youngest and least experienced leaders, but she's as clever as she is well-endowed. She managed to get herself into the good graces of one of Glaza's chief administrators. Then she only had to wait for him to leave a computer while he was still logged in under his superuser password—"

"And steal a few I.D. codes."

"Better than that. She got Glaza to generate new codes for our use, connected to identities we'd already constructed— imaginary officials based in remote areas so that they're difficult to check on. This way, the codes appear to have been created legitimately within the system. The one I just used made me a mid-ranking Pomoshchnik, but we can also be high-ranking Pomoshchniki and even Opyekuni. Of course, we have to be careful with the 'kuni. There are too few, they talk to each other too often."

Stepan shook his head. "Solntse's too sure of himself."

"Or else we are. I prefer to look at it your way. Now, let's see what he's got on the kids." They both looked at the screen. It showed a list of names, birth dates, class ranks, special talents, and I.Q.'s of all female Level 5 students in the three local Institutes. They were all accompanied by brief physical descriptions.

"I suppose we'll have to go through all of them," said Andrei.

"What are we looking for, specifically?" Stepan asked.

"Hard to say. All of these children are gifted, so I.Q. isn't really going to help us. But there are more telling criteria. Obviously we can rule out any non-Caucasian children. Also, we know that she was born in August. Other than that, anything that might link her to you or Sasha."

Andrei printed two copies of the list, and they took them back downstairs. Stepan studied his copy carefully, interested despite himself in what it might reveal. As Andrei had predicted, many of the children had unusual talents; fewer had birth dates that matched with Andrei's information. Slowly, they narrowed the choices.

"I have ten that match the hard data," said Andrei. "Maybe five of them seem likely."

Stepan sighed. "I've got about the same. I don't know how to narrow it down further. I know my talents and Sasha's, but one or the other matches all of these kids, and besides, there's no guarantee that her talents will reflect ours."

"There has to be something unusual about her, or Solntse wouldn't have risked keeping her. You'd think that she would stand out from the others in some way, even on a list like this." Andrei shook his head. "But that might be a foolish assumption, considering we have no idea what Solntse was looking for."

"Maybe not," Stepan said slowly. "As you say, for Solntse to keep her she'd have to be so unusual she'd stand out even on a list like this. If she is so extraordinary, then it's unlikely she's anywhere but Institute 1."

"That's one theory..."

Stepan was pacing the sagging floor of the apartment, his bad leg skewing the rhythm to iambs. "Well, such a child would also appear outstanding to others. Solntse wouldn't risk listing her publicly. She'd be too much of a liability to him, too easy a target."

Andrei was smiling wryly "So what do you suggest we do next?"

Stepan stopped in front of Andrei, staring at him but clearly not seeing him. "Begin at the beginning."

"Which is?"

"Her parents." They climbed back up into the bunker, and began with a wide search on Stepan's name, under the guise of a high-ranking Pomoshchnik. They came up with the expected reams of results.

"Now search within those," said Stepan. "Are there any matches with 'children' or 'Institute 1'?"

Andrei typed in the keywords, but came up with nothing. He turned to Stepan, whose face had taken on the set, determined aspect that it always showed when he was absorbed in an intelligence problem.

"Now what?"

"You might as well try Sasha."

Andrei searched, then cross-searched, but again there was no mention of a child in connection with Sasha's name.

"There's something we're not thinking of," Stepan muttered.

Andrei contemplated the screen. "If only we had some clue, something to help us think of what the child's name might be, or how Solntse might have classified her…"

Stepan wrung his mind for every bit of information he knew about Solntse, any word Sasha might have said to him which would give him a clue as to what she might have named their daughter. He repeated the facts to himself: Solntse ousted the second post-holocaust government, then set up his own dictatorship based on a revisionist reading of Plato's *Republic*. He hoped to rebuild the Russian country and culture under a strong leader, his commonly-known idol being Tsar Peter the Great. He praised Tsar Peter almost as vehemently as he criticized the American president who had resigned on the eve of the holocaust, Elisa Foley, the woman whom Sasha had so admired and to whom he himself was distantly related—

"Elisa Foley," he said abruptly.

Andrei looked at him questioningly. "The American president? There were no Elisas on that Institute list."

"Of course not! They never would have allowed it. But I think this is the right direction."

"All right," Andrei sighed. He typed in the name, and it produced over five hundred thousand references. "We've got to narrow it down somehow," he said.

Stepan was biting his fingernails, a habit he had incongruously forgotten during his years in prison. "Try to find a bio."

Andrei typed, read the results, then paraphrased: "She was born in New York City, the daughter of Norwegian immigrants. She went to a local high school—"

"Does it give a full name?" Stepan interrupted.

"She was born Elisa Pierson." He looked up at Stepan. "Pierson?"

"My great great grand something or other, but I don't think that's the right lead, either. Are there any other names?"

"Let's see…yes, a middle name. Sifte."

Stepan smiled. "Sifte indeed. Let's look at the Institute 1 files again."

Andrei requested the list, this time giving an Opyekun's code. The search yielded no 'Sifte.'

"There's still one rank higher," Stepan said.

"What makes you think we have advisors' codes?"

Stepan said nothing, just looked at Andrei with his cool, assured eyes. Andrei sighed, and began typing the complicated string of numbers that allowed Solntse's thirteen advisors access to anything stored in Glaza. In a few minutes, text began to unroll on the screen.

"Quick work, Stepan," Andrei said grudgingly. He looked at the text, and began to repeat it out loud. "Her name is indeed Sifte. Hmm, even here he's being cagey—it says her family was of Finnish origin. But she was born ten years ago on August 23, in Myortvograd. Supposedly her father died in the smallpox epidemic before she was born, and she was taken from her mother who was crazed and…tried to kill her?" Andrei and Stepan looked at each other, then both discarded this statement as another of Solntse's fabrications. "She was taken from the city when she was one week old, which coincides with Sasha's disappearance. They took her to Institute 1 two weeks later.

"Academic data...Sifte's I.Q. is off the scales. Her academic rank among her peers, as designated by the standardized testing, is in the first percentile. This child is obviously brilliant. The puzzling thing is that her class rank on her teacher's analysis—excuse me, her former teacher, Maria 3 Orlovskaya—is around the twentieth percentile." At the bottom of the screen were the words:

```
Replacement instructor, Isaak 1 Dmitriev
```

"Dmitriev," Andrei said. "Wasn't he that teacher they tried for murder a few years ago?" He shook his head. "I must be confusing him with someone else. Anyhow, it seems the girl is interested in political history. Her aptitude for historical analysis and synthesis is on par with an upper-level Institute 1 student."

"All of the evidence points in her direction," Stepan said slowly, as though trying to convince himself.

"I have to agree," Andrei replied.

Stepan looked at him with weary surmise.

10

The first change Dmitri instituted was to customize his students' assignments. In the beginning this puzzled Sifte, because she had always been told that Institute education was standardized to promote unity. However, she found her new lessons too interesting to worry about this for long, and soon she came to love him like most of her classmates, for his gentle competence and genuine interest in their wellbeing.

There was one mystery connected with him, however, which Sifte couldn't forget. The day after his arrival, she had decided to re-read the book on Elisa Foley. But when she went to find it, it was gone. She browsed through the other books half-heartedly, and was about to leave when her eye caught on something anomalous. She turned back to the shelves. The titles of the library books were always printed in standard Cyrillic letters, even those that contained text in foreign languages. The title that caught her eye now was also printed in this standard font, but it had an unfamiliar symbol on either side of it. It was like a pinwheel, but somehow more sinister. The title was: *The Rise and Fall of the Third Reich*.

Sifte didn't know the word 'Reich.' It sounded German, but she hadn't studied German. Pulling the book from the shelf, Sifte found that though the spine had been finished with the bland gray binding tape of the post-war publishing houses, the covers were made of black leather. She pulled the tape away to reveal the same title stamped into the leather in gold. This time, Sifte didn't pause to wonder how the book had come to be where it was. She took it to a table against the far wall and began to read.

The book was about a dictator in twentieth century Germany. He had intended to implement his theories on the superiority of what he called the Aryan race: a term apparently synonymous with Caucasian Christians. The methods he used to destroy aberrants were so horrifying that Sifte was reluctant to turn each page; yet she did turn them. The more she read, the more uneasy she felt, because she couldn't help but see the similarity between the Nazis' and the Institute cliques' persecution of anyone different from the super-race ideal.

It was not so much the persecution itself that bothered Sifte. To reject what was different was simply human nature. Rather, it was the fact that like many of the educated Aryans in Hitler's Germany, her teachers allowed and therefore indirectly condoned this persecution. In effect, this meant that Solntse sanctioned it too. It wasn't much of a leap to wonder whether he shared Hitler's ideas about the eradication of variants from the super-race.

Sifte had read enough to know that some of the most powerful nations in the world had joined together in the belief that these oppressed races did not deserve to be treated as inferior, and had helped them prevail. So by the world's standards, Hitler had been wrong—not just wrong, but wrong to a degree that had ravaged entire continents and caused his own country to implode. And however she tried to avoid it, Sifte could not discard the possibility that Solntse was equally wrong.

For Sifte this was not a liberating but a horrifying possibility. She had never felt the rapturous love for Solntse that some of her peers seemed to, but he was still the summation of her past, present and future. If Solntse were wrong, then her life had no meaning and no purpose. She didn't want to accept this; however, she could no more easily throw the book aside. So she read on until her free period was over and then, with equal parts reluctance and relief, she put the book back on the shelf where she had found it.

But when she climbed into bed that night and her hand came up against something hard under her pillow, she wasn't surprised. In the last few minutes before the lights dimmed, she curled around the volume, and opened to the page where she had stopped reading, too eager to continue to even wonder where the book had come from. Inside, she found a piece of paper with a few handwritten words on it. They said:

"Read it, and believe it. There is a reason why you should know these terrible things. But don't ever let anyone know that you know them, not even your closest friends. When you have finished this book put it in the cafeteria incinerator— this holds true for the ones to come as well—and don't ever ask me about them. You will know the answers in time, but in this place even the walls are listening. My life and yours depend on this remaining a secret."

There was no signature at the bottom of the note, but Sifte knew who had written it, just as she knew now that she hadn't imagined the emphasis in Dmitri's words that first day. Before she could resume reading, the lights went out. But Sifte lay awake for a long time in the darkness, clutching the dubious comfort of the solid volume to her chest, wondering what it all meant.

*

A month later, a viral epidemic swept through the school. So many children and teachers were ill that classes were postponed. Though Sifte remained healthy, she was miserable. She had no lessons to keep her busy, Cave wasn't any fun without Aleksei, and she had finished and incinerated the latest of Dmitri's books several days earlier.

She took to wandering the Institute's lesser-used hallways in search of anything distracting. She seldom saw anybody, and even less frequently anyone who bothered to send her back to her own part of the building. One day she found a locked door on the Level 8 floor which seemed to be operated by an old-fashioned key-card.

Lately Sifte had been so busy that she had forgotten her old sense of claustrophobia. Somehow, the locked door brought it all back, compounded by the wild new ideas Dmitri's books had suggested. Sifte wondered anew why they weren't allowed outside. The more she thought about the teachers' justifications, the less sense they made. If the land still held radiation, and the cities dangerous gangs and deadly diseases, then how was it that people still lived in those places? Even Solntse lived there. It had become increasingly clear to Sifte that her understanding of many things was being carefully guarded, and certainly guided; that more than locking things out, the Institutes were locking something in.

"Prisons," Sifte said out loud. She stopped walking and sat down on the floor's dark blue stripe. She shook her head as if to loosen the word, but it was firmly lodged. Glowering at the colored line, she wondered whether it would ever really end. From her earliest days, she had been told about the great work that she would take up when she graduated. But none of the graduates had ever come back to verify that promise, unless you counted the teachers, and they had never really left the Institutes.

Sifte got up again, walked to the elevator and rode it up to the news room, thinking she might find Dmitri there, and that he might be able to offer some kind of solace. He was hunched over one of the terminals when she entered. When he saw her he smiled, though she could not help thinking that it was forced.

"Still healthy, I see!" he said, with a joviality that seemed equally labored. "I thought that I'd see you here sooner or later. I must come up with something more for you to do while the epidemic continues."

Sifte scrutinized him as she always did when they spoke, for any sign of a hidden meaning, but his face was blank and serene. This serenity sometimes made her wonder if she had it all wrong, and her secret mentor was not in fact Dmitri.

"That would be good," she finally answered. "What are you reading?"

"News. I try to read it every day."

"Why?"

Dmitri half-shrugged. "It's good to be prepared."

"For what?"

"You never know."

"Another war?"

Dmitri smiled, but too late to hide his surprise. "Do you think there will be another war?" he asked, in the teasing tone an adult takes when asking a child a rhetorical question.

"Of course not," Sifte answered quickly, wondering how she could have been so careless. "There's no more reason for war."

"Indeed," Dmitri said, turning once again to the computer screen. "The Sun is wise; he gives us no reason to quarrel and keeps our country an island to avoid conflict with other nations."

"And there are no more nuclear weapons," Sifte reminded him.

Dmitri paused, then proceeded more slowly, as if he were afraid of choosing the wrong words. "Still—conflict is inherent to human nature. Though the military function of the Opyekuni is in this perfect state only theoretical, it is perhaps wise for the student Opyekun to understand war. What causes it, what wins or loses it. Solntse won't live forever, and there could come a time when Russia faces an outside threat. Then it would fall to the Opyekuni to truly act as guardians—not merely to fulfill the function of the philosopher-ruler, but also to physically defend the state."

"I suppose so," Sifte answered, while her mind raced across the reams of information she had taken in over the last month, much of which had covered the histories of Europe's wars. As in many of their conversations, she was aware now that Dmitri was speaking to her on two levels, and her mind dove to the challenge of his double meanings like a hawk to its prey.

"You said that there won't be another war," Dmitri began, in the tone he took during class lectures, "and based this assertion first—and here I interpret your words, so do correct me if I am mistaken—on the strength of Solntse's political ideology and ability to implement it, and secondly on the fact that there are no more weapons of mass destruction. Of course, we know that the first assertion is correct. But can you back up the second?"

"Do you think they didn't destroy all of them?" Sifte asked.

"I think they did."

"Then what's the problem? If there are no weapons, there can be no war."

Dmitri shook his head, looking at the screen rather than at Sifte. "Simplistic logic. There are few direct correlations when it comes to war. It's a state of mind; weapons are only instruments controlled by minds in such a state. Two minds can fight a war. Or one mind, divided."

He stared fixedly at the text on the screen before him. He appeared to have said all he meant to. However, Sifte was enough used to this multi-level banter by now to know that though he had finished speaking, he had not finished his lesson. His last few words rang in her ears: one mind, divided. Sifte leaned over Dmitri's shoulder. He was logged into a Glaza news room, the screen scrolling the latest headlines. A Myortvograd building had collapsed onto one of the old Metro stations, killing the people living in both the building and the station. An antiquated, overloaded plane from one of the Satellites had crashed onto the Vyborgside shanty-town, and the fires were still raging. A new synthetic virus would eradicate the Clones, a recent genetic engineering backfire of one of the Protectorate states, which were beginning to cause problems in southern Russia. None of the stories was anything special.

"I don't think I understand," Sifte said.

A strange expression passed over Dmitri's face: equal parts panic, plea, and desperate faith. "Too abstract?" he asked, with a smile like a searchlight. "Let's take a different tack, then. Consider America."

"America?" Sifte asked, shocked that Dmitri would pick the topic he must have known had been rubbing her raw since he planted that first book.

But he was already speaking again with kindly patience. "Americans are conditioned to hate what they don't understand. Actually, to be fair, they're probably only conditioned to suspect it, but suspicion turns to hatred soon enough. The holocaust is proof of that.

"Hatred is nearly impossible to overcome, Sifte. It's the strongest of emotions, except perhaps fear. Though often they are two sides of the same coin. Do you know why it's so difficult to subjugate hatred?"

He looked at her earnestly, and Sifte thought of all the times she had been taunted by Tanya for her foreign name or her odd scar. She thought of the intensity with which Tanya's followers clung to her, even when she was cruel to them. Then she considered the last time she had fought with Tanya and how she had gambled on her friends to help her win that fight. She had trusted them to support her, and they hadn't. Now she persecuted them with as much vitriol as she ever had Sifte.

"Because it's so easy to hate," Sifte said slowly, "and because when you hate, it takes over everything in you."

"That's right."

"Is it?" He raised his eyebrows, but said nothing. Sifte continued, "I think…I think you're right when you say that hatred is the most difficult emotion to overcome, but I don't think it's the strongest."

He scrolled down the news screen, as if he were only perfunctorily interested in what she was saying, but Sifte could sense him listening. She had begun to feel that the concept she was talking about was beyond her. Nevertheless, she drew a valiant breath and plunged on.

"What I mean to say is, hatred isn't a natural emotion, so even though it might be the easiest to feel, it can't be the strongest."

"If you feel it, it's as natural as any other."

Sifte sighed. "Then 'natural' wasn't the right word. I mean that hatred isn't…well…pure." She groped for an analogy. "If we were talking about chemistry," she said, "then hatred wouldn't be an element, it would be a compound."

Dmitri smiled. Sifte thought she saw something supercilious in that smile, but when he said, "Go on," she knew that she had hit one of his targets, and that this pleased him, regardless of his opinion of it.

"Hatred doesn't exist by itself. It has to start out as something else. I guess maybe the compound isn't even a good metaphor for it, because hatred is more one thing changed into another, than a combination of different things. Something catalyzed, but still itself."

"I'm not sure about that," he answered. "I think perhaps it takes on some of the catalyst, and is thereby altered. Still, I'm intrigued by your idea that hatred is essentially derivative. Can you tell me how this is so?"

Sifte paused again, choosing her words carefully. "I think hatred comes from fear or betrayed love. Which I'm assuming includes trust."

This time, Dmitri's smile was genuine. "Good girl!" he said softly. "Now back it up."

"Fear seems to come from two things—misunderstanding and threat. Only I guess in the end, the first is only an earlier form of the second. Like what you were saying about the

Americans. If you misunderstand something, you begin to make it into something else in your mind. Usually you don't make it into something good, so it becomes a threat. And it's normal to be afraid of a threat.

"Fear is a bad feeling, so when you fear something for long enough, you're going to begin to hate it for making you feel that way. And once you hate it, you'll try to fight it. I guess that's what you were saying, before. What you meant about war happening in the mind. It's like Tanya hating Aleksei. He looks different, maybe he reminds her of something she's already afraid of. He threatens her because of something that's in her head, that probably doesn't even exist, but it's still real to her. So she hates him. And because she hates him, she persecutes him."

Sifte paused, and before she could continue Dmitri asked, "And you?"

"Me?"

"You're not a favorite among the other children. Do you think the same logic applies to their view of you?"

Sifte looked at him for a long time. There had been one of the now-familiar rifts in the flow of those words, a slight pause before he said 'among the other children.' She saw what he meant: that it was not only the other children with whom she was not a favorite. She didn't know how to answer. In the end, she only said, "Yes, I guess it applies to me, too." She shrugged as though she accepted this as the only possible way for things to be.

"You also said something about love."

"Betrayal of love," she answered wearily. "I think the kind of hate that comes from love must have a lot of other things tied into it, because the love is still there in some way. But I still don't really think it's a compound."

"So you think it's elemental?"

Sifte was aware that this didn't really follow on her last statement, but she was glad enough to find herself on firm rhetorical ground that she answered, "Yes."

A half-smile was twitching Dmitri's face again. "What makes you think so?"

Again she answered without a pause, "Mila."

Dmitri appeared taken aback by this response. After a moment, he conceded, "Lyudmila possesses great strength and an unusual capacity for love. Not just love, but selfless love. Still—even selfless love is not necessarily elemental. Not pure, if you like."

"What do you mean?" Sifte didn't like the implications of this statement.

"Do you know anybody else who loves like Mila?"

Sifte automatically thought of Aleksei and knew that he didn't. It was difficult to say how. The only way she could think to describe it was that Mila loved her better than Aleksei did. Yet she knew that Mila and Aleksei loved her equally, and 'better' felt like a betrayal.

As if he had read her mind, Dmitri said, "Aleksei is different, isn't he."

"I don't know."

"Don't you think that Aleksei's love is as pure as Mila's?" Dmitri was looking at her with infuriating circumspection.

"I—I don't know," she repeated. "It's different. Not as easy to figure out."

"More selfish?" Dmitri suggested.

"No!" Sifte cried. "I didn't say that!"

Dmitri shrugged. "Less straightforward, then."

"Maybe," she conceded grudgingly.

"Compound, rather than elemental," he persisted.

It seemed he was taunting her, yet there was nothing goading in his look or tone. If anything, both were pleading. What for? she wanted to ask him. The right answer? A clue that she'd understood something he couldn't put into words?

"And tell me this," he continued. "Is there nothing selfish in Mila's love for you or Aleksei? Not even the desire to be loved in return?"

With those words, Sifte's view of her friend shifted. She didn't consider the desire to be loved a taint, and to suspect this motive in Mila didn't make her see her friend as any less well-intentioned. Yet at the same time, Sifte was aware that a chunk had been torn from her secret heart.

"I guess you're right," she said dejectedly.

Dmitri looked at her, surprised. "Right?"

"Love can't be an element."

Dmitri shook his head. "But we weren't talking about love. We were talking about war. And whether or not love is elemental, I think you'll find that the emotions that drive war, as you suggested, generally are derivative. Arguably derivative of compounds—that was my only point in this tangent—but derivative nonetheless. So continue. You were telling me about how hate derives from love."

Sifte's head was spinning. Nonetheless, she collected her fragmented thoughts enough to answer, "You can't kill love, you can only hurt it badly." Dmitri nodded. "I think that kind of hate, the kind that comes from love, is stronger than the kind that comes from fear, because it's based on betrayal. That's the kind of hate that causes civil war. Brothers fighting brothers. You might hate what he's done, or what he's turned into, but some part of you still loves him. And I guess if what you're saying is true, and a war can take place in a mind, then a civil war of the mind is the worst kind of war. You can't fight yourself and win."

Sifte had been looking at the floor as she made these last assertions. She had said everything in the same expressionless tone with which she answered questions in class. Yet when she looked up at Dmitri, what she saw shocked her. He had taken his glasses off, and his face had become haggard and old. When he realized that Sifte had stopped speaking, he made a valiant attempt at a smile.

"What can I say? You've made my point more adeptly than I could have."

A lump had formed in Sifte's throat, and she was suddenly afraid, though she didn't know of what.

"Don't look at me like that!" Dmitri snapped. "You won't be punished for having your own thoughts, no matter what might have happened before." He turned away from her. "You'd better go."

Sifte wondered what she'd done wrong. "Good-bye," she said tentatively, to his inert back. He made no sign that he had heard her. Creeping softly, as if through a sickroom, she left.

11

After Sifte's conversation with Dmitri, no new books appeared on the library shelves. She began to wonder whether she had failed some kind of test, and he had decided that she wasn't worthy of his secret tuition. Then one afternoon, as she was trawling the science section in case Dmitri had taken to leaving his lessons elsewhere, she found Aleksei waiting for her. His arms were crossed, his eyes fixed on her with determined anger.

"Is this what you're looking for?" He opened his book-bag and held it toward Sifte. Inside was a battered paperback. The title was in Spanish, and translated to, *The Spanish Civil War*.

Sifte sighed, but said nothing. She moved down the aisle of books as though she were still looking for something. Aleksei followed her. At the far end of the row, she pulled a book from a shelf and pretended to be looking through it.

"You shouldn't have done that," she said, as softly as she could.

Aleksei, too, picked up a book and pretended to be looking at it. "What's this all about?"

More loudly, Sifte said, "The calculus problems? They confused me at first, too. Come over here and I'll explain."

She led him to a table, took out her screen, selected one of the mathematical settings, and began typing what looked like calculus equations. She handed the screen to Aleksei. The equations made no sense.

"I'm not sure I understand, yet," he said.

"It's just these variables you're having trouble with," she said. "Have you ever wondered why we use Roman letters in math, and not Cyrillic?"

Aleksei looked at the equation again, and this time he saw it. The main variables spelled out two English words: "Not here."

"Oh, right," said Aleksei. "I see now." His eyes rested heavily on her. "What happens when you figure this into it?" He took the screen, typed something in, and then handed her another set of equations. The variables spelled, "Where?"

"I was just going to visit Mila. Come with me, we can talk about it on the way."

Aleksei looked at her for an uncomfortably long moment, then said, "All right. I just hope it'll be quiet enough in the infirmary. Maybe there's somewhere better." Under the table, he pressed something into her hand. Sifte didn't have to look at it to know what it was: a metal key-card. Heart racing, she put it in her pocket.

"Let's go," she said.

A librarian stopped them on the way out. With a too-wide smile, she asked, "And what were you two working so hard on?"

Sifte smiled back. "Just calculus." She showed her the screen. The librarian gave it a perfunctory look, and then handed it back to her.

"Such dedicated students," she said. Sifte smiled at her until the elevator door shut, then allowed her face to collapse into anxious relief.

"Sifte, what—" Aleksei began, but she shook her head, and with a look of deepening irritation, he kept quiet.

They got out at the medical section, but Sifte bypassed the infirmary, continuing straight to the locked door. Pulling the key-card out of her pocket, she slid it into the slot, and the lock's red lights flashed green. She pushed the release button and the door slid back, revealing a dark corridor with several other doors opening off of it. One of these doors was open, and a faint light spilled from beyond it.

"Sifte, is this really—" Aleksei began again, but she was already inside.

The lit room was small and square and empty. The cement it was made of had never been sealed or painted. On one wall was an opening for a closet, which had no door. There were electrical outlets on another. It smelled musty, as if it had been closed for a long time. The light came from a bare halogen bulb that hung by a cable from the center of the ceiling.

"Okay," Aleksei said, "I'm guessing teachers' quarters they never finished."

"Probably," Sifte answered.

"You mean you don't know?" The hurt and bitterness were clear in his voice.

Sifte sighed. "No, I don't. I don't know anything—I only suspect, and I don't suspect much at that. Look, Lyosha, did you read the book?"

He shook his head. "It's in Spanish. I got my translation program to do a bit of it—" Sifte groaned. "Don't worry," he said, apparently forgetting for the moment that he was supposed to be angry with her. "Once I figured out what it was, I stopped and erased the computer's memory."

"Was it a main terminal?"

"No—one of the laptops. I told you, don't worry! I know what I'm doing."

"No, you don't."

Aleksei bristled again. "Then how about filling me in?"

"I'll tell you all I know, but it isn't going to help much." Sifte took a deep breath, then told him the whole story, beginning with the book on Elisa Foley and ending with her strange conversation with Dmitri in the news room. When she had finished, they both stood in silence, neither looking at the other.

"Lyosha," Sifte finally said, "please don't be angry with me."

"You lied to me."

"I didn't! I didn't tell you, but that's only because I didn't want to put you in danger, too."

"That's not all, though," he said, the bitterness more pronounced. "A part of you liked it. Being singled out."

Aleksei's words stung Sifte, but she answered calmly, "Think that if you want to. The truth is, I didn't know where to talk to you even if I hadn't promised not to. He says that they watch us here, when we don't know they're watching. That talking about this in a public place is dangerous."

Aleksei's expression was still skeptical. "How could they watch us? And anyway, why would they want to? For that matter, what's all this even about?"

Sifte shook her head. "I don't know. I've had ideas, but they're only ideas."

"Like what?"

Sifte sighed. "Remember when I asked if you thought teachers could get sent away like students if they did something wrong? I've been thinking a lot about that since Gospazha Maria left. I've been wondering if it's true, and if maybe the thing she did wrong was us. The way she treated us."

Aleksei shook his head. "That's just paranoid. She was hard on a lot of kids. That girl who always back-talks, Anastasia. Any of the ones who were different."

Sifte gestured impatiently. "She was hard on Anastasia the way Tanya's hard on her, but in the end she gave her what was due. You, too. You always did well on your tests and reports, but Gospazha Maria kept trying to fail me for no good reason. Why would she try to fail me unless she wanted me expelled?"

"But why would she want you expelled?"

"I don't know. Anyway, it's not the answer—it's only the beginning of a whole new string of questions."

"Like what?"

Sifte began to pace the room. "Like, who are we? We don't know who our parents are, but other people might know; teachers might know. So, what if Gospazha Maria didn't like mine? Maybe enough to try to get at them by getting me expelled?"

"Do you really think a teacher would risk everything for that? Especially when neither you nor your parents would ever know that that's why you got kicked out of Institute 1."

"Okay, but assuming I'm on the right track, what if there's something about me that makes me somehow dangerous— to a teacher, to Institute 1, even to something bigger?"

Aleksei laughed. "You're not just paranoid, Sifte, you're an egomaniac."

"I'm trying to explain something that makes no sense!" Sifte cried.

Aleksei looked at Sifte the way she had seen him look at difficult equations. "I know," he said. "And you and I both know you're doing a better job than anyone else here could do—so maybe that's the point. Maybe all this is a test. Maybe they want to see what you'll do if someone tries to make you turn against them, and the way I see it, you're walking right into their trap. I think you should take that book and turn it in right away. Or give it back to Dmitri if you want, tell him the game's over. Give him the key and don't come back here. Just forget about it all."

Sifte looked at the real compassion in his face, and for a moment she wavered. Then she thought of the drawing she had found in the book on President Foley, the fundamental honesty in Dmitri's face, and she knew that neither could be fabrications.

"You're wrong," she said around the hard knot in her throat. "Please don't take my books anymore. Please don't tell anyone about this, not even Mila. And from now on, leave me alone."

Aleksei looked at her incredulously. "You can't be serious. This is crazy—"

"I mean it!" she cried.

He blinked at her for a moment, his mouth half-open as if he wanted to say something more; then he turned and left. Sifte sank down against a wall and didn't even try to stop the tears that spilled down her face. Yet she soon found the tears permuting into a feeling of resignation which, if bitter, was still better than the dishonesty had been. For the first time in

136

many weeks, she wasn't worried. In fact, for the moment she had reclaimed her capacity to shut her mind off, and she fell into thoughtlessness as a tired child might fall into a familiar bed. She tipped her head back against the wall, and let her eyes rest on the ceiling.

But after a few moments, something called her eyes back into focus: an inconsistency in one patch of ceiling not unlike the inconsistency that had alerted her to the presence of a new book on a familiar shelf. She stood up, straining to see. Finally, she found it. There was a lump in the cement a few feet from the cord that attached the light socket to the ceiling. She was too short to actually touch it, and there was nothing in the room to stand on. Sifte went out into the corridor, and began to search the other rooms. In one she found a packing crate full of plaster powder. She dragged this back with her, stood up on it, and looked more closely at the lump in the ceiling.

It was a wadded piece of gray paper. When she pulled, it came away with a drift of dust from the tinted plaster it had been tacked down with. Sifte opened the page, and was reading before she had even climbed down from the packing crate.

"First of all, let me assure you that you're safe here. The means they have for watching and listening to you don't apply in this room or the corridor outside, I've made certain of it.

"I know that you're unhappy. I also know that I'm at least topically the cause, and for this I'm sincerely sorry. If I knew a less painful way to teach you what you must learn I would certainly use it, but I don't think there is ever a painless way to learn a harsh truth.

"Do you remember the news report I showed you the day we spoke about war? You knew that I was trying to tell you something, though you didn't know what. You couldn't. So I'll explain it.

"You read that a Dead City building collapsed onto a Metro station, that it killed sub-race gangs living in both the building and the station. What I read was that the building was bombed on Solntse's orders, and while the collapse no doubt killed violent gangs, it also killed untold numbers of innocents. Old people. Sick people. Babies.

"You read about the crash of a Protectorate plane onto the shanty town. The plane was indeed antiquated, overloaded—but Russian, hijacked by the Soviet to evacuate sub-race people fleeing massacres in Kiev.

"Glaza also told us about a synthetic virus that would free us from the Clones. But the Clones are Russian too, Solntse's own mistake, and though the virus will no doubt kill them it will also kill much of the sub-race in the area, because they have not been inoculated against it.

"Does this information disturb you? Does it make you lose your precious composure? I hope that it does. Hate me for it, but think about it. To think is your responsibility, because one day you will have a great deal of power, but if you lose your capacity to feel horror at the violence man perpetrates in the name of justice, then the power will be worthless. You will belong to it, rather than the other way around."

Sifte looked away from the page. What do you mean? she wanted to scream at him. What do you want from me? She was furious at his circumspection, but she composed herself enough to go on reading:

"When we spoke last week of the nature of weapons, we left something out. People can be weapons, sometimes

138

without knowing it. There are things about you and some of your peers which make you potentially lethal weapons. Watch for those who would make you one, and for those who could become weapons against you. Don't be afraid, but always be aware. And please, destroy this letter like the rest."

*

Sifte had thought herself isolated before, but now she knew the true, terrible meaning of loneliness. Not only had she lost her only two friends—one to illness, the other to the murky trenches of betrayed trust—she was further removed from everyone now by the letter's confirmation of her worst fears. Vindication only intensified the unease Aleksei had planted with his suggestion that she was being set up. She lost her appetite and began to suffer from insomnia. Finally, on the eighth night after she read Dmitri's letter, Sifte couldn't stand the morass of her own mind any longer.

Sifte didn't go to Mila with the intention of unburdening herself of her secret. Yet when she threw back the covers of her dormitory bed and tiptoed past the other sleeping girls, along with her love and grief she carried the resolution that she must somehow make amends for her deception.

No one was watching Mila's room in the infirmary, and Sifte slipped easily inside. It was warm and dim, close with the smells of sickness and medicine. Mila lay against the sheets like a fragile aquatic creature the sea has flung up onto the shore, blue-white, her skin almost translucent, webbed with violet veins. Breathing tubes ran from her nose to the humming machine at the head of the bed, and I.V.

lines snaked from both of her arms. Her hair lay in two long plaits over her breast.

As Sifte stood over her, Mila opened her eyes. Sifte was frightened for a moment that Mila did not recognize her, but then she smiled, and curled one fragile hand around Sifte's proffered one.

"You came," Mila said in a voice shredded by illness and despair. "I've been asking for you. They said I was too sick. They said I might make you sick, too."

"I don't get sick often." Sifte forced herself to smile, but Mila had begun to cry, tears slipping from the corners of her eyes across the rice-paper skin of her cheeks and into her hair.

"Milyonka!" Sifte pleaded, feeling her own tears rising.

"I can't help it," Mila said, misunderstanding Sifte's horror as a reaction to the failure of self-control. "I hear them talking when they think I'm asleep. They say I'm going to die."

Sifte climbed up on Mila's bed and took her hands, squeezed them. "You heard them wrong!"

"I keep seeing things," she said, trying to wipe the tears away with one encumbered arm. "People. But I can't see their faces. They're so bright, they hurt my eyes…they come close, and then they're far away again. They have fingers like branches, so long and sharp…if I go to sleep—"

"Mila," Sifte said.

But Mila no longer had the strength to spare Sifte. "The doctor keeps giving me shots that put me to sleep. I have to stay awake. Help me stay awake."

"I will," said Sifte. "I'll stay right here." She lay down next to her.

"Talk to me," said Mila. "I might not answer you, but I'll be listening. As long as I can hear you, it's all right."

140

"What do you want me to say?" Sifte asked.

"Tell me about the dacha."

The dacha originated in a picture they had been shown while still on the nursery floor. It was a picture of an old-style summer cottage on the bank of a wide river, complete with fairy-tale gables and wooden fretwork. As small children they had imagined an entire world around it, given themselves grown-up jobs beyond it, filled it with the things they most wanted. These trappings varied, but the central idea never did. The dacha was only theirs, a place where they could shut the door on anything or anyone who wasn't welcome. They knew by now that Plato's philosophy forbade Opyekuni the kind of privacy and luxury they dreamed of. Nevertheless, they held on to the dream, still referring and even adding to it sometimes.

Mila had closed her eyes again and her hand jerked once, convulsively, in Sifte's. Fighting her panic back, Sifte began, "The dacha…it's by a river. All around it there are trees. There are no other houses in sight, no one else around for kilometers. We live there alone, you and me and Aleksei, and other people can only come in when we invite them. And all day long we do only what we want…"

All night Sifte lay there, building the dacha for Mila with soft words. She tried not to think of what Mila had heard the doctors say, but she was aware that a part of her had awakened to a grief more powerful than she had ever imagined she could feel, and which she did not know how she would bear. A few times Mila's breathing became so faint that Sifte had to put her head to her chest to make sure that it still rose and fell. Each time Sifte called to her, though, she answered. Somewhere towards morning, Mila's fever broke. Sometime after that, they both fell into true, deep sleep.

*

The day doctor, making his morning rounds, was angry to find Sifte asleep next to Mila, but he stopped short of admonishing the night doctor when he found that Mila's fever was gone and her chest sounded clearer. Still, the presence of the second child worried him. Mila's disease was virtually unknown territory, and he had been warned to keep Sifte healthy at all costs.

"I don't know how she got in here," the night doctor, Galena, was saying in anticipation of his anger. "I checked the room two hours after lights out."

"You should have checked again."

"You know I was on alone last night, Lev, with fifty beds filled!"

"Do you think there's a risk of infection?" he asked, in a more diffident tone.

The woman looked at the sleeping children and said, "She has the eye disorder, the lymph imbalance, and the last scans I took showed lesions on the heart and lungs. All of it suggests that the disease is already in the tertiary phase, and if it is—"

"Then she shouldn't be topically infectious," he finished for her.

"But given the drugs we've been using, she never should have reached this stage at all." Galena looked at Mila thoughtfully for a time. "Considering the disease resists the traditional treatments, then there's no reason to assume it will follow traditional paths of infection. If others are infected—"

"They won't be," Lev answered with finality. "Diseases evolve resistance, but seldom new modes of transference.

142

And she's not old enough yet for any of the remaining modes to be a danger."

"She will be soon enough." Galena sighed. "I don't understand why they keep her."

Lev half-shrugged. "She's the best candidate they have to pioneer the biological aspects of the purge. The best by far."

Galena shook her head. "It's such a gamble." She looked up at him. "I'm going to contact the supervising Opyekun and recommend again that she be removed. We can't risk losing others—especially not this one." She indicated Sifte.

Despite the authoritative tone she tried to take, both doctors knew that such a decision could only be made by consensus. Lev looked at Mila for a few minutes, and though his eyes narrowed, his look was otherwise unreadable. "No," he finally said. "She's here by Solntse's choice, and he knows best."

"Then she should at least be told. She's so close to that boy, Aleksei, you never know what could happen."

He shook his head. "She's too young. It will crush her emotionally. Wait two more years."

Galena said nothing else.

When the doctors left, Sifte opened her eyes. Mila was still asleep. She didn't know what the doctors were hinting around, but she knew that it was both sinister and serious. Most terrible of all, she realized that it was up to her to decide what to do next.

12

Neither Stepan nor Andrei broached the topic of Sifte for several days. This was partly because she posed so many dilemmas, but also because to discuss what was to become of her meant discussing what was to become of Stepan himself.

From what he had been told about Andrei's conservatism, Stepan suspected that Andrei would want him to leave the city. Andrei in turn had guessed that Stepan would want to stay, if not to try to find Sasha then to resume his work with the Soviet. As such, both were ready with well-prepared arguments when Andrei finally confronted Stepan about it.

"We've decided to help you," he said, so imperiously that Stepan had to work not to show his irritation, "but we believe that the best plan is to get you away from Solntsegrad as soon as possible." Stepan waited to hear the rest before he contradicted him. "You'll remain here in the meantime. You'll have no contact with the Soviet."

"Can't I attend meetings?"

"At the moment you're too much of a liability." Stepan nodded, still waiting to hear a compelling contradiction to his own arguments. "Getting you out of the country will be more difficult," Andrei continued, sighing. "We might be able to get you into Finland, perhaps even Sweden or England if you can get work at the docks, but it will take time. The officials have been watching the docks carefully, lately. Too many Soviets were escaping that way."

Stepan waited to make sure Andrei was finished, then said, "I'm not leaving."

"Have you considered that it might not be your choice?" Andrei replied, with well-controlled but detectable hostility.

Stepan shrugged. "You can keep me out of the Soviet and perhaps even make it difficult for me to stay in the city, but please consider whether that would really be to our mutual benefit."

"It's the Soviet I'm thinking of—not myself." He paused, then said, "This is about Sasha, isn't it. You still think you'll find her here."

"No," Stepan answered, "I'm sure that I won't. But I owe it to her to continue her work."

"You don't owe her anything."

"With due respect, Andrei, that's something only she and I can know."

Andrei paused, then said, "You want to work for the Soviet again?"

"I don't consider myself ever to have stopped."

"If this is true, you must be certain that it is the Soviet's interests you place first—before yourself, before Sasha."

"I have no other interest now."

Andrei looked at him with inert eyes. "You have one," he said. "Because of her, and only because of her, we might overlook your liabilities. Let me sleep on it."

He had slept on it for nearly a month though, and his silence was beginning to keep Stepan awake. He was tired of waiting for Andrei's reply, let alone his approval. Most of all, he was tired of hiding. Andrei's apartment had become as much a prison as Kronstadt had been.

So, at the end of his fourth week back in the city, Stepan took the first steps toward liberating himself. He waited until Andrei had left for an evening meeting, then he went to work. First he cut his hair as close to the head as he could manage with the pair of dull shears he found in the kitchen. Then he mixed up the bottle of brown hair dye that he had bought from a black-market dealer with the buttons from his prison doctor's coat, and rubbed it into his remaining hair. When it had set and he'd rinsed it out, he looked at himself in the scrap of polished metal that served Andrei as a shaving mirror.

He couldn't remember the last time he had really looked at his own reflection; he barely recognized himself. It was more than the dye or the lines on his skin, or even the stark bones of starvation. If anything it was the hollow, haunted look to his eyes, the grim set of his mouth. Prison had scoured away the last of Captain Steven Pierson.

For the first time in a long time Stepan thought about Steven. He tried to remember what it had felt like to be him, but he seemed as foreign now as the Russians once had. Anti-Russian sentiment in the West had grown steadily since the holocaust until it outdistanced the worst of Cold War animosity. Solntse had essentially kept his promise to confine his regime to the boundaries of his own country, and if he sometimes stretched the margins to the Protectorate or Satellites, or more lately Asia, the rest of world turned a blind eye. But America didn't trust the silent sinkhole that Eastern Europe had become. When the Western Alliance refused America's request to help wrest power back from

Solntse, the Americans decided to do it themselves. Unwilling to risk their place in the Alliance, they began to breed human weapons, the ultimate secret agents: young, strong, brilliant, and thoroughly inculcated with their country's propaganda. And of all of them, Steven Pierson had been the best.

His mission had been to infiltrate the Soviet and buy its cooperation with promises of American aid in securing the government for their party following a successful coup. Of course, American officials would control this government, but Steven would keep that to himself. He had wholeheartedly believed in the righteousness of this plan, and had even begun to make visible progress on it, when he met Sasha. In one clean sweep she had destroyed everything he had believed in.

His admiration for Sasha had been incomprehensible to him at first, because she was the opposite of everything he had ever valued. She had no aspiration to glory. She was willing to lay down her own body as a foundation for a new state in which her people wouldn't suffer. The people of his privileged country showed nothing like Sasha's passion for her own, ravaged one. Perhaps, Stepan thought now, it was this spirit which had turned him. He had wanted nothing more after their first conversation than to be a part of it.

Lying awake the past night, Stepan had thought about what he had said to Andrei when they discussed his leaving weeks before. He had asked himself whether it really was the Soviet that compelled him to stay in Myortvograd, or whether that mission was only a shield for Sasha's specter. After hours of tortuous thought, he realized only that he didn't know.

Now, in the tepid light of the approaching White Nights, his aim seemed clearer. He had arrived at his understanding of responsibility over gravel, on his knees, and he knew that he bore one both to Sasha and to her people. The child—or rather, whatever Andrei had planned in connection with her—was the most obvious path to fulfilling it, perhaps the only one that would allow him to keep Andrei as an ally. But first he needed to ascertain the true state of the Soviet, and he knew by now that he would never find out from Andrei.

Stepan cleaned the rime of dye out of the bathroom sink, rubbed his hair dry, and pulled his shirt and sweater back on. Then he went up to the bunker and took Andrei's handgun from its hiding place behind the desk and loaded it with bullets he'd taken earlier from Andrei's pocket. Tucking the gun into his waistband, he covered it with his sweater and then a battered jacket, and went out into the street.

The meeting was being held in the ruined Technological Institute. He hadn't paid much attention to the Institute during his first stay in the city, but he recalled the striking terra-cotta color of its walls. There wasn't much left of them, but the walls still formed a complete enclosure which was easy to guard and big enough to hold several hundred people. Beneath them was an extensive basement, where the Soviet was planning its central bunker.

The meeting was well underway by the time Stepan arrived. All eyes were fixed on the speaker, a short, stocky, dark woman who stood on a podium which was just tall enough to make her visible to all the gathered people, but not too tall to distance her from them. Though he had not seen her in years, Stepan recognized her at once. Olga was the first Soviet leader Stepan had met, and it was she who had introduced him to Sasha, her closest friend. Olga was one of the *pozabitiy,* the "forgotten ones:" gifted sub-race children whose parents had successfully hidden them from the Opyekuni, or whom the Opyekuni overlooked.

"You must remember that your lives are your own," she was saying, her plain features animated with sincere passion. "No man or woman has the right to rule you against your will. You tell me that this city is a living death—well, nobody keeps you here but yourselves! You are afraid of Solntse's power, you say." Here the crowd began to murmur angrily. "Yet you have none to blame for it but yourselves!"

Stepan smiled bitterly. He didn't doubt that the so-called sub-race was capable of revolution, but it couldn't be planned and plotted as the Soviet imagined. To succeed, a revolution must be fueled by outrage, but outrage is a force beyond control, and this terrified the Soviet. So they tiptoed on, preaching the kind of academic revolution Myortvograd's people could never engage.

"The Opyekuni came again yesterday," Olga was saying when Stepan tuned back in, "and they took more children. I see the mothers crying; I see the fathers praying, but tears and prayers are solitary comforts. If you wish to end this reign of terror you must leave behind your talismans of grief, your paralyzing fear, and band together to demand justice!"

Indeed, Stepan thought, but justice would mean little to a people who had never known basic human rights. Only anger would overcome their fear, and only unified anger would win a revolution. So, the question was how to loose and channel their anger? They needed the right battle cry from the right leader—someone equally oppressed by Solntse's regime, but educated beyond it; someone who understood just how much they had been denied, and who would appeal to a people who had lost their children.

"The Sun is only one," Olga said, holding up an index finger. "The Solntsegrad Opyekuni do not number more than one hundred. The super-race has grown weak and complacent. The decision is yours, whether to remain scattered in fear, or to join together in the faith that you can rise above injustice and persecution. They know that you have the strength to topple theirs—why else would they suppress you? But you must learn to believe in your strength. One wolf cannot kill a united flock. Join together, and you will be your own salvation!"

Stepan had always thought that a flash of inspiration was only metaphorical. Now he realized that this was only because he had never experienced it. For a moment it blinded him, filled the stale atmosphere of the crowded space with the ozone smell of lightning strike. He, too had lost a child to Solntse. If Sifte could be brought back to their side, she would be emblematic of all the lost children; she would command the people's hearts and minds as no leader could.

For a few moments, Stepan drifted on the high of inspiration; then the complications began to surface. Even the idea of trying to contact Sifte was impossibly daunting. If he could, and could make her believe him, how would he know whether or not she was capable of filling the role he'd imagined, and how would he be able to prepare her for it if she was?

In the shadows of these doubts another idea began to form. Quite likely, many of the Opyekuni didn't know about Sifte. The rest of the super-race didn't even know that Solntse had been feeding sub-race babies into the Institutes. If the super-race learned about the existence of Sifte Pierson, they would probably turn on Solntse. Then it wouldn't matter whether or not Sifte could be won over, or was the right leader for a sub-race revolution. The sub-race itself wouldn't matter. Disclosing Solntse's deception would ignite a revolution he couldn't win: the revolution of his own super-race.

Stepan knew that it was a good idea, but he hesitated. Any way he painted it, the fact remained that his idea would make the child a pawn—more a pawn than she was already. Stepan had learned long ago to use people without remorse, but though he might never know her and couldn't imagine loving her, he also knew that using his own child was something entirely different.

A loud crack tore through Stepan's reverie, and he surfaced to chaos. Andrei was on the podium, trying vainly to maintain order. People were screaming, pushing, trampling each other to find a way out of the enclosure that was suddenly full of flying bullets. Looking up, Stepan saw the silhouettes of officials on top of the far wall. On some kind of cue, they pitched the bodies of the Soviet guards into the crowd below, further stoking the panic.

"Shit," Stepan said to no one in particular, and pulled the gun from his waistband. He pushed away from the door, through which three hundred people were now trying to press themselves simultaneously. This was where the officials' assault would be concentrated. People were falling everywhere Stepan looked, and more officials were pouring over the walls. He waded toward the front of the room, thinking of Andrei and Olga. Along the way, he shot at several officials, but he couldn't see whether he had hit them or not.

Keeping close to the wall and its shadows Stepan approached the podium, which had toppled in the onslaught. The Soviet's flag had been hanging above it, the red ground with its white 'C.' A Pomoshchnik was tearing it down, replacing it with Solntse's black flag with its seven-pointed golden sun. To the side of the flag, about three meters from Stepan, Andrei was bending over a woman whose chest had been shattered by a bullet. Two officials approached him from behind. Squinting in the dim, flickering lamplight, Stepan aimed and fired. He hit both Pomoshchniki cleanly, and they fell at Andrei's feet. He turned. His face registered momentary shock, then anger before the Opyekun calm closed over it again.

"What are you doing here?" he demanded, crouching with Stepan by the wall.

"You're welcome," Stepan answered, ejecting the gun's empty clip and loading a new one. "Let's go."

"I can't just—"

"There are too many of them. And anyway, you forgot your gun."

Andrei glowered, but he followed Stepan around the wall until they found another exit. When they reached the street, they ran south-east into a section of the ruin where even the sub-race couldn't live. The officials were unlikely to follow them here. Still, they waited in silence for some hours before venturing out again. When they did, in the first dawn light, Andrei looked at Stepan.

"You're an idiot," he said, in the manner of a man unused to granting concessions, "but I suppose I ought to thank you for saving my life. As they say in your country, I owe you one."

Stepan smiled as a tinge of the past night's inspiration ran through him again. There just might be something left for him in the Dead City after all.

13

For the next few months, Mila was as well as she ever had
been. By September, when she walked with her class on their
ceremonial passage through the door that separated the lower
school from the middle, the doctors began to speculate that
she would stay that way. Everybody rejoiced in Mila's good
health, and she smiled and bore it, anything but relieved.

"I don't know," she answered when Sifte asked her why she
seemed apprehensive. "It's just a feeling I have sometimes,
that there's something the doctors don't want me to know."
She was too preoccupied to notice the flinch Sifte couldn't
quite hide. "And, well…" she continued reticently, "don't
you ever feel like something's wrong?"

Avoiding her eyes, Sifte asked, "Like what?"

"It's as if…well, as if there's something here with us,
beyond what we see. Something watching us, making us do
what we do…or don't want to do. In the daytime it's not so
bad, but at night I lie awake and…"

"And what?"

"I know it sounds crazy, Siftenka…but it's like I feel it
reaching for me."

"Feel…what?"

"Whatever it is. The presence. It's suffocating—" She stopped short, catching Sifte's anxious look. "Don't listen to me," she said. "It's just my morbid imagination."

But Mila's words reminded Sifte of something Aleksei had said to her once, which she had tried to put out of her mind. They had been in Mila's favorite greenhouse, the one that replicated a tropical forest complete with colorful butterflies and moths. In one corner a stream trickled into a pond where carp mapped in gray and orange hovered, mouthing bubbles. Small ground birds scurried in the undergrowth.

Suddenly Mila had cried out. In front of her on the path was a dead bird. Its matted form was crawling with maggots. Sifte had started to nudge the carcass under the plants, but Aleksei stopped her.

"Don't," he'd said, crouching down to look at it more closely.

"Why not?" Sifte had asked. Mila had hurried to the other side of the room, and sat staring into the fishes' pool, trying to maintain the appearance of calm. Aleksei had looked at her, and pity had crossed his face; then he'd looked back at Sifte with clear, emphatic eyes.

"It's the most real thing I've ever seen," he'd said. "You understand, I know you do—but Mila can't, because when she looks at it she sees herself."

Sifte had turned away in anger.

"Don't, Sifte," he had said, catching her arm. "I wasn't criticizing her—only saying that she can't be what we are."

Now, despite her current anger at him, Sifte had to admit that Aleksei had been right. Mila had been trying to tell her that she was losing the strength and will to keep fighting herself. Sifte thought about this all morning, and finally made a decision. At lunchtime, she pulled Mila aside.

"There's something I want to show you," she said.

"Okay," Mila answered, puzzled, "but why are you whispering?"

"Never mind. You'll see."

"Can I see, too?" Aleksei asked.

Sifte whirled on him. "What are you doing here?"

He regarded her with what looked like recrimination. "Why shouldn't I be here? Are you telling secrets?" His face was serious a moment too long before he smiled.

"Of course not," Mila said, "and of course you can come. Can't he, Sifte?" Mila had noticed the rift that had grown between her friends, but she still hoped that it would blow over without her interference.

Sifte sighed. "Fine." After lunch she led them through the hallways to the unfinished corridor, then opened the door with the key-card.

"Where did you get that?" Mila asked.

Avoiding her eyes, Sifte said, "It was in a library book."

"What was a key-card doing in a library book?"

"I don't know."

The room was just as they had left it months before. "Well?" she asked. "What do you think?"

Mila glanced around doubtfully. "It feels like no one's been here in years."

"That's why it's perfect," Sifte answered. "It's the only room I've seen here that isn't theirs."

"So maybe it can be ours," Aleksei said speculatively, and for the first time since their disagreement Sifte remembered why they had been friends.

"What can we do with it?" asked Mila.

"Well, first of all, we can keep things here that we don't want to share, or show to the rest of them," Sifte said. "We can decorate it if you want."

"Like the outside," said Mila, beginning to warm to the idea.

"Maybe there're things in the other rooms on this corridor that we can use," Aleksei added.

"I can get paper," Mila said. "Gospazha Zoya always gives me things like that. I can even go now."

"All right," Sifte said. "Here, take the key-card so you can get back in. Aleksei, let's look in the other rooms."

As soon as Mila was gone, Sifte turned to him and said, "She needs this. If you ever tell her the truth, I'll kill you."

"Sifte, you don't understand—" he began, but she had already turned away.

*

Aleksei and Sifte were dragging crates and paint cans into the room when Mila came back with an armful of paper and an apprehensive look. "What if somebody finds out about this?" she asked, putting the paper down on one of the crates. "I mean, we must be breaking about a hundred rules."

"Probably," Sifte replied, "but what's the worst they can do?"

"Expel us."

"They won't expel us for this. There's nothing here."

"But the paper and things Gospazha Zoya gave me—"

"You said yourself that she always gives you things like that."

"I guess so."

Sifte said, "Tell me what you want to make."

Mila's face lit up. She held up some big pieces of green paper. "Trees," she said. "I got some extra scissors so you can help." She unfurled a long, torn piece of blue paper. "Maybe a lake? Or a river—like the one by the dacha! And gardens. And I got some silver and gold paper, we can make stars."

"And airplanes," said Aleksei.

"And the sun," said Sifte.

"It will be just like the real dacha," Mila concluded.

*

Over the next few days, they began to put the scenery together. When they were done, they stood in the middle of a paper forest. Trees and flowers sprouted from the walls. Green paper reeds streamed with the current of the blue paper river. A silver moon and golden stars hung by strings from the ceiling along with Aleksei's airplanes, and on one wall there was a gold paper sun. A shade made of green paper covered the light bulb, throwing soft light over the room. The paint cans and plaster crates were covered by old towels and blankets.

"It's perfect," said Sifte.

"Just how I imagined the dacha garden," added Mila. "Well…almost."

"You know," Aleksei said, "we should plan to have a meeting here every once in a while—maybe once a week."

"Why should we do what you—" Sifte began.

"I think that's a good idea," Mila interrupted. "How about on Sundays? We all have Sunday afternoons free."

"Okay," Aleksei agreed. "Sifte?"

All of a sudden, Sifte tensed. She motioned to the others to be quiet. They could all hear running footsteps in the main corridor outside their hallway. They shut off the light and crowded into the hallway to listen.

"Stop it!" a girl screamed shrilly. "I don't have anything! Leave…me…ALONE!" Beneath the anger, her voice sounded frightened. The people had stopped running, apparently outside the door to their hallway.

"Give me those disks before I make you!" an older boy's voice demanded. "I know you have them! I saw you saving stuff, and it sure as shit wasn't your English lesson."

Mila, Aleksei and Sifte looked at each other in the dim light that filtered through the small window from the main corridor. "Rodya," Sifte whispered.

"And Anastasia," Mila added.

"I don't have them!" Anastasia cried, her voice breathless and thin.

"You do!" said another boy, whom Sifte identified as a crony of Rodya's, called Boris. "I saw you take them."

"You didn't!" cried a younger boy. "Nastya was only helping me with trigonometry. Why do you keep trying to get us in trouble?"

"Well to begin with, you're stealing classified information!"

"How could we?" asked the little boy with incredulous innocence. "It takes all kinds of codes to even get into classified pages. Who knows what you'd need to take stuff out? And even if I did know, I'm sure you can't store that kind of information on homework disks."

"Why are you so interested, anyway?" Anastasia asked. "Do you know something we don't?"

Rodya paused, then growled, "I'm gonna kill you, you little—"

"Don't!" said Anastasia's ally.

Rodya laughed. "Why not?"

"You wouldn't want to jeopardize your future, would you?"

"What are you talking about?" Boris asked with venomous suspicion.

"'When you are looking for your philosophic character you will look to see whether it has been, from its early days, just and civilized or uncooperative and savage,'" Anastasia's friend answered cryptically. "Book six, section two," he added after a pause, apparently for clarification.

"You're nuts!" Rodya cried.

"He really is nuts," Sifte whispered.

Aleksei shook his head. "It was from *The Republic*."

"Right," Sifte answered. "Only a crazy person would quote Plato to Rodya and think he'd get it."

"I'd rather be crazy than inbred morons like—" A sharp smack cut Anastasia off mid-sentence.

Mila winced. "We should do something," she whispered.

"What can we do?" Sifte answered. Mila didn't reply, but she didn't loosen her grip on Sifte's arm, either.

"Keep your hands off her!" the little boy shrieked.

"What're you gonna do, izmyennik? Quote more philosophy?" Mila, Sifte and Aleksei heard another smack, and then another.

"Stop it!" Anastasia cried. "Stop it, you son of a bitch!"

"Oh, shut up," Rodya said with languid irritation.

"You're really hurting him!" There was true fear in her voice this time.

"So give me the disks."

On Sifte's side of the door, no one breathed. Finally, Anastasia said, "All right."

"I knew it!" Rodya crowed. "Let me have it!"

"Here!" Sifte heard something small hit the floor just outside the door. "Misha's trigonometry work. I hope you find it interesting."

"Come on, let's go," Boris said. After a pause, the footsteps moved away.

"Are they gone?" the little boy asked.

"I don't know," answered Anastasia. She paused. "Yeah, I think they are."

"But they got the disk. Hey, I thought you had more than one."

"I do. I have two. Right here in my pocket."

"So what did you give them?"

She began to giggle. "A homework disk."

"Couldn't you have given it to them *before* they beat us up?"

"I forgot I had it." Anastasia's voice turned serious again. "We were lucky."

"Yeah. And when they find out we tricked them, they'll kill us."

"They're so stupid they'll probably think the math is classification codes."

"Still, we should get out of here."

"Where can we go? They'll find us anywhere."

There was silence for a moment, and then the boy, Misha, said, "Hey—look at this lock."

"So?"

"That card you found in your pocket the other day—it looked like one of those old key-cards. Got it on you?"

Mila, Aleksei and Sifte looked at each other in horror.

"Actually, I do," Anastasia said. "I've been too scared to leave it anywhere else. But if you really think it matches this door, you've been playing too many detective games."

"So what will it hurt to try?"

"I already told you, I think it's a trick."

"'We are called on to use our reason when our senses receive opposite impressions,'" Misha answered. [331]

"Glaucon in the prologue?"

"Socrates, book eight, section two."

Anastasia sighed. "Fine—but reason tells me it would be just like Tanya to steal a key-card and try to get me in trouble for it."

"That would be too much work for someone like her."

"We also haven't figured out the surveillance system. What if it catches us?"

"I don't think they'd waste surveillance on a door no one uses. Come on, it's this or go wait to get the shit beaten out of us."

Sifte, Mila and Aleksei could do nothing but watch as the door opened.

14

Sifte regarded the two children in the doorway. Misha was younger, two levels below them. He had a round face, dark skin, and slanting Kirghiz eyes, one of which was swelling. There was a cut on one cheek, and he was wiping blood from his nose. Anastasia's lip was swollen and bloody, the skin around her right eye beginning to bruise.

"I told you it was a set-up," she said to him.

"Don't be an idiot," Misha answered. "They're nothing to worry about."

She turned to Sifte. "How much did you hear?"

"Enough to get you into a lot of trouble," Sifte answered.

"Are you going to?"

"That depends on what it means."

Anastasia gave her a fatalistic look as she came inside. As soon as the key-card door was shut she turned to face them, eyes narrowed like an angry cat's. "How do you know that it's safe here?" she demanded.

"You explain—then we'll explain."

"Sifte—" Mila began tentatively, but Anastasia interrupted.

"I'm not saying anything until you tell us how you got in here."

Sifte shrugged. "The same way you did. I found a key-card."

"In your pocket?"

"In a library book. Look, come all the way inside. There might not be surveillance, but you never know who's outside the door." She led the way into the Dacha, as they had begun to call it.

The two new children looked around at the scenery. Despite herself, Anastasia's face lit up. "Did you do this yourselves?"

"Mostly it was Mila," Sifte answered.

"We just finished it before you…came," Mila said. Anastasia nodded.

"So, tell us what that was all about," said Sifte.

Anastasia narrowed her eyes again, but Misha said, "Just tell them, Nastya."

Anastasia looked at the floor for such a long time that Sifte began to think she wouldn't answer after all. Then she looked up, and in a strange, strangled tone, she asked, "Do you know what they're really doing here?"

"What do you mean, 'really doing'?" Aleksei asked.

"Telling children stories," Misha piped up, before Anastasia could answer.

"*The Republic*?" asked Sifte.

"Book three, section one," Misha concurred with a look of triumph. "'…we begin by telling children stories. These are, in general, fiction, though they contain some truth.'"

"Have you memorized it?"

"Most of it," Anastasia answered for him, with an impatient flick of her thin hand. "He likes to show off—just ignore

163

him. What he means is that there's a lot more going on here than they're telling us."

"Who's 'they'?" inquired Mila.

"The government, and the teachers they put in charge of running this place—and running us."

"Stop being so cryptic!" Sifte burst out, finally overwhelmed by the panic that had been growing steadily since the day Dmitri arrived.

"I can't!" Anastasia yelled back. "I don't know how to explain it and I don't even want to, so if you're not going to listen then just let us go!"

She and Sifte bristled at each other. For a moment Mila thought that neither of them would back down. Then Sifte relented. "Go on," she said.

Anastasia turned, began to pace. "To begin with, almost everything we've been taught is a lie."

"Then there isn't really a world outside of here?" Aleksei bantered, then regretted it when he saw the look on Mila's face.

Anastasia sighed. "I said almost everything. There is a world outside, and as far as I can tell it looks like we think it does, but otherwise—"

"It would be unrecognizable," Misha finished for her, with what sounded oddly like excitement.

Mila was shaking her head with slow persistence. Sifte couldn't look at her, or at Aleksei. She was both horrified and relieved that someone was finally vindicating her.

"I don't understand," Mila said. "Why would the teachers lie to us?"

Anastasia frowned. "Let me finish, and then you can ask questions." Once again she paused, then she said, "We've

164

always been told that we live here because it's too dangerous out there."

"'Children cannot distinguish between what is allegory and what isn't'," Misha interjected, "'and opinions formed at that age are usually difficult to eradicate and change.'"

"Book three, section one—good point," Anastasia agreed, without breaking stride. "All that stuff about the radiation and the gangs…it's the perfect way to shut us up. At first because we believe what they tell us, later on because we're scared to question it. Ask too many questions, you'll be expelled." Anastasia shrugged, but Sifte saw that she was far from indifferent.

"Or maybe what we're really scared of is what we already know," Anastasia continued. "Like the fact that being under water doesn't protect you from radiation. Be honest—how many of you have wondered about that?"

Tentatively, one by one, they nodded. Anastasia sighed. "I bet everybody here's wondered, but nobody ever says anything. That's what started me thinking that the reason why we never say anything is that we're afraid that if it's a lie then anything else could be, too. For a while I was just as afraid as anybody else. But I couldn't stop thinking about it, so I decided to prove myself wrong. I went looking for other discrepancies, to prove that there weren't any.

"The problem was, there were—everywhere. It started to seem like nothing about this place was what I'd thought. I wondered if I was going crazy, imagining things that weren't there. That's when Misha and I kind of…collided." Once again, in contrast to everyone else's gravity, Misha smiled.

"It's too long a story to get into now, but basically, we decided to get together and find out the truth. A few days ago, we did it." She reached into her pocket and held up two mini disks, the kind that could be used in the external drives of the computers to give access to information that wasn't stored in the mainframe.

Anastasia made a valiant effort to pull herself together, and then continued, "They tell us we're going to be Opyekuni when we grow up, but they don't tell us what that means." She clenched her trembling hands together, as if in supplication.

"What…does it mean?" Mila asked, in a near-whisper.

"Killing people—lots of people. Taking sub-race babies away from their parents to train as new officials—"

"I thought officials had to be super-race," Aleksei interrupted.

Anastasia pinned him with hot, bright eyes. "Do you think a few walled cities of a few thousand people could produce so many of us? They take us from wherever they can find us—slums, refugee camps, even other countries."

"Are you saying some of us are sub-race?" Aleksei asked.

"I'm saying that most of us are! But the sub-race is a lie, too. The only thing wrong with them is that their ancestors didn't make it inside the walls."

It was all beginning to fall into place in Sifte's mind. "So when you called Rodya and Boris inbred, you really meant it."

Anastasia smiled wryly. "The walls saved a lot of people at first, and those people became the super-race. For a while, they really were. I mean, they were stronger than anyone outside the walls because they could afford to buy the medicine and the food and whatever else they needed to survive. But that meant they never had to develop resistance to diseases and things, and since they bred only with each other they got weaker. At the same time the sub-race got stronger, because only the strongest people could survive all the radiation and diseases and other crap that came after the bomb. It's pure Darwin, and it's the reason why Solntse wants sub-race kids in his ranks."

"Why not just do it in a laboratory?" Aleksei asked. "Gene therapy or stem-cell manipulation…there are lots of possibilities that would be less trouble than your idea."

"That kind of thing would take a lot of money and a lot of people who know what they're doing, and our country isn't exactly overwhelmed with either. And it wouldn't change the fact that the sub-race is still big and strong. Stealing the best sub-race babies takes care of both problems at once."

"But we're only children," Mila said.

"No, we're not! We're just pieces of…I don't know…a machine. You already know that."

"And how did you get all this information?" Sifte asked.

"We wrote a Trojan Horse program to steal a teacher's password," Misha answered, "and used it to get into classified files."

"What kind of files?" Sifte asked.

"Well, to begin with, there's one for each of us. They tell where we came from, the results of a genetic test they do when we're a week old, and then year-by-year profiles on our development."

"But what's the point of it all?" Aleksei asked. "You started out by saying that we're being trained to kill people. What gave you that idea?"

Anastasia took a long time to answer. "It's not just an idea, and it's definitely not mine. I found a file—it's on this disk, you can check it if you don't believe me. Solntse wrote it himself. It's about something he calls 'Utopia'. It looks like some kind of long-term plan. He only gives details of the first part, and that's to wipe out the sub-race."

"Kill them all?" Mila asked tremulously. Nobody answered her.

Finally, Aleksei broke the silence. "I'm sorry, Sifte. You were right."

"What do you mean?" Mila asked, her eyes bewildered and poised to hurt.

Aleksei looked at her and sighed. "You know Sifte and I fought a few months ago. Well, this is why. Sifte told me she suspected something like this, and I told her she was crazy." Now he turned to Sifte, and she finally saw the plea for forgiveness that had been in his eyes all along. "But the truth is that I did believe you, and I was also afraid to. So I pretended I didn't. I'm sorry."

Mila sat in shocked silence, but Anastasia looked shrewdly at Sifte and asked, "How did you know?"

Sifte shrugged. "'The man who has a real love of learning will yearn for the whole truth from his earliest years.'" She smiled at Misha's surprise. "You're not the only one who's done your background reading." Her smile faded. Haltingly, she told them about Dmitri's books and messages.

"When you told me how you found the key-card," she concluded, looking at Anastasia, "I was sure Dmitri put it there. And I think his last message told me why."

"You think Dmitri knows what Misha and I found out?" Anastasia cried.

Sifte shrugged again. "I've given up trying to guess what Dmitri knows. But he probably at least suspects. Otherwise, why would he have given both of us keys to this place? It's probably the only place in Institute 1 where we can talk without someone listening in."

This only heightened Anastasia's panic. "It must be a trap!"

Sifte shook her head. "If it had been a trap, I would have been kicked out of here after the first time I came. The things I said to Aleksei were more than enough for that. I don't know why, but I'm sure Dmitri wanted us to know these things, and to find each other."

"But how did Dmitri know we'd believe him?" Mila asked. "Or that we wouldn't say something to another teacher?"

Aleksei shrugged. "Maybe he only guessed. When he swore Sifte to secrecy about the books, he probably knew she'd tell us eventually—he just wanted to buy enough time to convince her, first."

"There's only one problem with that theory," Sifte answered. "He left the first book the day he came here. He couldn't have known how I'd react."

"Maybe he did. That the first day, he said he knew about all of us."

"What will we do?" asked Mila.

Anastasia shook her head. "Nothing. If they knew that we know this stuff, they'd kill us. That's what they do to the sub-race kids who don't pan out." They looked at each other in half-disbelief. Mila finally broke the long silence with a sob. To everyone's surprise, Anastasia went and put an arm around her.

"I'm sorry," she said gently. "We didn't want to tell anyone about this, at least not so soon. But you heard us, so you had to know. What could I do?" After another long silence, Sifte said, "I think we should try to find out what this 'Utopia' is all about. Or do you already know?"

"No," Anastasia answered. "I've only been inside Glaza on the teacher's password long enough to get a general picture, and I don't want to do it again. They can trace transmissions from the main terminals."

"We'll need our own computer, then," Sifte said.

"We can't steal a computer!" Mila cried.

"Not a whole one," Sifte answered.

"What good is part of a computer—" Misha began, and then slapped his forehead. "Of course! Why didn't I think of that?"

"Don't worry," Sifte placated, "you'll have plenty more thinking to do if we're going to pull this off." She turned to Aleksei. "Lyosha, Dmitri knows you're interested in technology. Can you get him to give you access to the parts store?"

"Are you going to build a computer?"

"No," Sifte answered, "you and Misha are. If he can steal government passwords and you can build all those weird models, I think you can handle a computer."

"It might even be fun…" Misha mused.

"And once we find out exactly what's going on, we might have a better idea of what to do next. Okay?"

They all agreed, except for Mila.

"What's the matter, Milyonka?" asked Sifte

Mila looked up with troubled eyes. "These things you're all saying, they're only ideas. We don't really know what they're about."

Sifte sighed. "That's why we need to get access to Glaza."

Mila shook her head. "That's not what I mean. Maybe our lives now aren't great, but they are real. We know the rules. But if we find out things about ourselves, about everything, then we won't anymore. Maybe it's better if we never know."

"Do you really think you'll be able to forget about what you've heard?" Sifte asked.

"I think it will be easier than forgetting what we might find out."

Sifte didn't know what to say. She felt that much more was on the line than Mila's support. Or perhaps it was simply Mila's support; perhaps her faith delineated the difference between the plausible and the possible.

Then, for no reason that made sense to her, Sifte remembered the folded drawing that she had carried in her pocket since the day she found it in the library. She pulled it out, unfolded it, and handed it to Mila. "I think this was really meant for you," she said.

Mila took the drawing, looked at it for a long time. Then she stood up, and with a corner of tape, she pasted it to the wall. "All right, Sifte," she said, but her eyes remained fixed on the drawing's black spire and red sun long after the others had looked away.

15

It took Aleksei and Misha a month to steal the parts for the computer, and another to get it fully operational on the wireless network. Once it was up and running, though, they wasted no time in tapping into their classified files.

"Got yours, Mila," said Sifte.

"Let's see!" Mila cried, dropping her screen to come and sit by Sifte. Sifte moved aside to let her read. As she skimmed the computer screen, the color slowly drained from Mila's face.

"What does it say?" Aleksei asked.

Mila read to the bottom of the page before she answered. "They want me to build viruses that can wipe out city-size populations in a few days."

"Does it say where they plan to use them?" asked Anastasia.

"Sub-race shanty towns." Mila shuddered. "How can they think I'd do that?"

Anastasia's lips curled into a caustic half-smile. "They didn't plan for you to know."

"You couldn't do that kind of work and not know."

"But they didn't mean for you to know that there was anything wrong with it."

Mila was quiet for a few moments. Then she said, "I've been working on epidemiology for the last month. Making computer models of viral pathways, and things like that. They're theoretical, but somebody could use the results if they wanted to." For a moment, Mila's face was bitterly intent. Then she said, "I can't do any more work."

"You can't stop working," Anastasia said. "They'll realize you know something."

"They can do what they want to me," Mila answered. "I'd rather die than kill anyone!"

"And take us along with you?" Anastasia shook her head in disgust. "If we start trying to subvert them, we'll give ourselves away."

Again, they were silent. Then Aleksei asked, "What about the rest of us?"

"I don't want to look," Mila said, moving away from the terminal.

Sighing, Sifte resumed her place. "They have Nastya leading a band of undercover assassins. You'll be searching out and killing Soviet leaders in Myortvograd."

"Over my dead body I'll be killing Soviet leaders!" Anastasia cried indignantly. After a moment's consideration: "But I thought the Soviet weren't a real threat...aside from in Cave."

"Ironically—or not, I guess—Dmitri's had me reading about them for the last few days," Sifte said. "Apparently they're more of a threat than the teachers tell us. They're an offshoot of the group that overthrew the first post-holocaust government. Some of them hung on after Solntse got rid of their government. A lot of them are ex-officials, which mean they know things Solntse would rather the sub-race didn't. They're trying to raise a revolutionary army by educating the sub-race into their beliefs."

"How many of them are there?" Aleksei asked.

"No one knows."

"Have they considered counting them?"

"They've tried. But a lot of the Pomoshchnik squads Solntse sends in for raids never come out."

"That doesn't sound like the kind of thing Solntse would admit," Anastasia said, eyes narrowed skeptically. "I can't believe you got that out of your homework reading."

Sifte shrugged. "'Our first business is to supervise the production of stories, and choose only those we think suitable, and reject the rest.' It's all there, if you read between the lines."

"So basically," said Aleksei, "the Soviet stands for the same things we do."

"Well," said Sifte, "I'm not sure we're exactly socialists, but in terms of thinking that Solntse's methods are wrong and he should be stopped—yes."

"All right!" cried Anastasia. "I'm joining them! Well, at least we could try to find a way to help them."

Mila asked, "How are we supposed to help them if we can't do anything that might make the teachers suspicious?"

"We can figure that out later," Anastasia answered. "For now, let's see what the plans are for everyone else." They turned their attention back to the computer.

"Aleksei …" Sifte said, her fingers flying over the keyboard. She read the screen that came up, then said, "I don't know if we should tell you this, Lyosha. You might want to take them up on it."

"Sifte!"

"Oh, all right. They have you designing bombers."

"All right!" he cried.

"Lyosha!" cried Anastasia, glaring at him.

"Me next!" said Misha.

"Let's see. It's pretty general, what they've got here. I guess because you're so young still. All it says is 'Leading Strategics'."

"Oh," he said, disappointed.

"Don't worry," Mila appeased. "You'd be among the greatest military minds in history. Caesar, Napoleon, Alexander the Great."

"Hitler," Anastasia added. Misha punched her in the arm, and she punched him back.

"What about you, Sifte?" asked Mila.

"Yeah, what about you?" said Misha, turning his attention away from Anastasia.

Sifte looked at the screen, then said, "This has got to be a mistake." She typed names and codes again, but the result was the same. There was no detailed profile, as there had been in the other records. There were only a few words:

```
Integrate Utopia. Stage One: Eliminate Stepan
Pierson.
```

An inexplicable chill ran up and down Sifte's spine.

"Who's Stepan Pierson?" Misha asked.

"I don't know," she answered slowly.

"Why would they go to the trouble of training an Opyekun to assassinate one man? If he's so bad, eighteen years is a long time to wait to kill him."

Sifte shook her head.

"Maybe he threatens this thing, Utopia," suggested Anastasia.

"But we still don't know what Utopia is," said Mila. "Maybe it would help if we got more information about that."

"I already tried," said Misha, "as soon as the computer was up and running. There's nothing in Glaza that tells us any more than the document we already had."

"Then the best we can do is look up Stepan Pierson."

Sifte went back to the Glaza search engine, then typed in the name.

"No matches at all?" Aleksei said. "That's weird."

"Maybe it's classified," Anastasia suggested.

"Or maybe you're just not qualified," said Misha. "Let me try." He pushed in beside Sifte, re-entered Glaza under a new password. "Gospazha Alla's," he told their questioning eyes. "If anyone can get at this information, it's her."

"Check under Noviy Soviet," said Mila suddenly. "You said they're Solntse's main opposition, didn't you?"

Having no better ideas, Sifte did so. She found a list of all of the Soviet leaders considered to be of criminal stature. Stepan Pierson's name wasn't among them. Most of the names had only one or two links, but one of them, Aleksandra Kirillovna Umanskaya, had fifteen.

"Have any of you ever heard of her?" Sifte asked. None of them had. She followed the first link, and found herself confronting another list of files, the first of several pages' worth: Profile, Early History, Soviet Involvement, Andrei Kirillovich Umanskiy, Imprisonment, Connections.

"If Stepan Pierson's connected to the Soviet, then maybe there'll be some kind of cross-reference," said Aleksei.

"Which one should I choose?"

"We might as well find out who she is," Mila said.

Sifte chose the "profile" link. A few paragraphs appeared on the screen. She summarized them for the others, concluding with Sasha's incarceration in Schlüsselburg Fortress. "That was about ten years ago," she added.

"Is she still alive?" asked Anastasia.

"It doesn't say she isn't."

"It doesn't say anything about Stepan Pierson, either," Misha pointed out.

Aleksei said, "Try 'Connections'."

Sifte touched the link, and was confronted by another list of links. The last one was S. Pierson. "That was too easy," she said incredulously.

"And there hasn't been enough hard stuff to do lately?" Anastasia said. "Just open it!"

A new set of links appeared on the screen, among them: "Profile, History, United States of America, Western Alliance, Western Satellites, Southern Protectorate, A. K. Umanskaya, Imprisonment." Sifte chose the profile, and again paraphrased it for her friends. "They caught him and sent him to jail for treason," she concluded. "Kronstadt. They started hunting Sasha not long after and—" She faltered, looked inadvertently at Mila.

"Whatever it is, Sifte, just say it," she said wearily.

"She had a baby. They assumed it was Stepan's, and tried to take it—I guess we know why—but she killed the baby so that Solntse couldn't have it." None of them said anything, or even looked at each other. Finally, Sifte continued, "And then, almost a year ago, Stepan escaped." Now they crowded closer to try to see what was on the screen. They had been told that no one had ever escaped from Kronstadt.

A half-formed idea was nagging at Sifte. It had to do with Kronstadt. All at once, she remembered. The day Dmitri arrived he'd left a news report on one of the library terminals. Now she realized that it had been about this very escape.

No doubt it had been as studied a gesture as the others he'd made since then.

She filled the others in. "But the thing is," she concluded, "that report said they were close to re-capturing him."

Anastasia smiled derisively. "So what? They lie about everything else."

"It's still strange," Sifte persisted. "That was only a few months ago. When they took me to Institute 1, that couldn't have been how they meant to use me."

"It doesn't mean anything," Anastasia answered. "They probably change their minds a lot before we actually graduate."

"Even so, it'll be another seven years before they can send me after him. That doesn't make much sense."

"Maybe it's like the viruses," Mila suggested, "and you can do it from here."

"This is an assassination, not lab work! What could I do that no one on the outside could do better?"

They all considered this. Finally, Aleksei said, "Maybe we're thinking about it the wrong way. Maybe it's not about what Sifte can do, but about what she is." The others looked blank, but Aleksei looked at Sifte with rueful awareness. "Remember when I called you paranoid and egotistical?"

"You were right," she said, her stomach beginning to twist with apprehension.

"I'm starting to think I wasn't."

"Just say what you mean!"

Aleksei suddenly looked tired. "Look, can I sit there for a minute?" Sifte moved over, and he sat down in front of the computer. He began to sift through pages of files. Finally, he found one that appeared to contain a photograph.

In the picture Stepan wore his military uniform, already impressively strung with medals, but they weren't what caught Sifte's attention. It was the thin-lipped smile, the high cheekbones, the hazel eyes and blonde hair, the same she saw every day in the mirror. The room tipped and reeled.

Her friends stood at a slight distance from her, held at bay by the intensity of feeling bristling around her. "Sifte?" asked Mila tremulously.

"Sifte, what is it?" asked Misha.

"She should have killed me," she said flatly.

Anastasia took her by the shoulders as if to shake her. "Tell us what you're talking about!"

Only Aleksei said nothing, and Sifte realized that the picture was exactly what he had feared to see. His eyes were full of compassion, and it was on these that her own eyes rested when she answered, because she knew that if she looked at the innocent confusion on her other friends' faces, she would go to pieces.

"Stepan Pierson is my father. I'm the baby Sasha Umanskaya is meant to have killed."

"He looks like you," Mila conceded, "but it doesn't mean you're that baby."

Sifte couldn't answer. Instead, she jerked the sleeve back from her scarred left arm, showing them all the Soviet 'C.' Her friends looked at it mutely. For the first time in her memory, Sifte began to cry in the presence of others. She reached out blindly for support, and Aleksei caught her, held her.

"It's okay, Siftenka," he said. "It's going to be all right."

"It's not going to be all right!" she cried, pushing him away. "They want me to kill my father! I'd rather kill myself!"

Mila reached out, stroked Sifte's hair. "Now you see," she said softly, and with such resignation that Sifte paused for a moment to look at her before she crumpled again.

"You'll never have to kill anybody," Aleksei said grimly. "None of us will. Will we?" He looked around the room, his eyes hurt and defiant. They all shook their heads.

"The bastards!" Anastasia broke out. "How can they think they can use us like this?" She looked around, the beginning of a crusader's passion in her black eyes, written into every feature of her thin, dark face. "Look, if we're serious about fighting the system, here's our chance."

"What are you saying?" Mila asked.

"'The time for all serious effort is when we are young.'"

"Book eight, section four," Misha added.

"But I thought you said there was nothing we could do without putting ourselves in danger," Mila persisted.

"That was before I knew about him." She pointed to the picture of Stepan on the screen. "If we can find him, maybe he'll help us get out of here."

"But if they figure out what we're doing, they'll kill us!"

Anastasia shrugged. "Then we'd better make sure they don't figure it out."

16

"Stepan!" Andrei called down from the bunker. There was no reply. "Stepan, get up here!"

Stepan started awake, and for a moment he couldn't orient himself. He was in a dark room with a barred window, and for a nauseous, lopsided moment, he thought he was back in prison. Then he sat up, and the dim shapes of Andrei's apartment resolved around him. Now he remembered: they had been up all night working on a meeting strategy. He must have fallen asleep, missing the few hours of daylight.

He had been dreaming, and the dreams had left behind a sense of foreboding like a body on a riverbank. The last one had been about Sasha—or someone like her. The dark eyes of the woman with the knife had been hers, but not the look of detached cruelty in them as she pursued him through endless darkened tunnels.

Stepan stood up, walked over to the window and looked down at the handful of campfires in the street below, wondering where Andrei had gone. Over the past few months and the course of many arguments, Stepan and Andrei had finally arrived at a tenuous truce. Now Andrei allowed him to help with Soviet strategies and to attend smaller meetings.

Though he didn't like it, Stepan knew that Andrei was right to make him lie low. Solntse hadn't sent even a nominal search party after him, which was suspicious at best, and it would be better not to draw attention to himself until he had some idea of what Solntse was up to.

"Stepan!" Andrei called again, and all at once Stepan remembered what had awakened him.

He made his way up into the bunker. Andrei was sitting at the computer, his face ghostly in its blue light, staring at the screen with determined disbelief. Without a word, he got up from the chair and indicated to Stepan to sit down.

The text on the screen was an e-mail, the identification code at the top that of an Opyekun. The message read:

```
Andrei Umanskiy,

Ignore the ID code, it's fake. I'll explain
when I know I've reached you. I'll know it's
you if you know who I am, and why.

Sifte

P.S. Correspondence between our addresses is
encrypted and untraceable.
```

"Any thoughts?" asked Andrei.

"Obviously somebody was monitoring our transmission the day we searched for information on the child, and they're trying to get me to give up my whereabouts." He paused, studying the message. "I thought you said your system was foolproof."

"I never said that. Anyway, all that matters now is that the 'kuni are on to us."

"I don't think an Opyekun would have bothered to write this," Stepan said speculatively. "It would have made more sense to trace our network signal and arrest us."

"Then maybe it's Solntse playing games."

"It's awfully straightforward for Solntse."

"So, what? Do you think this actually came from the child?"

"At the moment, I think only that it came from someone other than Solntse or the Opyekuni."

"No one else knows about Sifte."

"If we can break into classified files, someone else could."

Andrei's eyes were quick and clinical as scalpels. A clot of images from his recent nightmare tumbled across Stepan's mind: Sasha's knife, her empty eyes, the gray specter of his own fear. For a split second, he wondered if he was missing something significant, even whether Andrei was the source of the message, was somehow setting him up. Almost as it formed, though, he crushed the thought muttering, "That way madness lies…"

"What?"

"Nothing."

"All right. Let's see if we can trace it." Andrei took Stepan's place at the computer, brought up a search engine, and typed in the identification of the Opyekun who supposedly belonged to the message's return address. "Nothing," he said after a moment.

"The official didn't write it?"

Andrei smiled his tight, cold smile. "The official doesn't exist."

"I suppose that doesn't really tell us much. Anyone could have fabricated an Opyekun identity." Stepan dragged his hands through his ragged hair. After a moment he said, "The author of the mail says that all correspondence between our addresses will be encrypted. We can check that, too. Go into Glaza as a ranking official—"

"—yes, yes, retrieve the message again." Andrei typed, and a new block of text appeared on the screen. For the first time since Stepan had met him, Andrei's face showed something other than inert assurance. "Amazing," he said softly, then moved out of the way so that Stepan could see.

The message on the screen read:

```
Leonid Larissov,

I have been to Dvortsovaya and Nevskiy. All is
as it should be. The Soviet is currently out
of sight, the sub-race quiet. There is no need
to concern yourself with Myortvograd at the
present time.

Pyotr
```

"What the hell is that?" Stepan asked.

Andrei shook his head. "An encryption program superior to anything on the market. Even robotic scanners wouldn't be able to detect anything amiss, because the message doesn't look encrypted. Who could possibly come up with something like this?"

The two of them looked at each other.

Before Stepan could speak the thought, Andrei said, "It's impossible."

"Not impossible. You yourself said that she's a genius among geniuses."

"But how could she know—"

Before he could finish, another message appeared in the inbox. Stepan opened it.

```
Andrei Umanskiy,

I know that you're there and receiving. You're
probably afraid this is a trick. So I'll trust
you, and hopefully earn your trust, by telling
you this:

My friends and I know that we were sub-race
babies, and that we're being trained for
terrible things. We know about Utopia. We found
plans for the first part of it. I'm supposed to
kill my father, Stepan Pierson. Check it if you
don't believe me. Follow the Glaza link below.

We don't want to be Opyekuni, and we don't want
to be part of Utopia, but we need help. If you
don't reply by this time tomorrow, I'll destroy
this identity and I won't try to contact you
again.

Sifte
```

Stepan looked at Andrei. "Utopia?"

Andrei's look of suspended disbelief had deepened. "I've heard it mentioned," he said. "It's supposed to be a master plan of Solntse's. No one knows what it's about, or even whether it's real or not."

"Then I don't think Solntse or the 'kuni would have sent a Soviet leader an e-mail about it."

"No—but I don't know whether I want to involve myself with whoever did."

Stepan considered this, then said, "They could prove valuable if they're on our side. Is there any other way you can think of to trace this message?" Andrei shook his head. "Then I think we should answer it."

"What?"

"Even if the encryption is a sham, sending one e-mail isn't any more likely to catch the censors' attention than anything else you do with Glaza. We don't have to give away any information about ourselves." Andrei said nothing, just glared at Stepan with the stubbornness Sasha had described so accurately. "If you're really worried, we can answer the mail then desert for a few days and see what happens. We can get someone to watch the place. And we can take the computer—that way no one will be able to trace anything." Stepan paused, then added, "I know your codes. I can find another computer."

Andrei looked at him coldly. For a moment Stepan thought that the other man might hit him. In the end, though, he only stood up and offered the seat in front of the terminal to Stepan. "If the Soviet goes down because of this," he said, "I'll kill you."

Stepan sat down, and considered the message on the screen. *I'll know it's you if you know who I am, and why.* It was clever—particularly the second part. It was unlikely that anyone would guess why Sasha had chosen the name.

"Having second thoughts?" Andrei asked, half-smiling.

Stepan began to type:

```
Don't destroy it. This is Stepan Pierson, not
Andrei Umanskiy. You're Sifte, my daughter, and
you were named for the U.S. President, Elisa
Foley.
```

He sent the message. There was a long pause, then a new message showed in the mailbox.

```
So it's you, Father.
```

When he read the words, despite all the lies he feared they might mask, Stepan experienced the same wrenching shock of pure, undefined emotion—and the same panic—he had felt when he first met Sasha. Andrei's eyes were also glued to the screen now, despite himself.

"Shit," Stepan said. "If only there were a way to find out... what about asking them to send one unencrypted message? The return pathway will tell us whether it comes from Institute 1."

"But not whether it's really Sifte writing. Just keep talking. Maybe something will come up."

So Stepan typed:

```
Did you write the encryption program yourself?
And does it work for real time?
```

The reply came more quickly this time:

```
Two of my friends wrote it. And no, it doesn't.
```

Stepan thought for a few minutes, then wrote:

```
How long have you known the things you just
told me, and how did you find them out?
```

Sifte replied:

```
It's too long a story to go into now. We don't
have much time.
```

"We're not getting anywhere," Andrei said. "You have to find out what she knows. If it's her, that is."

Stepan typed:

```
How did you find Andrei, how did you know he'd
know where I was, and how are you doing all of
this without attracting attention?
```

Sifte answered:

```
We didn't know Andrei would know where you
were. At first we didn't even know about
Andrei. He doesn't get as much Glaza air-
```

```
time as you. But we found out that Sasha had a
brother, and that he was still in Solntsegrad.
We thought he might have access to a computer.
So all we had to do was find his home address,
and see if there was Glaza activity coming from
it. If it's supposed to be a secret, we can
tell you how to block your transmission better.
```

"I have to say," Stepan said, turning to Andrei, "this is getting awfully detailed to be a fabrication."

"But nothing she's said proves she is who she claims to be," Andrei answered.

"Does it need to? This is good information."

Andrei didn't reply. They both turned back to the screen.

```
We used a Trojan Horse program to steal
teachers' codes and passwords and get into
classified Glaza sites, but obviously we
couldn't keep using them. So we made up a fake
Opyekun identity. We couldn't use the school
computers, so we had to build our own. We stole
the parts.
```

"That almost convinces me," Andrei said, smiling grudgingly. "Only a child of yours and Sasha's would have the audacity to build an unauthorized computer right under Solntse's nose."

```
Like I said, I don't have much time now. Please
tell me what you want me to do.
```

"Preferably not kill me," Stepan said to the screen. Then he turned to Andrei. "What should I tell her?"

Andrei's face was unreadable. "If only there were a way to tell…"

All at once, Stepan had an idea. "There is," he said. "Or at least a way to begin to. You know the English term 'red herring'? Well, let's drop one in her path. If someone moves on it, then we'll know she isn't on the level."

Andrei sighed. "Fine. But first, ask her what she knows about Utopia."

Stepan sent the question, and Sifte answered:

```
Not much—just that it's some kind of plan for
the future, and we're involved, at least in the
first part. Solntse is afraid of the sub-race,
and he's planning to destroy them using us as
his army.
```

Stepan paused. The words confirmed suspicions he'd had for years. He answered:

```
Please direct us to your sources when you can.
I'll be here all day tomorrow if you want to
contact me again. And send us a copy of your
encryption program. We don't have anything as
good.
```

Sifte replied:

```
We will. We'll send you the real-time program
too when we finish it. We have to go now, it's
time for our daily brain-washing ceremony.
Good-bye.
```

"Pretty cynical for an eleven-year-old." Andrei said dryly. "I guess we'd better pack. I want to be well away from here by tomorrow."

Stepan was scrolling back through the e-mails. "I don't think anything's going to happen, tomorrow."

"I know. But that would be some coincidence."

"I don't believe in coincidence."

"So, she's told us that Utopia equals genocide and the little geniuses are the bombs? It's what we suspected all along."

"But this is—"

"Still purely speculative," Andrei interrupted, exasperated. "And if this really is Sifte, and she really means all she says,

189

then she won't last long. No one can fool Institute 1, and when they find her out she'll go the way of the other sub-race failures."

Stepan regarded Andrei with his own coldness. "Did you only want me to help you get her killed, then?"

"What do you mean?"

"When this started you were adamant that I find her. I never thought to ask why."

"I didn't plan to decide that until I knew what she was being trained for."

"Well, now you do."

"What do you want me to say, Stepan?"

Stepan shook his head. "I intend to be good and sure that she is who she says she is before I do anything at all. But I want to know that if this is really Sifte, and she really does need help, then you'll give it."

Andrei scrutinized him for a few moments, then said, "There's something else. You're planning something."

"What could I possibly be planning?" Stepan answered evenly, though Andrei's astute observation had rattled him.

"Don't tell me, then," Andrei said coldly. "But don't forget that no matter whose side she's on, she's a loaded gun as long as she's at Institute 1."

Still staring at Sifte's last message, Stepan said, "Then we'll have to get her out of Institute 1."

Andrei's mouth tightened. "Don't forget that this isn't America. One life counts for little, here." Andrei turned to go, but half-way down the ladder he stopped. "I'm not as intractable as you think, Stepan. If we really have found Sifte, and she really does want to help us, then it might be to our advantage to let her. But I mean to be sure before we start plotting revolution."

PART 2

THROUGH THE FIRE

"Then think what would naturally happen to them if they were released from their bonds and cured of their delusions... and suddenly compelled to stand up and...look and walk toward the fire..."

Socrates to Glaucon
On the Simile of the Cave
"The Republic"

1

"Please choose your weapon," the cool, disembodied female voice instructed for the second time.

Sifte tore her eyes away from the shimmering image of a sub-race family huddled in the corner of the Myortvograd alley. Three guns rotated slowly in the air in front of her. Two were automatic: one a rifle of Middle Eastern make, the other a handgun, a prototype from America not yet for sale. The third was a German semi-automatic handgun discontinued at least two decades earlier. Sifte reached for it.

There was a ghost of a smile in the voice when it said, "A challenging choice, Sifte." She had chosen the gun because it had the least destructive capability. However, if the system chose to see it as enthusiasm, so much the better for her.

Sifte loaded the gun, trying not to flinch as the cold metal touched her skin. When they had still worked in pairs, weapons practice had been bearable. Since they had reached Level 11 they practiced alone. It wasn't the only thing about target practice that had changed. The chases were harder now, the adversaries more cunning, and their deaths more realistic. There was also pain. Before, it had been blocked as it was in the games, but now they felt any injuries as realistically as they saw them.

Sifte knew that it had probably made her a better fighter, and certainly a more ruthless one, but it had also made her afraid. She wasn't afraid of the pain itself, but when her mind was focused on pain she couldn't block her other thoughts, and she was constantly aware that the presence she had felt in Cave five years earlier might be waiting for such a lapse, might see just how much she was hiding.

"Are you ready," the console's voice said, its programmed arrogance precluding the intonation of an actual question.

Sifte took a deep breath. "Ready."

The ruined city solidified around Sifte. She looked at the sub-race family by the broken wall, dreading that one of them would produce a weapon from a fold of ragged clothing. However, they only huddled closer together at the sight of her Opyekun uniform. Sifte breathed an unconscious sigh of relief.

She picked her way carefully out of the alley and onto the main street to which it connected. It was a big street, probably a major thoroughfare. Often the streets in these settings were full of people—non-targets who, if accidentally shot, lost her points. This time the street was deserted, though cluttered by the ruins of what seemed to have been an open-air market. The wood of the carts and tables was half rotted away, and only gray, tattered rags of the awnings and parasols remained, drifting in the cold evening breeze.

Sifte moved warily among the toppled remnants of the market. Nothing moved but the ragged awnings. Long minutes passed,. Finally she saw a flicker of movement to her right. As she turned, three shots ricocheted off a wall a few inches to the right of her head. Sifte dropped to her knees behind an upturned cart in a spangled rush of adrenaline, and peered out through a crack in its weather-beaten planks. She saw no sign of the person who had shot at her. Almost directly across from her was another alley, and she decided that her assailant must have fired from its protection.

Creeping from cart to cart, she made her way across the avenue, then stood up carefully, and ran the few feet to the crumbling wall on one side of the alley. With her back up against it and gun arm raised, she inched around the corner. Two more shots whizzed by her head, and she fired two of her own into the alley. She heard footsteps running off in the opposite direction.

Sifte turned the corner just in time to see the man rounding another corner. In a second, she was off after him. She followed him into a smaller street which ran parallel to the avenue. Hardly any of the violet twilight filtered between the high walls; it was all shadows and black, gaping doorways. The man ducked into one of them.

Once he was out of sight, Sifte proceeded more slowly, her gun raised and ready. She knew now that the console would force her into the building her attacker had entered, that finding and killing him would involve some kind of intricate chase through a labyrinth of half-ruined hallways. It was a scenario she had been fed often enough in these practice sessions. She was already running through possible search patterns in her mind when she reached the doorway through which the man had disappeared. Though she approached it with caution, she didn't really expect that he'd be anywhere near the entrance. She paid more attention to the glassless windows above the door, which would afford a sniper a clear, point-blank shot. And then he stepped out of the doorway.

He was dead before he had the chance to finish raising his hands, before his smile of recognition could fully form. Then he was falling. He seemed to fall forever, his eyes fixed on her all the while. The worst of it was that they weren't reproachful, only sad, and also mildly inquisitive, his lips slightly parted as if he wanted to ask her why she had done it. And then he was at her feet, and Sifte could only stare down at him, oblivious to the cool console voice congratulating her on her quick reaction time. Her head was a wasp-swarm of rage and disgust that she couldn't begin to block. Because the expectant, recriminating face of the dead man at her feet was her father's.

*

"Shit," Sifte muttered. She turned from the screen of the Dacha computer, to which she had been all but riveted for three days. "Lyosha, come look at this."

The past five years had made a marked difference to Sifte's appearance. She had grown as tall as many of the boys in her class. What little baby fat she had had was gone, and her long limbs would have looked fragile if it hadn't been for the fine wrappings of muscle that their recently stepped-up physical training had given her. Lately she had been skipping meals; fatigue had worn bruised grooves beneath her eyes, and there were bluish hollows under her high cheek-bones. Her eyes had the look of something hunted.

Aleksei put down the printouts he was reading, and went to join her. On the screen was a Glaza file showing import and export records for the past few months. As he read, Aleksei ran a hand absently across the black bristles of his new military haircut. The starkness of his features without

197

the unruly black hair made their situation more real to Sifte even than the new version of weapons practice or the rigorous physical training.

"What is this?" he asked.

"Utopia."

"How do you mean?"

She tapped the screen. "According to this, a group of prisoners from Kronstadt was shipped to Institute 1 a week ago. I haven't seen them, have you?" Aleksei was silent, but his eyebrows had drawn together. "That's not all. There've also been a lot of shipments lately *out* of Institute 1."

"So...?"

"So, when did the Institutes start producing exportable goods?"

"Any idea what they were?"

"No, but they've all been classed as biohazards. They've also all measured under a half-meter square, and none have weighed more than ten kilos."

"Where were they going?"

"Siberia, the Caucasus...and Pakistan."

"Then it can't be weapons trafficking. No country in its right mind would risk the Solntsegrad Treaty's sanction penalties—"

"Sanctions don't pose much threat to a country that has nothing to lose," Sifte interrupted. "And having nothing to lose can make a deal with the devil look pretty appealing. India's been tightening its own sanctions on Pakistan for the last few years. I bet a few super-germs in the Delhi water supply would loosen things up."

"Have you found any more of this kind of thing?" Aleksei asked slowly.

"Why? Have you?"

Aleksei hesitated for a moment, then said, "Ask me that one again when we've got everyone together. I think it's time for an emergency meeting."

*

"That's everything I know," Sifte concluded, looking at her friends, who were crowded around the computer screen. She looked at Aleksei. "So what about you?"

Aleksei reached into his pocket and pulled something out. Five smooth, elliptical pieces of metal, no bigger than buttons, rested on his palm. He said, "Fly." The buttons sprouted wings, which began to oscillate. In a moment they were hovering like hummingbirds in front of Aleksei's eyes. "Formation A," Aleksei said, and they rearranged themselves into what appeared to be a battle formation.

"Where did you get them?" Misha asked.

"I made them. They started out as a kind of 3-D doodle. I was thinking about bumblebees and how physics says they shouldn't be able to fly…anyway, my aerophysics teacher saw one, and you can guess the rest."

"Nanobots," Anastasia said speculatively. "I wonder what they want with those?"

"You could load a lot of germs into one of them." He looked grimly at the robots, then said, "Sleep." They settled back onto his palm and retracted their wings. Aleksei pocketed them.

"So, what does it mean?" Mila asked.

Sifte sighed. "The sub-race works the logging industry and the farms and a million other things that keep the country going. If Solntse gets rid of them, he'll need to start trading for necessities. To trade he needs a product—"

"So he plans to trade in technology," Anastasia finished, her expression oscillating between disgust and fascination.

"You've got to admit, it's a tight plan. Especially since we'll be out of work once the genocide's over."

"And the prisoners?" Mila asked quietly. "How do they fit into this?"

They looked at one another uneasily. Finally, Sifte said, "It's just a guess, but I think they might be part of the training that starts when we reach Level 12."

"Which part?"

Sifte took a deep breath, then said, "Target practice."

Mila whitened, and the others fell silent. "There must be something we can do to stop it," she said.

"Yeah," Anastasia said. "Shoot ourselves."

"Remember, we're only speculating," Sifte said. "And nothing's happened to us yet that we haven't been able to deal with. We'll find a way through this."

"That's easy to say when you're still innocent," Mila answered, her tone caustic.

"What does that mean?"

"It means I know what was in those biohazard shipments." Mila looked up at them. Her face was white and hard as marble. "Viruses. Deadly ones, programmed to work on specific gene pools."

"You made them?" Anastasia asked.

"I worked on the preliminary research. I should have seen what it was. I could have tried to stop them—"

"And you'd have been dead before you even began." Sifte looked around at her friends' anxious faces and sighed. "Look, if all this is true, then it's a terrible truth, but it's one we have to accept." Mila turned away, and Anastasia's face tightened with anger. Only Aleksei would meet her eyes.

"Up till now we've been playing soldiers," she said, "but the war's always been real. Now it's real for us, too, and reality number one is that you can't fight a war without casualties. We can debate ethics all we want, but right now we only have two choices—survive Institute 1, or not."

"So you're saying we should sacrifice other people to save our own skins?" Mila asked coldly.

A spasm of what looked like pain crossed Sifte's face. "If that's the only option," she said softly.

Mila's face flushed with anger. "How can you be so callous?"

"That's not fair!" Aleksei cried. "You can't condemn her for facing the truth!"

"So you think we should go along with them?"

"I think we have to have faith that the good we'll do once we're out of here outweighs the worst of what we have to do to get there."

"'The good is the end of all endeavor.'" Misha said.

"But if we do terrible things," Mila answered, "do you think we'll have any faith left in what's good?" Her words sounded heavy to Sifte—laden, like Dmitri's, with secondary meaning.

"Isn't that the meaning of faith?" Aleksei answered.

After a moment Mila looked away. As the anger left her, she seemed to retreat inward on herself, almost to deflate. Sifte wanted to crumple with her, but she saw that if somebody didn't push them beyond this impasse, they would succumb to it. Through the dreamlike inertia that had settled on them she said, "This isn't something we can solve tonight. There are practical things to deal with now, beginning with our concentrations. What have you all been assigned?"

They looked at one another. Finally, Anastasia answered haltingly, "Political science."

"Engineering," said Aleksei. "Specializing in aerodynamics. But I think they're going to make me take a political science segment as well."

"Biological research," Mila said. "Otherwise known as genocide."

"All right," said Sifte, ignoring the barb, "that's concentrations. And I think there's one more thing we should cover before we go."

"Room changes," Anastasia pre-empted.

"Right," said Sifte. "We have to put in our requests next week. It makes sense for Mila and me to ask to room together, but what about Nastya and Lyosha?"

"I'm asking for a single," Anastasia said, "but I won't get it. They're reserved for the ass-kissers. Which means I'll end up in the lottery."

"And just think," said Misha, "you might get Tanya."

"I'm sure she'll coerce someone into rooming with her." Her look changed to anxiety. "Won't she? They wouldn't make me room with her, would they?"

"I doubt it," said Misha. "They seem to value her life."

"Actually, I've been thinking I'll put myself in the lottery too," said Aleksei. "Misha's too young, and otherwise, my friends are girls."

"So that's it?" Sifte asked. "Is there anything else we should talk about now?"

Nobody suggested anything. They began to disperse, since they had to be in their dormitories in twenty minutes. Mila hurried past Sifte without looking up.

"She'll get over it, Siftenka," Aleksei said when only he and she were left.

But Sifte wasn't thinking of Mila, rather of the glazed hazel eyes and aborted smile that were just as clear in her mind a week after the fateful weapons practice.

"Nothing," she said.

Aleksei studied her for a few moments. Then, abruptly, and with what looked to Sifte like disappointment, he looked away. "Just remember, there's nothing you can't tell me." Watching him leave, Sifte wished that this were true.

2

"She said yesterday that they've stepped up the training," said Stepan to Andrei, who was preparing food for a meeting. Andrei held to the belief that people are more willingly educated when their stomachs are full. In Stepan's more cynical view, providing food at the meetings only encouraged the attendance of those too lazy to help the cause: yet another misjudged holdover from the country's first bout of socialism.

"Who?" Andrei asked absently. "What training?"

Stepan flicked the desiccated carcass of a cockroach off the table impatiently. "Sifte and her friends. They've been counseled into concentrations, and soon they'll be moved to private rooms. But there are other things, too—stepped-up firearms practice, in-depth research on germ warfare...they know what's coming next."

Andrei didn't turn around, but the hand with the knife, poised to cut slices of meat, froze in mid-air. He stared straight ahead, out the tiny window. "They can't begin to imagine what's coming next," he said.

Stepan disagreed with this, given what Sifte and her friends already knew about Solntse's plans for their future.

If she didn't talk about its more immediate aspects, it was for a different reason. "She wanted to know what to do," he said out loud.

"What did you tell her?" Andrei had gone back to his preparations, but he moved more slowly now.

"To go along with them, of course." Stepan put down the meeting outlines which he had been skimming and joined Andrei at the kitchen counter. He had hoped that his words would shake some kind of feeling from Andrei, but Andrei only asked, "What is her concentration?"

"Besides genocide?"

"Rash judgments will help neither you nor her."

"History and political science," Stepan conceded.

"Well," Andrei said after considering this for a moment, "she's smart enough to stay out of trouble."

Stepan threw up his hands in exasperation. "She's not going on her first date, Andrei, she's being trained to destroy us!"

"What are you proposing?"

"It's time to take her out."

"We've been through this—"

"And I'm saying that now it's time." Stepan's face was set and stubborn, his tone adamant. "If she stays there any longer, we might not be able to save her."

There was another long pause. Then Andrei said, "Come upstairs. There's something I want you to see." Stepan followed him up to the bunker, where the computer was already running. Andrei opened a Glaza news page. The headline read: "Rebels Rally: Convict or Coincidence?"

"So," said Stepan with a dry smile, "they're onto me."

"Things were certainly quieter while you were in Kronstadt. Since you've been taking a more active role in meetings, we've collected more of a following. With more Soviet activity in the city, Solntse's taken more of an interest in us than he has of late. Two undercover Opyekuni were taken at a meeting three nights ago." Andrei paused, then sighed. "All this leaves me in a difficult position. On one hand, you are a great asset. But on the other—"

"I'm a liability."

Andrei sighed again. "But not in the way that you think. Some of the leaders are tired of waiting. They want you to make yourself known to the people, to prove that Solntse's system is not infallible. They think that this would spur the people to fight, and some of them even think—well, that you could lead them."

"What do *you* think?" Stepan asked.

"We aren't ready for revolution," Andrei replied, "no matter who's leading it."

Stepan smiled. "A diplomatic answer. At any rate, you don't have to worry. Even if I wanted to take on that kind of role, it wouldn't work. Your leader needs to come from your own people."

"So far, none of my people are up to the job."

Stepan thought for a moment, then he said, "Are you sure?"

"What, is it the children again? You can't possibly involve them in this."

"They're already involved."

"Not in any real way."

"No, but they're older now. Capable of more. If we could get them out, maybe they could fill some of the gaps in the Soviet. And if not…well, they might still be able to help us."

Andrei looked up at him questioningly.

"At the moment, the 'kuni are behind Solntse when it comes to incorporating the right sub-race babies. They could probably maintain control of the super-race if the information ever made the big time. But not many of them know about Sifte. If they did, particularly if her role in Utopia is a significant one, then even they might turn on Solntse. And without the 'kuni, the field's a lot more even."

"You'd use your own child that way?"

Stepan didn't meet his eyes. "I'd rather not. But there's no other way…"

Andrei looked at him for a long time. Then he said, "You're right. Losing the officials' support would certainly make it difficult for Solntse to hold on to power, but we aren't the only ones who would be vying for it. Right now we wouldn't win a coup."

"Of course not—which is why we need to be preparing an army now. To go ahead with this, we need the people to understand the reality of war, rather than the ideal."

"I've said nothing about going ahead with anything," Andrei said sharply, frowning again. "At any rate, you seem to have diverted my original point, which is that it would be better if you left the city for a while."

It was clear that Andrei was expecting a fight, and he looked entirely disconcerted when Stepan said, "Yes, you're probably right."

Stepan found it difficult not to smile at Andrei's look of consternation. Andrei knew that he was up to something, and also that there was nothing he could do about it. No doubt it would distract him throughout his speech that evening and probably cause him a sleepless night. However, Stepan doubted that even Andrei would guess the complexities of what he was planning.

"All right," Andrei replied, still looking at him with his sinkhole eyes. As he gathered up his bags of food and headed for the door, he said, "You aren't planning to tell Sifte any of this."

"Of course not," Stepan answered. "I wouldn't want to plant unrealistic hopes." He looked pointedly at Andrei. When he was gone, Stepan went up to the computer.

Two years earlier, Aleksei and Misha had come up with an encrypted chat program. Now they used it to communicate with Stepan under the guise of two Pomoshchniki. Sedov, Stepan's alias, was based in Kiev; Kalyuta, the children's, in Novosibirsk.

Someone on Sifte's end accepted Stepan's hail. With an eagerness that he would have thought impossible five years earlier, he typed:

```
S: Sifte?
K: Yes.
S: How are you? And things there?
K: Okay. I have to go in a few minutes, but I
have to tell you I think the officials are onto
you.
S: I know. Andrei's already worked me over.
K: You should listen to him.
S: It's difficult not to.
K: Stepan, do you understand how serious this
is?
```

Stepan paused, trying to picture Sifte's expression. His image of her was based on a patchwork of downloaded pictures, but still mostly invented. Right now, he saw her looking at the screen with grim determination, her forehead furrowed over her wide-spaced hazel eyes. No doubt she would have an anxious habit of some kind—biting her fingernails? Chewing her lip? Finally, he answered:

```
S: That's why I'm writing to you. I need to
leave the city for a while.
K: So you won't be able to write anymore?
S: I'll let you know before I leave. Nothing's
certain, I might know more tomorrow. Is there
anything else?
```

Sifte stared at her screen. She wanted to tell him about the
weapons practice session, but if there had been any kind of
warning in that session, it had been for her, not him. So she
answered:

```
K: No.
S: Then I'd better go. Goodnight, Sifte.
K: Goodnight, Stepan.
```

3

"Umanskaya!"

Sasha flinched, then looked up from the sun insignia she had been sewing onto an Institute jumpsuit.

"What is it?" she snapped.

The guard's eyes narrowed. "Take that tone with me, and it'll be more than you bargained for."

Sasha looked back down at the sewing, but this only increased her anger. She hated stitching the insignias, particularly on Institute uniforms, and she had no doubt that this was why she had been given the task.

"Your shift's finished," the guard said. "I'm taking you to your new cell."

"They're moving me again?"

"You don't like it? Stop preaching treason. Come on."

Sasha stood up. Her knees cracked, and a belt of fire ran across her shoulder blades. She had been sitting at the machine for twelve hours. Another woman silently took her place and began sewing where Sasha had left off. The guard guided her at gunpoint through echoing corridors. Finally, he stopped in front of a cell door and unlocked it, then pushed her inside.

There were two men in the cell. One was asleep facing the wall, snoring heavily. The other was Ivan Kiriyenko.

He had changed considerably since the last time she had seen him, a week after she set his broken leg. Five years of prison had scraped the excess flesh from his bones. His scarred face was stony beneath a scraggly beard. Their eyes met for a moment, and then both looked away again, waiting until the guard had gone.

"Don't try your games on these ones," the guard said to Sasha. "One's for Kronstadt, the other one hates women. He'll beat you senseless if you even look at him the wrong way."

"Thanks for the warning," Sasha said as the guard shut the door. She waited until his retreating footsteps faded, then she rushed to Ivan, crying, "I thought you were dead!"

"I will be in two days."

"You've had your trial?"

"There won't be one."

"Then why—"

Ivan interrupted, "The Sun moves in mysterious ways."

Sasha studied him. "Over the last few months they've been sending more and more prisoners to Kronstadt without trials. I think he's worried."

"Still the idealist, I see." Ivan smiled bitterly, shook his head. "It only means that the prisons are overcrowded. And, I suppose, that there's not much entertainment in the trial of a clear-cut traitor."

"That's it?" Sasha cried. "You've survived five years in this hell-hole, and you're going to accept their summons just like that?"

"You think there's an option?"

Sasha slumped down against the wall. "I think that if there isn't, I'd rather get shot down trying to climb the wall than sew another 'Sun of Truth' onto another fascist uniform."

Ivan gave a hollow laugh. "Still mad, I see."

"Meaning?"

"You still think there's a way out."

"Stepan got out of Kronstadt."

Ivan shook his head. "Stepan was trained to get out of Kronstadt. And he had help."

"Then I have to find help," Sasha answered. "There must be a way to get a message to someone on the outside."

"This can't be the first time you've thought of it."

"No. But it's the first time I've had access to somebody who can tell me how to do it."

Ivan sighed. "You think that I know how to get a guard to help you the way that I helped Stepan, but it's not that simple. You never finished your Institute training, you couldn't know...my last few years at the Kiev Institute taught me the meaning of fear."

"Some things are stronger than fear," Sasha said, with what seemed to Ivan to be a touch of derision. "Even Solntse's version."

"You still don't understand," he answered. "Target practice on superfluous prisoners, scientific experiments on sub-race children...at the end of Institute training, you're desensitized to atrocity. It's a kind of fearlessness, but there's a different terror that comes with it, and it's that which subjugates you to Solntse. You don't even imagine doubting him, because if you do then those children you poisoned are yours. The prisoners you shot are your brothers and sisters. You would go mad."

"Then why did you do it?" Sasha asked. Her voice was soft, even gentle, but the challenge in it was manifest.

Ivan didn't answer. His silence had a strained, deliberate quality. It was as if for every word he spoke, there was another he stifled. When she first met him, Sasha had suspected that he was hiding something from her. It was there in the way that he flinched when she touched him, the supplicating terror in his eyes when he looked at her. Now she was certain of it.

"What happened?" Sasha asked, fixing her unblinking eyes on his face.

Ivan didn't answer for a long time. It was only when he began to speak that Sasha saw how his hands trembled. "The first time I met Stepan, I nearly killed him." He paused, his eyes fixed on a distant past. Sasha didn't dare move.

"They're tradition, the beatings. They must be, because there's no other reason for them. Generally the prisoners aren't violent. Most are already broken. You torture them anyway. It's either that, or become one of them.

"We would taunt them, you know, try to get them going. It's easier to beat a man who stands up to you. But Stepan's group wouldn't rise. They just looked at us like they'd already seen hell…only Stepan was different. There was no defeat in him. There was even hope."

Ivan gave Sasha a bleak smile. "For this, I beat him to unconsciousness, but I might as well have saved myself the effort. I could still imagine his eyes. Full of absolution I could never accept. I knew they'd be no different when he came around. They would never be any different, and for that I despised him. So, even though I knew I was risking my job and perhaps my life, I went back to finish him.

213

"His face was covered with blood. That made it easier, I don't know why. I aimed, and realized the gun wasn't loaded. When I looked up again his eyes were open. I was right: they looked no different. Can you imagine, he still thought there was a way out—as if simply believing it was enough. And in the end maybe it was, because I hesitated long enough for him to say, 'I think my leg is broken. If you're not going to shoot me, could you please open my knee-locks?'

"I still don't know why I did it. I only know that nothing has been the same since." He looked at Sasha. "You want me to promise you a chance, but the most I can offer is a possibility that's as good a suicide."

"Tell me!" she demanded, and in her determination he saw the specter of lucid hazel eyes, clear despite the blood running into them.

"The doctors," he blurted. "Sometimes they've been known to help. But the prison Opyekun won't bring in a doctor unless your life is in danger, and he considers it worth saving."

"He will," Sasha said, the grim intensity on her face deepening. "The 'kuni still think I might be valuable as a trading piece. If they didn't, I'd be dead."

"Don't be so sure."

"What do I need to do?"

"Sasha, I can't possibly—"

"It's not your choice!" she cried.

"All right," he said. "Listen carefully." To his own surprise, Ivan felt a sense of relief.

*

"Guard!" Ivan called. "Come quickly!"

The cell door opened, and two guards stumbled in upon an all-too-familiar scene. In one corner crouched a pallid, heavy-set man, the one who had earned a reputation for torturing women. His face was scratched and bleeding, and there was blood on his hands. He was turning something in them fretfully: a piece of metal, sharpened into a cutting blade. One of the guards took it away.

The other two prisoners were in the opposite corner, the one who had been the Pomoshchnik holding the woman in his arms. She was covered in blood.

"What happened?" asked one of the guards.

"What did you expect, putting her in here with Artyomov?" Ivan answered in a trembling voice.

The guard glanced at the man he'd taken the knife from. Artyomov leered back. "Did she provoke him?"

"If you call sneezing provocation."

The ranking guard sighed. "Take him to isolation," he ordered the younger guard, jerking his head in Artyomov's direction.

When they had gone, he bent down to see to Sasha. Her right arm was shredded, and she seemed to have a head wound as well. "I suppose they asked for this, putting her in here," he said. He tied the rag around her arm, and picked her up.

Ivan saw something like pity glint in the guard's eyes as he lifted Sasha; perhaps also regret. "Where are you taking her?" he asked, but the guard didn't answer. The door swung shut.

4

Sifte was already late when she signed off the Dacha computer, but when she reached the classroom where Dmitri had asked her to meet him for her first Political Science tutorial, he wasn't there. She stopped in the doorway. Five chairs had been pushed into a circle, and four of them were filled. Anastasia and Aleksei sat next to each other. Aleksei was studying something on his screen, and Anastasia was trying not to look at Tanya, who sat diagonally across from her. Next to Tanya sat a boy named Nikolai, who was looking at the floor.

Sifte didn't know much about Nikolai, though he was in her year. He was tall and thin, with sparse, pale hair and eyes of a flooded-watercolor blue. He had a supercilious air about him that explained his lack of friends, yet he was missing the hardened detachment of the true outsider.

Sifte slid into the empty seat and asked, "What's this all about?"

Tanya looked up with a small, cynical smile. "I would have thought you'd know."

Ignoring her, Sifte looked at Anastasia and Aleksei. Anastasia shrugged. "I got a note from Dmitri telling me to meet him here." She shot a poisonous look in Tanya's direction. "He didn't say anything about anyone else."

Aleksei put his screen in his pocket. "That's what my note said, too." He gave her a slight, anticipatory smile and said, as if as an afterthought, "I imagine, though, that it all has something to do with that." He nodded in the direction of the room's terminal. It was set into a podium, facing the window in the opposite wall. The screen's light reflected off the window, along with what appeared to be a passage of text.

Nikolai got up to inspect it. His expressionless face took on a slight look of puzzlement as he read.

"Are you going to enlighten us?" Anastasia asked.

Nikolai regarded her coldly, then read, "'Social Democracy thought fit to assign to the working class the role of the redeemer of future generations, in this way cutting the sinews of its greatest strength. This training made the working class forget both its hatred and its spirit of sacrifice, for both are nourished by the image of enslaved ancestors rather than of liberated grandchildren.' Walter Benjamin."

"Who's ever heard of him?" Tanya scoffed.

"I have," Aleksei answered. Tanya reddened, and Anastasia smirked.

"So have I," Sifte added. "Dmitri assigned him to me a while ago. He was a German-Jewish writer who spent the most important years of his career in France."

"When was that?" asked Tanya, clearly annoyed that she hadn't been singled out for these readings, too.

"The late 1930's."

"A German-Jewish man must not have lasted long in late 1930's France," said Anastasia, who had recently studied the second world war.

"He didn't," Aleksei answered. "He and a group of other Jews tried to escape over the Pyrenees. He meant to emigrate to America, but the border guards wouldn't let them through. Benjamin poisoned himself that night." He paused, then added, "The border opened again not long afterward."

"He was a fool, then," Tanya said.

"Maybe he didn't have a choice," Aleksei answered.

"We always have a choice!"

Aleksei regarded Tanya, and her eyes faltered. "Not always," he said. "We of all people should know that."

"Do you find something wrong with our circumstances?" Nikolai asked of no one in particular, still not bothering to raise his eyelids above their laconic half-droop. There was something ominous in his look, nonetheless.

"I only meant that we didn't choose to be the elite any more than those who aren't chose not to be."

"Well I don't see what a 1930's German would know about socialism, anyway," Tanya interjected. "Hitler might have called his party the National Socialists, but everyone knows they were a bunch of greedy capitalists. The only real socialists back then were ours."

"Only you would claim squatters' rights on them," Anastasia scoffed.

"Hardly," Tanya answered, her eyes narrowing. "I only mean to say that Walter Benjamin wasn't in much of a position to comment on the failings of socialism."

"Why not?" Aleksei asked. "After the fall of the Weimar Republic, most of Germany was under socialist—"

"Yes, we've all done that reading!" Tanya said, then reddened again, and couldn't settle her eyes on him. All at once it occurred to Sifte that Tanya was in love with Aleksei. She had to stifle a smile when she considered how it must torment Tanya to harbor feelings for one of the foreigners she hated. However, it was also clear that Aleksei didn't see it, which could be dangerous.

"You're talking about the Social Democrats and the Christian Socialists," Tanya said, "both hybrids, neither revolutionary, and neither able to unify a divided and weakened country. Only true socialism could have done that."

"True socialism?" Anastasia repeated with a smirk. "Democratic Socialism *is* true socialism."

"No, it's not."

"Yes, it is. They might not have given themselves the label until later on, but the original socialists believed in implementing their ideology gradually, by democratic means."

"The first iteration of an idea isn't always the truest," Tanya answered.

"Then what is 'true socialism' according to you?" Anastasia demanded, clearly irritated that Tanya had said something intelligent.

Tanya shrugged. "The kind that works."

"None have worked for long."

"But some have worked better than others—the ones with quick and absolute implementation and a strong leader to maintain them. Stalinist Russia. Maoist China. Germany didn't experience true socialism until it came under our control after World War Two. So like I said, Walter Benjamin wasn't in much of a position to comment."

"Maybe not," Aleksei conceded, "all things being equal. But for the Jews things have never been equal. Democratic Socialism offers representative rather than autocratic equality, which the European Jews of that time might have been able

219

to access to their advantage. Besides, the alternatives were openly anti-Semitic."

"You're getting off track," Tanya complained.

Aleksei shook his head, without judgment so much as weariness. "Am I? What the Third Reich called 'National Socialism' bears a distinct resemblance to 'Social Democracy' as interpreted by Stalin."

"Did Stalin actually call himself a Social Democrat?" Sifte asked.

"I don't know."

They were all quiet for a few moments. Then Anastasia said, "This Benjamin—was he a philosopher?"

"Sometimes. Anyway, I'm pretty sure that quote comes from his 'Theses on the Philosophy of History.'"

"Right," said Anastasia, looking less sour as she began to be inspired. "Well, philosophers are purists. I doubt Benjamin was thinking about any specific socialist system when he wrote that. He was probably more concerned with the idea itself."

"And what, in your opinion, is the idea itself?" Nikolai reiterated—the closest he had come so far to showing interest in the discussion.

Sifte didn't know why—she hardly knew him—but she disliked Nikolai abruptly and intensely. And so, though she had promised herself that she wouldn't be dragged into this debate, she found herself answering for Anastasia. "No one can really do anything more than presume what he meant, especially from such a short quote, but it seems to me that he's blaming the socialists' flawed interpretation of their own ideology for its failures in practice."

"That's a pretty broad statement," Nikolai said, smirking, "especially considering how many brands of socialism existed at the time."

Sifte sighed, disliking him more by the second. "Fine. Let's say that Benjamin was looking at Russian socialism." Nikolai shrugged. "He claims that it's the memory of past injustices rather than the possibility of freedom from new ones that inspires an oppressed people to change their circumstances. He also says that the Social Democrats failed to employ this idea in motivating their most dedicated and useful followers, and as such failed to make their ideas work." She paused, then proceeded carefully, "What he doesn't say is that this kind of weakness becomes the foundation for a country's enslavement to a succession of nominally socialist dictators who are actually fascists."

"I don't see why someone now would be worried about that," Tanya said.

"Don't you?" Sifte rejoined.

"You might as well come right out and say it," Nikolai said with nonchalant venom, like a recently-fed but not-quite-sated snake. "Everyone knows the lot of you are just as bad as those reds you're criticizing."

"What do you mean?" Sifte asked, wondering where Dmitri was, and what had inspired him to call together this volatile group in the first place.

"It's obvious that you don't approve of Solntse's methods, you and your little group. The books you read, the films you watch, the positions you take in class—it's obvious. You should have been kicked out of here years ago. If I were you, I'd be down on my knees blessing Solntse for his mercy."

Anger flared in Anastasia's eyes, but before she could say anything Sifte said, "I'm not a traitor. I'm not even ungrateful.

221

I just happen to look at the whole thing more pragmatically than a lot of people here. We might be the chosen ones, but we'll be expected to show something for it sooner or later, and if you think that I disapprove of something…well, you're right. I disapprove of the fact that everybody pretends that's not the way it is."

"Well worded," Nikolai said. The smile was gone now, replaced by a look of calculation. "But I'd stop there, if you don't want to be turned in for blasphemy."

"Who gives you the authority?" Sifte asked calmly. A muscle in Nikolai's face twitched, and Sifte noted it with interest. "Anyway, we're talking about Benjamin, not Solntse. And I think he's wrong."

"How so?" asked Aleksei, his anxiety evident.

"I think endangered children are at least as compelling as broken grandparents when it comes to revolution. They're both emotional issues, but the children are the future of any people, and so that's where their faith and their guiding ideologies must originate…or topple. If a people is oppressed, and their children suffering—well, a leader would be foolish to disregard it."

She looked at Nikolai's, and saw understanding in his eyes. A shiver ran down her spine. "I hope you're not suggesting that the sub-race could ever threaten Solntse," he said.

"We're talking about Benjamin, not Solntse," Sifte repeated. "Though since you suggested it, I suppose it's relevant for us, as future Opyekuni, to consider the way it might relate to our own society."

"Don't ever think a few gutter-rats could threaten Solntse's system."

"I didn't," Sifte said softly. "You did." Their eyes locked for a moment, Nikolai's full of cold fury, Sifte's showing compassion, which surprised Aleksei. And then, without another word, she stood up and walked out of the room.

*

Alla turned to Dmitri, who sat beside her in the observation booth.

"Well?" she said, a smug smile splitting her angular face.

Dmitri appraised her, and seemed to come up short. "I didn't need proof that they're dogmatically incompatible." He stopped, waited for her reply, then realized that she was waiting for him to say something more. He hadn't felt true panic in a long time, but he felt it now. "I imagine that if they can't get along it will put a wrench in Solntse's plans," he added.

Alla's smile widened, becoming both condescending and sympathetic. "Once again, Dima, you miss the point."

"Which is?"

"Why is it that they don't agree dogmatically? Haven't they been educated in the same system?" She shook her head slightly, with a touch of regret. "Either you've been asleep at the post, or you've been up to something. Which is it?"

"Have you ever seen me step out of line?"

Alla looked at him with speculation, fingering her bloodless lips. "Something's not right. They're too sure of themselves, too righteous, which leaves me no choice but to find out why."

Dmitri's wavering panic took hold in earnest. "What are you planning to do?"

She looked at him, her face blank with a serene smile. "You've had your turn with them, Dima," she said, standing up. "Now it's mine."

5

"Ready?" Aleksei asked Sifte, when she met him at the door of the games room, where they were scheduled to play Cave.

In fact, she wasn't. She had been on edge since the terrible weapons practice, and even more so since the strange meeting Dmitri had called several days before. She couldn't shake the feeling that something was eavesdropping on her thoughts, and though she didn't know how it would be possible, the neural jacks were the only inroad she could imagine. However, even the thought of trying to explain this to Aleksei made her wonder if the strain of their dual lives was finally taking its toll on her sanity. It was easier to pretend it wasn't happening. So she followed him into the games room, sat down in the console and plugged herself into the computer.

"What *is* this?" Aleksei asked as the program opened. They stood in a narrow stone room without doors or windows, facing a wall with two full-length mirrors, one in front of each of them.

"Maybe someone's trying to tell us we've become narcissistic," Sifte said, looking over at Aleksei.

"The game's never had a sense of humor before. Or an obvious bent for moralizing."

Sifte turned back to the mirror and started. Now it showed a door in the wall behind her reflection. It was open, but beyond it was impenetrable blackness. She turned to look at the wall behind her, but it was blank.

"Do you see—" she began.

"An open door behind my reflection."

Sifte walked over to Aleksei, but her reflection didn't follow her. In his mirror, Aleksei stood alone.

"No wonder Nastya and Misha looked so creeped-out the other day," Aleksei said. He reached toward the place where Sifte's reflection should have been. His hand met its reflection and kept going, dissolving into itself. He turned to her, began to say something, but it seemed that once begun, the process couldn't be stopped. In seconds, Aleksei was gone, his mirror blank. Sifte put her hand to the mirror and met cold, solid glass.

Fighting panic, Sifte turned to her own reflection. "Take me too, then," she said.

"We thought you'd never ask," her reflection answered with a supercilious smile.

The reflection reached out of the mirror and took her hand. For a moment she seemed to be pushing through icy, viscous fluid, and then she was standing in a garden bright with sunshine and a profusion of flowers. The grass was the humming green of a fever dream, the sky the liquid blue of light through stained glass, and the hues of the flowers throbbed with an intensity the plants in the Institute greenhouses would never duplicate. Birds chirped and fluttered among the branches of the birch trees lining the garden's walls, and fat bees hummed among the blossoms.

Somebody was calling her from a copse of birches to her right. The voice was a woman's, familiar and unfamiliar at the same time. A narrow path led into the trees. The light that penetrated their spreading canopy winked and beckoned like the eyes of a sly child.

Under the trees the air was cool, lush as the garden foliage, so full of sounds and smells and nuances of breeze that it had a kind of obscure solidity. Sifte felt smooth earth under her feet, and looked down at them in surprise. They were bare. Except when she bathed or slept, she had never been without Institute 1's regulation black boots in her life. The feeling of the earth full of roots and insects shivered up through her skin. It was the most alive she had ever felt.

Her jumpsuit, she saw now, was also gone. Instead she wore a simple, sleeveless dress. The lightness of her freed legs was strange, but the most amazing thing about it was the color. Nobody at Institute 1 wore anything but gray. The only variations were the colored arm-bands the lower and middle level students wore, and the navy or black uniforms of the Pomoshchniki who occasionally visited the school. Her new dress, however, was blue—a bright shade, like the sky but deeper.

"Sifte!" the woman's voice called again, startling her out of her reverie. She looked up, and her amazement deepened.

The person walking towards her was Mila. Or rather, she was the woman Mila might have become if she had never known illness or grief. She wore a dress like Sifte's, but it was the color of her own blooming cheeks and sunburned nose. Her smile and the softness of her eyes showed the contentment of a peaceful life. Her hands were dirty, as if she had been digging in the earth.

"How…how are you here?"

Mila laughed, her brow furrowing at the same time. "What kind of question is that?" she asked. "You must have been in the sun too long. You have to be more careful. Come sit in the shade for a while. Lyosha's made kompot."

"He's here too?" Sifte's feeling of lightness, of floating somewhere to the side of herself, compounded.

Mila shook her head. "What's the matter with you, Siftenka? Are you sleepwalking?"

Sifte was wondering something similar. She followed Mila, who had turned and moved off along the path, apparently toward the house among the trees. She kept telling herself that she wasn't dreaming—that she was still in the game and must keep looking out for the purpose of the level. However, the heady air made it continually more difficult to retain a cerebral grasp on her surroundings, and ever more tempting to topple into them like the sweet dream they seemed to be.

They emerged again into the bright heat. Ahead of them, across another expanse of grass and surrounded by flowering plants, was the dacha that she and Mila and Aleksei had spent so many hours dreaming up as children. It was all there, from the peaked gables to the porch full of violet shadows. The walls were whitewashed, the trim a deep forest green. There was a swing in the porch, and Aleksei lay on this, reading.

He was no more the friend she knew than the rosy, healthy Mila was. His face had a similarly ageless appearance. His hair fell in a blue-black wing over eyes so dark that they took on a cast of heliotrope as he squinted at the page. When the girls came into the yard, he sat up and smiled.

Sifte found it difficult to look at him, just as it was difficult to look at Mila. It was as if a searing radiance had worked itself into every bit of them, from the golden filaments of hair that escaped Mila's plaits to the tendons running along

227

the top of Aleksei's feet like burnished piano wires. Even her wildest imaginings had not included the ravishing detail she saw around her now. It was as if someone or something had taken her ideas and made them more than a human mind ever could, realized them to the fullest measure of perfection.

All at once, she understood. These were the Platonic forms of her dreams. Yet to Plato, dreams were enemies, the shadows the philosopher-ruler had to recognize and rescind in order to prove equal to the calling. Despite the heat, she shivered.

Mila and Aleksei seemed to be waiting for her to do something. Sifte closed her eyes, and trying her best to block out the world around her she said, "End game."

"Siftenka, what are you talking about?" Mila asked.

Sifte opened her eyes again, as the panic she had felt once before began to claw inside of her. "Computer, end the game!" she demanded, but the house and the trees and the grown-up Mila and Aleksei all remained as tangible and seductive as before. Despite her growing fear, Sifte felt a part of herself that had been sleeping awaken. The game had only trapped her once before, and if she had ever doubted it she knew now that it hadn't been about a crossed wire. It had been a test, and this time she would learn who was behind it.

"Okay," she said, folding her arms across her chest, "what happens next?"

Mila's smile was gone, and Aleksei was looking at her anxiously. "I think maybe you should sit down," Mila said. "Lyosha will pour you a drink."

Mila helped her up to the porch swing. Aleksei handed her a tall glass of amber-colored liquid. She didn't want it, but when she tasted it she forgot about this. It tasted of mint and lemon, apples and honey.

"Can't you tell me anything?" Sifte asked Aleksei, searching his eyes for any shade of understanding.

"Anything about what?" he asked, with a tenuous half-smile.

Sifte sighed. "Never mind. Look, I'm not feeling well. Mila's right—I've been out in the sun too long. I think I'd better lie down."

"Of course," Aleksei said. "I'll go with you and make sure you're all right." He held out a hand towards her. The thought of touching him made her uneasy. Yet when his hand closed around hers, it seemed more real than anything she'd ever touched. She looked at him in surprise, but he only smiled at her again.

She caught glimpses of the dacha's rooms as they passed, filled with light the color of Mila's hair. One had a bay window with a view over molten water, another was full of tropical plants. There was a library with walls tiled in books, another room bare except for a grand piano sentient in the mellow light. Aleksei led her up a flight of stairs, then into a bedroom. The wooden floor was golden, with darker lines weaving along the grain. The bed had a plain white cover on it. On a dresser by the window a mirror caught the sun. The window itself had a view over the river.

"Do you need anything?" Aleksei asked, a puzzling tangle of emotions in his eyes.

"No," Sifte answered. "I think I'll just lie down for a while."

"Do you want me to stay?"

He reached out and ran the back of his hand along the side of her neck. She stared at him for a moment, stunned. In the end he precluded any decision, saying:

"You look like you need to rest. I'll come back and check on you in a while."

Sifte tried to smile as she imagined the Sifte in such a reality would, but she was well aware that it must be a poor replica. Her roiling emotions had finally settled into a deep unease. Aleksei didn't seem to notice. He turned and walked out, shutting the door softly behind him.

Sifte sank down on the bed. Once more she said, "End game," but it was an entreaty rather than a command, and she wasn't surprised when nothing happened. She was certain now that she had to break out of this reality, as she had the last time the game trapped her, but she didn't know where to begin. Then her eyes lit on the mirror on the dresser. She went and looked into it.

If Mila and Aleksei had seemed too bright to her, her own reflection was blinding. Yet she found that by focusing on just a part of it, she could keep her eyes steady. Gradually, as her focus cleared, she realized that her image was smiling at her.

"What is there to smile about?" she demanded.

"What is there to be angry about?" it answered. "You have everything your heart desires."

"But it's not real."

"'All that we see or seem is but a dream within a dream,'" it said in English.

"I would never have dreamed all of this."

"For all you know, you're dreaming now."

"You have to be able to imagine something to dream it. I could never have imagined these colors, these sounds and smells. And...and Aleksei..."

"Made you feel something you weren't expecting to feel," the reflection finished for her, with a knowing smile. "But that doesn't mean that it isn't real."

Sifte shook her head angrily. "Enough! Let me out!"

"Only you can do that." The reflection faded, and Sifte was looking at the face she saw every day in the ordinary mirrors of Institute 1.

She thought she knew what the reflection had meant: to escape the cave, she had to renounce the shadows. Yet she couldn't think of any other way to do this than to exit the game, and this was apparently impossible.

Her prior experience wasn't much help. The other time she'd been trapped, the game had taken what she didn't need, and as such had given her what she did. Relinquishing everything had been relatively simple when she had next to nothing. Here, though, the choices were endless. There was value everywhere, as far as the eye could see—and then, suddenly, she did see.

For years she had believed that the first test had been about abandoning what was most important to her. But maybe that logic had only worked by accident, and the test had really been about something else. If so, this problem and the first could be viewed in the same light. Then, there had been so little to see that sight itself became precious; now, there was so much that she couldn't see what she needed to. Only one thing could be real in this world of beautiful shadows, and Sifte knew what it was.

She leaned out the open window, towards the sun resting on the treetops like a wheel on a burning highway. "Let me see you," she said.

For a few moments, nothing happened. Then brightness began to engulf her vision, first with searing white light, then with red murk, and finally with darkness. Within it, the presence was waiting. Sifte asked:

Who are you?

I am the truth of all things.

Why am I here?

Nothing answered her, but the darkness thinned like smoke in a strong wind, until she could see. Once again, the city like a split heart appeared below Sifte. This time she didn't allow vertigo to unseat her. She let herself relax into the other mind, and found that it was like the city, divided between light and shadow.

Mine, said the voice, tight with proprietary glee. *And it can be yours, too.*

Sifte looked toward the darkened slum. It seemed to pulse faintly, diseased but not yet dead. *It isn't yours to give*, she said.

I am the Sun, the voice answered, suddenly cold. *I give and take as I please.*

If you were really the Sun, Sifte replied, *you would cast no shadow.*

She was falling through a howl of anger, toward the ruins of a palace and a sad, blackened angel. Faintly, she heard the wail of a newborn baby. One puzzling word blazed in her mind: home.

The moment before she hit ground, her eyelids jerked open. When her eyes focused and the feeling came back into her limbs, she realized that Aleksei was holding her—

232

clutching her, gray-faced, with tears in the corners of his eyes.

"Sifte...you were screaming...I unplugged you but you wouldn't come back...it was like that time when we were little, but worse—Sifte, what happened?"

To both of their surprise, she threw her arms around his neck and burst into tears. "They know. Lyosha, *they know*."

6

Sasha opened her eyes to the tainted darkness of a city night. The faint glow that filtered through the skylight turned the landmarks of her room to chiaroscuros. She was afraid for a moment, until she remembered that for the first time in many months, she was not alone.

Not alone…the words and their meaning flooded back to her, breaking into her consciousness like a warm wave. Reaching out, she felt the little bundle beside her, heard her breathing softly. She picked up the child and wept over her, because it had all been a dream—the years of darkness, pain and hunger, the hovering despair. Now the night was close and sweet, and she was lulled by it, by the even breathing of the sleeping baby.

Sasha sang to her, ancient peasant lullabies the women of Myortvograd still sang to their own children. She spoke to the baby about her father. It was important that she grow up knowing what he had been. In the years of her nightmare, Sasha had learned that there was nothing worse than not knowing.

All too soon the baby awakened and began to cry. Sasha tried to hush her, but she only cried harder. She gave her

her breast, but after a few moments the child turned it away. Sasha realized that, hungry as she was herself, she must have no milk to give the baby. Trying to soothe her, Sasha stood up, jogged her gently up and down as the ragged patch of sky began to brighten. When the sun broke over the edge of the skylight, the baby stopped crying and looked at it with wide, river-colored eyes that held Sasha, dragged her into their current.

The baby was growing heavy. Sasha put her down, and Sifte stood. She transformed as Sasha watched, as if years were passing in seconds. She toddled about on legs that grew continually longer and stronger. The sparse baby fat disappeared, left her face sharp and starkly beautiful. Sasha looked on helplessly, not knowing whether to rejoice or despair as time made her baby a woman, set that woman impossibly beyond her reach.

Then came the sound of the footsteps that Sasha had never forgotten. Sifte heard them too, and evidently she knew what they meant. "Mamushka," she said, and turned to her mother, reaching out her hand. There was fear in her eyes, and supplication.

Sasha reached out her own hand, but it seemed that the farther she reached, the farther Sifte's hand retracted, until it seemed many kilometers distant. All the while the sound of the Opyekuni's footsteps grew louder. Sasha ran after Sifte's retreating image, but it continued to outdistance her, until finally she collapsed in exhaustion. Darkness filled the sky like squid ink, seeping down around her as rough hands shackled her. There was only one tiny, flickering light in the midst of the vast, dark distance, which she knew was her daughter. As Sasha watched it, she tried to remember the brief hope the child had given her. As she concentrated,

Sifte's light grew stronger, widening and brightening until it engulfed her vision—

—and Sasha was awake, fighting her heavy eyelids for sight. But the light was too bright, and she closed her eyes again.

"Oh, no," said a man's voice, not unkindly. " We've just got you back. It seems you lost more blood than we thought. There's the head injury, too."

He shut off the light which he had been shining into her eyes, and after a moment Sasha found that she could see his face, though a speckled-granite film remained around the periphery of her vision. The man was middle-aged and mild-looking, with gray hair and eyes, dry, papery skin, and the long, gray coat of the prison doctors.

Sasha knew that she ought to be pleased that Ivan's plan had worked. She ought to hear the gentleness in the doctor's tone as a possibility, but she felt only overwhelming despair for the child she had dreamed. She turned her face to the wall, and to her own horror, she began to cry.

The doctor said, "Don't."

"Why not?"

"It won't help."

Sasha sat up. Her head pounded violently, and her right arm seared. She looked down and saw that it was bandaged from wrist to shoulder. A string of images flashed through her mind: crazed eyes, a gap-toothed leer, the burning pain of a dull knife in her flesh.

"What do you know about it?" she asked bitterly. "You've devoted your life to those who've taken mine. You must know that to me, you're no better than a murderer."

"I'm afraid not," he answered, his eyes faltering from hers. "I'm sorry."

Sasha was too surprised to respond. The doctor turned from her, but the briskness didn't hide the disappointment in his eyes. She wondered whether she had imagined it, or if the bump on her head was making her see what wasn't there. It seemed too much to hope that this doctor would be the one she was looking for.

"What's your name?" she asked.

"Krieger," the doctor replied, not looking at her.

"You're German?"

He turned toward her again, still not meeting her eyes, and handed her two small, white pills. "Russian, now. I came here during the Satellite wars, and pledged my allegiance to the man who granted me asylum."

Sasha's hope grew stronger. Someone who had not grown up with Solntse's propaganda might be more easily swayed from it.

"What are these?" she asked, regarding the pills dubiously.

"Codeine," he replied. "You don't have to take them, but I'd recommend it. The pain will get worse before it gets better." He finally looked at her, and his eyes searched hers with a hunger of which she doubted he was aware.

"They wouldn't kill me so kindly," she said, swallowing the medicine. She paused, then asked, "What happens now?"

Krieger was silent too long. "They don't tell me their plans for prisoners. I only treat them."

Sasha watched him. Something was wrong. "What about my arm?" she probed. "And my head?"

"Both should heal with time," he answered brusquely. "I'll remove the stitches in a few days."

"You?" she asked with studied disinterest. "Not another doctor?"

He seemed to see through it, looking intently at her as he answered, "They brought you to me, so you're my responsibility."

He bit off the end of the word as if he regretted it, but again, his look was equivocal. Sasha wondered whether he guessed the truth. She said nothing more, and the doctor seemed suddenly very busy with something on the other side of the room. A few moments later the door opened, and a Pomoshchnik entered.

"Come on," he said to Sasha, without looking at her. He took a set of blinders from his pocket, and Sasha's stomach clutched. Prisoners were never blinded for an internal move.

The Pomoshchnik put the blinders on her. They pressed lightly on her eyelids, cool and not necessarily uncomfortable, but Sasha could only think of the old custom of laying coins over the eyes of the dead. A tremor of dread ran through her. She tried to concentrate on Krieger's oblique promise to see her again, hoping that it hadn't been a platitude. If she was going where she thought she was going, then that promise was the only hope she had left.

The Pomoshchnik led her outside, toward the water, and then onto a boat. They crossed the thin strip of Lake Ladozhskoye that separated Schlüsselburg's rocky island from the mainland. When they docked, she was led to some sort of vehicle and into a narrow compartment, where she was seated on something hard. Her arms and legs were strapped down. She fought the rising claustrophobia by thinking of the dream from which Dr. Krieger had awakened her. She found that when she thought of the light that was her daughter, the panic subsided. It was almost like the meditation she had learned at Institute 1.

With the thought of Institute 1, Sasha's mind strayed. For the first time in many years, she contemplated her expulsion from the Opyekun training program. She had never been told why she failed, though she suspected that it was a result of many intangibles rather than any concrete defect. What she was certain of, however, was that the expulsion had been the first in the long line of narrow escapes from death which constituted her adult life.

Though she hadn't realized it at the time, Sasha knew now that if she had been one year older, Gospazha Alla would have killed her. With one more year of training, she would have known too much to be allowed to exist as anything but an Opyekun.

Yet in a way, she had become an Opyekun after all. The Soviet had taught her most of what she had missed in the last three years of Institute 1, and nothing could have hardened her like life in Myortvograd. For a moment she smiled to herself at the irony; then the engine of the vehicle jerked to life, and her smile foundered. That she had become an Opyekun without Solntse's blessing was precisely why she was being taken to the slaughter—for she had no doubt anymore that sooner or later, this journey would end in the Kronstadt quadrangle.

But why now? she asked herself, as she had asked Ivan. It couldn't have been the fight, since technically Artyomov had started it. And there was no way that anyone could know she had planned it unless—

A hollow opened in her gut. She couldn't believe she hadn't anticipated it. She had always known that Ivan lacked the brutality required to make a successful Pomoshchnik. It was why he had helped Stepan. But if he could turn from Solntse, surely he could turn back.

239

Sasha wanted to be angry at him, but she knew that she had only herself to blame. Perhaps she had been in prison too long: she had lost her ability to reason passionlessly. She tried to blank her mind again, but she couldn't. Sasha had always been able to sense direction, and she had felt the truck turn west. They were heading to the docks, to Kronstadt and the killing wall.

Once she had stood against a wall in a Myortvograd alley with a Pomoshchnik gun to her head, waiting for the tearing red end to everything. Andrei had come unexpectedly and shot the man a moment before he would have shot her. Sasha didn't believe in premonition. She had known as she pressed her cheek to the burned bricks that she was about to die. It was the miraculous salvation she hadn't been able to believe. It had been the same when she gave birth to Sifte, and she had hemorrhaged. The midwife had given her up—or that was how Sasha had understood the woman's sigh of resignation as she dropped her rags and herbs and began rocking back and forth on her heels and keening softly, her eyes closed in her crumpled witch's face. Though at that moment Sasha had felt sadness for the baby, who would certainly die without her, she had felt none for herself. Then the bleeding had stopped, so unexpectedly that the midwife gave Sasha a look that was near reproach, apparently for reversing the rightful order of things, and forked her fingers at her to ward off evil.

But the peace she had previously found in the face of death eluded her now. Sifte had stolen it. Any way she turned, Sasha met the same conviction that she must live.

The codeine was working by now, and she fell into an uneasy half-sleep. When she awakened, though, and was shoved at gunpoint out of the moving cell, she began to understand what her newfound reticence toward death might mean. She heard none of the bustle she associated with the docks. Instead there was silence, and the feeling of age. There were cobbles beneath her bare feet, and though she could hear water, it was contained and distant. She was led up a ramp, and she heard a gate shut behind her. A man's thin, jeering voice called out, "Welcome to the Fortress."

7

Tanya grew lovelier with each passing day, or so her many admirers told her. But she was shrewd as well as beautiful, and she understood the manipulative power of beauty. The right kind of smile could turn other people's wills to the shape of her own, and she had already found this useful. Now she waited in the corridor outside the newsroom to put her faith in her beauty to its first real test.

It was nearly twenty-two twenty, and soon the corridor lights would dim. Any students caught in the corridors after twenty-two thirty without a pass would be punished, for, as Tanya had recently learned, the teachers had secrets, and at some point during the day they had to discuss them.

Nikolai left the newsroom soon after Tanya took up her position outside it. She had made certain that he was the only one there. That hadn't been difficult. Sifte was the only other student who would have been in the newsroom so close to lights-out, and Sifte was in the infirmary sitting up with Mila who was, mundanely enough, ill again.

Tanya had positioned herself at the bend in the corridor. As she had anticipated, Nikolai showed signs of surprise and discomfort when he saw her. She smiled, and greeted him.

"Tatyana," he said, the officious tightness of his manner making the greeting an indictment.

"Tanya," she said, then waited just long enough that he was on the verge of squirming before she continued, "I wanted to ask you a question." Her face was void of emotion, though a powerful and unsolicited emotion was beginning to stir beneath the surface.

"Well?" he said gruffly.

"You know Aleksei?"

"I know several Alekseis."

"And you know the one I mean."

"If you're hoping for information about him, the most I know is what I learned at that farce of a tutorial Dmitri called. In other words, no more and probably significantly less than you do. Now, I need to get back to the dorm, and so do you."

He tried to push past her, but she caught his arm. He began to wrench away from her, but then he caught sight of her eyes—wounded, tremulous—and stopped. He regarded her with cold fury and, though he would never have admitted it, fear. It was not fear of Tanya, but of the question she had just asked, because in fact he had learned some fairly significant things about Aleksei since that meeting, and he would have done just about anything to make certain that no one else did.

"Not yet," Tanya was saying, in a voice that seemed to Nikolai as remote and spindly as the voices on the oldest of the film clips. "And anyway, I only want to know what you think of him."

"Not much," he replied.

"That's all?"

243

His torpor seemed to freeze and shatter into bitter anger. "No, that's not all," he said. "He makes me sick! I don't know how he can think he's above the rest of us, given that dirty skin. The only one here I hate more is his friend Sifte. They look right past us like we don't exist, like they're too good for us. And they're only foreign scum, scraped up after some pathetic civil war or other!"

Despite her interest in this unexpected venom, Tanya felt a twist of anxiety. The interview wasn't going as smoothly as she had planned. "Perhaps they *are* too good for us." She had aimed for sarcasm, but she couldn't keep her own pain from imparting more poignancy to the words than she had intended. However, Nikolai appeared not to have noticed. He seemed preoccupied, and impatient to get away from her.

"What do you want from me?" Nikolai asked, his eyes moving to the clock on the wall.

"I want you to be his friend."

"What?"

Tanya smiled. "Not really, of course. Just pretend to be, until you figure out what he's up to. You see, I think he's working against Solntse." She had lowered her voice confidentially. "And I think you think so, too."

Nikolai smiled incredulously. "Aleksei and his friends might have radical ideas, but there isn't much they can do with ideas, here."

Finally, they had circled back around to the scene Tanya had rehearsed. She waited for him to finish, feigning interest in his words, then said, "You misunderstand me. I think that Aleksei and Sifte and their friends are actively working against Solntse."

Nikolai's manner was still dismissive. "I suppose you think they're plotting revolution."

"Actually, yes."

Nikolai's confidence hitched almost imperceptibly before he rejoined, "Don't be ridiculous." Despite his protest, Tanya saw that he was worried. He began to walk in the direction of his dormitory. "Where would you get an idea like that?"

Tanya shrugged, no longer trying to hide her impatience. "I've lived with Sifte and Mila and Anastasia for years. They often go missing together for long periods of time. And they're so secretive, always reading books or news reports for hours on end…they're up to something, I'm sure of it."

"Then why don't you find out what you need to know from them?"

Tanya smiled as if at a slow child who has asked a particularly moronic question. "Because they don't trust me. In fact, I think it's safe to say they despise me."

"And you think Aleksei trusts me?"

"Not yet." Her voice had lost its persuasive simper, becoming coldly methodical.

Nikolai shivered despite himself. "You want me to spy on him."

"Clever boy."

"How am I supposed to do that?"

"By requesting to room with him."

This took Nikolai aback. "Under what pretenses?" he finally asked.

"Under none. Why should they question you?"

Nikolai studied her. There was something more to all of this; he could see it when she looked at him, an evasive fish in the blue pools of her eyes. "Even assuming you're right about all of this, why do you care? Surely if you've noticed

245

something, the teachers have. And if they're traitors it's the Institute's problem, not yours."

A flash of bright scales; she lowered her eyes. "Won't you just accept that I have to do this, and I can't do it without your help?"

"Why me?" he asked.

Tanya smiled. "They'll never question your motivations."

"What do you mean?" he demanded.

Tanya watched his panic blossom. She hadn't anticipated this reaction, and it threw her. She knew she had missed something important, but she couldn't change her course now.

"You never make trouble," she answered. "You're good at blending into the background." Tanya read the flood of relief she saw on his face as agreement, and to cement it, she played her trump card. "Of course," she said, "there will be something in it for you." She lowered her eyelids, but kept her eyes fixed on his.

"All right, I'll do it," Nikolai said, with an off-handedness that further confused Tanya. His mind was clearly on something far from her not-so-subtle suggestion.

"Good," she said anyway, and smiled at him. "We'll talk more later."

Nikolai said nothing, but shook free of her hand, which had tightened on his arm as they walked. He moved off quickly toward his dorm. It had been easier to convince him than she had imagined, despite the glitches. She smiled, though the pain to which she had become accustomed was there as always, even in the elation of her victory.

*

246

Aleksei let his small box of possessions fall to the bed with a clash when he saw who occupied the other one. He had always disliked Nikolai, and since their odd debate several months earlier, he didn't trust him either.

Realizing that he had been staring, he said, "Nikolai, right? I'm Aleksei."

The other boy sprawled gauntly on the bed by the far wall, his laconic eyes wandering over something on his portable screen. "Yes," he said, "I remember."

"So," Aleksei said, grasping at the first words that came to him, "you've chosen that bed?"

Nikolai looked at the bed on which he lay with his few possessions. "If it makes no difference to you," he replied.

"It isn't," said Aleksei, his unease deepening. He began to unpack his box. It held his own screen, a book on twentieth-century airplanes which the tutor from his former aerophysics elective had given him, a book of the Christian Psalms which Dmitri had given him when he passed Level 9, a watercolor painting of the Dacha done by Sifte when they were seven, a fragment of an old poem copied out of a library book by Mila, a model of a fighter jet, and five new gray jumpsuits with sun insignia stitched in gold on the right breast pockets. He put everything away while Nikolai watched him with a fish's flat, passionless eyes. As far as Aleksei could tell, Nikolai had no relics of his dormitory life. He wondered whether he had any friends at all.

"What now?" Aleksei said, after he had finished.

"Wait for dinner," Nikolai said.

"I suppose," agreed Aleksei, beginning to feel desperate.

"What are you studying?" Nikolai asked abruptly.

"Aerodynamic engineering, with an extra segment in political science."

247

Finally, Nikolai's interest seemed roused. "That's an unusual combination."

Aleksei shrugged and sat down on his bed facing Nikolai. "It was recommended."

"Was it," Nikolai said. He paused after his non-question, as if he expected Aleksei to answer it anyway. He turned his eyes back to his screen and said, "You know, I don't think they've ever done that before. Mixed the disciplines when assigning a concentration. 'One man could not do more than one job or profession well,' and all that."

Aleksei shrugged uncomfortably, feeling that Nikolai was somehow holding him accountable for this aberrance. "Well, maybe it's a new thing. A few of my friends have had the politics segment added on to their concentrations, too."

"Anastasia and Sifte."

Aleksei tried to detect any hostility in the watery face, any secondary motive for these probing questions, but all was blank. "That's right. What are you studying?"

"Politics," said Nikolai with a strange, atrophied smile. "I'm sure it's entirely coincidental."

It took Aleksei a moment to realize that this was sarcasm. When he did, he laughed, and once he began he couldn't stop. It was half hysteria, built up over years of suppression and let loose by the shock of this bizarre situation. It took him some moments to realize that Nikolai was laughing with him, perhaps with equal panic, perhaps because he also realized that he had no choice but to play blindly into Solntse's hand. Aleksei was overwhelmed by a sudden feeling of compassion for Nikolai, made more powerful by its unexpectedness.

"Well," he said with more composure, "we'll never really know why the teachers make the choices they make for us."

"No," Nikolai replied. He didn't sound convinced but he looked at Aleksei with slightly less disdain. "No," he said again and then sat up. "I guess there's nothing left to do but wait for the next thing, now." Then he added, "For dinner, I mean."

Nevertheless, Aleksei was struck by the irony of the remark.

*

"Be careful," Sifte warned, when Aleksei told his friends about his new room-mate in the Dacha that night.

"It sounds like he's got his hooks out already," Anastasia agreed.

"I doubt he's that creative," Aleksei said. "I mean, he's not exactly the world's warmest guy, but I don't think he's so bad. He's an outsider…like us."

"He's nothing like us."

"With all due respect, Nastya, you can't know that."

"So we should invite him to our next meeting?"

"Of course not! I'm just saying we shouldn't make enemies on principle."

"That's true," said Sifte, who wasn't pleased with what she was hearing on any side, "but I think Nastya's right about not trusting him. I looked into his history after that meeting Dmitri didn't show up for." She paused, trying to find the words that would appease everybody. "The most distinctive thing about his file is its lack of information. But it does say that he's got two super-race parents, and that might mean something."

"Yeah," said Anastasia, "that he's one of their bootlickers."

"We're all their bootlickers," Mila said, breaking out of her reverie. She was paler than ever, having just spent two weeks in the infirmary. Like so many of her observations, the perfect, simple truth of it rendered them silent.

"Anyway," said Aleksei after a moment, "it's not like I've told him the first thing about any of you, let alone what we're up to, and I'm not planning on it. I'm just saying that we shouldn't automatically hate the super-race just for being the super-race."

"'You must see it has no touch of meanness,'" Misha said. "'Pettiness of mind is quite incompatible with the constant attempt to grasp things divine or human as a whole and in their entirety.' Book six, section two."

"Flawed logic," Anastasia replied, to Aleksei rather than Misha. "We know the super-race is degenerate." Looking at Misha, she added, "Barely human, never mind divine."

"Like the sub-race?" Aleksei retorted. He shook his head. "I can't believe what I'm hearing. We say that we support freedom and equality, so we should be willing to accept anyone, no matter who their parents were. If we can't, then we're as bad as Solntse."

"I'll accept anyone you want, Lyosha," said Anastasia. "I'm just saying that I won't let them into our secrets!"

"I wasn't *asking* you to!"

"Stop it," said Sifte. "Let's not fight about things that haven't happened yet."

"Yeah, well, I'm off to bask in solitude," said Anastasia, who had managed to get her single after all. "I'll see you tomorrow." Misha followed her out.

When they were gone, Sifte let her face fall into her hands. "What is it, Siftenka?" Aleksei asked anxiously. "Really, I'm not going to say anything to Nikolai."

Sifte looked up at him, shaking her head. "Of course you aren't. It's not that. I don't know. It's nothing."

"It's everything," Mila amended. Sifte looked at her for what seemed the first time in weeks, and she was not pleased with what she saw. Mila's face was drawn and pale, her eyes dilated and unusually bright.

"Everything," Sifte repeated speculatively, looking from Mila to Aleksei and then back again. She sighed. "We should go. They'll miss us soon."

He got up and left, but neither of the girls followed him. The curling paper stars swayed faintly in his wake. Mila regarded them sadly. They had outgrown these childish representations of their wishes long ago, but they were still young enough not to be able to take them down.

"Let's have wind-chimes in our room, Sifte," she said.

"What use would they be without wind?"

Mila took off her glasses. Her eyes were dreamy and distant. Sifte knew that look, and it frightened her no less now than it had the first time she had seen it, when the ten-year-old Mila had come too close to dying in her arms. "One day this sea will be a desert of salt," she said. "Only the skeleton of this place will remain, and the wind will blow through it, and then they'll sing…" Mila frowned, as though troubled by her own prediction.

"'And if ever in this country they should want to build me a monument,'" Sifte said softly. The words weren't her own, but came from a piece of a verse by one of the pre-war poets, which they had found in one of the few literary books Dmitri had allowed them in the relentlessly political secret curriculum of their childhood. They had all loved this snip of poem, and had committed it to memory.

"'I consent to that honor,'" Mila continued, then trailed off. "I consent to that honor," she repeated after a moment, with tears in her eyes. "Not me," Mila said, looking up at them from the fragments of the broken spell. "You'll be the one with the monuments, Sifte."

Sifte shook her head at the finality of Mila's words, the unspilled tears. "None of us can tell the future," she pleaded, uncertain whom Mila was condemning.

Mila's eyes were sad, but no longer terrible. "Siftenka—" she said, her tone almost supplicating. Then she stopped. As much as Mila wanted to confide in Sifte, and be rid of the weight of her hopeless secret, she knew that Sifte would not understand it, and that lack of understanding would make her already tremendous pain unbearable. "Let's go," she finished, and turning off the light, they shut the door behind them with a finality that neither could ignore.

8

Sifte was already waiting at the Dacha computer when Stepan hailed her.

```
S: It's set now, Sifte. I'm leaving
Myortvograd.
K: When?
S: Soon.
K: Where will you go?
S: I don't know.
K: You mean you won't tell me.
S: For your own sake.
```

There was a pause, and then Sifte typed:

```
K: Will you take us with you?
```

The cursor blinked the passing seconds, and her anxiety deepened. Nevertheless, she felt relief at finally having asked the question she had been worrying over for so long. At last he answered her.

```
S: This is something I've considered often.
In the past, the danger to you has always
outweighed my own desires.
K: I can't believe that anything's more
dangerous now than staying here. We think
they're starting to use some of our work.
```

```
S: Why?
K: We found files that suggest they're
producing bioweapons at Institute 1. Some of
the work we've been doing lately matches up.
S: Anything else?
```

Sifte couldn't bring herself to tell Stepan what had happened at that terrible weapons practice session, and she didn't know how to explain what had happened in Cave. Finally, she answered:

```
K: A little while ago, Dmitri arranged a
meeting with me. But he didn't show up. When I
got there Aleksei and Anastasia were waiting,
and also two other students from our year.
One's a girl who's always hated me. The other
one is called Nikolai. I don't know him well,
but he's strange, creepy. And he has super-race
connections. Now they've put Aleksei in a room
with him.
S: None of that necessarily means anything.
They could just be tests - I've heard similar
stories. And as for the weapons, you knew that
kind of thing was coming.
K: But we always thought we'd get out before
we actually did anything. It's a big blow,
especially to Mila.
S: And you?
```

Once again, Sifte saw the image of Stepan's dead face. She pushed it back but it hovered at the periphery, a righteous ghost demanding absolution. With shaking hands, she typed:

```
K: I'm in a different position from the rest of
them, because of you. I have a father fighting
for the Soviet, but they only have their
principles. I don't know how long we'll be able
to hold it together in here. Things are already
strained.
```

There was another excruciating pause. Sifte watched the cursor blink. Finally, his message came:

```
S: I couldn't possibly get you all out at once.
```

This condition was another specter she had tried not to see. Yet while her heart sank at the prospect of betraying her friends, the part of her that was an Opyekun told her that she would be justified in accepting Stepan's condition. Her position at Institute 1 had always been more precarious than the others', and if the target practice incident had taught her anything, it was that she would be powerless to keep her secrets if she remained at the school any longer. So she answered:

```
K: Then take me alone. When I'm out, I'll be
responsible for getting the rest of them.
```

It was Stepan's oldest dream for his daughter, yet now, faced with its reality, he hesitated. Getting to the school would be difficult, spiriting Sifte out of it more so, yet the only serious obstacle was Andrei's certain disapproval. He would probably excommunicate Stepan for attempting it, but then, Andrei had been restricting Stepan's activity more and more of late anyway. Any hope he'd had that Andrei would see the light about Sifte was long gone. Andrei would never abandon his caution, and the very idea of Sifte, of the cataclysm that would ensue if she were to publicly expose Solntse's treachery, defied it. So he answered:

```
S: All right. I'll contact you when everything
is ready. In the meantime, be careful. And look
out for Aleksei.

K: Why?
S: Just a hunch. I have to go now.
K: Good-bye, Stepan.
```

Stepan shut off the computer, and its hum faded into the matted silence. He looked up at the clock. It was nineteen-forty-five. He would have to leave as soon as Andrei returned with his supplies. He would remain in Myortvograd for a few weeks to work on the Technology Institute bunker, then he was to leave the city indefinitely. And then, Sifte. Stepan sighed.

"Have you told her that you'll be leaving?"

Stepan jumped. Andrei was standing over the trap door, his face cratered with shadows in the dim light, his eyes hooded. "Yes," Stepan answered, flustered and suddenly anxious.

"There's something else," Andrei said. "You've told her that you're going to get her out."

It seemed pointless to lie. Stepan nodded. Andrei didn't fly into the rage Stepan had anticipated, but a cynical smile crept over his face. "So," he said, "the American in you finally rears its ugly head."

"What do you mean by that?"

Andrei shrugged, shifting his weight to his left leg. "Solntse is bad, doling out professions of Platonic justice on one hand while he corrupts it with the other. But the American perversion of democracy is far worse. You sing the praises of equality and majority rule while every last one of you works towards his own ends with a megalomaniacal lust," he spat the word through white lips, "at least as profound as Solntse's!"

"Is that what you really think?" Stepan asked, standing to face Andrei. "That I'm doing this for myself?"

"Why else would you be doing it? I've listened to you for years, Stepan—your pet fantasy about your daughter liberating us and all the rest. But if you mean to go through with it, you certainly don't have the Russian people's best interests in mind."

"Solntse is systematically destroying the Russian people! Is it in their interest to let him carry on?"

"The people aren't ready for revolution."

Stepan's anger finally erupted. "They'll never be ready, the way you creep along with your intricate plans and stultifying circumspection! Solntse is about to turn his army loose on Myortvograd, and by the time you've choreographed our so-called defense to absolute perfection, there won't be anything left to defend. Don't you see, the only chance you have is to act before Solntse does!"

"And how are we supposed to do that? March into the Fortress and demand justice?"

"Why not? For fuck's sake, Andrei, get your head out of your textbooks for a minute and look around!"

"All I do is look around," he interjected coldly.

"But do you see?" Stepan tugged at his ragged hair; his goldwater eyes were bright with anger and inspiration. "Don't you realize that for every five half-hearted followers you gain at a meeting, you lose ten to starvation, or disease, or simple bloody apathy! The people need something to believe in, someone to follow, and it's not going to come from a nineteenth-century ideal!"

"And you think you can provide what's missing?"

"I think their children can."

"The people at Institute 1 are no longer their children," Andrei said with unmitigated assurance.

"Five of them are, and they're willing to die for your cause."

Once more, he shifted his weight almost imperceptibly. "Suppose for a moment that you succeed in freeing those children. What exactly are you going to do with them?"

"Put them in charge of your army, and win back this country."

Andrei smiled again with unguarded derision. "They're seventeen years old. Their training has been entirely theoretical. Why would they succeed where everyone else has failed?"

"Because they're smarter, and they're closer to the other side, and they'll appeal to the people in a way that none of us can!"

"It's no use, is it?" Andrei said, and for the third time, his solid stance pitched slightly to the left. A glacial smile crept over his face. "It's a pity. You have all the qualities of a great revolutionary, except patience."

For what happened next—or rather, for his narrow escape from what might have happened—Stepan could only thank the sixth sense that his own ruthless training had instilled in him. In the split-second before Andrei raised the gun, Stepan understood the meaning of that final shift of weight, lowered his head, and barreled towards Andrei's stomach. The force of the impact knocked Andrei to his knees. He was only winded, but the pause was enough for Stepan to pin the wrist of his gun-hand, wrench the weapon free, then hit Andrei across the back of the head with it.

He fell forward, almost into Stepan's arms. Stepan lowered him to the floor. He made sure that he was still breathing, then bound Andrei's hands and feet. He thought about taping his mouth, but realized that Andrei would die before he would give away the location of the bunker and the precious computer—even conscious, he wouldn't make a sound. Anyway, it wouldn't come to that.

Stepan took the gun and a few clips of ammunition, and some of the food Andrei had left out in the kitchen. He knew that he ought to cross the river and lose himself in the vast misery of the Vyborgside shanties, but at the moment he couldn't bear the thought of the tunnels. So he wandered the side-streets around Nevskiy instead, weaving between the smoky fires. He elicited no curiosity in the people he passed, nor any visible fear. There was only a vague, shadowy longing, something akin to jealousy. Yet despite their abject despair, every pair of eyes echoed Sifte's plea for freedom.

By the time he reached Dvortsovaya Square, Stepan had given away most of his food to begging children. Once he would have been able to ignore their pleas, but now he saw his daughter's face in each of theirs. He gave the last of his bread to a child dragging one withered leg behind her and leaning on a patient old mongrel. The child was so thin that Stepan could have circled her thigh with his thumb and forefinger, but she gave half of the bread to the dog before eating any of it herself. Stepan watched them limp away into the shadows. Gradually, he came back to himself and realized that he was looking at an image from a dream: the shattered wall of what had once been the General Staff Building behind the Winter Palace, on which the faint bands of a graffiti rainbow were still visible, along with the words, "I know there's dark in all things, but I find the light, and struggle on."

Nearly two decades had passed since he had turned his back on that frail message of hope, but Stepan felt as though he had never left it. He knew that it was pure folly even to go near the place again, let alone spend the night there, but the past hour's events had left him feeling sick and drained, and he could not resist the brief, bright memory of Sasha that their old home proffered.

The ladder had disintegrated long ago, so he lowered himself down through the hole in the roof and then dropped the last few feet to the rubble-strewn floor. He lit a candle. The room was empty, except for a pile of rags in the corner. Stepan curled up on this makeshift mattress, with the blackest heart he'd had since he abandoned Sasha without explanation or apology eighteen years earlier. The memory of her Byzantine eyes rose up as stealthily as the shadows. He found himself praying to her specter like an icon—for forgiveness, and for guidance—and he fell asleep with her image still flickering like a stern-faced archangel in the candle's smoky shaft of light.

9

Stepan awakened at dawn, appalled with himself. It was bad enough to have told Andrei of his plans; to have come to his old home, and left the candle burning all night, was beyond logic. He hid the traces as best he could, then scrawled a note stating where and how to find Andrei. As his food was gone, he gave an urchin a candle in exchange for delivering the note to the nearest bunker. He watched from a hidden doorway to make sure that it was delivered, and then melted into the ruined streets.

He used the Aleksandra Nevskogo Metro tunnel to cross under the river, and made his way north-east until the river was out of sight. Then he found an abandoned room to hide in and waited out the day.

When he came out of his hiding place that evening, he found the streets all but deserted. He made his way to the rebuilt ground floor of what had once been a high-rise apartment building. The front door was open. A flat-eyed woman with a shaved head sat in the doorway nursing a dirty child. Stepan stepped past her into the unlit corridor, counted doors until he found the right one, and knocked.

A peephole's coin of light flashed briefly into the darkness, then he heard the rattling of locks.

"Stepan!" Olga cried once she had let him in and closed the door again. She kissed him on both cheeks. "Come in, sit down."

It had been several months since Stepan had last had the chance to speak with Olga. She seemed to have aged even in that time. Her short, plump form seemed weightier, her kind, dark eyes exhausted. Stepan sat down at the rickety table as Olga took out an unmarked bottle and two glasses. She filled both, pushed one toward Stepan, then sat down with him.

He sipped the vodka, sighed, and said, "Look, I wish there were time to catch up, but there isn't. I'm here to ask your help in a serious matter. If you want nothing to do with it, then say so, and I'll go. Just promise you won't turn me in until I have a chance to get out of the city."

Olga smiled, swallowed her vodka, and re-filled her glass. "Plots are more Andrei's department, aren't they?"

Stepan smiled bitterly. "Not this time." He felt the handle of the gun in his pocket.

Olga emptied her glass and filled it again, keeping her shrewd eyes on him all the time. "Well?"

"What can you tell me about my daughter?"

"So…you know about her," Olga said slowly.

Stepan couldn't tell whether this was news to her or not. Either way, he knew that he was treading dangerous ground. He swallowed his vodka to hide his unease and said, "I want to know what you know about her."

Olga re-filled his glass, her expression guarded. "Not much. I was there when she was born, and I visited Sasha a few days later. Those were the only times I saw the child. I don't know where she is now."

"Institute 1," Stepan said.

Olga looked at him blankly for a few moments, then said, "What's the game, Styopa?"

He sighed. "I've been in contact with her for the last six years. She and a group of her friends discovered Solntse's plans for them and didn't like what they found. They learned that I was Sifte's father and tracked me down to ask for help."

"If I didn't know you better—"

"You'd say it was impossible? I thought so too at first."

"How have they managed to keep it a secret?"

"They have an ally on the teaching staff. And they're very clever. In fact, by every account, Sifte is the most gifted child they've ever had at Institute 1—which is no doubt the only reason why she's still alive."

"Even so, if the super-race found out, all hell would break loose."

"Precisely," Stepan answered, looking at her pointedly.

"So you plan to make her the catalyst."

Stepan smiled grimly. "The general, too, if she's willing."

Olga looked at him for a moment, then took out a cigarette—poor quality, but a luxury in Myortvograd. "Well," she said, lighting it in the flame of the kerosene lamp and blowing poisonous-looking smoke at the cracked ceiling, "I haven't heard anything I'd turn you in for, yet." She looked at him with startling directness. "Of course, Andrei wouldn't approve of this plan." Stepan thought he kept his face blank, but Olga's smile was mocking. "It's a pity you're men. Take Sasha and me. Our ideologies often clashed, but we never tried to kill each other over them."

Stepan sighed. "How did you know?"

Olga smiled again. "You and Andrei are stunningly unoriginal in your choice of confidant. He came here this morning, looking like shit and asking for you. Turned the place inside out before I could convince him you weren't here. He wouldn't tell me what happened, but he said that if you came here I should throttle you. Luckily for you, I believe in hearing both sides of a story. And while you're picking your jaw up off the ground, you might as well give me the gun, because both of us know you couldn't do it to me any more than you could do it to him."

Sheepishly, Stepan put the gun on the table between them. Olga picked it up, and disengaged the clip. She weighed it in her palm, then threw it into an overflowing garbage pail with surprising vehemence. After another moment's deliberation, she pitched the gun after it. Then she turned back to Stepan, swallowed her third glass of vodka, and re-lit her cigarette.

"Now," she said calmly, "why don't you tell me what happened."

Stepan sighed. "Last night Sifte asked me to get her out of the Institute." He paused, trying to determine how best to explain the urgency of the situation, then said, "She's been playing both sides for a long time, but it's getting too dangerous."

"And the fact that taking her out may well launch a civil war is only incidental."

"Incidental, but not 'only.'"

"Well, I'm not sure I approve of your motivations, but I do agree that Institute 1 is no place for Sasha's child." Olga sighed, and the dark grooves under her eyes seemed to deepen. "Look, Styopa, I loved Sasha like a sister, and her baby couldn't mean more to me if she was my own. I want to help Sifte, and I know that you think this is the way to do it."

"But?"

"I'm dubious about your motivations."

"What does that mean?"

Olga tilted her head in equivocation, then said, "It sounds to me like you mean to use Sifte for your own ends."

"How can you—"

"Because of what you just said." Olga's plain, kind face was serious, her dark eyes searching. "And what Andrei told me about your last conversation."

Stepan shook his head impatiently. "She wants to help! She's been asking to help since she was eleven years old!"

"And what if the Soviet won't let her? You'd better believe that if Andrei has reservations, a lot of the others will too."

"That's only speculation. The danger she's in at the Institute is real. It's now."

Olga looked at him with unwavering eyes. Finally, she said, "I'm still not sure that I agree with you, but I do believe that anything is better for Sifte than what she's up against now. So, what do you want me to do?"

Stepan frowned. "Nothing, until I see what happens when Andrei tells his story."

Olga smiled again, though this time it was supercilious. "For a clever man, Styopa, you show a remarkable lack of insight."

"Meaning?"

"Andrei's a proud man, and he'll be embarrassed to have been defeated. Also, a part of him respects you despite your differences, and though he might have done something hot-headed last night, I think he understands your value enough that he won't risk alienating you entirely now. He'll keep your secret. I wouldn't even be surprised if you ended up working together again before this is through."

Stepan was smiling. "You're a pain in the ass, Olga, but you're a wise woman."

"So, what do you have up your sleeve for me?"

"For the moment, I only need to know you'll help."

"You have my word. Now, I have a meeting to run. Come back tonight and we'll put a plan together. Unless you need a place to stay?"

Stepan stood up. "I'll find one."

Olga smiled again. "Which means you already have, and you don't want me to know where it is because it might put you in danger."

"You're not very charitable. I was thinking that it might put *you* in danger."

"Fatherhood has made you soft. Or maybe I've just turned cynical." He was already half way out the door, but he turned back to her when she said, "Walk carefully, Stepan." He nodded. But when he shut the door, she was not smiling.

10

"Aleksei," a female voice called softly.

He stopped, looked around, and saw Tanya sitting in one of the window seats in the apogee of the corridor's ellipse. They were high enough up in the building that a silver-green tease of light would penetrate the window during the day. Now, though, Tanya stood out against the dark camber like a misplaced Madonna. A smile slipped across her full, petulant lips.

Aleksei shifted uncomfortably. "Tanya. Did you want something?"

"Perhaps." She narrowed her robin's-egg eyes as her smile widened.

He stood waiting for her to elaborate. When she didn't, he asked, "Well?"

She laughed. "Relax, Aleksei. We don't have to be in our rooms until twenty-three-hundred now."

"No, but I have a lot of work to do. So if you don't want anything—"

Tanya stood up, and this alleviated some of his nervousness, though he couldn't think why it should. "Actually, I did want something," she said.

"Well?" he asked, this time with the beginnings of impatience.

"You're rooming with Kolya," she said, on the tail of this thought.

"Is he a friend of yours?"

If she caught the tone of Aleksei's remark, she chose to ignore it. "I wanted to talk to you about him."

"As you've said."

"I wanted to tell you to be kind to him."

Aleksei scrutinized her, wondering what she could possibly be up to. "I hardly think he needs you to look out for him."

"Maybe not, but he's had a hard time, and it will be to both your benefit if you're aware of it."

Aleksei sighed. "We all have a hard time, Tanya." He began to push past her, but she caught and held his arm such that he would have had to hurt her to break free.

"It's been harder for him than for most," she said.

Aleksei disliked her more with every moment that passed; disliked especially her hand on his arm, and the way that it made him notice her beauty. "How so?" he asked shortly.

Tanya's eyebrows contracted almost imperceptibly before she smiled and said, "People expect a lot of him." She leaned toward him conspiratorially, and Aleksei recoiled. "Sometimes I even wonder if somebody bought him his place here, because you know, he really isn't up to the work."

Despite his distrust of Tanya, Aleksei had known Nikolai long enough to realize that the last part of this statement was true, and this made him reconsider the rest. "How do you know all of this?" he asked.

Tanya lowered her voice, leaned closer to him, "Some, I guessed. The rest, he told me himself. He tells me lots of things, like—" She broke off, as if realizing that she'd said too much.

"Like what?" Aleksei asked.

"I really shouldn't be telling you this."

The cunning in her eyes was clear. Though Aleksei suspected that she did know something he might find interesting, he didn't doubt there would be a price for it. So he said, "If that's all, I have to go."

Tanya tightened her hold on his arm and said, "Wait. I'd better tell you."

Aleksei sighed. "Go on, then."

"He asked to room with you."

Aleksei was in the process of disengaging himself from her grasp, but this stopped him. "Why?"

"Because you have such close friends, and he has none."

"Except you," Aleksei reminded her.

"Of course," Tanya continued, almost seamlessly, "but I'm not a boy. I think you impressed him that day in Dmitri's non-tutorial."

Aleksei frowned. "I don't remember saying anything particularly impressive."

"That's just it," Tanya continued. "You're even-headed. You judge on content rather than appearances. He needs a friend like that. I don't know everything about Kolya, but I know enough to be sure that things will go well for you if you're kind to him, and perhaps not so well if you aren't."

Aleksei searched Tanya's face, but it was as slippery as polished marble. Every time he thought he'd pinned something down, it evaporated. Whether or not her intentions were treacherous, though, what Tanya had said about Nikolai certainly seemed to be true. His sense that

Nikolai was as frightened and confused as he was himself had increased as he got to know him better.

"I think I understand," Aleksei said, more to himself than to Tanya.

No, you don't, she thought bitterly. But you will. She turned and left him still looking through her.

*

While Aleksei walked back to his room adrift in roiling thoughts, Sifte sat alone in front of the Dacha terminal's blank screen, hands clutched together as if in supplication. She had managed to maintain her calm for the first few days after Stepan promised to help her escape, but then two weeks passed without word from him, and worry began to crack her composure. She had e-mailed Andrei as a last resort, but he didn't answer her, and finally she gave in to her anxiety. Either the officials had caught up with Stepan, or he had reconsidered his promise to her. She couldn't decide which would be worse.

She waited until twenty-two hundred hours. Then, just as she went to shut down the computer, a hail appeared on the screen. It came from an unfamiliar address, registered to a Pomoshchnik named Sevastyanov. Too fraught to consider the possible implications, she accepted the hail.

S: Sifte. It's Stepan.

K: Where were you?

S: There's not time to explain now. Are you alone?

K: Yes, but probably not for long.

S: I only have a few minutes anyway, so listen
carefully, and destroy this message when you've
memorized it. One week from today, at precisely
one-hundred hours, a fishing boat will land
at the east side of the Institute near the
helicopter pad. The captain will answer to the
name Vanya, and he'll expect you to show him
the scar on your arm. He'll only wait five
minutes, so be on time. Don't take anything
with you, don't leave anything that can be used
to trace you, and needless to say, don't tell
anyone any of this.

K: I'll have to tell the others. They need to
be prepared for the fallout.

S: It's safer if they know nothing. Otherwise
they'll be treated as conspirators. Please
trust me on this, Sifte.

Sifte stared at the screen for a long time. Finally, she
typed:

K: All right.

S: I have to go now, I'm not safe here, but
there's one more thing. Whatever happens, don't
try to contact Andrei. Things have come up.

K: I already wrote to Andrei.

S: Did he write back?

K: No.

Stepan's pause was long enough to seem ominous. Finally,
he wrote:

S: Just don't try again. I have to go now.

K: All right. And thank you, Stepan.

S: Good luck.

The screen blanked automatically, as Aleksei had programmed it to do when a chat connection was broken. Sifte erased the correspondence from the computer's memory, and then sat staring at the blank screen, with little more peace of mind than she'd had before. That was how Anastasia and Mila found her ten minutes later.

"I can understand getting hung up on Glaza, Sifte, but a blank computer screen?" Anastasia smiled at her. "Maybe the pressure of our double life is getting to you after all."

Sifte looked up at Anastasia, wondering when her smile had become a woman's. It seemed that overnight, the sarcasm that had characterized Anastasia as a child had refined into wit. Mila's face had changed as well, but where Anastasia's personality had blossomed outward, Mila's seemed to have carved a deeper channel, until her face was entirely inscrutable, even to Sifte.

Sifte sighed, and Anastasia said, "It'll be over soon." Sifte said nothing, chilled by the irony of her words.

"What were you working on?" asked Mila.

"Nothing," Sifte answered.

"You expect us to believe that?" Anastasia asked.

Sifte smiled. "Believe whatever you want. But I'm telling you, it was nothing important. Just a problem that's been bugging me for a while."

"Statistics?" Mila asked. "That's been giving me trouble."

"Never mind," Sifte said, standing up to go. "I'm tired of working on it, anyway. Want to go back now, Milyonka?"

She shook her head. "Nastya and I were going to do some work, first."

"All right, then. I'll see you later."

If she could have seen the looks that followed her out the door, she might have worried more still.

*

"Kolya!" Tanya called down the corridor. Nikolai cringed at the sound of the voice, but stopped nevertheless. When Tanya caught up to him she was flushed from running, and this, like the breathlessness, had a certain charm. "Kolya," she said again, catching up to him.

"Not now," he said. "I'm tired."

"This will only take a minute."

"Well?" he demanded. The way she waited expectantly, as if for him to tell her something rather than vice-versa, annoyed him more than anything about her.

"I was…" she faltered. "I was wondering how you were getting along with Aleksei."

"Well enough."

Apparently, Tanya decided that flirtation was wasted on Nikolai. Dropping all affect, she proceeded with a slight shrillness: "Good. I want you to find something out for me."

Nikolai sighed. "This isn't more of your conspiracy theory, is it?"

Ignoring the sarcasm, she continued, "Aleksei spends a lot of time away from your room, doesn't he?"

"So do I."

"Yet he's never in any of the obvious places. The library, the film room, the news room…"

"How do you know that?"

"Never mind. What I want to know is where he does go."

273

Nikolai's look of disdain deepened to ridicule. "You don't want me to ask him?" He laughed, seeing that this idea had indeed crossed her mind.

"I thought you'd become friends," she answered.

"What gave you that idea? We get along well enough, which I'll admit surprised me…" He trailed off, seeming to forget about her for a moment. Then he recalled himself and resumed speaking, now with reproach in his tone, "Besides, if we were friends, do you think that I'd tell you his secrets?"

There was anger on Tanya's face for a moment, then she smiled voluptuously. "Why shouldn't you?"

"Why *should* I?"

Tanya reached up and kissed him. At first he resisted, but soon she felt him weakening and finally complying. She pulled away, smiled at the shock and bewilderment in his eyes, and spoke before it could fade.

"I want you to find out where he goes, and tell me. Never mind why," she added, seeing the question on his face. "You wouldn't care if you knew. Please?" She lowered her eyelids, pouted a little.

"Whore," said Nikolai in a grating whisper, pulling roughly away from her.

"Tell me as soon as you know," she said, almost sweetly.

11

"What's wrong, Sifte?" asked Mila, looking away from the wind chimes that hung above her, limp as bodies on a gallows.

Sifte looked up from her book, startled. "Why do you ask that?"

"You only study this late when you're trying not to think about something." Mila sat up on her bed, the angles of her body stark even under the coarse canvas jumpsuit. "Besides, you haven't turned the page for the last half hour."

"I've been thinking," Sifte said.

"About Stepan?"

"Yes…about Stepan." At least that wasn't a lie. Sifte hated lying to Mila more than any of her friends, not least because she had a feeling that Mila suspected the truth.

Mila sighed. "You're keeping something from me. Something that's hurting you."

"It's nothing you can help with. I'm sorry, Milyonka…I can't tell you more than that."

Sifte could feel Mila's eyes moving deftly around the blockades she had built, as the sea moves around boulders. "Can't?" she asked softly. "Or won't?"

Sifte drew a breath, expelled it slowly. Without quite knowing where she was headed, except away from the one secret she must keep at all costs, she began, "Remember when I said we'd have to accept the things they're going to make us do here if we wanted to get out?"

"How could I forget?" Mila answered, her voice neutral.

"Well I've been thinking about it a lot, and the more I've thought, the more I've realized that I was wrong."

Mila shook her head in mild puzzlement, but said nothing.

"Not long ago, I wouldn't have said something like that. I wouldn't even have thought it. But lately it's been easier and easier to think like that—to think like them. I'm turning into one of them, Mila."

"Not just you," Mila said softly, but Sifte plunged on as if she hadn't heard her, propelled too quickly now by the force of her own unburdening to stop.

"A long time ago I told you about how I got stuck in Cave," she said, "and how something seemed to be there with me. But I didn't tell you it happened again, not so long ago—the last time I played with Lyosha. And the thing inside—this time I talked to it. I saw through it, and I have to think that it also saw through me. And then...in weapon's practice...Mila, I killed Stepan. They made me kill Stepan. They know about me."

"You think they're reading your mind?"

"I don't know. It feels that way."

Mila gazed at her for a long time, unblinking. Then she said, "They can't be. If they knew, you wouldn't still be here. They're only guessing. We'll be more careful."

Sifte stared at the book on her bed, choosing her next words carefully. "It seems to me we've gone beyond that. I'm thinking...maybe I should stop for a while."

Mila's eyes were clear but menacing. "Stop?"

"Stay away from the Dacha and the computer and the books and all of you. I'm dangerous to you—to everything."

"Are you mad, Sifte? Even if it were possible for you to just…disengage yourself like that, we could never hold it together without you."

"What have I got to do with it?"

"You're the voice of reason! You're the only one who manages to get us back on track when we start fighting—and lately, we seem to be fighting most of the time. In fact, I think you're the only one everyone's still speaking to."

"What about you? No one has an argument with you."

Mila looked away, and said, "Maybe not an argument."

"What do you mean?"

Mila's eyes were filling. "Do I have to spell it out for you, Sifte?" The silence hung tangibly in the air between them. "All right then—have you noticed that Aleksei doesn't talk to me anymore? Oh, he speaks to me, but only when he has to, and he never looks at me. So you see, he must know, and not want to know that I'm in love with him."

It wasn't really a surprise. For Mila to fall in love with Aleksei seemed natural, even obvious, but Mila's face was sad, tinged with bitterness, not the face of a girl confessing her first love to her best friend.

"I'm sure he just doesn't understand," Sifte said. "How could he not love you?"

A fleeting smile crossed Mila's face. It showed up the despair with the raw immediacy of a flashbulb, and also something else, something Sifte had never seen there before. It was hard and glittering, and so unlike Mila that Sifte could not place it at first.

"Don't you know?" Mila asked, with the same bright-faceted coldness in her voice, but no real incredulity. Sifte found herself shaking her head. Mila laughed with more than a hint of malice, and said, "You're supposed to be so smart, Sifte, but you can't see what's right in front of your face. Aleksei only wants you."

"Oh, no," she said. "It can't be...it can't—"

"What?" Mila interrupted. The hostility was gone, leaving her haggard and hopeless. Sifte didn't know how to answer her. She wished she were gone already, but she knew that even that wouldn't end this misery.

Mila looked at Sifte's bent head with resignation. "Don't, Sifte," she said. "You haven't done anything wrong. Love isn't fair or logical. You can't change that."

When Sifte looked up, her face was hard and determined. "Can't I?"

"Don't even think about it, Sifte," she said. "Hurt him and you'll hurt me worse than he ever could."

"But I don't want it!" Sifte cried with venom. She was on her feet, trembling. "Once he knows that, he'll love you like he should!"

"No!" Mila cried. Grabbing Sifte's arms, she forced her back onto the bed with a strength Sifte wouldn't have imagined she had. She held Sifte until she was certain that the impetuous moment had passed. Then she let go, retreating behind a cynical smile. "You really would have done it, too, wouldn't you."

"What do you mean?" Sifte demanded.

"Rushed to him and commanded him to change his mind. His heart." She fairly spat the word, though her face as she spoke it was more afflicted than angry. "Even if it was that easy, we could never be together."

Sifte shook her head. "What do you mean?"

Mila's smile shriveled inward like a frost-bitten blossom. "I'm dying."

"Of course you're not! You've been so much better the last year, how can you say—"

"Better at hiding it, maybe. I'm dying, and you can't argue it away. I won't live to be twenty. Or if I do, my life will be worse than death."

"Why do you think this?"

Mila paused, then said, "Do you remember that time you came to see me in the night, in the infirmary, when we were children?"

Sifte went cold. "Yes," she said softly, her eyes fixed on Mila's.

"Well, the next morning, when you were still asleep, I heard something. The doctors were talking about me. I didn't understand it then, but I couldn't forget about it. Last year, working on some research, I started to have an idea about what those doctors might have meant—and why they wouldn't tell me about it.

"I went looking for my medical records. I couldn't find them anywhere. But then I turned up some information about my mother." She looked at Sifte as if she expected her to interrupt or argue, but Sifte could only stare at Mila with mounting horror. Mila took a shuddering breath, and then plunged onward. "Her name was Anna. She was a singer— sub-race, but so pretty that she was allowed to perform in Solntsegrad. The first reports I found said that she died of pneumonia. But I dug deeper, and found out that was only partly true. She had pneumonia when she died, but that's not what killed her."

Mila's voice had taken on a flatness that told Sifte she was having a hard time controlling it. "A sub-race performer doesn't earn enough to stay alive. So to feed herself, and later on me, my mother sold herself. She died of syphilis—a resistant strain, not uncommon in Myortvograd. And she gave it to me."

Mila paused, but before Sifte could say anything she continued, "I don't know who my father was; I don't think my mother knew. Sometimes I don't think he was a man at all, but some piece of Solntse's evil." Mila looked up to watch Sifte's shock deepen. "That's why I can't think that everything will come out all right, the way the rest of you can. You will be all right. You were born to parents who fought that evil, and you'll follow in their footsteps. But my mother was his whore. No matter how hard I work to do good, it will only turn bad in the end."

"That's not true!"

"It *is* true!" Mila cried, her composure evaporating. "Don't you think I checked on those exports? Well guess what, you were right. They're already testing bioweapons on sub-race villages in the south."

"We've been through this already. Preliminary research isn't the same as—"

Mila shook her head. "This was different. Recent. They asked for a vaccine. I was looking so hard for all the ways they might trick me into making germs, I didn't see the obvious." She saw that Sifte still didn't understand, and sighed. "They asked me to come up with a vaccine against a mutant strain of cholera. I didn't know that they mutated it. My vaccine provided the missing links they needed to make it work against a sub-race immune system."

Sifte stared at the waffle pattern of the gray bedspread, as if the repetitive weave would contain her rage. "Where did you read this?"

"Somebody told me." Mila smiled a weak, cynical smile, and Sifte didn't press her further. She didn't have to.

"Don't you see, she lied to you! It was the only way she could hurt you, and hurting you was the only way she could hurt me!"

Mila shook her head. "She didn't lie. I checked. Anyway, she did mean to hurt me."

"Tanya's never had a grudge against you."

"She does now—or thinks she does."

"What—" Sifte began, then remembered. "Aleksei," she sighed. "We have to tell him."

"Better not," Mila answered with a wry smile. "All the attention might go to his head."

"This is serious, Mila!"

"Don't you think I know that?" she snapped.

Sifte covered her eyes, as if shutting out sight could also shut out the barrage of sinister implications hurtling around her. When she looked up again, Mila had turned her face to the wall.

"Mila," Sifte began.

"There's nothing you can say," she said, her voice leaden.

Sifte looked at her across the schism that had suddenly opened between them. Then, sighing, she stood up, moved toward the door. Just as she was about to leave, Mila spoke again.

"You do love him, Sifte, whatever you might think right now. Do what you have to do, but please don't hurt him."

Sifte slipped out through the door and closed it softly behind her.

12

Sifte found Aleksei at the Dacha. He looked up quickly, guiltily, from the computer screen, as Sifte closed the door behind her.

"You won't find anything," she said. "I wiped the memory."

Aleksei switched off the computer, leaving the room to the austere light of the single bulb. Some time ago the green shade had fallen off, and nobody had bothered to replace it.

"But I expect you already knew that." Sifte walked toward him, never taking her eyes off his. She paused, searching his face for the new emotion. She didn't have to look hard.

One side of his mouth twitched into an approximation of a smile, but even that miscarried. His shoulders hunched forward, and he looked not at her, but at the dark screen. "You're leaving, aren't you."

Though she had expected them, hearing the words was still a blow. She nodded, unable to look at him.

"Are you going tonight?"

"I can't tell you that."

Finally he looked at her. "Something's happened, hasn't it? Something besides this?" He gestured to the computer. Sifte nodded. "Come on, Sifte. I never could read your mind."

"I had a fight with Mila."

"What about?" he asked, his forehead furrowing.

"It's not important, really." Now she couldn't look at him.

"It was about me," he said grimly.

"See, you can read my mind."

"I didn't read your mind. I just know…"

"That she loves you," she finished, when it was clear that he wouldn't.

"I…I guess maybe I thought…" He trailed off, turning away from her. "If it would help for me to tell you what I—"

Sifte couldn't help smiling. "Don't flatter yourself—I said we fought about you, not over you." He looked at her, then turned away again, coloring. Sifte relented. "Lyosha—"

"What would you do if I asked you not to go?" he interrupted.

"Go anyway."

His smile was sudden and brilliant as a cloudbreak over water. Something in the way his head tilted slightly downward, as if his own joy abashed him, moved Sifte, made her look at him more closely than she ever had. What she saw shocked her more than anything that Mila had said. Aleksei was beautiful: a beauty which transcended symmetrical bone structure and clear eyes, went deep inside of him. More than that, his face at that moment was colored by the depth of his love for her. It terrified her.

Still, she didn't pull away when he took her hands, twining his dark fingers with her light ones. His eyes moved over her face, and though a part of her ached to look away, another longed to look back. When he kissed her, blood pounded through her with the violence of a sea-storm. She felt her resistance weakening until she found herself kissing him back. And then she was trembling, shaking uncontrollably in his arms, close to tears.

"Sifte, I'm sorry…"

"No," she said, unaware that she was clutching his shoulders hard enough to hurt him. "You haven't done anything wrong." She heard the words, and realized with a guilty jolt that they were Mila's. She let go of him, looked away in confusion. "But I can't be what you want me to be— not when it's so unfair to her."

Aleksei's eyes were both soft and hard when he answered her. "That's the nature of love, Sifte. It defies everything, even justice."

Sifte shook her head. "But couldn't you try—"

He shook his head. "I'm in love with *you*! I'll never love anyone but you."

"How can I love you when I know how it hurts her?"

There were many things Aleksei wanted to say, arguments he'd imagined over the course of sleepless nights to confound this protest, which he had known that he would hear sooner or later. Yet when finally faced with it, he didn't speak any of them; for it was this very integrity against which he would argue that he loved most in Sifte.

"I know that you can't," he said finally, but he couldn't keep the bitter disappointment out of his tone. He sat down again by the blank computer screen.

Sifte stood looking at his averted face. She knew that it might be for the last time, and her heart ached that it should end this way, but she couldn't see an alternative.

"I'll be back for you, Alyoshka," she said softly. "Till then, take care of them…and yourself."

"I love you Sifte," he replied almost inaudibly, without looking at her. "I'll always love you."

Sifte wanted to answer him as he deserved to be answered, but for the first time in her life her courage failed her. She knew very well that she would regret those unspoken words, possibly forever, but for the second time in an hour, she turned her back on a ravaged friend and fled. And perhaps, had she not been as distraught as she was, she would have remembered the warning she'd come to deliver, or noticed the shadow by the Dacha door that slipped away nearly as quickly as she.

*

Sifte didn't bother to turn on the light, knowing the workings well enough by feel. She even knew where the right disk was in the file drawer. As she pulled it out, she had the uncanny feeling that she was the last one to have touched it. Was it five years ago? Ten? She slipped it into place in the drive, and then sat down to watch.

The city grew out of the vast, flat plane: the old capitol, the true capitol, its fairy-tale onion-domes fenced by the vertical lashings of skyscrapers. Like evil raptors the missiles stooped from the bright summer sky. There was a pause, then the city blossomed into a plume of fire that lit the world with terrible glory, before the sky collapsed.

The image flickered for a valiant moment, and then the screen went blank. Sifte cried in the dark, violent, soundless sobs that tore the earth from the graves of her heart. She felt

285

all of the ghosts of her life rise up at once, glare at her with eyes like the craters that had been cities.

She cried for those cities, for seeds ungerminated and loves unspoken and children unborn. She cried for the babies who had lived, never to know childhood. Mila had been right to call herself doomed, yet wrong to think that she was the only one. They were all Solntse's children, their hearts rooted in his shadow. They had been fools to think that they could challenge him.

At that moment Sifte imagined that she had nothing left to lose. Her hatred for Solntse had taken on a life of its own, dreams of freedom and justice replaced by a consuming determination to destroy the man she saw as her own destroyer, without consideration for who or what else she might ruin in the process. In the wake of her tears Sifte lay down on the film-room floor and slept her final night at Institute 1.

PART 3

THE SUN

"The final thing to be perceived in the intelligible region, and perceived only with difficulty, is the form of the good; once seen, it is inferred to be responsible for whatever is right and valuable in anything, producing in the visible region light and the source of light, and being in the intelligible region itself the controlling source of truth and intelligence. And anyone who is going to act rationally in either public or private life must have sight of it."

Socrates to Glaucon
On the Simile of the Cave
"The Republic"

1

Sifte passed the next day in a daze. After classes were finished, she went to the library and stayed there until twenty-three-hundred hours. As she had hoped, Mila was asleep by the time she returned to her room. Her friend seemed a crumpled husk, and it was clearer now than ever that the Mila she had grown up with and loved was sinking into the wallow of her own tortured subconscious. Sifte was almost glad that she wouldn't have to witness this disintegration any longer.

She collected the few things she wanted to take with her: a drawing of an airplane by Aleksei, a copy of Mila's favorite poem, and the picture she had stolen from the book about Elisa Foley so many years ago, which she had retrieved from the wall of the Dacha. Once she had everything in order, Sifte sat down on her bed to wait. She had figured out an escape route using the floor plan she found in the library; she hoped that it was accurate. She planned to start out at half past midnight, which didn't leave much margin for error, but she couldn't risk hanging around in the hallways any longer than necessary.

Sifte looked at the clock, and sighed. It was only a quarter past the hour. Then she looked down. A small package, wrapped in paper of the same nondescript gray as the bedspread, lay on her pillow. She picked it up, and broke the seal. Across the room Mila shifted in her sleep, mumbling softly. Sifte waited until she was still again, then finished unwrapping the package. Inside was the book on President Foley.

For a moment time buckled, and Sifte felt that if she were to look up, the small white room with its two monastic gray beds would melt into library shelves, and she would be a child again, her future still simple and certain. Her shoulders lifted as if the weight she had carried so long had never rested on them. Sifte realized that she was holding her breath, and that a part of her would rather stop time at this moment of imaginary possibility than allow it to continue into the certain turmoil that awaited her.

But Sifte had only arrived at this moment because she couldn't live in a suspension of time, or belief, or disbelief. So she opened the book to the blank page which had once seemed so exotic, and found an inscription written in Dmitri's close, careful hand.

Dear Sifte,

Would you believe that I began this letter when you were ten years old? I've known that you would leave this way since I met you, and I've tried to prepare you for your calling. Sometimes I think I've failed; other times, I believe you learned everything you needed to know when you first read this book.

Be guided by its words. Face your destiny without fear or regret. There will never be a better time, and you will never have another choice. I pray that we will meet again, in a kinder world than the one you go now to face. But if we don't, remember that I love you as my own child, and love, as you once told me, is stronger than anything.

God go with you,
Dmitri

Sifte read the inscription twice, half-hating Dmitri for guessing her heart so accurately. The wind chimes swayed softly as Sifte stood, pitching faint harmonics into the silence. She gathered her few possessions, and shut the door quietly behind her.

The hallway was empty. A door in the sharp curve of the ellipse led to one of the service stairways that ran up through the building. The lock would normally restrict student access, but years before, Aleksei had figured out a way to manipulate the security system to recognize them when and where they chose. Sifte had programmed this one to recognize her.

Inside, a slatted metal staircase ran away from Sifte in both directions until it was lost in the vaulted shadows. She climbed up one flight, then slipped back into the main building. The hallway was identical to the one she had just left, but the stripe on the floor was white. Beside her was a window, and she found herself wishing that it was daytime, so that she could see the sun. Then, with a dizzy feeling of dislocation, she remembered that if all went well she would see the sun rise the next morning for the first time in her life.

And then she heard voices, nearby and moving in her direction. She ducked back into the stairwell, panic beginning to churn. As far as she knew the only access to the outside lay at the top of the White Level corridor, and it could only be reached by the elevators or the corridor itself. Though the service stairs continued above the landing where she stood, she didn't know where they let out.

Soon the speakers were close enough to identify as Alla and Dmitri. Sifte sucked in her breath and flattened herself even further against the wall.

"*I* know she's up to something," Alla was saying with cranky petulance, "and I hardly ever see her. *You* work with her every day—you must have seen something!"

"We've been through this," Dmitri answered wearily. "You can't fence an intellect like Sifte's. She might make correlations that enter into dangerous philosophical territory, but that doesn't mean she'll believe them to be morally correct, let alone act on them. If Solntse wants her, he's going to have to accept that."

"If she'd been properly monitored, she wouldn't have the basis for dangerous ideas!" the woman snapped.

Dmitri sighed. "Sifte isn't like any other child you've taught, Alla. Build the walls around her as high as you want, she'll always see beyond them. You find this frightening; but stop being afraid for moment and imagine the value of a mind like that to Solntse and to Russia's future. Besides, an entire generation of Opyekuni have been trained in relation to Sifte. Take her away, and you lose everything."

To Sifte's dismay, Dmitri and Alla had stopped in front of her door.

"That's better than letting her turn them against us."

"What are you suggesting?"

"That we separate her. Test her. And if she proves false to us, deal with her accordingly."

A leaden silence followed. Finally, Alla said, "Solntse knew that he was taking an enormous risk in choosing her. He must have prepared for the possibility of losing her. But whether he's prepared for it or not, losing Sifte is far better than allowing her to corrode his plans from the inside out."

"You sound as though you believe she's actively plotting against him," Dmitri said, with what Sifte considered laudable incredulity.

"She's as dangerous if she's innocent," Alla answered, with an intake of breath that indicated this was not the end of the thought. Nevertheless she paused, and Sifte could almost feel the tension between the two teachers seeping through the door. "But I have reason to suspect," she continued, "by virtue of a report from one of her peers, that she might be involved in something of the sort."

"Tatyana," Dmitri said grimly.

"I don't see that it matters. But if you must know the details, then come to my quarters. We shouldn't be discussing this here. Let's use the service stairs—I'd rather no one knew we've been up here."

Sifte bolted up the final flight of stairs, then crouched by the door at the top, which had not been on the library's floor plan. Now the teachers were on the landing below. Sifte cursed her luck, but not as violently as she cursed it when she realized that they had begun to climb the staircase, rather than descend.

A ventilation duct let out above the door. Sifte climbed up on the stair railing. Balancing precariously on the thin strip of metal, she felt inside the opening. The sides of the duct were smooth concrete, offering no handholds. There was only one possible leverage point, the frame of the door's small window. It seemed barely enough for a toe-hold, but it would have to be. Still clutching the edge of the vent, Sifte put one toe on the narrow sill and hauled herself up. She bent her knees, then thrust upward with all her strength, flinging herself into the tube.

"Is someone there?" Alla wheezed. Sifte froze.

"Maintenance?" Dmitri suggested.

"At this hour?"

Sifte didn't wait to hear more. She crawled as fast as she could in the dark, constricted space. She wondered whether it really had been Tanya who had spoken to Alla, and if so, what she had said. It didn't seem likely that Tanya would suspect what they had been doing, let alone possess any evidence. Then Sifte thought of the incisive points that Tanya had made during their staged debate, the influence she clearly had over Mila, the pride wounded by Aleksei's indifference. Perhaps she was a good deal more dangerous than any of them gave her credit for.

Sifte crawled on in the dark for what seemed an eternity, and then it began to grow murky. Soon there was light enough to see by. Abruptly, the vent ended, connecting to a larger duct which ran perpendicular to it. Sifte hung over the edge for a moment, looking down into the shadows. Then she looked up, into the face of the full moon. The air from the vent smelled fresh and sharp, unlike anything she had ever imagined. She could hear waves breaking against the outer walls.

A rusting ladder ran up the inside of the vertical shaft. Sifte managed to pull herself onto this and climbed to the top. When she tried to open the grate, however, she found that it was fixed in place by four rusty screws. Clinging to the ladder with one hand, she pulled a button from her jumpsuit with the free one. With its edge, she was able to twist the screws out. Then she pushed the grate aside, grabbed the outer lip of the vent, and pulled herself up and out, glad now of the stepped-up fitness regime they'd all complained about.

For a moment, Sifte thought she'd gone mad. She couldn't register the vastness and movement that surrounded her. All around her, dark water swirled and churned chips of moonlight. Her face was wet with the spray tossed up by the wind. The air was colder than anything she had ever felt, but the sky was clear and spattered with stars, more beautiful even than the wildest excursions of her imagination. The scenery so overwhelmed her that, for a moment, she forgot her purpose. The sound of a motor sputtering to life reminded her. She ran to the edge of the platform, in time to see the little boat pulling around the curve of the Institute's wall.

"No!" she cried. "Wait!"

The man at the wheel looked around, put the engine into neutral, but kept a wary distance from the wall.

"Vanya?" she called down to him.

"Yes," he answered.

"It's me." She pulled back the sleeve of her jumpsuit. She doubted that he could see the scar from so far away. But though the dark partially obscured his face, she could see that he smiled.

"Well then," he said, "welcome to the world." He pulled up to the wall, and she dropped down into the boat. Then he turned it around and pulled out the throttle. In seconds, the place that had been her entire world was lost on the pitching horizon.

2

Sasha awakened screaming.

It had been a nightmare of the cave. 'Cave' was her own term, chosen because the dreams' fruitless infinity reminded her of the Institute game she had never been able to win, and because they generally landed her in something like a cave. She didn't know what the nightmares stood for, or even whether they were anything other than a sleep-induced tour of her own agonized consciousness. However, every time they released her, there was a twinge of pain in her neural jack, and because of this she suspected that they were not true dreams at all, but Solntse's newest attempt to break her.

Whatever their origin, the nightmares came every time she slept, and they were always the same. They began with mazes: wide, dark corridors lit faintly red, which led eventually to a room with mirrors on the walls, all showing further mazes, each lit a different color. Pick a mirror, step into the next maze—slightly narrower, slightly dimmer—until the next hall of mirrors, and the next level. She would follow the mazes for hours, it seemed, until the corridors were so narrow that she could barely move through them, so dimly lit that she could barely see to move.

Just as claustrophobia threatened to reduce her to senselessness, she would turn a corner and find herself in a kind of cavern. On its far wall would be a mirror, but when she stepped up to it, the face it showed was never her own. There were only a few faces in actuality, and they shuffled in a seemingly random pattern. Still, each managed to seem unique every time, and each subsequent cave more horrible than the last, though she would have thought that by that point, the horror of her life had transcended stratification.

The most recent cave had been Stepan's, a Stepan so horribly like and unlike the man she had loved that he could only have been a synthesis of her tormentors. He would smile and invite her into the cave, with such tender earnestness that she ran to him time after time, though the outcome never changed. Once inside, the smile would twist into contempt. In the looking-glass cave lurked a Stepan who would beat her, rape her, try his very best to convince her that what good she remembered was false.

Wide awake now in the pitch black, Sasha wrapped her arms around her frail, bruised body, unable to erase the dream images. There was never any light in the cell. She had lost track of time long ago, and now she could feel her ability to distinguish between dream and reality disintegrating too. Solntse had finally found a way inside of her, and in this impregnable darkness she couldn't hope to fight him.

Life, waking and sleeping, had dissolved to a hell of hunger and pain. The only variations were in degrees, there was no longer any respite, so what was the point of staying alive? They would never let her live anyway, not after what she had done, but nor would they let her die. When she stopped eating, they put in a tube. When she tried to cut her wrists with cement shards they bandaged the wounds, tied her down, sedated her, and locked her up again.

Sasha knew that sometimes she cried, though she could no longer feel enough to sense tears flowing. Every once in a while she wondered what it was that she cried for. It certainly wasn't for her own misery—she had accepted and relinquished that long ago. Nor was it for others'. She was too weak now, too much a prisoner of her own mind for compassion. Sometimes she comforted herself with the thought that her tears were for Sifte, because it was Sifte who deserved them the most, wherever she was. Sasha knew now that she should have killed her as she'd meant to the day the Opyekuni took her.

In her heart, though, she knew that it wasn't really Sifte she cried for, either. If anything, she cried because once, in some distant dream, she had given everything she had to the empty shell of a country she had mistaken for something worth saving.

*

Andrei was tired and aggravated. The night's meeting had been particularly frustrating, not due to the presence of too many of Solntse's sympathizers—the bane of his early career, before he had learned to accept them as weak, frightened people who would follow the strongest leader blindly—but precisely because there had been none. He would have welcomed any voice other than his own, even a challenging voice. Instead there had been row after row of blank faces, staring at him throughout his speech without the slightest sign of comprehension.

When he stopped speaking, the silence closed in like fog. A few people stayed afterwards to talk, but he recognized all of them from past debates, and their questions and assertions were flat, like the faces of the crowd that filed away as silently as it had congregated.

Andrei was so distraught over this last in a string of increasingly ineffective meetings that he didn't notice the man at the back of the room until he had picked up the last of the lamps and was about to leave. The man was seated in the farthest corner, almost hidden by shadows and clutter, as though he feared recognition.

"If you please, tavarishch," the man said, extending a smooth, slender hand as Andrei whirled in surprise, "I was wondering if you might stay a moment to discuss with me a matter which I believe you will find to be of great significance, to yourself and perhaps to your cause as well."

At the sound of the man's accent, Andrei's eyes narrowed. His figure was unimposing, small and gray and bespectacled, modestly though well-dressed. He was clearly not of the same class as the people who had just left the burned-out basement, probably not a resident of Myortvograd at all, and just as obviously not Russian.

"German, are you?"

"Don't let that deter you. I come here as a friend." Andrei nodded slightly, but said nothing, and after a moment the little man took a deep breath and continued, holding Andrei's eyes as a terrier holds a rabbit.

"I have reason to believe," he said, "that a woman by the name of Aleksandra Umanskaya is your sister?" Andrei stared at him, and a flicker of a smile crossed the man's face. "You are wise to conduct yourself with discretion. There is no need for you to reply—only listen carefully." He paused, drawing a breath which seemed somehow shallower than it ought to be, then continued even more rapidly and quietly than before.

"As of this morning your sister was alive, and I have every reason to believe that she still is, but she won't be for long. She was for many years an inmate of Schlüsselburg prison, but she has recently been moved to isolation in the Fortress. She is being held on charges of high treason and the murder of an official. Unless unequivocal evidence in her favor is produced—and I assure you that it is unlikely that she will be allowed to testify even if she is able—she will go to the firing squad in one month. To be completely frank with you, I do not believe that she will survive that long."

Andrei's face had gone from gray to red to gray again in the course of Krieger's speech. The two men stared at each other for a long moment, and then Andrei asked, "Who are you?"

For the first time since he had approached Andrei, Krieger averted his eyes. "It does not matter who I am. It only matters that you believe what I tell you."

Andrei sighed. "Obviously, you've broken orders and put yourself in great danger to tell me this. Either that, or you're lying. All things being equal, the latter would seem the more likely of the two possibilities. However, I happen to have had one or two pieces of information recently that would suggest you're telling the truth. Assuming for the moment that you are, what I really want to know is why you've put yourself in danger on the off chance of helping a dying criminal?"

Krieger sighed as well and took off his glasses. Without them, his face retreated into his general colorlessness, so forgettable that it became memorable. "I have been a prison doctor a long time," he said. "Until a short while ago,

301

I believed I had seen every kind of criminal that exists in Solntse's Russia. Some of them deserve the title, some do not. I never dared pass further judgment than that. After meeting Sasha Umanskaya, however, I lost my neutrality. I think that this country cannot afford to bury her so soon." He paused, drew another strained breath, and said, "I have also come to care for her personally, and I do not want her to die. Without your help, Andrei 1—or Andrei Kirillovich, if you prefer—she will die, a more horrible death than even you can imagine."

Andrei sank into the nearest chair. "All right," he said. "I'm listening."

Krieger straightened, seemed to breathe a sigh of relief down the length of his frail body. "She is in the first sub-level of the prison underneath the cathedral. As you must know, the Fortress is guarded by two hundred of the best Pomoshchniki and twenty Opyekuni at all times. The only conceivable plan to free your sister hinges on my authority to order a transfer within the prison, and your ability to arrange a sabotage as she is being moved."

Andrei considered this. "How can I be certain that you aren't merely a plot to trap and kill me?"

"I don't suppose you can. In this city, things are seldom what they seem."

Andrei studied the doctor's face. The man looked like a fading pencil drawing, as though something was erasing him from the inside out. Yet his voice and eyes had sparked when he had spoken of Sasha.

Andrei had no illusions. He knew that this was more likely to be a set-up than not. Yet the fight he had had with Stepan had changed him in ways he had not thought he could change. Since that night, or more accurately, since he awakened bound with his own ropes and realized he had nothing but his unyielding principles to blame for it, he had begun to doubt those principles. He would never be ruled by passion like Stepan or Sasha, but he was no longer convinced that passion was inferior to logic when it came to fighting for one's beliefs. Perhaps, he ruminated as he looked at the doctor's face, the butt of his own gun had knocked sense into him. Though Andrei was not given to humor, he found himself smiling at the idea.

The doctor, apparently mistaking Andrei's smile for acceptance, smiled back. It transformed him. Apparently this little man did not merely care about Sasha, he loved her. Though he worried that this in itself might derail the doctor's best intentions, Andrei knew what he had to do.

"How will I contact you? And when?"

Krieger shook his head. "You will not be able to. We must make our arrangement now, or never."

"How long does she have?"

"Her trial won't begin before next week. I'd give it five days. After the verdict, perhaps another week for the paperwork to be put in order. So we'll say three weeks until the firing squad. If she lives that long."

Andrei sighed. "When will you order her move?"

"Whenever you wish it. Although I'd have to advise it sooner rather than later."

"Is five days too long?"

"I shouldn't think so. Sunday, then. Plan on the evening, eighteen-hundred hours—the guards take a tea break then, so there will be fewer of them around, and of course the night is always good cover. I'll leave a map of the prison, with her old and new cells marked, in this Glaza file," he handed Andrei a piece of paper with a file number on it, "as well as a more specific time frame. The password is 'tavarishch.' You will have to supply a way into Solntsegrad, as well as a way of defending yourself and any others you bring along. Surely you know of the flood tunnels running under the city?"

Andrei frowned. The Soviet had used them before on some of their more desperate projects. It was a last-ditch option, but probably the only one now. "I know them," he said.

"Good. I hope that you know them well because they connect with the basement of the prison. One of Solntse's mistakes, in my humble opinion, was choosing one of the old buildings for his headquarters. I'll tell you also that they will not move her with fewer than ten Pomoshchniki to guard her—not since the incident."

Andrei looked at the doctor. "Incident?"

Again Krieger smiled, apparently despite himself. "It would have been better for her if she hadn't done it, but I can't say that I blame her. He was a low-level guard in the Fortress. A man known for tormenting the women." His smile died. "He tried to rape her." Krieger paused, staring at his hands, and then continued, "I've never been sure why Solntse uses the Fortress for his most dangerous prisoners. The romance, I suppose, but its history makes it a liability. Kronstadt—now that's a prison. State of the art, nothing to break or malfunction, or be used against its staff—except by certain of your more notorious colleagues."

Andrei looked at the doctor with quick suspicion, but the little man only shook his head and smiled his watery, rueful smile. "Come now, you know that your friend's continued freedom is not due to Solntse's ignorance of his whereabouts. But that is another matter. As for Sasha, the age of the Fortress helped her…or perhaps not, depending upon how you look at it. She ripped a piece of metal from a window frame and stabbed the guard in the throat with it. I saw the man myself not long after it happened. He was already dead." He shook his head again. "It was worth a death sentence in and of itself, but she'd also been plotting an insurrection of sorts while she was in Schlüsselburg."

"Is that where you met her?"

Krieger sighed. "Yes. I saw her there for injuries inflicted by a cell mate. Unfortunately, it was part of a plot. They questioned the accomplice, and he broke. Hence the Fortress for Sasha."

"How long has she been there?"

"About six months. At first, they put her in semi-isolation in the Trubetskoye Bastion. They questioned her about Stepan Pierson, and about a child they allegedly had together. They seemed to think she'd been in contact with one or the other of them. She wouldn't admit to anything, so they began depriving her of food. She never complained—in fact, they say that by then she had stopped speaking at all. Out of frustration, that guard began to beat her, and when he tried…well, who wouldn't fight back?" Krieger's voice had begun to shake, filling Andrei with pity.

"I'll do my best," he told Krieger. Then, feeling that he somehow owed the man more comfort than that, he asked, "Will I see you again?"

"Who can say?" answered Krieger, with a smile of strange sweetness. He touched Andrei briefly on the shoulder, then slipped out as quietly as he had come.

3

They traveled for a period in silence, during which Sifte studied the man at the helm. He was medium-height and sturdily built, with a kindly, broad face, fair hair, and something subtle and foreign in his look, which after some time she identified as freedom. For all the oppression of Solntse's regime, this man had never lived in a cage.

"Put this on," he said, pulling a heavy, dark coat from beneath one of the bench-like seats that ran along the sides of the boat. "And these clothes, when you feel up to it. You'll have to dump your uniform overboard, but I don't imagine you'll count it too much of a loss."

"No. Thank you." Sifte took the woolen bundle from him. She had been too full of adrenaline to think of the cold; now she realized that she was shivering. Vanya looked straight ahead at the empty sea as Sifte stripped off her jumpsuit, weighted it with a stone Vanya had brought, and tossed it into the water. She put on the thick trousers, sweater and coat, heavy boots, hat and mittens.

"I'm decent now," she said to the man's back, when she realized that he was not going to turn around unprompted.

Vanya looked at her and began to laugh. It was a slow, low sound like the sea between high cliffs. He said, "The apple truly doesn't fall far from the tree. Not only are you the spitting image of your father, you also have the same manner. Insolent. Your eyes demand answers."

Sifte looked down at the dark water, embarrassed and pleased. "Did you know my mother, too?"

Vanya shook his head with a touch of regret. "I joined the Soviet too recently for that. I don't really know your father, either. I mean, I heard him speak a few times, without knowing who he was. They try to keep him a secret, you know. Well, of course you know. The first time I met him was last week, when he told me about the plan to get you out of the school."

"Why you?" Sifte asked after a moment of consideration.

Vanya shrugged. "Olga chose me, I suppose because of the boat. Olga's an old friend of your father's. Your mother's too, I hear. Anyhow, I'm a registered fisherman, which makes me less conspicuous than another hired boat. And for the moment, you're Anna, my daughter."

Sifte looked at him with heightened interest. If he was a fisherman, then he was sub-race. Nothing about him fit with the abject image in the Institute simulations and textbooks. Then again, Vanya had a regular job and would be better off than many.

"What's the plan, then?" she asked.

He shrugged again. "I only know my part in it. It's safer that way. I'll take you as far as the village of Vasilovo, where Olga will meet you. Where you go after that is up to her." He paused, contemplating her, then continued, "I'll warn you now, even landing won't be easy. No doubt by the time we reach coastal waters someone will be looking for you. Do you know, you're the first escape in the history of Institute 1?"

"I never thought about it."

"At any rate, if all goes as planned we'll land north of Solntsegrad, in Zelenogorsk, beyond the northern Badlands."

"Badlands?"

"I guess they wouldn't teach you about Badlands. They're deserts…places where nothing lives or grows. Nobody knows why, but of course most people think it's a side-effect of the bombs. Even the officials don't like to go near them."

"What about officials? We're bound to run into some sooner or later."

Vanya sighed. "We'll cross that bridge when we reach it." He paused again, as if appraising her. "You'll be safer with this." He lifted a semi-automatic handgun from another hiding place under the benches, along with three clips of ammunition. "Can you use it?"

"I haven't practiced much with automatic. They like us to learn precision."

"Then this will be easy. Don't hesitate to use it if you're in doubt. Do you think you can?" Sifte knew that he wasn't questioning her technical ability. She took the weapon and hooked it into the waistband of her trousers, stuffing the clips into one pocket of her coat. Vanya smiled in approval.

Sifte sat down on one of the benches, resting her head on her arms, which were crossed on the bulwark. The water rushed by beneath her, tiny phosphorescent creatures lighting up in the boat's wake, mirroring the stars that blazed overhead. This world was a far richer tapestry than she had ever imagined, and she wished that Mila and Aleksei could be on either side of her to share it. Everywhere she turned, she saw the stricken look in Aleksei's eyes the last time they spoke, and the quiet despair in Mila's. She wondered if they could ever forgive her. She tried not to wonder whether they would have the chance.

In an attempt to escape these thoughts, she concentrated instead on the broken reflection of the moon, the tiny glowing creatures that winked and faded in the boat's wake. Before long, her eyelids drooped, and her tense, exhausted body relaxed into sleep. Vanya laid her out gently on the bench, covering her with his own coat. She stirred, mumbling what he thought must be a name, and then she was silent.

Only then did Vanya allow his own terrific anxiety to surface. His face seemed suddenly haggard and careworn, even old. Nevertheless, his big hands were steady as he turned the boat north, and prayed that they would make it.

*

Sifte awakened at the change in the motor's timbre; they had slowed to a crawl. There was a reddish glow on the eastern horizon which stained the water beneath it, and between them she could just make out a black line. Her heart leapt to her throat.

"Is that land?" Sifte asked Vanya, pointing to the line on the horizon.

"Mother Russia." His smile was oddly rueful. "We'll be there in a couple of hours. Are you hungry?"

Again, Vanya had pre-empted her need: Sifte's stomach was suddenly pinched and rumbling. She took the bread and cheese and smoked fish that Vanya offered her and ate all of it.

"Well now," he said, "you've got your sea-legs quickly for a child who's never even smelled the ocean."

"Maybe it's because I've lived all my life under it," she suggested, and when Vanya laughed, she rewarded him with one of her rare, reluctant smiles.

"You even smile like Stepan!" Vanya cried. After a moment's consideration he added: "You don't give anything away, do you?"

Sifte shrugged. "How come you've slowed down?" she asked after a moment.

"Sea's too rough to go faster. Looks like a storm coming in from the west."

"How bad?" Sifte asked, clutching the edge of the bench as the boat rolled again.

"No worse than a hundred others I've seen." He smiled at her reassuringly. "Don't worry. We'll get there."

For a time Sifte drifted, watching the hairline of land on the horizon thicken. A light snow began to fall. Sea and sky were cold and leaden, a world away from the past night's idyll.

"Now," Vanya said softly, "I think I'd best show you how the gun works."

Sifte's gaze snapped upward. Far off on the gray water, she could see a black spot moving toward them.

"How do you know it's not another fishing boat?"

"Too many years having my catch confiscated for Pomoshchnik dinners," he answered tersely, then took the gun she held out to him. "You load the ammunition here," he said, demonstrating with one of her clips of bullets. "Safety on, safety off. Adjust the sight here, if you need it. Got it?" Sifte nodded. "Good. Use the bullets sparingly. These are all you'll see for a while."

Sifte took the gun back. "Now," Vanya sighed, "let's crank up this old motor and see who's so eager to meet us."

Despite his efforts to hide it, Sifte could hear the anxiety in his voice.

The snow grew thicker as they neared land, whirling and howling around the boat like broken ghosts, but Sifte never took her eyes from the approaching vessel. Vanya's attitude turned grimmer by the moment, and Sifte was almost glad when he let out a low curse, in that it broke the horrible tension.

"'Kuni," he said, peering through binoculars at the boat which was now less than five hundred feet away. "Now, child, you must be strong as you have never been strong, but don't let them see any effort. Remember, a fisherman's daughter is seen and not heard. Speak only to answer their questions. Don't look them in the eye, and use your weapon only as a last resort."

The only Opyekun Sifte had ever seen was Gospazha Alla, and Alla had softened with age and her comfortable post. These men who boarded Vanya's boat stood straight and tall in dark gray coats and matching, fur-lined hats, with heavy black boots that disappeared beneath the hems of their gray trousers. Their faces were inert as sculptures. Sifte was glad that Vanya had instructed her not to look at them. Their very proximity revolted her. It was her first true understanding of what she had been destined to become.

One of the Opyekuni stared at Sifte's bowed head, the other addressed Vanya. "Please state your name, rank and occupation," he said in a hard, dull voice.

"Ivan Ivanovich Kuznetsov," Vanya replied, assuming the frightened, groveling tone of the ignorant faced with authority. "Sub-race, fisherman."

"And the girl?" Icy blue eyes probed Vanya's face.

"My daughter."

311

"Name?"

"Anna."

"Age?"

"Is there some kind of—"

"Age!" the second Opyekun barked.

"She's—she's just sixteen, sir."

Both Opyekuni regarded Sifte skeptically. She didn't shift her position, or even lift her eyes from the deck of the boat.

"Let us see your papers."

Vanya produced two sets of forgeries.

"These appear to be valid," the second Opyekun said slowly.

"Yet she looks—" the first Opyekun tilted Sifte's chin upward, so that her eyes met his own. "Older than sixteen," he finished, speculatively.

The silence bore down with all the weight of the bruised storm clouds overhead. The boat pitched and tossed violently, and still no one moved or spoke. Sifte wondered how she had ever managed to convince herself that she wasn't afraid to die.

"In what town were you born, Anna Ivanovna Kuznetsova?" he asked.

"In Zelenogorsk, sir," she replied. It seemed to Sifte that someone else was speaking through her.

"Your mother's name?"

"Lisaveta Aleksandrovna, but she's dead now, sir." She struggled to keep her voice soft and even.

"Why are you here now with your father?"

"I've worked on this fishing boat since I was a child."

The eyes of the first Opyekun bored into Sifte's own until she thought she would go mad with the effort not to flinch.

312

Then he looked at the second Opyekun, who stood by Vanya, tensed and ready to strike at the first sign from his comrade.

And then the world crumbled. The first official nodded almost imperceptibly to the second, then reached out with uncanny deftness and pinned Sifte's arms behind her back. In the same instant, Vanya had the man's neck in his hands, and then the second Opyekun was drawing his gun. Sifte was not aware of a train of thought, only that she was jerking her elbows upward into the solar plexus of the man holding her. When his grip on her arms loosened, she tore free, ripped the gun from beneath her sweater.

For a long time afterward, she could not remember anything about the next sequence of events beyond the sound of gun shots, and a few disjointed images: a flock of frightened sea birds scattering into the air, the torn white of the snowflakes against the slate-gray water, the red trail of blood on the boat's deck, curving and zigzagging with the erratic motion of the waves. This last image held her mesmerized. She stood staring down at the pattern of crimson on white until rough brown hands intruded, breaking the spell, and lifted the gun gently from her own. She looked up into Vanya's eyes, blue as day and brimming now with compassion and respect and behind these, a shard of fear.

"They're both dead," he said. Only then did Sifte register the two bodies sprawled behind the blood-trail, one bleeding from a wound in the chest, the other with a blackened gash in his skull oozing dark blood and something yellow.

Sifte looked up at Vanya, her mouth open but no words emerging.

"I shot the one who was holding you," he told her. After a pause, he added gently, "You killed the one who would have shot me. You saved my life, Sifte."

313

Sifte nodded, and sat down on one of the benches, still looking at the bodies of Solntse's Opyekuni. "They never seemed...quite...real," she stammered. "Until now."

Vanya sat down beside her. "It's like that the first time you kill someone, and it's never really like that again. I don't know whether that's good or bad." He looked at her carefully, and again she saw that trepidation in his eyes. "Are you going to be all right?"

"Yes," she answered, wondering what she had done to make him look like that.

"You know we have to move on now, as quickly as possible." She nodded. "Sit there, then, while I take care of them." Sifte remained obediently seated as Vanya weighted the Opyekuni's clothing with pieces of an old engine and dumped the bodies overboard. He set their boat adrift, and threw water over the deck of his own to wash away the blood. Then he started up the motor again, and pointed the boat toward land.

The storm had blown them closer to shore. By the time they were within rowing distance of the beach, they could barely see through the whirling snow, and the bitter wind cut straight through their heavy clothing. Vanya lowered the row-boat over the side and helped Sifte into it, then cast his own boat adrift, too.

"We need to find shelter," he told her as they landed on a grayish beach that faded into a forest of spindly pines. "The town is out of the question now. If it's not already crawling with officials, it will be soon. Come on, we have to hurry." Vanya took her hand and helped her up the beach and into the trees, with what Sifte soon realized to be a good deal of foresight. Among the trees the wind's teeth weren't as sharp, and the snow wasn't as deep.

"There's a farm about a kilometer east of here," Vanya told her. "There should be outbuildings where we can hide."

Sifte nodded and pushed on through the deepening drifts, concentrating on her feet in their thick felt boots, lifting first one, then the other out of the snow, losing a little more feeling each time. Before long, the world was nothing but a monotone of white and the madman's howl of wind, and Sifte wondered when she would give up believing that it had ever been anything else. She began to slump into the deepening drifts. Vanya gripped her elbows and pulled her upright, turned her around to face him.

"Can you make it another few minutes, Sifte?"

She nodded, although she knew that he doubted the truth of her affirmation as much as she did. They stumbled on, Vanya holding tightly now to Sifte's hand. They climbed a hill, and then the trees thinned out, and they were looking down into a shallow, white valley, in which they could make out the dark hulks of buildings. Vanya was tugging at her hand. Sifte followed the sensation blindly.

The barn door was sealed with snow, but Vanya was able to force it wide enough to allow them entry. He pushed Sifte inside first, and then followed her, pulling the door fast behind them. The air that greeted them was sweet with the smell of hay and blissfully still. Dim light filtered through the screen of snow on the barn's single window. It was enough for Vanya to locate a lantern and matches, and put them to use. He hurried back to find Sifte huddled on a pile of hay, shivering violently. He led her to a stall half-full of hay bales, and shook one of them out to cover the dirt floor.

"Take off your coat and boots," he said, "before the snow melts. You'll be in trouble if you get wet."

Sifte fumbled with the buttons of her coat. When Vanya saw that her frigid fingers were useless, he knelt and unbuttoned them for her. He helped her out of her boots as well, and then wrapped a horse blanket around her.

"What about—"

"Don't worry about any of it, now," he interrupted, squeezing her icy hands in his. "They won't look until the storm is over; the going is too hard, there are no tracks to follow. They know we couldn't have made it far. Sleep now, if you can. We have a long way to travel, yet."

"Will it be all right?" Sifte's voice was tremulous. The childish supplication in her eyes finally dispersed the images that had haunted Vanya since he had watched her fire nine rounds into the official's head, with uncanny precision and the rigid, remorseless face of an Opyekun. He smiled, leaned down, and brushed the fine hair back from her forehead, thinking of the real Anna Kuznetsova, whose face he had begun to forget, though she had not yet been dead a year.

"Of course it will," he said, as he had said to Anna.

Sifte nodded, and shut her eyes. She knew that he was lying, but she had seen the skittish look leave his eyes, and the immense relief of this delivered her into a warm drowse. Within minutes, she slept.

4

"*What!*" cried Anastasia.

"She really went without us?" Misha asked.

Mila lowered her eyes, and Aleksei looked grim.

"It was the only way," Aleksei said. "She'll come back for us."

"You mean you knew about this?" Anastasia raged.

"I suspected."

"Why didn't you say something?"

Aleksei sighed. "I thought she must have her reasons for not telling us."

Anastasia turned away in disgust. "What about you?" she asked Mila.

Mila shook her head wearily. "I didn't know any more than you, Nastya." But she didn't meet Anastasia's eyes as she said this.

After another taut, elongated silence Aleksei drew a breath and said, "Look, whatever she did, she did for us all."

"'The conviction that they must always do what is best for the community,'" Misha said ruminatively.

"Oh, shut up," Anastasia snapped. Then, to Aleksei, "Well, thanks to Sifte's magnanimity, we're sitting on a sinking shitheap. Anyone got any ideas what we're going to do about it?"

Over the last two sleepless nights, Aleksei had tried to think of all the possible answers to this question. He answered now without missing a beat. "First, we destroy everything—the Dacha, the Glaza files and passwords and all the records of our correspondence, and when that's done we've got to destroy the computer, too. Probably no one will even realize she's gone until after the first class…but we need to come up with a story before they start asking questions."

"And pulling out our fingernails," Anastasia added, with a dark look.

Mila answered in a cold, clipped tone, "They wouldn't waste the time."

Aleksei looked at Mila as if she had slapped him. She looked back at him, unblinking, remorseless. He said, "If Sifte joins up with Stepan, then we've already accomplished more than we ever thought we could. If we can hold out long enough for her to get to the city, then even if we die for it, we haven't died for nothing."

Misha looked sullen, Anastasia furious, and Mila's face had pinched inward around a small, bitter smile.

"Don't look at me like this is my fault!" Aleksei cried. His face was hard and proud, yet also oddly vulnerable. "Each of us swore loyalty when we started this—"

"To each other!" Anastasia spat back.

"Yes, but first and foremost to what we all know is true and right. Sifte believes this is the only way; how can you condemn her for that?" Aleksei faltered for a moment, then found his courage again, and continued in a tremulous voice, "Or if you do, then go turn yourselves in. Say you always thought Sifte was an izmyennitsa, and you only went along

318

with her to get more information. You'll be the heroes of Institute 1."

His face twisted with disgust. Once again he paused, waiting for anyone to say anything, but no one even moved. He sighed. "Look, whether or not we really understood at the beginning how far this could go, it's gone that far, and it'll still go farther. If you don't think it's worth putting aside what we want to give Sifte the greatest chance she can to help…well then I'd rather you did go turn yourselves in. Just give her—and me—a couple more hours before you do it."

Nobody was looking at him now. Aleksei felt a hollow, heavy despair. Despite his passionate defense of what she had done, at that moment he hated Sifte for shouldering him with this responsibility. Yet as he thought it, he knew that if there had been any selfishness in Sifte's decision to go without them, it had been their own fault. Already he was buckling under the weight of the others' dependency, yet Sifte had borne it since she was a child and had never let them see how she must have suffered.

"If you don't plan to go to the teachers," he said, looking at each of them squarely, "then we can't waste any more time."

"I can't imagine a story anyone would believe," grumbled Anastasia, but there was a note of defiance in her voice.

"It's better than pretending we don't know anything."

"Then it has to be simple."

"Right. And play into their own fears…like, a teacher's been giving Sifte trouble. Accusing her of treason."

"Simplicity itself," said Anastasia. "Which teacher are you planning to scapegoat?"

"Sifte never told us?"

"And how did she get away?" asked Misha. "There would have to have been a supply boat or something yesterday."

"There was," Anastasia said, finally warming to the idea. "I've been keeping a watch on the shipping schedules since Sifte found that thing about the biohazards. I bet Stepan knew it, too. And speaking of Stepan, there've got to be people here who suspect that Sifte is his daughter, and they probably know about Solntse's plans for her. No doubt any officials he sends to investigate will be clued in to that, and this story will plug right into their own fears."

"One of us is bound to slip up sooner or later," said Mila.

"If you have a better idea," said Aleksei, "let's hear it."

She glared at him for a moment, and then looked away. There was a long silence, then Misha said, "It's time for class now. We'd better go."

No one moved; they were still caught in the inertia of Sifte's wake.

Finally Aleksei said, "Come on. Take whatever you can hide and put it in the incinerator now. Come back for the rest whenever you can get away."

They each crammed something into their book bags, and one by one, they left the Dacha.

5

"You're certain they're not coming back?" Tanya whispered.

"They're all in class," Nikolai answered sullenly. "There's no reason to whisper."

"Is it locked?" she asked, touching the door with a near-reverence that only irritated him further.

"See for yourself, you have the key-card. I'm going."

"But I don't know where to look!" she cried.

"I've done what you asked." He pulled away from her clutching fingers. "Now leave me alone."

"Fine," Tanya said, opening the door. She saw nothing in the hallway itself, but a thin strip of light was visible underneath one of the closed doors. She moved toward this.

Nikolai said, almost hopefully, "If there's anything in there, it'll be locked."

But the door opened easily, and from inside the room Tanya called back, "It should have been—they've got some kind of lock here. I guess they forgot, in all the excitement."

"What excitement?" Nikolai asked.

Tanya didn't answer the question, but said, "This must be headquarters." She fingered the paper trees and flowers almost reverently.

Nikolai took a step inside. "It's crazy," he said gruffly.

Tanya turned to him, her eyes for once unguarded. "You think so?" she said. "I think it's beautiful. Pitiful, but beautiful."

"They hardly need our pity," Nikolai said. He wasn't certain why he had said it, particularly as he suspected they would soon need it very much.

"There must be something more here than old boxes and kids' drawings."

"I thought I saw the light from a computer the other night, when I followed him here."

"Where could they be hiding it?" Tanya asked, examining the walls, the floor, lifting paper scenery to look behind it. Finally she opened an old packing crate, and lifted out a small computer.

"How did they get that?" Nikolai asked.

"My guess is they built it…it's a mess. But we'll know soon enough." She smiled at him over her shoulder, but there was sadness along with the acidity in its perfect curve, which confused Nikolai. He didn't answer, but she didn't seem to expect one. She set the machine on the crate and turned it on.

"Shit!" she said. "It wants a password. What could it be?"

"Just about anything," Nikolai said dismally.

She turned, and seemed to see Nikolai for the first time since he had showed her the door to the hallway. "You know him," she said, her eyes locking with his. "Think, Kolya. What would he choose?"

"How do you know he chose it? Why not one of the others?"

She rolled her eyes. "It's Aleksei who tutors kids in the lower-level computer lab, Aleksei who takes the programming electives, and Aleksei again who's on good enough terms with what's-her-name in the parts store to borrow a key and help himself to the ingredients for a computer when no one's looking. This is his baby."

"You're smarter than you look," he grumbled.

Tanya gave him a saccharine smile. "Don't forget it. Now, suggestions?"

"Try inversions of their names," he said tentatively, after a moment.

Tanya did this, but the cursor still flashed its intractable demand.

"What about last names?" Nikolai suggested.

"None of us have last names."

"We did once."

"Do you honestly think they know them?" There was a derisive languor to the tone with which she asked this question that made it sound less than rhetorical.

"I don't know!" he snapped. Then, trying to reassert his calm, he said, "Why are you in such a hurry?"

"Haven't you noticed anything odd this morning?" Tanya looked at him, and he looked blankly back.

"Go ahead, spell it out."

Tanya looked levelly at him. "Sifte's gone."

Nikolai's forehead furrowed. "Kicked out?"

"No, she ran away." Her condescending smile dissolved into bitterness Nikolai didn't understand. "And do you know why she went? Because she'd rather risk death than be here any longer."

323

Nikolai couldn't help thinking that there was a shade of wistfulness in Tanya's voice, though it was as inexplicable as the bitterness. "She and her friends aren't like the rest of us," she continued. "We've always thought we're better than they are, because they're mixed race or had parents from the provinces or some other godforsaken place. But they make their lives, they do something, while people like you and me sit here and accept what comes to us, good or bad." She looked up at him with terrible eyes. "They're free. That's what all this means."

"They're no better than I am," Nikolai contradicted with terse petulance.

"Oh no? Then why are you helping me destroy them, when Aleksei's the only friend you've ever had?"

Nikolai's mouth tightened. "You never said anything about destroying anyone."

"I didn't think I needed to."

"If that's what you want, then I won't help you any more!"

Tanya smiled again. "Yes, you will. Because I know your secret, and you'd sell more than a friend to make me keep it."

It seemed to Tanya as if a glacier was moving over Nikolai, closing last around his eyes. He paused, then said, "Pierson."

"What?" Tanya asked.

"The password."

Tanya typed. "There!" she cried. "How did you know?"

Nikolai shrugged.

"Now, we'll check for unauthorized Glaza traffic."

"How do you plan to do that?" Nikolai's face and voice seemed worn.

She flicked an impatient hand toward the screen. "Every time you go through Glaza, the system makes a record of the correspondence, listed under the password. Every transaction run through it since it was set up is recorded there. So, we go into Glaza and check the records for this password."

"You can't just do that. You have to have a high level of access to read the log file on any system—probably only the Opyekuni can do it in Glaza."

Tanya smiled, and pushed him aside. "Well then, isn't it lucky that I happen to have a couple of Opyekun access codes?"

She entered Glaza using a code she had memorized, then folded her arms across her chest as a new channel opened up. Nikolai looked at her with a mixture of anger and disbelief. "How did you get that?"

Tanya shrugged. "A reward for good behavior."

"I thought this was your personal crusade."

"It is. But it happens to coincide with a bigger one, so…"

Nikolai's scowl deepened. "Who are you working for?"

"I can only tell you that my orders come from Gospazha Alla."

"Why her?"

"She needs the evidence, but she isn't allowed to interfere this way."

Nikolai shook his head. "You're even more deluded than I thought," he said.

Tanya flushed, and snapped, "What do you mean by that?"

"Gospazha Alla, not allowed to interfere? Believe me, if a teacher has the slightest suspicion of an izmyennik in our midst, Solntse will condone just about anything that teacher wants to do to prove it. Either this is about some personal grudge of Alla's, or they're involved in something so dangerous she's afraid to touch it."

"Why would she be afraid?"

"I don't know. Maybe it would imply she'd been slacking on her duties. Did you even bother to ask what exactly she's looking for?"

"Of course! She gave me a long list—a lot of which we've already found."

Nikolai shook his head. "So far, we haven't found anything except a computer they might have stolen, and seeing as they haven't actually taken it out of Institute 1, it's a stretch even to call it stealing."

"Well, well, haven't you turned liberal under the influence of the rebel rat."

Now it was Nikolai's turn to color. "Hardly! But I think that if this is something Alla is afraid to be associated with, then maybe we'd better think twice about getting involved."

Tanya sat down in front of the computer in a petulant huff. "Fine, I'll do it myself." She glared at the screen for a few minutes, until Nikolai realized that she had no idea how to do what she wanted to do. He turned to go, smiling to himself, and then Tanya spoke again, in the thin, wheedling tone he'd come to loathe.

"And I'll make sure to tell them you didn't have anything to do with it."

Nikolai stopped. "What do you mean?"

"Just that," Tanya answered, fixing him with her perverse child's eyes. "When they ask why you've been sneaking around here, and why you chose Aleksei as your room-mate, I'll tell them it had nothing to do with Sifte's plot to escape."

Nikolai stepped towards her menacingly. "You won't attach my name to this!"

Tanya shrugged. "When they ask me what I know about your dealings with Aleksei and Sifte and the rest, I'll have to tell them the truth."

Nikolai balled his fists and then opened them again several times, as if speculating whether it would be better to throttle or hit her. In the end he did neither, but said, "I suppose this is why they chose you for this little mission. Being a mendacious bitch just comes naturally to you."

"Call it what you like," she answered in the same confident, unruffled tone, "it gets me what I want, quickly."

"A bullet in the back is quick too."

"Sneer if you want to, but it works."

"Does it?"

"You're going to help me, aren't you?"

After a moment, without looking at her, Nikolai sat down at the computer.

He typed slowly, curiously dreading what he would find, but the search came up with nothing. He almost smiled. "See," he said, "the only transmissions come from public computers."

Tanya was chewing her lip, her eyebrows bunched together. "I just can't believe that. Why would they go to all the trouble to get into Glaza in the first place if they weren't going to use it?"

Nikolai sighed. "Glaza's good for a lot of things besides correspondence. Maybe they only wanted information."

"But without the access code of an Opyekun, they couldn't get to any of the information they would be interested in."

"How do you know what they'd be interested in?"

"What made you choose 'Pierson'?" Tanya's look was icy and probing.

Nikolai sighed. "Anyway, if they're resourceful enough to find the parts to build a computer undetected in a small, closed environment, they're probably also resourceful enough to find high-level access codes. Maybe they even found a way to block any records of their transmissions from appearing in a log like this."

"Either that, or somebody's been helping them…" Tanya's gaze had drifted from the computer screen, but all of a sudden, it snapped back. "What was that?" she asked. "Their first class isn't over yet." They listened. There was a sound in the hallway outside the room. They looked at each other, and without another word they ran, Nikolai into the closet, Tanya behind a stack of packing crates.

Misha came in, red-faced, disheveled and breathing hard. He looked wildly around the room, but not carefully, or he would no doubt have realized that something was wrong. He moved straight toward the computer, typed something, and the lights on the transceiver began to blink. Tanya was thinking so hard about how she and Nikolai would retrieve that message, that she only just had time to wonder why the boy was picking up a book on twentieth-century Russian composers at a time like this, before he smashed in the monitor screen with it.

He seemed barely aware of what he was doing. He ripped the front off the processor, and without even unplugging the machine, he began pulling wires out of it. He swore as a shock ran up his arm, then he ripped the power cable from the wall and continued his work. Only when he started pulling memory cards from their sockets did Tanya realized what his purpose was. She leapt out of her hiding place, and Misha froze.

"You almost got away with it," she said, smiling at him. "But you see, you can't fool Solntse. Give me the cards."

Misha only remained frozen for a moment. Then, with a look of hatred and defiance that Tanya would remember until the day she died, he picked up a shard of glass from the broken screen. "I'd rather slit my own throat," he said, backing toward the door. "But first I'd slit yours."

In truth, Misha had little idea of what he was doing. He had bolted from his class in a sudden panic, imagining a situation not unlike the one in which he now found himself. He had had to duck out of sight of a group of officials heading in the direction of Dmitri's classroom, where Anastasia and Aleksei were in their morning lecture, so he knew that no one would come to help him. He was so shocked to find all of his worst fears coming simultaneously to life that Tanya could have overpowered him easily. But she saw only that he would kill her if he could, and perhaps, crazy as he was, he actually could. She hesitated a moment too long. In that moment Misha turned and fled.

On his way to the Dacha, Misha had been careful to appear natural, but he no longer pretended to be anything other than what he was: a terrified child running for his life. He ran as hard as he could toward the cafeteria incinerators, aware that people were following him, no longer able to care. He reached the chute just as their hands closed on his shoulders, and with one last desperate effort, he sent the cards toward the inferno, then sank back, sobbing with relief, into their reaching arms.

6

Stepan had decided to stay in the city until Sifte's escape attempt was resolved one way or the other. To keep him out of trouble while she was gone, Olga had put him to work on the Technology Institute bunker. One morning, while he was repairing weapons taken from Pomoshchniki in recent conflicts, the bunker door burst open. Stepan rose, ready to fight, but when he saw who it was he froze. He looked down at the guns. He'd left a belt of bullets attached to one he had been testing earlier. It was only a few feet away from Andrei, but well out of Stepan's own reach.

Andrei caught his glance, and smiled. "Relax. I'm not here to kill you," he said, a touch of irony in his voice.

"How did you find me?" he asked.

Andrei snorted. "How has no one *else* found you! Imagine going to *that* place, on *that* night. And then to Olga, of all people. I suppose you expected to find sympathy for your cause. The rumors say you found it, too. Are they true?"

"What do you want?" Stepan asked coldly.

Andrei glanced into the hallway, then shut the door. "Listen to me carefully, and don't make a commotion. I don't want anyone else to hear what I have to say." He paused, with a grave look that made Stepan think automatically of Sifte. But Andrei said, "I've just learned that Sasha's in isolation at the Fortress, and we have a chance to get her out."

Stepan couldn't think of words to express what he felt at that moment. Finally, he said the only thing that came to mind: "Who told you this?"

Andrei paused, tilting his head in the familiar gesture that meant that he was about to censor the truth. "A prison doctor. For obvious reasons, he wouldn't tell me his name."

The hope in Stepan's eyes crumbled. "Since when do you trust an official?"

Andrei sighed. "I don't, as a general rule. But I trust this one."

Stepan smiled his deprecation. "I can't believe I'm hearing this from you, of all people."

"Precisely. You know I don't commit to anything unless I'm sure it's legitimate."

Stepan's forehead furrowed. "How can you possibly be sure—"

"Listen to yourself!" Andrei cried, throwing up his hands. "There was a time when you would have given your life for her!" Stepan wouldn't meet Andrei's eyes. "It's Sifte, isn't it," Andrei said. "You've gone ahead with your bloody-minded plan, and you don't want anything to get in its way."

"That's not it!" Stepan cried, then shook his head in confusion, wondering whether he had really come to value Sifte over Sasha.

"Never mind. There are others who will be willing to help."

Stepan looked at him for a long time, then sighed. "You know I'll do it," he said. They were silent for another moment, then Stepan said, "But why the change of heart? I thought the individual didn't matter in your book."

Andrei smiled faintly. "Let's just say a certain knock on the head has changed my view on some things."

Stepan went back to work on the guns. Carefully avoiding Andrei's eyes, he asked, "What did he say about her?"

"She's been in isolation. She won't speak, or eat. She's dying, Stepan."

"She always said that she'd rather die by her own hand than theirs," Stepan said, to himself more than Andrei.

"The idea is that she won't die at all. Be at my place, Sunday morning, eight-hundred hours." Andrei studied Stepan's pinched face, and then said, "She's going to make it."

Stepan didn't answer. He was already lost in self-righteous fury, and this gave Andrei the first true hope he had felt since his conversation with the sad prison doctor.

*

It was a little after ten in the morning when they left Andrei's flat. Three others joined Andrei and Stepan. Svetlana, a farmer's daughter from the Finland border, had only been with the Soviet for two years, but had proven herself as devoted to the cause as anyone. Vasili was a metal worker who as a teenager had heard Sasha speak, and had never looked back. Yuri had joined the Soviet when he was twenty, around the time Stepan had been arrested. He knew the streets and a good deal of the tunnels inside-out.

The sky over Nevskiy was a uniform gunmetal gray that made the buildings look insubstantial, two-dimensional, like a child's cardboard cutout of a city. It was also very cold—the turgid cold that meant snow was coming.

"It'll be warmer in the tunnels," Stepan said to reassure them, but also himself. Cold could slow them too much.

They made their way in a loose group to Vladimirskaya Square, where they scattered to enter the Metro station separately. Stepan waited until the others were inside, then he crossed to the entrance with its crumbling neo-classical façade, startling a flock of mangy pigeons. He watched them arc five feet above the dirty pavement and then settle listlessly again, to resume pecking at nothing. He found this somehow dispiriting, and with a sense of deep foreboding, he entered the station.

Stepan made his way past the dark ticket counters, toward the Soviet-era mosaic of workers on a field in the wall over the defunct escalators. The mosaic had lost most of its colored tiles, leaving a ghost of the picture sketched in plaster and cement with a few incongruous flashes of color. The escalators were crowded with people, and lit only dimly from the fires in the station below. He pushed his way to the bottom, past the old guards' booths, the gaping, glassless fronts of kiosks looted long ago and littered with plaster and gold leaf that had fallen from the ceiling.

Finally he reached the lowest level, and found the others. They passed quickly down the platform toward the tunnel, trying to close their ears to the echoing cries of the sick and starving. At the entrance to the closest train tunnel, two Pomoshchniki were standing guard. Stepan said to Svetlana, "You're on."

Svetlana took something from her pack and left the rest with Stepan, then made her way toward the stairs. Before she could even make it back to Stepan, people near the stairs were wailing as acrid blue smoke filled the station. One of the Pomoshchniki was already running toward the cause of the commotion. The other moved about ten feet away from the tunnel entrance and stopped, straining to detect the cause of the commotion. Yuri knocked him out with the butt of his gun before the man even realized there was anyone behind him.

"Idiot," Stepan said to himself, as he jumped with Svetlana down onto the tracks, and hurried toward the tunnel.

An old man lay on the cusp of its darkness, a broken cup by his withered left hand. It was empty. "I saw an angel," he rasped, as Stepan stepped over his legs. "I saw an angel come down from heaven…he took the dragon and chained him up for a thousand years…"

"What's he saying?" asked Yuri.

"It's from the Christian Bible," Andrei answered. "The Apocalypse."

"Fitting," said Vasili.

"Come on," said Stepan, pressing a coin into the old man's hand and then stepped into the obscurity of the tunnel.

"God go with you," the beggar said, smiling toothlessly after them. Stepan didn't know whether it was the smile or the words that made him shiver.

They made their way past the fork where the train lines had once split and into another tunnel which was taller and narrower. For a while, they moved along with relative ease, using the flood tunnels only to bypass stations. The smell in the tunnels was almost overpowering, and they were filled with fetid water and sludge which in places reached Svetlana's thighs. They moved on this way until they passed the Gorkovskaya station on Petrogradskiy Ostrov. They were inside the walls.

When they reached the turnoff just before the Petrogradskaya station, Stepan looked at his watch. It was one. They were making good time. They entered the flood tunnel, turned on a flashlight, and took a moment to become acclimated. Then they began to move forward, with Yuri leading the way. Movement was harder than it had been in Myortvograd. The tunnels were smaller, the slop in them thigh-deep on Stepan, waist-deep on Svetlana. Nobody spoke.

"Wait," said Yuri after about an hour, jarring them from the watery silence. They all stopped. "We ought to have come to the Kronverkskiy Proliv turn by now."

"Could we have missed it?" Stepan asked.

"I don't think so. I've been watching carefully."

"And this is the only steep curve in this section of the Petrogradskaya tunnels," Svetlana said. "It has to be here."

Stepan sighed. "All right then, let's backtrack, and see if we find anything." They turned around, so that Andrei was in the lead, and pushed back the way they had come. After about ten minutes, Svetlana stopped them.

"Here," she said, and Andrei turned his flashlight on the wall. There had apparently been an opening in the wall once, but it had been bricked over.

"What now?" asked Vasili.

"Yuri, this is your department," Stepan said.

"If we follow the Kronverkskiy Prospekt tunnel the other way," Yuri said, "there should be another entrance to the tunnels under Zayachiy Ostrov."

"What about cutting through the Gorkovskaya station?"

Yuri shook his head. "It's too close to the Fortress. It'll be guarded."

They turned around again, and made their way back up the curved tunnel. They followed Yuri's route, and came to an unexpected fork. Andrei checked his compass, and advised that they follow it to the right. They wove through a series of capillaries, and though Stepan's sense of foreboding was deepening, he made himself trust Yuri's instincts. Finally, they came out into the broader tunnel. It was after three. They stopped briefly for food and water and then continued on their way.

They crossed under the waterway separating Petrogradskiy Ostrov from Kronverkskiy Ostrov, then another which brought them underneath Zayachiy Ostrov, the Fortress' island. There, the sewage thinned out. By the time they reached the tunnels under the cathedral, it was only ankle-deep. It was almost sixteen-hundred hours when they reached the entrance to the Fortress' sublevels. Two hours to spare—Stepan breathed a sigh of relief.

They rested for an hour and a half, then ate and drank more of their food and water, reserving a bottle of water and a loaf of bread for the journey back. There was enough water emerging from gutter drains that they managed to clean off the sewer scum and change into their Pomoshchnik uniforms before they went inside.

"We'd never pass an inspection," Svetlana observed, looking at her mud-caked boots.

"The idea is that we won't have to," Andrei answered.

He shoved the drain-grate aside, crouched down, and negotiated the short tunnel into a store-room in the basement of the prison. Once inside, he stretched his cramped limbs, and cleaned the sewer muck off his boots with a rag. The rest of them did the same, then Stepan looked into the corridor outside. It was lit like an inquisition room, but there was no one in sight. He ducked back into the storeroom, heart racing and throat tightening with anticipation.

"Are you ready?" They all answered in the affirmative. He turned and left the room before they could see his agitation.

There were no guards along the first part of the corridor. They stopped before the surveillance station and Andrei went inside. Two low-ranking Pomoshchniki, jackets unbuttoned, were playing cards at a table. A half-empty bottle of vodka stood between them. They looked up at the unforgiving face in the doorway through a haze of cigarette smoke, then scrambled to their feet to salute him.

"You are wanted at Stock Station B," Andrei told them. "Immediately."

"But sir—" one of them began.

"Who will watch the screens?" the other finished for him.

"You didn't seem to be particularly concerned with surveillance a minute ago," Andrei answered sternly. "I'll take care of it. You are to unload all of the boxes onto the shelves. Don't show your faces again until the job is finished. I suggest you take your orders without further argument, or I will be forced to report your negligence."

"Yes, sir," the first guard groveled.

"We're going now, sir," said the other. As he was passing through the doorway, though, he looked down at the residue of muck on Andrei's boots. "Trouble in the tunnels, sir?" he asked.

Andrei barked, "What do you know about that?"

The guard shook his head in deference. "Nothing, sir— I'd only heard that there were rats in the tunnels again." His broad face broke into a grin. "The red kind."

"We've examined the surrounding area. There's nothing down there but the product of silly imaginations like yours. Now get to your new post."

The guard wasted no more time. When he was gone, the others joined Andrei.

"Yuri, start the loop, then catch up with us," Stepan said, then hurried toward the stairs.

The sublevels in Solntse's prisons were populated hierarchically, with those prisoners he considered the most dangerous closest to the top. As a result, the guards here were more alert.

"You are both wanted in Medic for a difficult transport," Andrei told the two Pomoshchniki keeping watch on the stair landing.

"But sir, we have orders not to leave our post unattended tonight for any reason—"

"That's why we're here," Andrei replied coldly.

"I never had a message from Akhunin, there must be a mistake—"

"There is no mistake. Should I report you both?"

"Come on," the guard said grudgingly to his companion, who left them with a hostile look. As soon as they were out of sight, Stepan, Vasili and Svetlana followed Andrei up to the first sublevel. Just before they reached the top of the stairs, Yuri caught up with them.

The guards at the next landing insisted on verifying Andrei's order. Stepan shot the first as he was reaching for his radio, and Andrei killed the other before it dawned on him what was happening. Svetlana took their weapons, and Vasili and Yuri dragged the bodies down to a second sublevel storage room, then ran back to join the others. It was seventeen-fifty.

Yuri and Vasili moved to the end of the corridor, Stepan and Andrei to the middle, and Svetlana took her position in the stair landing. At seventeen fifty-three, two Pomoshchniki appeared at the turn of the hall. At seventeen-fifty-five, Yuri and Vasili opened the transport doors. At exactly eighteen-hundred hours, the doors of the transport elevator opened, and the seven guards disembarked with their prisoner.

Yuri and Vasili began speaking with them, telling them that there had been a change of plans. Svetlana held her breath, trying to keep her hands from shaking. Andrei and Stepan strained for a glimpse of Sasha, but it wasn't until the escorting guards pushed by Vasili and Yuri that they could see anything. For a moment, Stepan's heart stopped, then it pounded with a rage more terrible than any he'd felt.

Sasha's hair was cut close to her head. A bare patch on the right side marked a large scar, still red enough to have been recently acquired. Her tattered gray shift hid a body that was little more than a skin-covered skeleton. Bruises showed deep brownish-purple on her yellow, desiccated skin, like the rings under her eyes. The eyes themselves were the worst: they were open but unseeing, like the eyes of the people dying in the Myortvograd gutters. Stepan looked at Andrei and saw his own chalky face, clenched in horror and anger, and at that moment he forgot Sifte, vowing to die before he let them touch Sasha again.

Yuri and Vasili were arguing with the guards now, but they continued to move closer to the part of the corridor where the others waited. While Stepan fought to control his rage, Svetlana crouched down further into the shadows of the landing, finding a guard in her gun sight. She had never killed anyone at close range before, but when she looked at the ravaged husk of the woman from the pamphlet pictures, she felt she could have killed them with her bare hands.

Then she noticed something odd. The guard talking to Yuri seemed to be listening to something that the rest of them could not hear. His eyes narrowed, and he turned toward the door they had just come through, his hand half-raised to the back of his neck, from which something dark protruded. Then he was turning back to Yuri, raising his gun.

Faster than Svetlana could think the two shots were off, the two guards falling to the floor. At the turn of the corridor, the other two fell. The guards by Sasha looked around in confusion, and began firing randomly. Sasha lifted her head as the bullets flew around her, shattering into walls, ringing against the metal stairway, but her eyes remained vacant. A bullet drove into Svetlana's shoulder. She felt the bone shatter, and blood spread out across the navy wool of her jacket. Two more guards fell, and then Stepan and Andrei were out of their hiding places. Sasha's eyes locked on the figure of Stepan. She clenched her fists, closed her eyes and screamed.

All at once, the gunfire stopped. The one Pomoshchnik left alive was out of ammunition, and he turned and fled down the corridor. Vasili and Yuri had both fallen, Andrei's leg was bleeding, as was Stepan's arm. He didn't appear to notice. He was bent over Sasha's still form, but Andrei was shaking him.

"Come on!" he cried. "Stepan, there isn't a mark on her, it's just shock. We have to get out before that guard sends in the 'kuni!"

Stepan scooped up Sasha's tiny body and the two men fled to the landing. As Andrei checked Yuri and Vasili, he caught sight of Svetlana lying in the corner. "Get up!" he cried, pulling her to her feet.

"I'm hurt…" she began, indicating the pool of blood.

"You can die just as well in the tunnels, but you can't stay here to lead them to us. Come on!" He hauled her toward the stairs.

"Wait! The guard—his neck—listen!" She managed to grab the stair railing with her good hand, and held fast. Somewhere, a siren began to wail. Andrei glared at her. "That guard—look at his neck! *Do it!*"

Andrei looked at her a moment longer, then ran back to the guard she had indicated, turned him over. Again, Svetlana saw the dark thing at the base of his skull. Andrei wrenched it free, then ran back to her and pulled her down the stairs after him.

"What is it?" she gasped.

"My worst nightmare," he answered through gritted teeth.

They fled to the lowest sublevel, where Stepan had been cornered by the two surveillance guards they'd sent away. One was holding the disk with the video loop.

"So you think we're stupid, huh?" he said, glaring at them with bloodshot eyes.

"There's no shipment at Stock Station B," the other added.

"Out of the way!" Stepan snarled, hitting him across the back of the head with the butt of his gun and his one free arm. Andrei shot the other as he drew his weapon.

"That's the end of my ammunition," he said.

"Take their guns," Stepan answered. Andrei grabbed the guards' weapons, then ran after Stepan and Svetlana, who were already in the storeroom. He shoved back the grate, pushed Svetlana into the tunnel, helped Stepan inside with Sasha's still body, and then climbed in himself. He pulled the grate closed, just in time to hear the first officials reach the bottom of the stairway.

"Go!" he whispered harshly, pushing the others ahead of him. Svetlana was crying silently, but she went. Stepan didn't seem to notice the blood pouring from his cut arm; he cradled Sasha against his shoulder like a baby.

Behind them came echoing voices: "They're in the tunnels—get the gas!"

They pushed themselves faster, moving toward Gorkovskaya station. There was no point in backtracking to Petrogradskaya, since all the stations would be heavily guarded now, and without Yuri they couldn't find an alternate route quickly. They soon lost the voices of their pursuers, and after another half-hour they stopped to rest. Andrei passed the water bottle around, and turned on the flashlight to assess their wounds.

"Jesus," Stepan said when he saw Sasha's face. Her eyes were open, but staring straight ahead, with pupils like ice holes in a winter pond.

"She's catatonic," Andrei said grimly. "We've got to get her out of here—not to mention the rest of us. Let's get moving."

"Wait," Svetlana said. She had torn her blouse into strips with her teeth and one working hand. "You need something for your leg."

Andrei looked down at the dark gash in his right leg. He had forgotten about it, but Svetlana was right: he would bleed to death quickly wading in thigh-high sewage. She poured a little water onto one of the rags and cleaned the cut as well as she could, then helped him bandage it. She did the same for Stepan's arm.

When she was finished, Andrei looked at the clammy pallor of her skin, the tight set of her jaw. He could not believe that the girl had gone so long without complaining. "Sit," he said, and peeling the clothing away from her own wound, he began to clean it. For a moment he thought she would faint from the pain, then she pulled herself together.

"What was it?" she asked. "The thing in his neck?"

Andrei took it out of his pocket and put it into her good hand. Stepan bent to look at it too. It was a small, black plastic box, with what looked like a neural plug attached to it.

"It looks to me like a transceiver."

"Does that mean—" Stepan began.

"Any number of potential disasters," Andrei snapped, "and right now it's the least of our worries." He pocketed it again, then tied a sling for Svetlana's injured arm, and bound it to her chest. "Can you go on?" he asked.

"Is there a choice?" she replied, and to her surprise, he smiled.

"You'll be a fine leader, if we make it out of here," he told her.

Her mouth set grimly, and she didn't reply. They set off again into the dark.

Time dispersed. It was like being in prison, Stepan thought. There was no day or night, nothing to mark the passing hours. Only his wrist watch kept time in any kind of perspective.

Near twenty-two-hundred hours, Andrei stopped them again. He raised his head, turning in a slow circle. "Do you smell that?" he asked.

"Tear gas," said Stepan.

"But faint," Andrei answered. "Either they've been here already, or it's coming from Gorkovskaya. If it's in the station—"

"Let's hope it's not," Stepan finished.

343

They continued on, and the smell of gas grew stronger the closer they came to the station. By the time they were near enough to make out the dim lights of the train tunnel they could barely breathe. Svetlana began to stumble.

"I'm the least injured," Stepan said. "I'll see what's going on. Take Sasha back to the last turn and stay there. If I'm not back in fifteen minutes, find a different route, and go on without me."

Stepan expected Andrei to argue, but he only nodded and took Sasha. When they were out of sight, Stepan covered his face with a piece of his bandage and moved toward the station.

A few meters from the entrance, he tripped over something. It took a moment for him to register what it was, but when he did, he sprang away in disgust. Lying across the passage was the body of the old man who had spoken to them when they entered the tunnel at Vladimirskaya. There was a bullet wound in his chest, and his right hand was open, palm up, showing the tail side of the coin Stepan had given him, stamped with Solntse's seven-rayed sun. He stepped over the dead man, wondering how the body had come to be so far from Myortvograd, intrigued now despite their desperate situation. Slowly, he approached the entrance to the station.

Several voices carried out into the tunnel. One of them was saying, "Now clear the bodies to the sides…there's plenty of work here. By The Sun, if that guard weren't already dead, I'd wring his neck!"

"Imagine leaving the tunnel unguarded," someone answered, "and for a smoke bomb too—such an old trick!"

"We could have had a riot on our hands. I've never heard of so many getting through before."

"What about the ones who broke into the prison?"

344

Derisive laughter. "What about them? They're rats in a trap. Fyodor 16! Look sharp! The work's just begun…"

The officials moved away. Stepan inched closer to the mouth of the tunnel, and the station opened before his view. The platform was littered with sub-race corpses. Yet terrible as the slaughter was, their exodus from Myortvograd was a triumph over Solntse, and it revived Stepan's flagging spirits.

However, the station was also overrun with Pomoshchniki. An armed sentry passed in front of the tunnel entrance, and Stepan ducked back into the shadows. He retreated along the passage until he found Andrei, Svetlana and Sasha. Sasha was still motionless, Svetlana was gray, and even Andrei's face was beginning to tell the pain of his injuries. Stepan wished he had better news.

"It's chaos," he said. "That smoke bomb we set off—the guard left his post too long, a whole slew of people from the station got through to Gorkovskaya. They're all dead. The station's full of officials."

Svetlana shut her eyes, and Andrei sighed heavily.

"I overheard them talking," Stepan continued. "All the train tunnels are guarded, and they're going into the tunnels soon if we don't come out. We have to find another way."

"They'll be patrolling the streets too," said Andrei.

"In Solntsegrad, yes," Stepan agreed.

"You don't think they'll look in Myortvograd?" Svetlana inquired.

"Not yet. They assume our only way across the river is the tunnels."

"Is there another way?" Svetlana asked, leaning back against the slimy wall with resignation.

"There is one possibility," Stepan said. "Though not a great one."

"It's probably the only one." Svetlana's eyes were on the stagnant water around her feet.

Stepan looked at Andrei. "It's been a cold autumn. How solidly do you think the river's frozen?"

"The water down here isn't frozen."

"But remember, it's warmer down here."

"The Vyborgside people haven't moved onto the ice yet," Andrei said doubtfully. "That's usually the best indicator."

Stepan frowned. "It takes thicker ice to hold a camp than a few moving people. But if you have a better idea—"

"No," Andrei answered, his face sharp and shadowed in the thin light. "And if we're going to try it, we've got to go now. The river is narrowest at the south end of Vyborgskaya Storona. It's also far enough away from Petrogradskaya that they might not be looking there yet. If we can get there through the flood tunnels, we might make it."

Stepan's mind was too numb to imagine the many pitfalls that could undermine this plan, and Svetlana was beyond caring what happened to her, as long as it meant an end to the grinding pain. So they started off again, Stepan carrying Sasha once more. This time they relied entirely on the compass for guidance through darkness pierced only intermittently by the pallid flashlight beam.

Finally they reached what Andrei thought was the right spot. He raised a sewer cap, and a shower of white powder drifted down around them. "Snow," Svetlana said, like someone dreaming.

They climbed out onto a wide, deserted street: the Arsenalnaya, outside the Solntsegrad wall. This part of the city did not belong entirely to Solntse, but it was patrolled frequently by the Pomoshchniki. Stepan thought that it was odd that the street should be so deserted, but there was no time to consider the implications.

The snow-covered Neva was impossible to read. Andrei stepped out onto the ice first, then ran out about ten feet. It held. Svetlana and then Stepan, drooping now with Sasha's weight and his own leaking blood, followed him out onto the frozen river. All at once a floodlight came on, flickered over them.

"They're crossing the river!" a distant voice cried.

They began to run. Stepan was aware of footsteps following them, and at the same time he heard the guttural report of shifting ice. Oh, dear God...he began, but could not recall any prayers, so he kept repeating the three words over and over in his mind. Bullets whizzed by his head, and he could hear the breath of the man pursuing him. The ice groaned and creaked. The opposite bank was near, and Stepan looked not at the breaking ice or Sasha's blank face, but at the thousand flickering fires of Myortvograd, which he had never thought could look so welcoming. As he reached the shore, the ice behind him gave way. The pursuing Pomoshchniki slipped and fell and were swallowed by the snowy river.

Andrei and Svetlana were already limping into the shadows when Stepan reached the embankment steps. He stopped long enough to fire at the few Pomoshchniki who had managed to find their footing again. Then he turned and followed Andrei's dragging footprints. He did not stop running until he was safe underground in the new bunker, twenty hours after they had left.

347

7

The officials took them to a small, bare, Maroon Level room, and seated them in a row of chairs against the far wall. None of them spoke or looked at each other. One of the Pomoshchniki sat down in an empty chair. The other beckoned to Aleksei, who got up and followed him, still without a word.

The Pomoshchnik led Aleksei to the room next door, but stayed outside when he entered. It was a long room, with a window which gaped blackly at him from the far wall. When Aleksei looked at it, the circling vultures of panic threatened to land. Instead, he looked at the people in front of it. Dmitri was there, sad and bespectacled, and Gospazha Alla, with a sourly triumphant smile tugging at her crepe-skinned face. Between them was a woman in a gray Opyekun's uniform.

Dmitri indicated to Aleksei that he was to sit facing them, across from the Opyekun. Something in the quality of the light, or perhaps of the officials' expressions, suddenly made him feel more angry than frightened. He glared at their jackal's faces.

"Aleksei," Alla said in a thin, curt voice, "this is Opyekun Natalya Apraksina." She nodded at the female official.

Despite himself, Aleksei looked at the Opyekun with interest. This was the first time he had seen one in person, other than Alla. Apraksina looked back at him with gray-blue eyes which were surprisingly free of the hostile suspicion he saw in Alla's, but which were also devoid of any other emotion. Her hair was gray, her face finely lined, but with an ageless quality that Alla's lacked. For the first time, it struck Aleksei as odd that he and his peers had never had any contact with the officials whose ranks they were destined to join.

"We have no reason at this time to suspect you of any serious transgression," Alla said. The words sounded flat and rehearsed, and Aleksei wished that she could at least have the decency to tell him the truth. "However, as you were one of Sifte's closest friends, you will understand why we must question you now."

Aleksei nodded. Alla studied him for a moment with obvious disapproval, and then said, "Very well. How long have you been friends with Sifte?"

"Who can say when friendship starts?"

Dmitri nodded slightly, but avoided Aleksei's eyes. Despite this, the tiny encouragement of the nod revived the boy's sinking heart. The Opyekun began to take notes on a hand-held screen bearing Solntse's insignia on the back.

"Would you say that she is your best friend?" Alla continued.

"Among my best."

"Did your relationship with Sifte ever take on a more… intimate character?"

Though her voice remained steady, Alla's eyes flickered away as she asked this. Aleksei's remained steadfast, boring into her like core-cutters. "Are you asking whether I've slept with her or whether I love her?"

Apraksina's lips twitched upward for a moment. Aleksei noticed this, and found to his surprise that he felt not hatred for her, but a grudging kind of respect.

"Which do you think more pertinent to the situation at hand?" Alla snapped.

"I don't see how either is especially pertinent to Sifte leaving."

"One tells things to a lover she might not tell a friend."

Aleksei sighed. "I never slept with Sifte, and I didn't know she was going to leave."

"You must have had *some* idea of what she was thinking."

Aleksei looked at her; she wouldn't meet his eyes. "I often wished I did."

Alla regarded him for a moment with deepening scorn before she continued, "Aleksei, we are not as rigid as you probably think. We've known for years that you and your friends are working outside the Institute's standard codes and practices. We let you carry on in this assumption of intellectual and moral superiority because we recognize that original thought can be a strength in a budding Opyekun."

Out of the corner of his eye, Aleksei caught Dmitri's derisive half-smile. He wondered how long his teacher had been shielding them from Alla's suspicion, and how many of his liberal words she had co-opted. He felt both pity and gratitude for Dmitri at that moment, and realized with shame how much they had taken his support for granted.

"Now I see that we ought to have stopped these activities long ago," Alla concluded.

"Activities?" Aleksei repeated absently.

Alla pursed her parchment lips, aware and irritated that she didn't have Aleksei's full attention. "Call them tendencies, if you'd rather, for the moment. How well do you know your *Republic*?"

Aleksei stifled a smile, thinking of Misha. "Fairly well."

"'The mind must, while it is still young, remain quite without experience of or contact with bad characters, if its condition is to be truly good and its judgments just'," she quoted, as if it were an indictment. "'This is why people of good character seem simple when they are young, and are easily taken in by dishonesty—because they have nothing corresponding in themselves to give them a sympathetic understanding of wickedness.'"

She appeared to consider this a question. Aleksei said, "Book three, section two."

"That's all you have to say?" she asked, as if his answer had been a considered insult.

"I'm not sure I understand what you wanted me to say."

"You and your friends were never simple," she snapped, "which points to some inevitable conclusions."

"Just because we're hard to figure out doesn't mean we've done anything wrong."

"You are exclusive and secretive, which suggests you have something to hide."

He looked back at her steadily. "You'd be secretive too, if you'd spent your life defending yourself against people looking to fight you because you're sick, or your skin's a different color, or you're just plain smarter than they'll ever be."

Alla's eyes flinched from his. "You spend quite a bit of time, presumably together, away from the main rooms of the school."

"How can you say that?"

Alla smiled and flicked a switch on the wall behind her. The lights in the room went off. All at once, Aleksei's assurance vanished. The darkness of the glass behind the adults was dissolving to reveal a picture-window which looked into the newsroom.

"'We must watch them closely from their earliest years'," he said, with a bitter smile that resembled Nikolai's uncannily.

"Indeed," Alla answered. "You see, every child who makes it here is genetically capable of becoming an Opyekun…but there's far more to being a Guardian than gold in the soul. This is how we are able to determine who is fit, and who is not. We have watched you and your friends carefully: first, because you were so very promising, later because we saw that there was something more to your friendship than the usual bonds among Institute children. Something which suggests that you have been misled, or forgotten your duties?"

Aleksei didn't answer, and after a moment, she continued, "We know about your secret room and your computer. We are aware that you know quite a bit more about many things than you let us see. Believe me, things will go better for you if you tell us all of it now." Alla flicked the switch again, and as the room brightened, the glass darkened.

Aleksei smiled, and there was no trace of bitterness left in it, nor was there any hope. "Do you really not know why she left?"

"Aleksei," Dmitri said, precluding Alla's retort, "you have to understand the position Sifte has put herself in, not to mention all of you, by running away. We aren't accusing you of having a part in it, but she has committed an act of treason. If there is anything at all that you can tell us to help us find her, please do so, for her sake as well as your own."

"You're right," he said to Alla, rather than Dmitri. "I loved Sifte. And in one way or another, I know she loved me. Why would she have told me where she was going, knowing that I'd end up here?"

Alla and Apraksina exchanged exasperated looks; Dmitri never took his eyes from Aleksei's. Finally, Alla stood up, and opened the door. "Take him down," she said to the Pomoshchnik standing outside, "and bring in the next one."

"Dmitri—" Aleksei began.

"It's beyond me," Dmitri answered, with a voice like a sinking ship. Aleksei looked at him for a stricken, speechless moment before the Pomoshchnik led him out. At that moment, the last living piece of Dmitri's heart died.

*

When Aleksei was gone, Apraksina turned to Alla. "You shouldn't have shown him the window so soon. Now he distrusts us."

"We gave him no reason to," Alla said. "He must have something to fear."

"Haven't we given him a reason?" Dmitri demanded.

"What, then?" snapped Alla.

"Weren't you listening to him?"

Her look was coldly incredulous. "You think that they would turn against us just because the other children called them names?"

Dmitri took off his glasses, revealing vehement eyes in a gray, sagging face. "Have you forgotten that they *are* children? All children have a breaking point."

"Are you implying that it's my fault that this has happened?"

"That's enough," Apraksina interjected, unruffled, almost laconic. "Ethical arguments are irrelevant at this point. We know that Sifte Pierson is gone, and that her father must be behind it. We must assume that she and her friends know about him, and perhaps know of our plans for them, and that they don't approve of them—in which case, the ones left behind are ticking time bombs. We must defuse them before it's too late."

"What are you suggesting?" Dmitri asked numbly.

Apraksina shrugged. "Trying them for treason, to begin with."

"There's no evidence of treason!"

Alla's smile was a caricature of benevolence. "There will be soon."

Dmitri wondered what new trust or innocence she had betrayed to achieve her ends; but whatever treachery was yet to come, it could be no worse than his own. He wondered now how he could he ever have thought to subvert Solntse's plans with contraband books, cunningly chosen quotations. He had only taught the children to hope for an impossible redemption. Realizing the vastness of his own failure, he also realized, at last, a despairing kind of peace.

"Who's next?" asked Apraksina.

"Anastasia Malinowskaya," Alla replied, looking down at the screen in front of her.

"Not the daughter of the advisor?"

"She was born only a year before he died. I knew him in his youth. He was a brilliant man, a great Opyekun. She's like him, a spitfire. We had the highest hopes for her—"

The door burst open, cutting Alla off in mid-sentence.

"Let me go!" Anastasia spat. Her hair had come loose from its pony-tail, and it whirled like Medusa's snakes as she wrenched free of the Pomoshchnik's grip. Dmitri couldn't look her fierce, doomed bravery in the eye; instead he looked at his screen.

The Pomoshchnik put three disks on the table in front of Apraksina. "We found these on her. They aren't standard issue, so—"

"Thank you, you did well," Apraksina interrupted.

Anastasia's eyes had seized on her teacher. Dmitri finally raised his own to meet them, and then wished he hadn't. Underneath the outraged defiance was pure terror. He had never known Anastasia to be afraid of anything.

"Dmitri," she asked, "what's this all about?"

"Sit down, Nastya," he answered gently. "We'll explain everything."

8

Sifte awakened certain that something was wrong. She reached out to the place where Vanya had been sitting when she fell asleep. His coat was still spread out on the hay, but it was empty and cold. She thought that she remembered him lighting a lantern, but the darkness now was complete.

She lay still, listening. The wind keened around the barn, whistling through knotholes in the old wood and chinks where the boards weren't quite flush. Besides this and her own shallow breathing, Sifte heard nothing. She was beginning to wonder where Vanya could possibly be, when she heard a distinct thud, nearby and to the right, as if something heavy had knocked against one of the outside walls. It was followed by a man's muffled cry, and then a single gunshot. Sifte swallowed against a dry throat.

Sifte took the gun out of her waistband, then sat up with her back to the wall, her eyes straining into the compact darkness. A moment later the barn door creaked open with a blast of frigid air and snow. She saw a figure silhouetted against the vague light of the stormy sky: a man, with the neat lines of an official in uniform. He was carrying a rifle.

He shut the door behind him, and the barn retreated into darkness which seemed all the more impervious after its brief reprieve. Sifte pulled her knees up and rested the gun between them to stop her hands from shaking, wondering why she was so much more frightened now than she had been when she faced the Opyekuni on the boat. She didn't move and barely breathed, focusing on the senses that would help her locate her stalker in the darkness. It seemed she waited for hours like that. And then, a few feet to her right, she heard the unmistakable sound of a safety catch being released.

A Pomoshchnik. No Opyekun would have come into the barn with his gun's safety still on. Her confidence returning in a flood, Sifte ducked and dived towards his ankles, toppling him as he aimed and fired at the space where her forehead should have been. As he scrambled for his gun, she pinned his arms with her knees, pulled off his bulletproof helmet, put her gun to his temple and fired.

Sifte waited for the dislocated horror she had felt that morning to return, but Vanya had been right: she felt only vague disgust at kneeling on a dead body. Clumsily, she stood and backed away from the dead Pomoshchnik, and then a hard arm closed around her throat, while another pinned her arms to her sides and pulled her backward into a short, stocky body.

For a moment, Sifte panicked, and fought against a strength she couldn't hope to master. Then she realized that though this second Pomoshchnik had her immobilized, he held no weapon against her. In fact, he was speaking to her. She slackened her body and listened carefully.

"Institute 1 doesn't leave much meat on your bones, does it?" He laughed. "Still, you're not bad. Lemkov was a fool to try to kill you before getting the most out of you."

The brutal detachment that had taken possession of Sifte that morning closed over her like a skin of ice. It was so complete that she found herself calmly assessing the ways the man could have discovered what she looked like, as she wrenched sideways and toppled both of them to the ground. She kicked the gun out of his hand, still gripping her own tightly. He caught her arm and tried to pry it from her fingers, then, when he found that he couldn't, he twisted her arm behind her. Sifte felt the pain, but it didn't reach her mind or cloud her thinking. Concentrating on the feel of the metal in her hand, she waited for the precise moment when it slipped away, and then, with a massive thrust, rolled on top of it and the Pomoshchnik's arm.

He lost his balance and his grip on Sifte's weapon, but only for a moment. Then he was back on top of her, trying to turn her over. She didn't like presenting him with her more vulnerable front, and the gun dug into her spine, but she couldn't let him have the gun. Once again, she shunted the pain to an annex of her mind, and fought to maintain her position.

The Pomoshchnik was trying to pin her legs with his knees. He was heavier than she was, and stronger, but Sifte had the advantage of better and more recent combat training. She began to lessen her struggle by increments, to give him the impression that she was tiring, until she lay still underneath him, breathing hard.

"That's better," the man said, with the same unpleasant laugh. Sifte waited until he shifted his weight to try to turn her over, then kicked hard into his groin. He fell to the side in shock and pain.

"Izmyennitsa bitch!" he cried.

"Born, raised and trained," she said as she stood up, grabbed her gun and looked for the door. She had been close to the back wall when the Pomoshchnik caught her. Choosing the direction that felt the most like empty space, she ran. Within a few feet, though, she stumbled over something on the floor and fell, dropping her gun and jarring her injured arm as she hit the ground. It was the body of the other Pomoshchnik, and the assertions of pain from the one still living had ominously ceased.

As panic and pain began to eat away at her composure, Sifte felt desperately for her weapon. Her hand lighted on the face of the dead official, and she was about to jerk it away, when she realized that his eyes were covered with something hard. All at once, she knew how the other Pomoshchnik had known what she looked like, and that only a crumbling stable wall had saved her from being killed by him.

Sifte tore the goggles off of the body and pulled them on. Sifte's only experience of infrared goggles had been in Cave or target-practice simulations. The real ones worked better. Looking out through a crack in the wall, she saw the living Pomoshchnik's swirling mass of colored light and shadow approaching her purposefully. He had found his gun.

Sifte was hidden by the half-wall of the empty stall, but only for a moment longer. Looking around again she located her gun, still glowing faintly with the residual heat of her hand. She picked it up, leaned around the wall, and fired twice at the Pomoshchnik. He fell, screaming. Sifte was far from impressed by this lack of discipline. She came out from behind the wall and shot him a final time.

Only then did she realize how badly her hands were shaking and how much her right arm hurt. She slumped against the wall that had saved her several times that night, breathing deeply for a few minutes until the shaking stopped. Then she felt her right arm and hand carefully. The last of her fighting detachment had left her, and the pain was sharp. She couldn't feel any broken bones, however, and decided that it must be a sprain. It was bad, but not bad enough to stop her.

Sifte stood up, pulled on her damp coat and boots and made her way toward the door. Outside there was only the blank gray of snowy ground and sky still thick with storm. A few hundred feet away, a snowmobile was parked. Two sets of footprints led away from it, splitting as one moved into the barn and the other around it, already indistinct with new snow.

When she found Vanya on the far side of the barn, with his hands tied behind him and a bullet hole in his left temple, the adrenaline-charged courage left her. She slumped down beside him. For a long time she watched the snow pile around his body, her mind and heart too overloaded to think or feel much but a deep, dull sadness.

After a time, Sifte realized that she was growing cold, and that this was as dangerous as the possibility of more Pomoshchniki arriving. Unfolding her bruised and now stiffened limbs, she dragged Vanya's body into the barn with her good arm and laid him on his coat. Through the goggles, he was the same dull red as the walls and floor and hay. She pushed the goggles away from her eyes, then leaned back against the half-wall in blessed darkness, to decide what she ought to do next.

Vanya hadn't told her anything about the farm—more to the point, whether its people would be the type to report dead officials, or quietly dump them in the nearest river. She had to assume that if he had known them to be sympathizers he would have taken her to the farmhouse instead of the barn. So, she couldn't afford to leave Vanya and the Pomoshchniki in plain sight. Sifte knew that she couldn't bury the bodies in the frozen ground, even if she'd had the strength to wield a shovel. Then she slipped the goggles back over her eyes, and realized that she had been staring at the solution all along.

There was enough fuel in the lantern for her purposes. She searched the pockets of Vanya's coat, and then, gingerly, those of his inner clothing. Finally, she found a book of matches. The first expired in a draft from the door she had left ajar. Cursing, Sifte moved into the shelter of the stall, and this time she got the wick to take the flame. She turned it up until it was glowing brightly, and pushed back her goggles again, blinking with relief at the natural light.

More than anything, Sifte wanted to tip the lantern and run, but first she took Vanya's compass, and searched the pockets of both Pomoshchniki until she located a set of keys. She untied Vanya's hands, threw away the rope, and placed his gun in the right one. She also replaced the weapons of the Pomoshchniki, and arranged the three bodies to make it look like they had killed one another in a stand-off. Then, bending first to kiss Vanya's cold cheek, she broke the lantern's globe, and held the flame to the pile of straw on which he lay.

She didn't have much trouble figuring out how to start and control the snowmobile, since both Cave and target practice had simulated them. She found that the Pomoshchniki had left behind a bag containing cheese and bread, an insulated bottle half-full of tea, and another bottle which contained a strong-smelling clear liquid. She knew that this must be the vodka they had all heard about at Institute 1, but had never been permitted to try. Sifte tipped the bottle to her lips, and nearly choked on the fiery liquid. She put the bottle back in the bag.

Turning her attention to the snowmobile again, she started it up, and followed its original tracks to the strip of forest she and Vanya had walked through earlier. Once inside the trees, she stopped and looked at the compass. Vanya had pointed out Vasilovo on a map on the boat. Unfortunately, he had not brought the map with him. Since they had not landed in Zelenogorsk as they had planned, Sifte had no idea where they were now relative to the village she was trying to reach. The most she knew was that they had headed east from where they had landed. Vasilovo would be further east still, and probably some distance north. Taking a deep breath of the sharp, lucid air, she started the snowmobile, and set off east.

Several kilometers from the woods, Sifte stumbled across a road. It ran north-south, and after following it north for a few kilometers, she came across a sign that pointed her in the direction of the village. She kept off the road as much as possible, not knowing how frequently it was traveled or by whom, but she always kept it in sight. Her spirits were beginning to lift, and she actually thought she might reach the relative safety of the inn by morning, when she saw the bobbing lights of vehicles on the road ahead.

The road was lined by a row of spindly birches. Sifte ducked behind these and cut the motor on her snowmobile. A few minutes later, four jeeps with the sun insignia on their doors passed above her. The spray of snow they sent into the trees drove into her face like needles.

When they had passed she tried to start the snowmobile again, but the engine spluttered and refused to catch. It took her fogged mind several minutes to realize the obvious: it was out of fuel. Sighing, she got back down and began to kick snow over the snowmobile. In a few minutes, it was lost from sight. Then she set off on foot.

Sifte had thought she was tired before, but she had soon passed what she would once have called the threshold of her endurance. The one apparent blessing of cold and exhaustion was that she barely felt the pain of her sprained wrist anymore. When, after about an hour, the sky began to grow lighter, Sifte wondered if she were entering the first stages of hypothermia, not knowing that she had already passed them. Then she looked at the watch, and saw that it was nine-hundred hours. Her second dawn.

Moments later, another convoy of sun-emblazoned jeeps sped along the road, heading south. With a cold despondency growing in her guts, Sifte plodded onward. But when Vasilovo finally came into view, the cold inside her froze solid. The village was crawling with officials, and though their shapes were still indistinct in the dim, old-lace snow light, some of the uniforms were gray. Opyekuni.

Sifte slid back against a tree trunk, as desolate as she had been in the two most desolate days of her life. Her tears were freezing in her eyelashes, but she was too cold and tired to care. She slid into the snow, until she was lying flat, looking up at the snowflakes falling towards her. They burned into the slits of her eyes; she closed them.

Warmth unfurled in her limbs as sleep wrapped insidious arms around her. She met it like a lover. She couldn't remember a softer bed than the snow where she now lay, nor any desire more tempting than her present one for oblivion. And then, just as it was about to take her, the picture of Vanya's face—still and pale, with the scorched thumbprint of blood at the temple—slid into her head. She jerked awake, and was teetering on her numb feet before she could think how she had managed to stand.

The creeping drowse was still fighting to claim her. Trying to think clearly, she removed the small pack she carried and opened the bottle of tea. It was as cold as she was. With tears leaking again from eyes still half-sealed with ice, she rummaged in the pack for anything she had overlooked, anything that might save her; but her hand only closed on the bottle of terrible clear liquid.

With nothing else left to try, Sifte tipped the bottle to her lips and swallowed. The stuff still tasted atrocious, but the very burning awfulness of it startled her out of the deadly drowse. She made herself swallow one more mouthful, waited to make certain that she wasn't going to throw it back up, then replaced the bottle in the pack and turned again towards Vasilovo.

Making herself take the first few steps was the hardest thing she had ever done. Then she began to feel better. In fact, she felt a good deal better than she had in hours. The fire from the bottle had settled in her stomach, and seemed to be working its way out into her limbs, driving back the false warmth of hypothermia and bringing some real heat back to them. More than that, the pain of her injuries seemed not quite so bad, and her situation no longer felt entirely hopeless. Perhaps, she thought, there was merit in vodka after all.

Vasilovo was surrounded by a black rim of pine forest. Under this cover, with its shallower snow drifts, Sifte found herself a third of the way around the town's perimeter within half an hour. By that time, the storm seemed to be lessening. She stopped again to assess her situation. Though she felt better, she knew that she would have to find shelter and warmth soon, or she wouldn't be able to stop herself lying down in a snowdrift again.

She couldn't see many Pomoshchniki at this end of town, but she didn't know whether this was a good or a bad sign. Sifte was no longer convinced that she would find safety at the inn even if she could locate it. She was at a loss until she gained the top of a small hill, and saw, not a half kilometer away in the trees, the tarnished onion domes of what must once have been a pretty church.

Solntse's followers avoided churches and other places where the old religions had been practiced as meticulously as devotees had once attended them. This wasn't a guarantee that they wouldn't search it, but it was a less likely target than anywhere else Sifte had seen. She made her way towards it as fast as she could, checked to make sure no one was watching, then climbed in through a broken window at the back.

Perhaps she should have realized that in a town with a Soviet refuge, others might have cause to flee an invasion of officials. But Sifte had never been as mentally and physically taxed as she was at that moment. The row of thin, suspicious faces she met when she turned from the window was one shock too many for her depleted body and mind. For a fraction of a moment, Sifte found it in herself to be appalled at what she was about to do. Then, she fainted.

9

The Pomoshchnik put blinders on Aleksei and led him to an elevator. They rode down several floors, walked a short distance, and then entered another elevator. This one sank past the point where the building should have ended, and disgorged them into an echoing hallway. The Pomoshchnik opened a door, pushed Aleksei through it, and took off his blinders. Just before the door slid shut Aleksei caught a glimpse of the corridor, bright with the clinical light of a hospital, its monotonous integrity broken only by a line of identically mute doors.

Aleksei looked around his cell. It was clean but cheerless, made of unfinished cement like the hall outside. There was no furniture, and an observation window swallowed its far wall. The Pomoshchnik ordered him at gunpoint to take the laces out of his boots. At this, Aleksei couldn't resist a cynical smile.

"Even if there was anything to hang myself from," he said, "do you think I'd spare you the trouble?" The Pomoshchnik only pushed him against the wall, checked his pockets, then left him.

A perfunctory inspection of his cell told Aleksei that there was no mechanism to open the door from the inside, and breaking the window would be pointless, if it was even possible. He sat down beneath it with his back against the wall, and did what he had been trained to do—thought out his situation calmly.

He was certain that Alla still needed him for something, or thought she did; otherwise, he would be dead. Still, he didn't deceive himself. He knew that he was living on borrowed time. He sighed, shut his eyes, and blanked his mind.

A few hours later, the door opened again. It was Dmitri. He looked at Aleksei for a moment with eyes like drill-holes in a deadwood face, then he looked at the floor.

"Aleksei—" he began, with the voice of a drowning man, then seemed not to know how to continue.

Aleksei stood up. "That's it, then," he said.

Dmitri looked up at him. "It's not what you think, Lyosha." Something glinted in the beds of his eyes, like the slick of poisonous water at the bottom of a dead well. "Follow me." It was not lost on Aleksei that he made no mention of blinders. He turned and walked out the door. After a moment, Aleksei followed.

The door to his cell was the last in a line of ten, spaced evenly down the hallway and facing the others he had seen when the Pomoshchnik delivered him. Dmitri was already half-way down the hall, walking quickly with his shoulders hunched forward.

They entered the elevator, and Dmitri punched a white button. As they traveled upward, Dmitri looked at him, and this time Aleksei was close enough to see that his eyes weren't in fact hollow, but burning lightlessly with rage that verged on madness. Just before the lift stopped, he said:

367

"Don't martyr yourself, Lyosha." And, as the doors opened, "Forgive me…"

Before Aleksei could decipher the meshed emotions on his teacher's face, strong hands had grasped his arms and were pulling him into the room beyond the elevator doors. It took a few moments for his eyes to adjust to the brightness, which was more sudden and intense even than that of the sublevel hallway. When they did, his borrowed calm evaporated.

The room was long and narrow and entirely white, so pristine it could only have been newly painted. The only furniture was a bench running along the length of one wall. On this bench, evenly spaced, sat Aleksei's friends. Misha, his hands covered in dried blood, looked fixedly at Aleksei as he came in, and raised his eyebrows, as if he had something to tell him. Anastasia glared at the Pomoshchnik who held Aleksei's arms. And Mila watched him with a madwoman's eyes, drifting and darting in turns.

The Pomoshchnik pushed him onto the bench beside Mila and then went to stand in front of the wall opposite the elevator, in which there was another door. The elevator opened again, and Alla stepped out. She walked to the center of the room, straightened and looked at them with cold anticipation.

"You all know how to stick to a story," she said. "Apparently not all of your training has been wasted." She paused, and the vaguely triumphant smile Aleksei had come to hate turned her lips. "However, if you cannot quell your passion for independence, you will never be Opyekuni. I'm willing to allow you to resume your training if, and only if, you can convince me of your loyalty."

"I don't suppose you'll take our word for it," Anastasia grumbled.

Ignoring her, Alla continued, "This test is generally the last before graduation. However, as you've all proved so very advanced, we've decided to graduate you early—if, of course, you prove up to scratch."

"And how do we do that?"

Alla smiled. "Book four, section one."

They all looked at Misha. In a trembling voice, he said, "'We must choose from among our guardians those who appear to us on observation to be the most likely to devote their lives to doing what they judge to be in the interest of the community.'"

Alla smiled. "You might make a Guardian yet."

Once again, Aleksei found himself unaccountably calm as Alla walked to the far end of the room and the Pomoshchnik stepped aside to allow her access to the other door. She pushed a button beside it, and it parted to reveal another elevator. Inside, framed like a twisted nativity, was a trembling tangle of prisoners.

As they stumbled from the elevator and the Pomoshchnik shoved them into place across from the wall with the bench, Aleksei realized the full horror of the situation. It would have been bad enough to kill the boy with the Arab skin and hunted look, but that boy stood in front of Mila. Anastasia faced a boy like Misha, Misha a girl like Anastasia. His stomach leaden with nausea, Aleksei dragged his eyes upward to look at the face of the girl across from him.

It wasn't Sifte. She was about Sifte's age, with the same white-blonde hair and similarly spare features, but she was shorter than Sifte, frailer, and her eyes were gray and sad.

"Just in case the rules aren't entirely clear," Alla said, "I'll spell them out. Do it neatly, and you'll go straight to join Solntse's intelligence team where, thanks to your friend and her good luck, you're about to be badly needed. Refuse, and you'll be the next group of targets."

"'We mustn't exercise any form of compulsion in our teaching,'" Anastasia said bitterly

Alla smiled, and Aleksei realized that she was actually enjoying this. "Your attitude isn't helping your cause, Anastasia. Remember, I've given you a choice." She reached into a pocket of her gray jacket, and took out a handgun. "Now, who'd like to begin?"

None of them answered. "All right, then," she said. She looked at all of them in turn, and then shoved the gun into Mila's hands.

Mila stared at it as if she had never seen anything like it before. Alla watched her with a python's eyes. Aleksei wanted to grab the gun from Mila, fire it at Alla's insipid smile, but he could only watch helplessly as Mila turned the gun over in her shaking hands, released the safety, and looked up at the ragged boy in front of her. Tears were pouring down her face. With the same dreamlike sluggishness, she drew her firing arm upward. For a moment, Aleksei thought she might actually do it.

Then, with a quickness as eerie as her previous languor, Mila turned the gun to her own temple. A split-second before she fired, Aleksei broke free of his paralysis and wrenched her arm upward and away, so that the shot hit the ceiling. A fine sifting of plaster dust powdered the floor, gray against the glaring white. For a moment Aleksei stared at it, transfixed. The he tuned back in to the outrageous unreality of his surroundings

The dark-skinned boy cowered with his head in the blond girl's lap, while she keened like an animal. Anastasia slumped against the wall, Misha had his bloody hands over his face,

370

and Mila struggled for control of the gun with feverish strength. Finally Aleksei pinned her arms, and only then did he realize that she was speaking. In a low, hopeless voice, with tears still running from beneath her closed eyelids, she was repeating three words like a mantra, "Let me die."

"Shut up," Aleksei whispered. "I need you to help get us out of this."

He pulled the gun from her fragile fingers and turned on Alla, who was glaring at him with shocked, furious eyes. "Give me that!" she cried, reaching toward the weapon. "Give it to me or I'll order him to shoot you!" She jerked her head backward at the Pomoshchnik, who had his rifle trained on Aleksei's heart.

Aleksei smiled at her. "No, you won't."

"I'm not like Dmitri," she snarled. "I'll watch you die gladly, izmyennik brat!"

Still staring her steadily in her face, Aleksei lowered the gun, and offered it to her. Alla's face contorted with rage. "You're playing a dangerous game, Aleksei."

He looked at her calmly and said, "Solntse doesn't know about any of this, does he? You want to scare some answers out of us so you'll have some for him when he finds out you let Sifte slip through the cracks. But it's not going to work."

Aleksei and Alla stared at each other for a moment longer, he calmly, she shaking with rage. For a moment he thought that she would back down. But when she took the gun from him, her hands were steady again.

"You're right—I need answers," she said softly, weighing the weapon in her palm. She took Mila's arm, led her away from him as easily as an adult leads a dumb and docile child. She turned her to face Aleksei. Mila's eyes were wide and vacant as a room after a death. When Alla put the gun to her head, she didn't seem to notice.

"No!" Aleksei cried, dragging his eyes away from the hypnotic horror of Mila's. "Not her!"

"Ah," Alla said to him. "Now we have something you'll play for." She pulled Mila toward her gently, almost lovingly. "Let's begin with you telling me where Sifte has gone."

Mila blinked, and her blank eyes froze. "He'll never tell you that," she said, and though she spoke the words to Alla, her bitter smile was for Aleksei.

"Mila," he pleaded.

"Don't bother," she answered.

Alla's look was a gambler's. Before he could second-guess his judgment, Aleksei said, "I'm not sure I'd gamble with Sifte's best friend, if you need information as badly as I think you do."

The mad inspiration in Alla's eyes flickered for a moment, then died, diminishing her to the mean old woman she was. "It might have been quick and painless, Aleksei," she said, "but you've just bought yourself and all your friends the most miserable death I can imagine."

"We'll hold our breath," Anastasia said, as Alla herded them into the prisoners' elevator with the Pomoshchnik. This elevator had only two buttons, one white, one gray. The Pomoshchnik pushed the gray button. Alla turned toward the line of prisoners, a vengeful fury further contorting her wrinkled face. A moment before the elevator door slid shut they heard the first shot and subsequent scream.

10

Sifte rolled over sleepily, pulling the blanket closer to her body and her knees toward the warmth of her stomach. She had been dreaming—a nightmare of snow, a cold so deep it was pain, death hovering at the edges. But it was over now. She was about to drift back into sleep, when a woman's voice said, "Not yet, Siftenka. First, drink this."

Sifte lurched up, her heart pounding in her ears with an underwater intimacy. With bleary eyes, she took in crumbling splendor: water-stained whitewash, flaking gold leaf, painted saints blackened by smoke and time, all vacillating in a dim and unstable light. Her back and arm throbbed with dull pain. Her wrist had been splinted, her gun and her outer garments were gone.

A tiny woman sat cross-legged on the floor, by the blanket where Sifte had slept, holding a ceramic cup whose blue-on-white flower pattern was cross-hatched with mend-marks. A ragged red scarf held her gray hair. Her face was lined, but it seemed marked more by hardship than by years; her eyes were clear blue. A small oil lamp flickered and smoked by her right knee. At the edge of its faint pool of light, four children slept wrapped in blankets like Sifte's: woolen, rough but clean.

"Where are my things?" Sifte demanded.

"I'm sorry," the woman said. "We had to take your clothes off, or you would have died. Hypothermia. The men took the gun. You won't need it here, anyway."

"Where is 'here'?" Sifte asked, her voice wavering despite her effort to control it. "And who are you?"

"Masha," she answered. "And we're in the sacristy of Vasilovo's old orthodox church." The woman held the cup towards her. Sifte regarded it with overt suspicion. The woman sighed. "You were nearly dead when they brought you to me. Why would I kill you now?"

Sifte took the cup, sipped at its contents, then spat them back resentfully. The woman laughed, a sound as mellow as the gold on the ikons. "It doesn't taste good, but it will do good," she said.

"What is it?" Sifte asked.

"Arnica mostly, for the bruises and the sprain. Willow bark for the pain. A couple of other herbs that might help and won't hurt...oh, and vodka. That never hurts, either. Drink, Sifte."

Sifte took a hesitant sip from the cup, then said, "How do you know my name?"

The woman was smiling again. She had the kind of face that seemed to settle naturally into a smile, her cheeks tightening to ruddy plums above it; but the sadness never quite disappeared. "You told me, in your delirium. Don't worry, you have nothing to fear from us. It seems to me that we fight the same enemy, tavarishch."

Sifte's eyes locked onto the woman's again. "You're Soviet, then?"

374

The woman shrugged. "I don't believe I need to label myself to know what's right and what's wrong…but the others like to call themselves Soviet. A couple even go into the city for meetings, from time to time."

Sifte sipped contemplatively. If nothing else, the liquor was filling her once again with a sense of well-being and warmth. She felt she could never be warm enough again.

"Do you live here?" she asked.

The woman shook her head. "It's only a hiding place. We've never used it—the officials don't usually bother patrolling this far north."

Sifte studied the woman, but her face was inscrutable. "Why are they here, then?"

"I thought you might know."

Sifte shook her head, and quickly changed the subject. "Are the children yours?"

"The oldest girl, there, is my Varenka," Masha answered, with a tenderness that sent a pang of longing through Sifte. "The littlest boy and girl, the ones sharing a blanket, are Sonya and Arkadiy, a brother and sister whose parents were both killed a year ago, poor things. And the other boy is Lyosha."

The name drove into Sifte with the force of a fist. She tried to think of something more to say, something which would not touch too close to her aching heart, but no words would come.

As if she'd heard Sifte's thought, Masha said, "This is a wild country for a young girl to walk alone." Sifte looked at Masha, the non-question inexplicably bringing tears to her eyes. Masha took it all in, and patting Sifte's hand, she said, "I'm sorry. No one should be made to speak of pain until they are ready. Instead, let me tell you what we already know about you.

"You're what Vanya went away for, and although we don't know who you are, we know that you must be of the greatest importance to our cause for Vanya to have given his life for you. Yes, we know about that too, and the Pomoshchniki in the barn, and what it must have cost you even to come this far. We also know that they wouldn't be looking for you, and you couldn't have avoided them so long, if you weren't something special."

Sifte stared at Masha incredulously, and after a moment, her half-smile back in place, Masha continued, "You'll meet the others soon. They may question you, but they won't press you hard. Our own survival depends on secrecy, so we understand secrecy in others—as long as we're convinced that it doesn't put us in danger." Now Masha's face was serious. "More to the point, as long as Yevgeniy is convinced."

"Who's Yevgeniy?"

"He's our unofficial leader. Lyosha's father. His wife was killed in a raid on Zelenogorsk when Lyosha was only two. Yevgeniy was forced to watch. A lesson, they said." Masha sighed. "No doubt you can understand how much he hates Solntse and his so-called philosopher-rulers, and why he keeps such careful watch over us."

Sifte shook her head. "How can I convince him that I'm loyal to the Soviet if what he already knows about me isn't enough?"

The look of antipathy on Masha's face deepened. "Don't worry about that now. You need to rest."

Sifte had begun to relax into Masha's easy companionship, but these words set her on edge again. "I want to know what you're planning to do to me."

"Sifte, please understand that Yevgeniy's a good man and devoted to the Soviet cause. If it seems he takes his loyalty to an extreme—"

"Enough," Sifte said. She couldn't stand to listen to the mixture of fear and adulation in the woman's voice, and there was no way she'd rest again wondering what awaited her beyond the sacristy door. "Where are my clothes?"

Masha sighed more deeply still. "They won't be dry, yet."

"They'll be dry enough."

Masha got up, disappeared into the shadows, and returned a few minutes later with Sifte's clothing. She helped her to dress, as Sifte's splinted arm made it difficult. When she was finished, Masha looked at Sifte a moment longer, as if trying to decide what she could say to change Sifte's mind. Finally, she turned on her soundless, felt-booted feet, and led Sifte to a door at the far side of the room.

A man and a woman, both armed with antiquated handguns, trained their weapons and wary eyes on Sifte as the door opened. Both were young, probably not much older than Sifte herself, though they had the same world-weary eyes as Masha. They also clearly respected her. At a wordless signal from her, they lowered their weapons and let Sifte pass into the body of the church.

Blue and gold paint curled in swathes from the ceiling, and the pews and wooden floor had been wrenched out, probably for firewood. The few remaining ikons were rotten, their faces black, and the windows had long ago been broken and covered with paper and rag. On the altar, near the window she had climbed in through—now as carefully sealed as the others—sat four more people. They had a map spread before them on the floor, but their eyes were on her as she walked toward them.

There was a thin, middle-aged woman with dark eyes reminiscent of Anastasia's; a boy close to Sifte's own age, with orange hair and freckled skin; a middle-aged man with black hair and limbs that seemed impossibly long and thin; and, rising slowly to his feet like a wary cat, a dark man with cold eyes and an authoritative manner, whom Sifte had no doubt was Yevgeniy.

She walked up to him and demanded, "What do you want from me?"

With a thin, joyless smile he answered, "I suppose that depends what you want from us."

"No doubt you saved my life, and I'm grateful for that." She paused, trying to read his expression. It wasn't just equivocal, but seemed to changed every second, and she found this as confounding as the studied blankness of the Opyekuni. "But now I need to be on my way, so if you'll give me my things—"

Yevgeniy laughed. "We can't possibly let you leave until we know what your intentions are."

"I have no intentions that concern you."

The man pressed his lips together, then said, "You've seen us. You could identify us. Your intentions and ours are inevitably linked."

Sifte folded her arms across her chest, and regarded him as coldly as he did her. "Then you're going to keep me as your prisoner indefinitely?"

"It would be easier to kill you."

"Zhenya!" Masha said sharply.

Yevgeniy looked at Masha for a moment, then turned back to Sifte. "You seem to have impressed Masha."

"She said it was you I'd have to impress."

"Well then," Yevgeniy said, spreading his hands wide, as once a priest might have done in his place, "impress me."

"You're going to have to be more specific."

"All right. Who are you, and what was so important in Vasilovo that you'd risk death to get to it?"

"You already know my name," Sifte answered, in case they didn't, "and I was sent to meet someone in Vasilovo. A friend—Soviet. At the inn called The Firebird." The Soviets murmured to each other at the mention of the name. It was the reaction Sifte had been hoping for.

"The Firebird has served us well for a number of years," Yevgeniy conceded, frowning. "Unfortunately, it was raided yesterday. Every official in Russia probably knows about it by now. So you'll have to do better than that—Sifte."

Sifte pulled back the sleeve of her sweater and turned her forearm toward the light of the two oil lamps that were holding down the corners of the map. Even Yevgeniy's face registered interest when he saw the scar. Before this could fade, Sifte said, "My mother did it, when I was a baby. She was Soviet, and wanted to make sure that I would always remember it. I have."

Yevgeniy looked at the scar, and then back at Sifte. Now there was emotion in his eyes, but also madness. She took a step backwards, but he grabbed her scarred arm, and drew her so close to him that she could smell the liquor on his breath. He looked hard at her for a few moments, then he said:

"All right. Now you'll prove it." He bent down and picked up her gun and coat from a pile on the floor. Sifte stared at them, but didn't take either one. Yevgeniy dropped the coat at Sifte's feet, but he kept the gun. He strode up what had been the church's main aisle, toward the front door, indicating to Sifte to follow him.

"Zhenya," Masha said, with soft authority, "she's ill."

He turned to her with a smile of strange, almost childlike glee. "If she's who I think she is, it won't matter. And if she's not, it's better to find out now."

Sifte looked at Masha. Masha said, "There's nothing I can do."

Sifte picked up the coat and pulled it on awkwardly. Masha made no move to help her this time. Feeling the others' eyes on her back, she made her own way up the aisle and joined Yevgeniy where he waited by the door. He gave her the same strange smile he had given Masha, then let her out.

*

It had stopped snowing, but the sky was still murky with cloud. Sifte followed Yevgeniy through the darkness with silent trepidation. She thought about trying to lose herself in the woods, but she knew she didn't have much chance of making it to the city unarmed and without food or a compass. She was too weak to take the gun by force.

Just as she was beginning to tire, they reached a clearing. At its center was a small wooden shed, as badly in need of repair as the church. The door was secured with an old-fashioned padlock. Yevgeniy unlocked it, then he opened the door. An overpowering smell of urine drifted out. He gestured Sifte inside. She looked at her gun in his hand, and decided not to argue.

He followed her in and lit a lamp. Two Pomoshchniki lay bound and gagged against the far wall. The face of one was covered with dried blood from a gash in his forehead.

The other's coat was soaked dark, his skin gray-green. Both looked up at Sifte with hopeless eyes. They were little older than she was, dying and terrified, and despite herself, she felt a wrench of pity.

"We caught them yesterday morning," Yevgeniy said coolly. "I kept them alive because I thought we might need bargaining pieces. But I think you'll put them to better use."

He was holding the handle of her gun toward her and had another gun cocked and pointed at her.

"My hand—" she began.

"I'd bet my life that you'll do as well with the other."

"I won't kill without reason," she said, tucking her left hand under her useless right arm.

Yevgeniy appeared to be considering several answers before he chose one. "We know about the Opyekuni in the boat." Hearing these words, the Pomoshchnik with the bloody face looked at his companion. Yevgeniy kicked him, after which he lay still.

"I had to kill him," Sifte said, wondering how he could possibly know these things.

"Did you have to use ten bullets?" Yevgeniy smirked. Sifte looked at him in confusion, which only made his smile widen. "You mean you don't know you fired ten rounds?"

"I…I wasn't thinking clearly."

"You seemed to be thinking clearly enough when you left that barn near Zelenogorsk. You've been well trained by someone, Sifte, and I'm pretty sure it wasn't your Soviet mother. What I don't know is which side you're working for. If you don't prove to me that you're on mine, then you'll die with them." He jerked his head at the two Pomoshchniki.

Drawing a deep breath, Sifte reached out with her left hand and took her gun from Yevgeniy. She saw that he had emptied it of all but two bullets, and this confirmed what she already suspected: that even if she did what he wanted her to do, he still wouldn't trust her. She might save her own life by killing the Pomoshchniki, but she would be a slave to Yevgeniy's paranoia, like Masha and the others.

"Get on with it!" he barked.

Sifte turned to the boys again, hardening her heart against them, for she too was going to use them. She raised her arm, making sure that it shook visibly, aimed her gun somewhere in between the Pomoshchniki, and fired both rounds quickly. As she fired, she allowed the kickback to jerk her hand to the left, so that she missed. Then she dropped her gun and backed away, screaming with studied hysteria.

As she had hoped, Yevgeniy's uncertainty undermined him. He looked at her, hesitating too long, then pushed her aside and shot the officials himself. When they were dead, he turned to her again, anger and panic fighting for control of his face. He pulled her up off the ground and began shouting at her to control herself. She only screamed more loudly than before. He reached to slap her face, and at the same moment she ducked, grabbed his gun while he was unbalanced, and knocked him to the floor. The room was suddenly, deadly quiet.

To his credit, Yevgeniy didn't grovel or plead. He only looked at her with his haunted eyes and said, "Do it quickly."

"I already told you I don't kill without reason," Sifte said, keeping the gun trained on him.

Yevgeniy shook his head. "Haven't I given you reason?" He indicated the dead Pomoshchniki.

"I told you, I'm not one of them. But I don't think you'll ever believe that, so you don't leave me much choice."

Gesturing with the gun, she said, "Kneel, and put your hands on top of your head."

"I thought you said you weren't going to—"

"I'm not," said Sifte, as he knelt. "But I can't let you stop me, either." She hit him on the back of the head with the butt of his gun.

*

When Sifte returned to the church, she handed Masha Yevgeniy's gun, and the others cowered in a corner as she explained what had happened. "I guess you'll go and find him," she said, "but please, give me a day before you let him come after me."

Masha nodded silently. She handed Sifte her pack, with all of its original contents but the vodka, plus some extra food, water, and rolls of bandages. Masha didn't follow her to the door, but when Sifte was a hundred feet away from the church, she heard Masha call after her, "God go with you, Siftenka!"

Sifte turned. She couldn't see anything but shadows in the church's foyer. Sighing, she set off south through the dark, silent woods, as the gibbous moon surfaced from its sea of clouds.

11

Stepan greeted the guards inside the door of the Technology Institute, then moved past them into the semi-darkness. He made his way to a door on which a fading sign cast an empty threat to those unauthorized for entry. He opened it, and felt his way down the stairs. A strip of light showed underneath the door at the bottom, and he made a mental note to cover this when he had a spare moment. He went inside, passing rooms where recruits were sorting and stacking supplies, then on into the living quarters. The door to Sasha's room was slightly ajar and the light was on, but no sound came from within.

In the days since they had taken her from the prison, Sasha's physical health had improved quickly. She had even resumed some of the motions of living. More importantly, she had stopped cowering when Stepan came near her. If that had continued, Stepan wouldn't have been able to bear being with her. However, she still hadn't spoken, and when she was not lying with her eyes closed pretending to sleep, she sat cross-legged on the floor, staring at the blank wall in front of her, still as a bodhisattva. If it hadn't been for her eyes, Stepan would have been tempted to think that there was in fact something transcendent about her state. But they were flat and murky as the bed of a silty river.

The self-trained doctor who had tended their wounds had told Stepan that there was no physical basis for Sasha's catatonia. Stepan was little comforted by this advice; he found little comfort in anything since Sifte had failed to arrive.

Stepan had known that her travel plans couldn't be exact, but the news was worse every day: two scuttled boats off Repino, three men's bodies in a burned barn not far away, Pomoshchnik occupation of Vasilovo, and no word from Olga. He knew that one of the bodies in the barn must have been Vanya's, and though no one had reported a girl's body, it was unlikely that Solntse would have allowed the information on public news channels. No Soviet group between Repino and the city had reported any sightings of her, and this was strange at best. At worst, it looked like a cover-up.

Sighing, Stepan pushed Sasha's door open. There wasn't much in the room—a sleeping pallet, a couple of rickety chairs, a table made of reclaimed wood resting on broken cinder-blocks—yet it was luxury compared with the one he and Sasha had shared in the General Staff Buildings. The first few nights after they had taken her from the prison, Stepan had slept beside Sasha on the pallet, hoping that this might thaw her icy silence. But she had huddled as far from him as possible, like some trapped, feral animal. She didn't sleep; he knew it by the rhythmic click of her eyelids as she blinked, faint and persistent as a bird pecking at seeds. Each of those wary shutterings erased another of his hopes. After the third night, he slept on his own.

Now she was sitting on the floor in her familiar, contemplative pose, but she turned her head slightly when he entered. This was something new. Stepan forgot about his worries for a moment. He crouched down, still a good five feet away from her, and said, "Sashenka?"

At that moment, the door opened and Andrei came in. If it hadn't been for the pronounced limp, Stepan would have said that he was in a hurry. He brought the cold of the street in with him, and it curled around them for a moment before dispersing.

"Didn't anyone teach you to knock?" Stepan asked angrily, as Sasha resumed staring at the wall.

"Privacy is a Western luxury," Andrei answered. "I didn't interrupt anything?" He looked at Stepan with infuriating acuity.

"She was—" Stepan began, then stopped. The pallid gesture of recognition was as likely to have been a product of his own imagination as anything else. "Nothing," he finished. "Do you have news?"

"If you have vodka," Andrei answered. "If you don't, I might kill you."

Stepan would have called this an attempt at humor, except that Andrei's face was agitated, even more unsmiling than usual. As Stepan poured out two glasses, Andrei lowered himself painfully into a chair, and lifted his bad leg onto another. He accepted the glass Stepan proffered, drained it in one swallow, and screwed up his face.

"That's appalling."

Stepan sat down across from Andrei. "You never were much of a drinking man. It must be good news." Stepan couldn't keep the hope out of his voice.

"That's one more point on which I imagine we won't see eye to eye." He re-filled his glass from the bottle Stepan had set on the floor between them.

"Sifte?" Stepan asked eagerly.

Andrei drank and re-filled his glass again before he answered. "Well, your girl hasn't ridden in on a white horse, but I think it's safe to say you got your way."

"There's been news of her?"

"Not exactly. But a friend in Vasilovo informs me that they uncovered a snowmobile with Solntse's crest by the side of the road yesterday, just outside of town. It was in good working order, but out of fuel."

"It doesn't mean that Sifte left it."

Andrei raised his eyebrows, and looked at his empty glass contemplatively. "No." He paused. Good ascetic that he was, the liquor had gone straight to his head, flaming his cheeks with color for the first time in Stepan's memory. "But there were tracks leading all the way back to that burned barn, two or three days old."

"That's better."

"Then, two Pomoshchniki and one civilian were found dead this morning in an abandoned woodcutter's shack, also outside of Vasilovo. There were three new sets of footprints connecting the shack to an old church nearby: two leading there, one leading back. The church had recently been inhabited, but apparently abandoned in the last day or so. The footprints leading back to the church were a woman's."

"You think Sifte killed the civilian?" Stepan asked with obvious disdain.

Andrei filled his glass for the fourth time, but now he sipped the liquor as daintily as a lady. "I think Sifte went out of her way not to kill him. The officials, too. Very Platonic of her, don't you think? The Pomoshchniki had been shot point-blank with an antique, but there were also two stray bullets in the wall from a different gun. Incidentally, they matched the ammunition you gave to Vanya." Andrei lapsed into silent contemplation not visibly different from Sasha's.

"So the man shot the officials," Stepan prompted, when it was clear that Andrei had lost his train of thought, "and then himself?"

"The man froze to death." This time, Andrei's smile was almost beatific. "You know, this reminds me of that children's game—do they play it in America?—where you're told the outcome of a situation and have to guess the story leading up to it. Yes, you must have it in America. It's good training for lawsuits."

Stepan sighed. The last thing he was in the mood for at the moment was a litany of his birth country's faults. "Do you think we could stick to the—"

"Do you remember a young man called Yevgeniy?" Andrei interrupted. His eyes were beginning to glow with the fire of drunkenness. It was clear to Stepan that in some perverse way, Andrei was enjoying himself, or at least enjoying dragging Stepan through every muddy rut of this story before telling him what he wanted to know. "He was hanging around Myortvograd a couple of years back, a firebrand, wanted to be a leader, patently unstable? He wanted to reform us, had an idea about members 'proving their loyalty' he'd borrowed from Solntse. It involved capturing Pomoshchniki alive, bringing our recruits in and giving them guns..." He trailed off, his lip curling in disgust.

Vaguely, Stepan recalled a pair of wild, grief-ridden eyes. "You packed him off somewhere. North, I think—"

"Siberia, was the idea," Andrei answered. "He only made it as far as Vasilovo. He got a rag-tag band together there. Apparently he ran his ring like an Institute. Worse, probably—at least Solntse feeds his flunkies. Anyhow, his only injury was a mild concussion. My guess is, he wanted to recruit Sifte to his group, and she had other ideas."

"So she locked him up to freeze to death?" Stepan asked incredulously.

"I rather think we have his friends to thank for that—but it's only a guess. At any rate, no one's been able to find any of them to comment on the theory, so that's all it really is." Andrei looked at Stepan over the rim of the glass with eyes that were unnervingly astute, even drunk.

"There's more, isn't there," Stepan said, finally tossing back his own glass, and re-filling it.

Andrei looked at Stepan for a long time, then said, "Institute 1's disintegrating."

"How poetic."

Andrei shrugged, stretched his injured leg a bit. "Actually, it isn't, but that's beside the point. They're evacuating students and staff, dumping data, burning files, the whole bit. I doubt Solntse would scuttle his precious think-tank, unless—"

"Sifte made it."

Andrei's smile inverted. "Sifte's caused quite a stir with her little stunt. Rumors are flying fast and furious on Glaza, though to both your credit, no one appears to have guessed the truth yet. Turns out you were right. There were a lot of suspicions in regard to Sifte, and they're coming out faster than Solntse can contain them. He's panicking. He's clearing other schools and government offices that are too close to borders, or might otherwise be hard to defend. He's also shutting down parts of Glaza, apparently to try to slow down the gossip mill. Calling it massive system failure, of course." Andrei's look stopped Stepan's smile. "Needless to say, all of this has fired up the Soviet. They're beginning to organize for war, if you can call it organization, which is a good thing, since it looks like war's on the agenda whether I like it or not."

Stepan had shoved out of his chair, gripped Andrei by the shoulders. "Where is Sifte?" he demanded.

"I've told you all I know."

"Have you heard from Olga?"

"You know that I would have told you if I had."

"What about the other children?"

Andrei's look went cagey again. "What about them?"

"Any friend of Sifte's is going to be at the top of their hit-list. Have you heard anything from them?"

"There was one scrambled transmission I couldn't do anything with—"

Stepan swelled with anger. "Come on." He dragged Andrei toward the door.

"Where are we going?"

"Where do you think?"

Stepan looked at Sasha as he opened the door. She leaned toward the wall with the door in it, her head cocked slightly, as if she were listening to something. "We'll be back soon," he told her, and then wished that his business at that moment had been anything but desperately urgent, because she turned to look at him, and the eyes that met his held a spark of recognition.

*

Back at Andrei's, they read what news they could find on the rapidly-decreasing number of Glaza channels. Little of it was useful, and none of it was comforting. A bulletin had been posted an hour before, officially closing Institute 1 due

390

to 'structural problems,' and assuring people that all students and personnel would be safely evacuated.

"I'll bet," Stepan muttered. He scanned for any news of Sifte, but came up with nothing. "Now, what about that message?" he asked, relinquishing the keyboard to Andrei.

Andrei retrieved it. The message had come through one of the channels the children had used to communicate with Stepan recently, but it was a string of gibberish. "Most likely, Glaza police didn't like what it said," Andrei suggested, "and unwrote it."

"Then why bother sending it to us? Look, the characters are Cyrillic, there aren't any numbers—this doesn't look random. It looks like something typed by somebody who was afraid someone might be looking over his shoulder. You must have done work on cryptograms at Institute 1."

Andrei shrugged. "Of course, but it wasn't really my area of interest. I remember some of the common codes, but this doesn't fit any of them."

Stepan narrowed his eyes, willing the letters to resolve into something that made sense. Then, all at once, they did. "Speaking of kids' games," he said, "do Russian children play the one with the mirror and the message written backwards?"

Andrei smiled. "The only children with access to mirrors are already on to the Enigma by that point. What, you think the kids flipped their own encryption code to write this?"

"That'll teach you to drink too much," Stepan said, smiling without joy or even humor. "Look—he simply wrote it backwards."

"But even backwards, it doesn't make—" Andrei began, then stopped himself when he saw his mistake. Misha had written the message backwards, in phonetic English, spelled with Cyrillic characters. It was convoluted enough that a simple scan wouldn't detect treason, but simple enough that anyone or anything set to look for complicated algorithms would miss it. It said:

"No time left. Sifte got out but we're in trouble. Someone betrayed us, no I.D. Please help. Misha."

Stepan found himself humbled yet again by the prospect of a child who could retain such presence of mind in the face of such danger.

"I hope it's not one of their own group," Andrei said.

"I think he would have known that. Still, it doesn't look good for them." He stood up. "You try to find out who the spy was, and how much the Institute knows. I'll be back soon."

"Where are you going?" Andrei demanded.

"To try to find Sifte."

He didn't wait for Andrei to protest. He ran down the stairs to the street, burst out into the fast-falling night. He had taken a few steps in the direction of the Church on the Spilled Blood—a group of Soviet leaders was meeting there soon, and they were the most likely to know anything about his daughter—when he remembered the look on Sasha's face when he had left the bunker. On pure instinct he turned and began to walk back in the direction of the bunker, and then, finally, to run.

392

12

For a few hours, Sifte walked through forest. She kept to the cover of the re-growth as much as she could. Though she knew that dead trees were better than none at all, she didn't like walking among the skeletons of those particular war casualties, which seemed to retain an air of reproach. Occasionally she had to stop and wait in the shadow of a tree or rock as a low-flying airplane passed overhead. However, if the planes' purpose was to track her, the officials obviously didn't know that they were so close. Each made a perfunctory sweep over the open ground, then passed out of sight.

Sifte had crossed several roads since she left Vasilovo. They were all deserted, and only the first bore fresh tracks. Sifte didn't know what to make of the lack of traffic, and after a while it began to worry her. No matter what she told herself, she couldn't shake the feeling that she was being watched. At first she imagined that Yevgeniy or one of the others had followed her. But Yevgeniy could never have caught up with her so quickly, and she doubted that the others would have had the gumption. An official wouldn't bother to stalk her through this wasteland. They would either shoot her on the spot or make her an easy prisoner.

The further south she traveled, the more the woods thinned out, and her paranoia grew. She stopped more and more frequently, certain that the faint echo she strained to hear had been thrown by something other than her own movements. The couple of times she doubled back, though, she found no tracks but her own.

Finally even the flimsy epilogue to the woods petered out. As far as Sifte could see ahead was a plain of absolute topographical uniformity, unmarked by roads or walls or even the tracks of animals. These could only be the Badlands Vanya had spoken of. Scratching at the snow, Sifte uncovered a familiar patch of cracked black earth, and shuddered. From her hazy memory of Vanya's map, Sifte figured that a good forty kilometers of Badlands separated her from the city. There was no way around them—not, at any rate, on foot. They stretched all the way to Lake Ladozhskoye in the east, and to the Gulf in the west. Crossing them directly would make her a crippled hare to the officials' circling wolf-pack. She thought miserably of Olga, wishing she had even a clue about what the woman had planned to get them past this.

There seemed no option but to backtrack to one of the roads, follow it, and hope it would take her to a village where she could find some kind of help, or at least a way to contact Stepan. Sighing, and fighting the exhaustion that was stealing over her again, Sifte turned around, and found herself face to face with her pursuer.

She had her gun out in an instant. It took her considerably longer to realize that the woman in front of her held no weapon, and that she was, at least topically, a far cry from a Pomoshchnik. She was short and stocky and dressed as roughly as Sifte was herself. She raised her hands in surrender, and pulled her scarf from her broad, plain face. She was smiling.

"Your father's a hair-trigger too," she said in a mellow voice.

Sifte's head swam. She kept the gun trained on the woman until she said:

"Put the gun down, Sifte. I'm here to help you."

Sifte lowered the weapon. "Olga?" she asked tentatively, before she could think better of it.

The woman laughed again. "Shoddy training, for Institute 1." Sifte half-shook her head. "First rule in determining a stranger's loyalties: don't offer any information. But then, I imagine you're a bit off your game after what you've been through in the last few days. You've done pretty well, all things considered." The woman stepped toward her, and Sifte took a doubtful step back.

Olga sighed. "Yes, I am Olga, but I'm afraid it's going to be hard to prove it to you at the moment." Her voice still had an edge of laughter in it, but it was governed now by conciliation. "My bag, which unfortunately contained our papers, was seized in Vasilovo. Thankfully I wasn't, but it derailed things a bit. If Masha wasn't so astute, I never would have found you at all."

Sifte shook her head again. "But if you knew Masha—"

"I didn't know Masha until about twenty minutes after you left her. It seems you said something about me while you were ill, and she put two and two together. She seemed eager to help you. A force of nature, that woman; sometime you'll have to tell me what you did to deserve her gratitude. Right now, though, we need to get out of here. They're on our trail."

She turned, and began retracing Sifte's trail through the dead trees, careful to step only in the old tracks. Sifte stood indecisively, watching Olga retreat.

Olga turned and said with clear impatience, "If it makes you feel any better, I never carry weapons."

Sifte raised her eyebrows. "Given your line of work, that seems odd."

Olga laughed. "So everyone says. But in 'my line of work' you've got to have a principle or two, or you really would go crazy." Sifte still hesitated. Olga sighed. "You can try to cross the Badlands—keeping in mind that it will be light in a few more hours, and it looks like it will also be sunny, for a change. Frankly, I wouldn't bet on your chances, but it's up to you."

Olga's face was open and frank, with no sign of the officials' studied coldness, or of Yevgeniy's volatility. Her eyes were kind, but there was a sediment of grief in them, which a Pomoshchnik or Opyekun would never show.

"I'll go with you," Sifte said, and Olga turned and trotted off into the woods again.

"Try to keep to one set of tracks," she called back to Sifte. "It will confuse them for a little while, at least."

Sifte found that she had to push herself to keep up with Olga, despite the woman's roundness. "Where are we going?" she asked.

"I'll tell you more when we're closer. Sound carries a long way out here."

A short time later they veered off of Sifte's old track to the north-east. They reached a narrow road running through a thick pine forest free of the deadwood that had unnerved Sifte earlier, and here Olga slowed. The moon had set, and there was a streak on the eastern horizon the color of gas flame. It made Sifte think of Mila, and the subsequent lump rose in her throat.

"Dawn is lovely out here," Olga said softly. Sifte nodded, and looked at the snow growing brighter under her feet, losing herself in the monotonous rhythm of walking. Then, abruptly, Olga reached out and stopped her.

"We're here," she said.

Sifte looked up and around. They were still on the narrow road. The trees, buckling under the weight of the snow, nearly obscured the sky, but a narrow ribbon of blue was still visible between them. The color had thinned as the sun neared the horizon, but it had not lost its intensity. Silvery light hovered around them in the absolute stillness.

Sifte couldn't see anything that looked like a destination. Her suspicion returned, and she turned to Olga, who was looking calmly down the road to the east. "What's so special about 'here'?" she demanded.

Olga turned back to her, smiled. "What? Oh yes, I said I would explain, didn't I. Sifte, I know that this all seems mad, but I am who I say I am, and I'm going to do all I can to fulfill my promise to your father." She paused, then added, "And your mother."

Sifte looked at Olga in the blooming light. Her red cheeks and round, clear eyes exuded honesty. "You knew my mother?"

"She was my best friend," Olga answered as she took off her pack and brought out an insulated bottle. She opened it, sipped the contents, and made a face. "Cold—but better than nothing." She offered the bottle to Sifte. Sifte was so thirsty from walking that she didn't mind cold tea. She waited for Olga to continue, but Olga had taken out a packet of cheese and meat. She broke off a couple of pieces and then handed them to Sifte before she elaborated.

"She was also one of the best leaders we've ever had," she said, chewing thoughtfully. "Did you know that we've already met, you and I?" Sifte stopped chewing, and Olga smiled at her surprise. "I held you when you were only a few hours old."

Sifte chewed the rest of her mouthful and swallowed. Olga was once again looking off to the east, with an expression of growing anxiety. With her own stirrings of anxiety, Sifte pulled the mitten off her left hand, peeled back her sleeve so that the scar was exposed, and then said:

"Did she really do this?"

Olga blinked at the scar for a few moments, then she took Sifte's arm gently in her hand, and turned it back and forth in the hovering light. Finally, she let go. "I don't know," she said, but the equivocation in her tone told Sifte that she was thinking much more.

"Did she mean to kill me?"

Olga met Sifte's eyes, but it was several moments before she answered, "You can't imagine what it's like for a mother to see her child taken as a slave to the man who's destroyed her life. If she did try to kill you, Sifte, she was trying to save you the only way she knew how. Keep that in mind when you judge her."

Sifte smiled bitterly. "I suppose I'll never have the chance."

"Don't be too sure."

Sifte's eyes jerked toward Olga. "What?"

Olga drew a deep breath, and let it out slowly. "I've had news to suggest that it might not only be your father you'll meet in Myortvograd."

A sudden noise in the silence of the forest precluded Sifte's rash of questions. It was the rumble of a large engine. Olga's strained face flooded with relief. "Come on," she said, and without waiting for Sifte to reply, she picked up her pack and pulled Sifte with her along the road.

A big truck bearing Solntse's seal and carrying a load of tree-trunks pulled into view. Olga broke into a run, and Sifte followed her, too unnerved by Olga's revelation to wonder why they would be waiting for a truck with Solntse's seal. The driver put on the brake, but left the engine idling as he jumped out. He was short and stocky like Olga, with the same broad face and ready smile. They embraced, laughing.

Olga turned to Sifte, who had caught up with her, and said, "This is my brother, Grigoriy, and luckily for us, he's due to take a wood shipment into Solntsegrad this morning. We're going with it."

To Sifte's surprise, Grigoriy embraced her as he had his sister, and kissed both of her cheeks. "Good news," he said to both of them, as he led them around to the back of the truck. "They were successful." He looked at Sifte, then Olga.

Olga sighed, with what sounded to Sifte like relief. "I haven't told her all of it," she said. Then, turning to Sifte, she added, "It looks like you'll meet your mother after all." Sifte shook her head in confusion, but Olga was already focused on Grigoriy again. "Stepan and Andrei?" she asked.

"Both alive. Yuri and Vasili were shot. Olya, there's no time for this now—come."

Grigoriy climbed up onto the pile of wood and gestured to them to follow him. He loosened lines, shifted a few logs, and then pulled upward on another. It came away, revealing a wooden box fashioned out of the same wood he was hauling. Two blankets were spread on the bottom.

"It won't be comfortable," he said, "but it's the best we could do."

Olga sighed. "Well, it's not too far to the city from here. Anyway, it will give me time to fill Sifte in on the latest developments."

"I can't take you all the way to Myortvograd," Grigoriy said, "but if all goes well, this will get you past the roadblock."

"Roadblock?" Olga repeated, with a catch in her voice.

"Yes," he answered, avoiding Sifte's eyes.

"Let's not waste any more time, then," Olga answered.

There was just room in the box for both of them to lie down. Sifte fought claustrophobia as she listened to Grigoriy re-stacking and tying the load. When the truck jolted forward again, Olga reached out and took her hand, and Sifte wondered how she ever could have mistrusted her.

*

The next two hours seemed like as many years. Progress through the snow was slow, and at times Grigoriy had to stop and dig them out of a particularly deep bank. Finally, the motion of the truck smoothed and they speeded up.

Olga told Sifte all she knew about the plot to free Sasha. Then she described the early days of her friendship with Sasha and Stepan. As she spoke, Sifte was reeling. It was more than the sudden reality of the people and places she had imagined for so many years. She had realized that joining their world meant taking up her long-vacant place in the snarled web of lives that converged on her. She dreaded it and longed for it at once.

Yet the more real this new world became, the more she felt the absence of her childhood friends. They seemed as distant and unreal as the outside world had once seemed. She worried that they wouldn't forgive her for leaving without them, unable to consider the possibility that they wouldn't have the chance. Sifte was so lost in these thoughts that she didn't realize the truck was slowing until it had stopped.

Her good hand moved instantly toward her gun, but Olga caught it and squeezed it. "Be still, Siftenka," she whispered, "and if you have any gods, pray to them." Mila's sweet face came into Sifte's mind again, and she clutched Olga's hand.

The truck jerked slightly as Grigoriy jumped down to an official's summons. Sifte couldn't make out all of their words, but they seemed to be discussing papers, then a shipping order, and then someone was scrambling on top of the load.

"It's all fresh wood, the full load," she heard Grigoriy say from above. "It's going to the Vyborgside depot."

"We've been instructed to check all loads coming in from the north," the woman's voice said. "Please step to the side."

Logs came away, and red-tinged sunlight filtered through the cracks in the box. Neither Sifte nor Olga breathed, but Olga let go of Sifte's hand and didn't stop her when Sifte reached for her gun. Someone stepped onto the top of the box. Sifte tightened her hand around the gun. Just as she began to wonder how much more strain she could stand, whoever had stepped onto the box stepped off it again, and uttered the two sweetest words she had ever heard: "All clear." They began to push the logs back into place.

Sifte released her breath in a dizzy rush. "Good girl," Olga whispered, and Sifte could tell by her voice that she was smiling. "The worst is over, now."

Within minutes, they were moving again. "How much longer?" she asked.

"Not long," Olga answered. "Now listen to me carefully, Sifte. The river's frozen, so it shouldn't be hard to cross, as long as we're far enough away from the patrols. We'll have to go separately, since they know me, but I'll point you in the right direction. Once you're across the river, you're as safe as you'll ever be in this city. Ask directions to Muskovskiy Prospekt. The bunker is in the basement of the old Technological Institute. Our guards will be looking for you. If you have any trouble, go to Andrei's place. You have the address?"

"Yes," Sifte answered, as the truck slowed to a stop.

"I'll meet you in the bunker tonight." She paused, listened as Grigoriy began to untie and shift the load once more. "Will you be all right?"

Sifte smiled. "Yes. Thank you, Olga."

"Thank you too, Sifte."

Sifte wanted to ask her what she was thanking her for, but before she could, Grigoriy opened the top of the box. "Quickly," he said. "I've already caused a stir."

Sifte stood up. They were in a cavernous building with openings that seemed to have been made with large vehicles in mind. A crowd of ragged children had surrounded them. In the corners of the building, adults huddled close to smoky fires.

"A factory loading bay, once," Olga told Sifte. "Luxury accommodation now." She and Olga jumped down from the wood pile. Grigoriy embraced and kissed both of them again.

"Good luck," he said, with an oddly wistful look.

"You too," Sifte answered. "And thank you."

"Give my regards to your parents," Grigoriy said, as he swung up into the truck's cab.

Olga and Sifte watched until he turned the corner and disappeared from sight. Then Olga began stripping off layers of clothing and dividing them among the children. "No one wears so much clothing here," she explained. "It will make you stand out." She kept her trousers, sweater and boots, and one scarf, which she wrapped around her head so that it hid most of her face. The children ran off with their new possessions, looking back over their shoulders as if they feared that Olga would change her mind. Sifte did the same, though she was careful to tuck the tokens of her old life into the clothing she kept.

"Ready?" Olga asked, when Sifte was finished. Without waiting for her to reply, she strode toward one of the doors.

The first thing that Sifte noticed was the sky. A bronze haze of smoke dulled the blue. She looked at this for a few moments, then, with a feeling of foreboding, she followed it down to its source.

That first sight of the city seared itself into her vision. No Institute movies or pictures, or anti-sub race propaganda could have prepared her for the debasement that spread like a cancer over every accessible inch of ground. Clusters of dirty people with xylophone ribcages showing starkly through their clothes, mangy dogs, half-naked, blue-lipped children, greasy fires pouring out storms of smoke—the same few images seemed to permute endlessly, miserable camps receding to the indistinct horizon.

For a moment, Sifte wondered if she had made a hideous mistake, if Solntse was right to want to expunge this abject wretchedness from his country. Then she remembered Olga, and Vanya, and the others who had helped her over the last few days. All of them had come from this. She herself had come from it.

"Sifte?" Olga said softly, touching her hand.

Sifte turned, blinked at her. "I—I'm sorry—" she began, but Olga interrupted with a sad smile.

"No, I'm sorry. I should have prepared you better. I can't imagine what it must be like to see this, not having grown up with it. This is the worst of it, anyway. It's not so bad in the city proper." She took a breath, then sighed. "We have to separate now. The river's there."

She pointed to an expanse of dirty snow scattered with more makeshift camps. "They move onto the ice for the winter to give themselves more space. Keep your eyes open for officials, though I doubt you'll meet any out there, and don't use your gun unless you absolutely have to. Take care, Sifte." Olga smiled at her reassuringly, then set off along the river. Within minutes, she was lost in the warren of camps.

Sifte looked across the river. The twisted shapes of ruined buildings beckoned to her dubiously from the other side. Dreamlike and distant in the thick haze, she could make out the faded carnival colors of the two remaining onion domes of the Church on the Spilled Blood.

Sifte made her way out onto the frozen river. It was bigger than she had imagined it, and somehow hostile; she crossed as quickly as she could. She knew that she should find her father right away, but the city had hypnotized her. Instead she walked south, entranced by the vastness of it, the sheer number of people. She had never imagined that the world could be so big, yet she knew that this city was as tiny compared to Russia's sprawling expanse as Institute 1 was to the city.

As Sifte moved further into the city, the camps thinned out and partially-intact buildings replaced them. They were still far from hospitable, but they were an improvement on the shanties. Considering this, Sifte began to realize that there were gradations of poverty in Solntse's society just as there were gradations of privilege. She was wondering about her teachers' reasons for keeping this information to themselves, when it occurred to her that perhaps the teachers didn't realize that there were class divisions within the sub-race. She wondered how many of them had actually been to Myortvograd. If she could have such a violent reaction when she had consciously chosen to embrace it, then she doubted that someone who had been taught to hate and fear it could face it at all.

Sifte worked her way back toward the river, crossed the Moyka and emerged into Dvortsovaya Square. When she looked up at the angel on the Aleksander Column, a chill went down her spine the way it did when she listened to certain pieces of music, or when Mila's eyes went distant and her words cryptic.

She crossed the snowy cobbles, passed the toppled mansions of Millionaya, and finally stood on the Dvortsovaya Embankment. Across the frozen river, the Fortress cathedral's spire drove up like a dagger through the heavy heart of the setting sun. Its center was black, but the gilt edges and the weathervane angel at the top radiated light. Without taking her eyes from the steeple, Sifte pulled the picture from her pocket and opened it up. She looked at it, and then at the realization of it in front of her. For a moment, one was a perfect reflection of the other. Then the horizon bit into the sun, and the city receded into shadow. The steeple stood black against the smoke-streaked sky. A wind had come up off the Gulf, swinging the angel's hailing arm east. Sifte closed her fist around the drawing, and the old paper crumbled to dust.

For a moment the pieces hung in the air around her, and then they were gone.

She turned back to Myortvograd and its flickering campfires. She felt as if the picture's dust had infiltrated her, so that she no longer moved of her own will, but by the collective wills of all the unknown ancestors connecting her to the child who had drawn her destiny in a time unimaginably distant. Though she had never before set foot on these streets, she walked them as if she had known them her whole life. Mother, guide me back to you, she thought—then shuddered, because the thought was no more her own than her suddenly purposeful movements into the pondwater twilight of the ruined city center.

People fell silent as she passed. Her head-scarf had fallen away, and small children reached toward her hair, the brightest thing they had ever seen. The older ones shrank away in terror. Though she did not wear the uniform, they recognized in Sifte the mark of the Opyekun.

Finally, Sifte found herself in front of a door to what looked to be a long-deserted ruin. All but the ground floor had been destroyed, but she could still make out the dull orange of the walls. On the crumbling doorstep sat an old woman, her head in her hands and her eyes closed. Sifte reached into her pocket for a crust of bread she had stuffed into it that morning. She held it toward the woman and said, "Please, babushka, tell me what street this is?"

The woman looked up at her, but her eyes were hidden in the hollows of their sockets. She was silent for a long time. Finally, she took the bread and said, "They're inside."

Sifte pushed the door open onto a dark hallway. Strong hands grabbed her arms. She didn't struggle, just turned to look at the man on her left, illuminated by the dim evening light from the open door. He seemed made of wire and bone, his eyes unnaturally bright. She smiled, and he backed away. The man on her right had let go before she even turned to him.

"Which way?"

Slowly, they raised their arms and pointed into the darkness ahead. Sifte moved forward, her throat tightening with every step she took. She opened a door and found stairs in front of her, followed them down into what must once have been the building's basement. Just ahead of her, a strip of light showed under a door. She reached toward the doorknob, but before she could touch it, the door opened inward onto a blaze of light.

13

The cell block Aleksei and the others were taken to was structurally identical to the one in which they had waited for Alla's test, but this hallway was filthy, reeking of old urine and blood and rotting food. It was also uncomfortably warm.

"We're near the incinerators," Anastasia said. The Pomoshchnik leading them slapped her across the face. She glared at him, but said nothing else.

He herded them into a squalid cell, the last on the right-hand side of the corridor. The piles of rags on the floor looked recently occupied, and the bucket that served as a toilet hadn't been emptied. There was no observation window. The Pomoshchnik shoved the last of them—Anastasia—into the cell with unnecessary force, so that she stumbled to her knees. She whirled and spat at him, but it only hit the door as it closed behind him.

They huddled in a group in the center of the cell, staring dumbly at each other. The fluorescent light overhead buzzed and flickered as though uncertain whether it should waste its energy lighting this place.

"So," Anastasia finally said, "that went about as well as we could have expected."

"What now?" Misha asked.

"About ten minutes ago," Aleksei said, "I was fine-tuning a brilliant plan that hinged on breaking the observation window—"

"And killing the fascist pigs behind it with your bare hands," Anastasia interrupted with a cynical smile, "or maybe an exceptionally dull shard of glass? Way ahead of you on that."

Aleksei looked at Mila, expecting a jibe, but she had sunk back onto the pile of rags, shivering. He bent over her, felt her burning forehead and racing pulse.

"Shit," he said.

"You should have let me die," she said through dry lips.

"And I thought that was an act to buy time," Anastasia said, looking at Mila with an expression that could have been irony or anger.

"What for? We're already dead."

Anastasia shook her head. "I would have thought you'd be the last they'd turn."

Even as Mila glared at Anastasia, her eyes filled with tears, and then Anastasia burst into tears as well. They cried for a few minutes, clutching each other, then Anastasia dragged her sleeve across her wet face. Aleksei let out the breath he hadn't realized he was holding.

"So," Misha finally said, looking tentatively at Anastasia, who sat cross-legged now with Mila's head in her lap, "nobody has a plan?"

They looked at each other hopefully. Finally, Aleksei answered, "This was my plan B, so it's kind of sketchy. And contingent on a lot of other things going our way. In fact, if I handed this in as a tactics assignment—"

"Just spit it out," Anastasia said.

"Okay. I think that if Alla really is trying to cover all this up until she has a good answer for Solntse, then she'd involve as few officials as possible. All I've seen are Apraksina and two Pomoshchniki."

"So there aren't many officials," Misha said. "We're still in the sublevels with seventeen floors of enemies on top of us…with the possible exception of Dmitri."

"You can forget about Dmitri," Anastasia said.

"I wouldn't be so sure," Aleksei answered.

"Either way," Misha said, "our position is shit."

"Right—so they can't be too worried about us finding a way out of it."

"Honestly, Lyosha, if *that's* the point—" Anastasia began.

"It's not. The point is, Alla sent us down here with one Pomoshchnik. Why would it be different when they come to get us again?"

Misha looked dubious, and Mila was clearly suppressing a comment. Anastasia said, "So basically," Anastasia said, "you're saying we should overpower the guy when he comes to get us, take his gun and…what?"

"Hope that one gun is enough to get us into the main elevator."

"You're right, Lyosha," Anastasia said after a moment's consideration, "that plan is ludicrous. Still," she added with a wry smile, "I'd rather go out fighting."

"Guardians are soldiers, after all," said Misha.

"And in the meantime?" Mila asked, her eyes on the flickering light.

"Rest," Aleksei said.

"And hope no one has to pee," Misha added.

*

Anastasia shook Aleksei awake. She had a hand clamped tightly over his mouth. He sat up, glaring at her, and she let him go, hissing, "Not a word."

Aleksei had been dreaming of the greenhouses. He was with Sifte. She was looking down, as she had looked at the dead bird so long ago, but this time with horror on her face. When Aleksei followed her eyes, he saw not a bird at her feet, but Mila. Her skin was white with a lazuline tinge, her lips purple. A dark stain was spreading across the front of her white smock.

The dream and the abrupt awakening left him shaking. He looked over at Mila. An ominous pallor had replaced her feverish flush, but she blinked at him with clearer eyes than she'd had in a long time. Then he heard the unmistakable report of a gun. Their heads clocked identically towards the sound, like sunflowers to light.

"How long has it been going on?" Aleksei whispered.

"That's the fifth shot we've heard," Anastasia answered.

"But we were all asleep for a while," Misha added with a shaking voice. "So we don't know."

"And they're coming closer. Any last words?"

Aleksei's mind raced as he listened to the intermittent cracks. Suddenly, he smiled. "She did it," he said. He didn't realize he had spoken the thought aloud until Anastasia asked:

"Want to fill the rest of us in, oh holy oracle?"

"Sifte made it," he said.

"That's a bit of a leap," Mila said.

"I don't think so. You saw how carefully those prisoners were chosen. Alla wouldn't kill them off unless they posed

411

some kind of threat. Soviet prisoners could only pose a threat if the balance of power is shifting in favor of the Soviet. It can't be coincidence that it's happening now."

They were all silent, considering this. Then Anastasia said, "It sounds to me like three guns. What do you think the chances are that four of us can take three of them?"

Aleksei's smile broadened, and after a moment the rest of them smiled with him. He said, "Our best chance is to wait on either side of the door. Do what you have to do to get out. If any of us gets shot—"

Anastasia put her hand on Aleksei's arm. "Lyosha, we know."

They took up their positions on either side of the door, Aleksei and Mila on the right, Misha and Anastasia on the left. In the silence, the buzz of the light seemed almost as loud as the reports of the guns. Aleksei counted ten, twenty, thirty, shots. They were only a few cells away now, close enough that he could hear the muffled cries of fear and pain.

Then, abruptly, the shooting stopped. They waited, not daring to look at each other. After a few minutes, they heard the sound of muffled footfalls moving toward the elevator, then all was silent again. Finally they looked at each other.

"False alarm?" Anastasia offered. Aleksei glowered at her, but she smiled at him with thin defiance.

"I think we'd better find out," he answered.

"And how do you plan to do that?" Mila asked.

Aleksei smiled. "Plan C. You're going to love this."

*

They pulled the metal handle off the foul bucket, and bent it four times for strength. Then they took turns chipping away at the part of the wall by the side of the door where the lock ought to be. It took three hours, during which they stopped intermittently to listen to the increasingly peculiar sounds coming from overhead. The cement muffled things too much to make out voices or individual footsteps, but now and again a crash would shudder down to their level, and twice they heard the faint wail of emergency sirens. The temperature in the cell was also increasing.

"Never heard sirens before," Anastasia said, wiping sweat from her reddened face. "Looks like you might be right, Lyosha."

"What's with the heat?" Misha asked. "Do you think this is what the bitch meant by a horrible death?"

Aleksei shook his head, and went back to chipping concrete. "I'd say they're filling the incinerators."

"If they're shooting prisoners and burning evidence," Misha said, "doesn't that kind of suggest—"

"That they're clearing out."

"Then how come no one's come?" Mila asked. "I can't believe they'd have forgotten about us after what happened earlier."

"Conveniently forgotten," Anastasia answered, as Aleksei's makeshift chisel finally hit the metal box containing the lock's wiring. "It does fit nicely into the horrible death category."

"It's screwed shut," Aleksei said, looking at the lock.

"This should work." Anastasia pulled a button from her jumpsuit and handed it to him. He unscrewed the back of the box.

"Has anyone got any idea how to override this thing?"

"One," Misha answered, a barely-repressed smile tightening the corners of his eyes and mouth. As Anastasia had done, he pulled a button off a pocket of his jumpsuit.

413

"Spider," he said. Four metal filaments shot out of the sides of the button. It walked around the perimeter of his palm.

Aleksei cocked an eyebrow. "That's plagiarism."

"No, improvements. I was going to tell you once I'd perfected it." He grinned at the metal bug, then at the others.

"How imperfect is it, exactly?"

Misha shrugged. "I had to change some things to make it small enough. It can't fly, but it can do wirework. I think. I've never tested it."

"No time like the present," Anastasia said dryly.

Misha placed the bug in the box and said, "Open." The bug felt around with its filament legs for a moment, then scuttled into the workings of the lock. After a few minutes, the door slid open, and the bug reappeared. If Aleksei hadn't known better, he would have said that it looked expectant. Misha picked it up again, beaming, and pocketed it.

"Take care of that," Aleksei said, "we might need it again." He paused, peered with the others into the empty hallway, then said, "Look, I'll see what's going on up there, and then we can decide what to do next. If I'm not back in half an hour, assume I'm not coming."

"You're not going alone," Mila began.

"There's no time to argue." Before any of them could stop him, he was off into the sickly shadows of the corridor.

"Wait!" Misha cried, running after him. He pressed the nanobot into Aleksei's hand. "You'll need it to get up the elevator."

"Thanks," he said, pocketing the button, then turned back toward the elevator.

The cell doors were open, and those that weren't empty were a bloody mess of still, emaciated bodies. Aleksei didn't

414

look too closely. As Misha had predicted, the elevator to the white room was I.D. locked, but the bug disabled it as easily as it had the first. It seemed days since Aleksei had ridden away from the white room. He wondered whether this warping of time was what drove prisoners mad.

As the door opened, Aleksei flattened himself against the wall of the elevator, but the room was inhabited only by the dead. The bodies of the prisoners sprawled where they had fallen. Aleksei passed into the other elevator. He decided that he would be safer getting out in a corridor rather than a common room. He pushed the yellow button, flattening again as the doors opened, but the corridor was empty.

Even at night, Institute 1's silence had always seemed full, perhaps for the awareness of so many breathing bodies. The silence now was one of total desertion. Aleksei looked into classrooms, dormitories, bathrooms. All bore the same signs of hurried departure: scattered clothing, papers, books, disks and screens. It made sense, he thought, as he walked back to the elevator. They would evacuate the youngest children first and use the older ones to help clean up.

Aleksei checked the lower level corridors, and found all of them as deserted as the first. But beyond the door to the middle level, on the maroon corridor, he encountered the first signs of life. There didn't seem to be any children, but as he crept along, he heard a group of teachers talking in a classroom.

"We've done enough," a woman was saying in a high, frightened voice. "Let's get out while we can."

"I still think we're jumping the gun," a man answered with pompous irritability. "So the izmyennitsa reached the city. What can one half-trained Opyekun do?"

"Haven't you heard?" asked another man, who sounded as frightened as the woman who had spoken first. "People are saying she's Stepan Pierson's daughter!"

"I've heard," the other man snapped, "and it's ridiculous. Do you really think the Sun would have brought such a child here?"

"I know what I've seen," the woman answered. "Other children have turned against us, but Solntse has never thought it was cause to evacuate his most important school— or court-martial top students on speculation. Something's very wrong up there, and I think the sooner we get out of here, the better."

Aleksei made his way back to the elevator, once again filled with elation that defied all the grim certainties of his situation. As he stepped out of the elevator into the sublevels, he was optimistic. Soon Institute 1 would be deserted, and once it was they could contact Sifte. They might even be out by the next morning. In his exhilaration, Aleksei had forgotten Alla's threat.

14

To Sifte, whose eyes had grown accustomed to the darkness, it seemed that the tiny woman who stood a few feet from her was the source of the brightness. Even when her eyes began to adjust, the illusion remained. The woman was so frail that the light seemed to pass through her. It flamed her short, sharp brushstrokes of red hair into the halo of an avenging angel, but her dark eyes receded like cyclones.

"Mama?" Sifte heard herself say.

Sasha stared at Sifte for a moment, impassive. Then her face crumbled in fear and grief. "You're not here!" she cried in a voice rusted by disuse, redoubling as if from a blow.

Sifte didn't know the specifics of what went on in the Fortress prison, but she knew enough to realize that Sasha's mind might well be broken. She took a step into the hallway. The woman stepped back, her eyes wide and terrified.

"Sasha," Sifte said softly, reaching a tentative hand towards her. When the woman made no response, she said, "It's Sifte."

There was a flash of curiosity in her eyes before distrust closed over them again. "Sifte's dead."

"Didn't Stepan tell you I would come?" It occurred to her

as she said it that Stepan might in fact believe her to be dead, given the rumors her bloody journey had no doubt spawned.

"You can't be Sifte," Sasha insisted, still backing away. Then, for no apparent reason, she stopped and scrutinized her. "But you look like her," she said, almost wistfully. Then her expression changed again, this time to acrimony. "He's sent you to kill me."

Sifte wanted to shake the woman, to scream at her, but she clung to her patience and said, "I'm not here to hurt you."

Sasha smiled bitterly. "Then you can't be my daughter."

"Why not?" Sifte asked.

"Because if my daughter were still alive, then she would wish me dead."

Heart sinking like a wrecked ship, Sifte pulled back her left sleeve. Sasha looked at Sifte's scar for a long time, the expression on her face shifting as quickly as light on water on a windy day. Then she looked up at Sifte. It was as if a sea wall had broken, and the torrent of grief it had held back came pouring through all at once.

"You really are Sifte," she sobbed. Sifte nodded, unable to speak for her own welling tears. Sasha crumpled to her knees, wept into her daughter's open palms. "Then forgive me," she said. "Please, forgive me."

*

When Stepan reached the Technological Institute, he found the street door wide open. The guards weren't at their posts. With increasing foreboding, Stepan shut the door and made his way along the pitch-dark corridors. He found the missing guards by the open bunker door, straining to hear the words of the muted voices speaking somewhere inside.

"Back to your posts!" Stepan growled, but he didn't reprimand them, because he was listening to the rise and fall of the voices now, too. Both were women's; one he would have known if he'd been separated from it for a lifetime.

With the peculiar detachment that comes with sudden grief or joy, he watched his feet move him to the closed door of Sasha's room, his hand grasp the old-fashioned doorknob, turn it, push it open. The two women fell silent when they saw him. They sat facing each other on the mattress, balancing teacups and slabs of black bread and cheese on their knees. Both of them regarded him silently for a moment, and then the girl put the cup and bread aside, stood up and moved towards him.

He had pictured her height, but not the disarming fragility of her long limbs. He was prepared for her well-controlled expression, but not the eyes, colored like his own but deep with the paradox of innocence and wisdom that had once told him that Sasha was unique among women. Sifte's silver-blonde hair was tangled and grayed with dirt, there was more dirt and dried blood on her clothes and bandaged arm, and her face had the pallor and violet hollows of deep exhaustion. But she was alive.

"Stepan," she said softly, and stepped forward into his embrace. Stepan hugged her tightly for a long time, unable to feel anything but overwhelming, all-consuming relief. Then he saw Sasha watching them, arms tucked under each other across her thin chest, smiling tentatively.

"Sasha?" Stepan asked, as if he feared that his presence or the sound of his voice would send her back into the terrible trance of the last week.

"That's right," she said, her voice roughened but still her own. "I'm back."

419

*

For a while they talked—or Stepan and Sifte talked, Sasha mostly listened. They rushed to fill in the missing pieces of their stories, aware that they didn't have much time for this. Sifte told her story as briefly and modestly as possible, but Stepan managed to tease out a more accurate picture of what had happened in the days since they had last been in contact. He was appalled at the trials the girl had faced, but proud of how well she had done. Sasha's story was even briefer. Stepan and Sifte were aware that she left out a good deal, also that Sasha might never be able to tell them the rest.

Finally Sifte looked at Stepan, and asked the question she had no doubt wanted to ask all along: "What about my friends?" Stepan sighed. "You're going to tell me that they're dead."

Before Stepan could reply, Andrei limped in. "I don't think so."

"You!" Stepan cried. "How long have you been listening at the door? I suppose the night watch was there with you."

Andrei smiled less frostily than usual. "Not anymore," he answered. "I fired them. By the way, we really need to soundproof this place. And cover the crack under the door." Andrei's smile tightened as he looked at Sifte. "I don't always eavesdrop, but I wanted to know what I was up against." He leaned forward stiffly, kissed Sifte on both cheeks. "I'm Andrei Kirillovich Umanskiy."

"Of course," Sifte said. "But what do you know about my friends?"

Andrei laughed with more sincerity than he had smiled, and sat down in the chair Stepan vacated. "She really is like you—both. Glad you're feeling better, Sasha." He looked her

420

up and down, then turned back to Stepan. "Once again, your timing is impeccable. Twenty minutes ago Glaza coughed up its last gem, but it was the one we were looking for: a list of everyone who was evacuated from Institute 1."

"Slow down," Stepan said, looking anxiously at Sifte. "I haven't had time to explain to her about that."

"I already know." Sifte said. "Sasha told me all about it."

"So, you *were* listening, earlier!" Stepan said to Sasha.

"I've been listening the whole time," Sasha answered, in a tone that told him she didn't plan to elaborate.

"Please tell me," Sifte said to Andrei, her face beginning to show strain as well as exhaustion.

"None of your friends were on the evacuation list," Andrei said.

"So what makes you think they're alive?"

"They aren't listed with the dead."

"Look, I'm not up to mental gymnastics right now. If my friends weren't evacuated and they aren't dead, then where are they?"

Andrei gave her an appraising look. "My guess is, they're still there." Sifte shook her head, and Andrei sighed. "In Myortvograd, there's an old legend that Solntse's important buildings are rigged with self-destruct mechanisms. I've just confirmed it. I don't imagine I need to tell you why he wants to destroy Institute 1."

"What about how?" Sifte asked.

Andrei smiled with his old, sober cynicism. "You recall the windows?"

In fact, Sifte had thought a lot about Institute 1's windows since she overheard the conversation between Alla and Dmitri the night she escaped. There was only one way that

Alla could have known the things she seemed to know about Sifte and her friends.

So she answered, "I recall pieces of glass we were told were windows to the outside, which actually connected to observation rooms, from which the teachers watched us when we thought we were alone."

"You saw one of these rooms?"

Sifte shrugged. "No. But I'm sure they're there."

Andrei's eyes narrowed. "You're right. And yes, most of the windows are used for observation. But on every floor there is one which is real. Its frame is held in place with electro-magnetic locks. The control mechanism is in the Fortress. It works on a timed countdown system, depolarizing one window every hour. The window frame collapses, with obvious results. Given there are seventeen floors in Institute 1—"

"Sixteen," Sifte interrupted.

"Sixteen that you know about," Andrei rejoined, "plus a sublevel you don't. As far as I can tell the countdown started an hour ago."

"That's bad, but not so bad," Sifte answered speculatively. "They'll go to the roof, and we'll find a way to get to them."

Andrei sighed again. "You still think Institute 1 is founded on the sea bed."

"Isn't it?"

"No. It's floating, and it's held in place by chains. Filled with air, it floats. Filled with water, well…"

"How come no one ever told us this?"

"The only reason for it is the self-destruct contingency. Solntse wants everyone to believe he's infallible."

Sifte dropped her head into her hands.

"Maybe I'm missing something here," Stepan said, "but wouldn't it have been easier just to have built explosives into the foundation?"

"Easier," Andrei answered, "but illegal. Part of the non-aggression treaty Solntse had to sign to build Institute 1 in international waters stated that no mechanisms of war could be used, stored, traded or produced there."

"I'd say he's doing all of the above, even without explosives in the walls," Stepan said.

Andrei flicked his fingers impatiently. "Whatever your rose-colored Western view of things might suggest, Stepan, nobody cares what Solntse does out there as long as there's no danger of it blowing them up."

Sifte fixed Andrei with eyes that reminded him of Sasha's. "I do," she said coldly. "You two can stay here and argue if you want to. I'm going to—"

"Save your friends," Andrei finished for her, with a hint of condescension that made Sifte seethe. "I figured you'd say that, and since I can't stop you, I'm going to help you. But there's something else you should know, first. Your friend Misha sent a scrambled S.O.S. the day after you left. It said there was a traitor in the ranks—well, a traitor to your operation. He didn't know who it was, but he suspected that this person knew you and what you were up to, and would be a danger to you all. Now, there were two other names missing from the evacuation records. Do you know Tatyana or a Nikolai, both your year?"

Sifte shut her eyes on the suddenly-swimming room. "I should have known."

"The girl looks like a nasty piece of work," Andrei said, "but not particularly interesting. Typical Solntsegrad brat. Nikolai, though…what do you know about him?"

Sifte shrugged. "Not much. He was Aleksei's room-mate for a short time. Kind of a smart-ass, but not actually that smart. A bit of a superiority complex."

Andrei smiled grimly. "Not surprising, considering he's Solntse's son and heir."

Sifte paled still further. "*What?* But then, why would they leave him there?"

"I don't think they did. They probably wanted him off the records for some other reason. Quite possibly to protect him, and this Tanya, whatever she has to do with all this. But it means you're in more danger than any of us imagined."

"Okay," Sifte said. "Now, how are you going to help me save my friends?"

"I'm going to do it for you. You're staying here."

"No, I'm not. I got them into this, I'm going to get them out."

Andrei looked at Stepan, but Stepan only shrugged and said, "I'm not going to stop her. Besides, her help will be valuable if we need to go inside."

"I know Institute 1 well enough," Andrei bristled.

"Yes, but Sifte knows her friends," Sasha said softly. They all looked at her in surprise. She had been so still and silent throughout their discussion, they had nearly forgotten she was there. "Sifte will go."

Andrei sighed again, looking at Sifte with a mixture of annoyance and respect. "You'll be no use if you don't rest, and at any rate there's work for me to do before we can go anywhere. Stepan, come with me. Sifte, get some sleep. We'll be back to get you when we're ready."

Sifte wanted to argue, but a part of her knew that they were right. Her head was thick with fatigue, the periphery of her vision gray. So she watched them go, then sank gratefully onto Sasha's bed. The last thing she remembered was Sasha pulling the covers up around her chin.

*

Sasha awakened her from troubled dreams a few hours later. Sifte gulped a cup of scalding tea, but she couldn't make herself swallow anything solid. Throwing on a threadbare coat Stepan had produced when he returned to the bunker, she followed him and Andrei out into the cold, dark morning.

The city had changed. It was as if the people of Myortvograd had awakened from a long sleep to realize that entire lifetimes had passed them by. They gathered around blazing campfires, talking with animation. Over and over again the same disembodied words sprang from them like the sparks their fires sent up into the ageing night: hlopoti, izmyeneniye, boyna. Trouble, change, war. It was difficult to tell whether the change in Myortvograd's people was a result of fear or anticipation, but either way it was a relief.

Like the shanty town, the docks lay outside the walls of Solntsegrad, on Gutuyevskiy Ostrov. Technically, they fell under Solntsegrad's jurisdiction, and very little got in or out of his port that Solntse didn't know about. However, the black market had always been expensive to maintain, and without sub-race workers who would spend a day loading or unloading ships for a loaf of bread or a few eggs or beets, it would have been insupportable.

By the time Stepan, Sifte and Andrei reached the island, the docks were in a state of chaos. Pomoshchniki scrambled to control bands of sub-race workers who had taken advantage of the past day's confusion. Bands from the city and surrounding countryside had heard of the upset and poured in to take what they could, while they could. They had broken open warehouses, were tearing apart boats and machinery for their precious parts. They'd set strategic fires, apparently oblivious to the guns the Pomoshchniki were using liberally.

"We really don't have much time," Andrei said. "Solntse will close the port soon—he's started already. All of the big ships are gone."

Yet there was still an array of smaller boats of various shapes and sizes, docked or moored in the harbor. Stepan and Andrei were surveying these.

"Why aren't they trying to take them?" Sifte asked.

Andrei looked at her with distracted puzzlement. "Who, take what?"

"The people," she said, gesturing to a sub-race group running past, pockets and bags surreally bulging with peaches. A Pomoshchnik ran after them, brandishing a gun which had run out of ammunition. "Why don't they take the boats and get out of here?"

Stepan gave her a look that was part incredulity, part pity. "It doesn't occur to them," he said. "They can't imagine any world but Solntse's."

Stepan watched Sifte struggle to understand this. He wished there were an easier way to explain to her the mentality of an uneducated and subjugated people, but such understanding only came through long exposure to the same subjugation. Even now, he couldn't entirely grasp it. But he understood the look on Sifte's face well enough, so her next question didn't much surprise him.

"Then how will they fight?"

"A lot of them won't," Andrei answered bitterly, before Stepan could. "They'll run, or they'll stand like sacrificial lambs while—"

"Andrei!" Stepan snapped.

Sifte watched her father and her uncle stare each other down. In all the years she had communicated with them, she hadn't realized that they were rivals. It seemed to her that however many of her illusions toppled, she was no better able to anticipate the next. The world around her became more distorted by the moment, and she found it increasingly difficult to remember her reasons for wishing to join it. All at once, she understood the sub-race's inertia, and she wondered what she was doing here.

"Sifte?" Stepan was saying, with a solicitous hand on her arm. "Are you all right?"

She looked at the madman's hope in his eyes and found yet another reserve of courage and energy she had not thought she had. The world around her resumed its familiar proportions, solidified under her feet.

"I'm fine," she said, still slightly dazed, with the irony but without the bitterness. "Have you chosen?"

"That one," Andrei said, pointing to an open-decked boat at the end of the dock. It had two big outboard engines.

"It's going to be cold," Stepan said doubtfully.

"It's also going to be fast," Andrei retorted, already limping towards it. "More importantly, they don't appear to be paying much attention to it at the moment."

He was right. The majority of the activity was concentrated on the bigger docks where the main warehouses were. The only people within firing range were sub-race, hungrily eating their spoils.

"They'll be sick tomorrow," Stepan observed.

427

"Most likely they'll be dead tonight," Andrei answered, dropping down into the boat.

There were no keys, but Andrei hot-wired the motors. As they were pulling away from the dock, a band of Pomoshchniki finally spotted them, and began firing, but they were beyond accurate range. They kept their heads down for a few minutes, and then there was only the open water and cold air. Sifte leaned into the sharp wind with relief.

"Why aren't they following?" she asked.

"I expect there are others waiting," Andrei answered.

"I don't think so," Stepan contradicted. "Solntse needs all the help he can get on land. And if the Institute's about to self-destruct, he'll have ordered everybody out of the vicinity."

For once, Andrei didn't argue, and this silent concession comforted Sifte more than any spoken assurance could have. He urged the boat on faster, and Sifte glued her eyes to the horizon, daring it not to produce the angular crown of Institute 1 one last time.

15

Time was meaningless in the cell. After a while the flickering strip-light died, and sometime later the heat did too. Then Anastasia let out a piercing shriek and leapt away from the door, against which she had been sitting.

"Water," she said. "There's water coming in here!"

The puddle was inching across the floor. Aleksei tasted it. "Seawater," he said.

"But how did it get in here?" Mila asked.

"I don't know, but I think it's time we got out."

The water in the corridor was several inches deep. White emergency lights had replaced the dull fluorescents, and they cast electric moons onto the water, threw shadows sharp as flints over the walls and ceiling. The current grew stronger the closer they came to the elevator, and for a sickening moment Aleksei thought they really were doomed to drown in the sublevel. Then he saw that the water was coming from the last door in the left-hand row of cells. A perfunctory look inside showed that this cell had an observation window. It was broken, and dark water poured through it.

"So it really is a window to the outside?" Misha asked, bewildered.

"I don't think so," Aleksei answered. "If it was, the pressure would have ripped this whole wall out."

Mila pushed the call button for the elevator. Apparently it was running on the emergency generator, because the doors slid open. They didn't look at each other as they rode up to the white room. It was lit by a single emergency bulb, but it was still dry. They hurried past the pile of bodies, and took the main elevator up to the first floor—the nursery.

The place was a fever dream of half-remembered artifacts. The toys, the books, the tiny furniture were as they remembered them, but diminished by time and surreal in the stark light. Looking at a wide, black window smudged with children's finger- and nose-prints, Aleksei suddenly missed Sifte terribly. The others stood in a tight, defensive group, peering out at the brightly-colored room with aversion.

"Okay," Aleksei said. "The water's going to rise quickly, assuming it's coming in at the sublevel. We'll need to get as high up as we can. But first we should try to get a message to Stepan or Andrei if the transceivers are still online."

"What about figuring out where the water's coming from?" Mila asked.

"Or finding a way out of here?" Anastasia added.

"And food," said Misha.

Aleksei looked at them. He didn't like the idea of splitting up, but they were right—all of these things were equally important. "Okay. Misha, you find a computer and try to reach Stepan. Anastasia, have a look for a boat. Mila, if you can get some food and water, I'll go up to the newsroom and try to find out what's going on outside. Where should we meet?"

"The library," said Anastasia. "It's high up and there's computer access."

"Okay?"

They all nodded. As they waited for the elevator, there was a loud crash behind them. They turned to see a wall of water and debris rushing toward them from the far end of the corridor. Then the elevator doors opened and Aleksei shoved them all inside, slammed his hand against the button for White Level.

"What are the chances of two windows blowing out by accident?" Anastasia asked shakily. Nobody answered.

The elevator juddered to a stop at the top of the middle level. They managed to pry the doors wide enough to get out. Aleksei took Misha's button from his pocket, and put it to work disabling the lock on the door to the upper level.

"Okay," he said as they waited, "the elevator's obviously out. Use the corridors, or the service stairs if you can get into them. Do what you can as fast as you can, then go up to White Level." They nodded mutely, and went. Aleksei got the bug to unlock the door to the service stairway, and took this short cut one floor down to the newsroom.

He knew that something was wrong the moment he stepped out into the corridor. Several of the emergency lights were broken, and there were bullet pockmarks in the walls. Cautiously, Aleksei rounded the bend in the corridor with the window seat where Tanya had waylaid him on a night that seemed to belong to another lifetime.

The door of the newsroom was ajar, braced by the bodies of two teachers Aleksei had known only by sight. A single running screen cast phantom light over their faces, their hands stiffened around their guns. Aleksei pried them from their fingers, pocketed one, and released the safety on the other. He stepped over the bodies and into the newsroom, and when he saw what waited there, his hope nearly died.

Two blown-out monitors gaped like screams. Between them Dmitri's body slumped over the keyboard of the one left running. His right arm hung limp, a gun dangling from one frozen finger. He had shot himself in the mouth. Half of his face rested in a viscous puddle of blood, but the upward-facing half was clean, even peaceful.

Dmitri's left hand had fallen onto the keyboard, and the terminal screen had filled with slashes. Aleksei lifted it from the keys, and brought up the previous screen. It was a news report. Reckoning by the date the computer currently displayed, it had been posted the previous day. It informed the Solntsegrad public that the traitor who had escaped Institute 1 had been apprehended and shot outside of a village called Vasilovo, north of Solntsegrad.

For a moment Aleksei contemplated following Dmitri in his desperate fate. But the lucid cold of the gunmetal against his palm jolted his logic back into place. He felt sick at the thought that he had nearly walked into the same trap Dmitri had. But then, Dmitri had probably been told that all of them were dead, had perhaps even been shown the tangle of bodies in the white room that looked so like them. He would have been too much in the clutches of despair to wonder why, if the report's content was true, Solntse was still evacuating Institute 1.

Aleksei tried to initiate a search for corroborating stories, but the radio link appeared to have been severed. Instead, he traced the news report. By the time he located the source, he was shaking with fury. It had not originated in a Glaza newsroom at all, but at Institute 1. The codes were Opyekun.

He raised the gun in blind rage and shot five rounds into the terminal. Then, with a slightly clearer head, he looked down at Dmitri. He wished that his last words to his teacher had been kinder, but he didn't deceive himself by thinking that this would have saved him. Aleksei suspected that the seeds of Dmitri's suicide had been sown long before he had known anything about Sifte or the rest of them. He bent down and kissed the man's vellum cheek, then retrieved the gun from his bent finger, and turned his back on that ruined life.

*

When Aleksei got to White Level, the others were waiting. They had found a common room with a wall of windows. They would let in light if there was any, but now it was dark. They leaned on a wooden table, on which they'd spread out bread and cheese and cold, cured meat, but none of them touched it. They looked up at Aleksei with defeated eyes.

"Your news can't be worse than mine," he said.

"Try us," Anastasia answered.

Aleksei sighed, put the three guns on the table, and said, "Dmitri's dead. Shot himself over a fake news report that Sifte had been caught and killed."

"How do you know it's fake?" Mila asked.

"Because I traced it back to Alla."

Anastasia said, "We can definitely beat that."

Aleksei waited, but for once in her life, Anastasia appeared to be incapable of saying anything else. Finally, Misha said, "We're sinking."

"Sinking?" Aleksei repeated.

"The building is, to be specific," said Mila, whose face was glowing with fever again. Her lips stretched into Tanya's smile. "The windows are collapsing."

Aleksei shook his head. "I thought the windows were fake."

"Some are real," Misha answered.

"One on each floor," Mila continued. "Made with magnetic frames that depolarize on schedule—one every fifty-two minutes. Kind of like a time bomb, only more organic. The whole building will be full of water in about fifteen hours."

"How do you know this?"

"Misha found out when he tried to contact Stepan. There was a countdown sequence showing on all the main terminals, no link to Glaza, so he did some research—the book kind. Turns out there's a self-destruct mechanism built into all of the schools…but then, who really cares about the details now." Mila smiled again. Aleksei couldn't look at her.

"The roof will stay clear," he argued. "It'll be cold, but we can survive up there for a while if we're prepared."

The others exchanged a look. Anastasia said, "You don't think they'd go to all that trouble unless they meant it, do you?" She sighed. "Institute 1 isn't built on the ocean floor, like we've always been told. It's free-floating, chained down. It'll sink once there's enough water inside."

Letting out a long sigh, Aleksei said, "Can't we disarm the mechanism that releases the windows? Delay it at least?"

Misha shook his head. "I tried. The detonator, or whatever you call it, isn't here. And anyway, like I said, we're cut off from Glaza."

"They must have left boats."

"We looked," Mila said. "There's nothing in the docking bay."

"There has to be another way."

"Lyosha!" Anastasia wailed in exasperation. "It's over!"

"It's not over!" Aleksei answered, slamming his hands on the table. "If we have to build a boat from these tables and sail out of here with bed sheets, we'll do it or die trying!" He looked at them all in turn; none of them argued. "Okay. First we're going to eat. Then we're going to scour this place from top to bottom—well, the parts that aren't under water—and try to find some way out of here."

"And why should we listen to you?" Mila asked shrilly.

"Because if we'd done things your way, we'd be dead by now."

"We'll be dead in a few hours, anyway."

Their eyes locked. The cold intensity in Mila's made him falter, but the next moment he was furious. He knew where the hatred came from, but Mila had no right to hate him for not loving her, any more than he did to hate Sifte. Aleksei picked up Dmitri's gun and offered it to her.

"Why wait?" he asked.

"Aleksei!" Anastasia cried.

"If it's what she really wants, then let her do it and spare us the misery."

Anastasia's eyes and Misha's were filled with horror and anger. Mila looked at the gun with an expression of icy calculation that was more Opyekun than Aleksei had ever seen any of his friends look. She took the gun from him, weighed it in her palm as a housewife might consider a piece of fruit in a market. Then, quite suddenly, the look faded. She put the gun back on the table, looked at Aleksei for a moment with eyes like blown-out candles, then walked out of the room.

Anastasia got up to follow her, but Aleksei caught her arm. She whirled on him angrily, but he said, "You don't understand and there isn't time to explain. Please do whatever you can to get us out of this alive. I'll bring her back." Reluctantly, Anastasia let him go.

He found Mila in the Dacha, which had been cleared of all their things. She sat cross-legged under the light with her head in her hands, but her cheeks were dry.

"Come on, Milyonka," he said, sitting down by her. "There's no time for fence-sitting."

She was silent for so long that he thought she wasn't going to answer. Then, in an even voice, she said, "I was hoping to die with some kind of dignity, but thanks to you, that's out of the question."

"What are you talking about?"

Mila looked up, searching his face. "Sifte really didn't tell you?"

The last time he had spoken to Sifte had been barely a week before, but the memory was already cracked and darkened almost beyond recognition, like the ikons in the archives. Drawing a deep breath, he said, "I know that you love me, Mila. Sifte and I did talk about it once, but she didn't have to tell me."

"So you really don't know."

"If you have something else to say to me, then say it, and I just hope it explains what's going on with you, because I don't know how much more of the new Mila I can take!"

"Plain and simple, then," she said, her tone hard. "I'm dying of syphilis. It's a resistant strain that's generally confined to the sub-race. I got it from my mother, who was a prostitute, thanks to Solntse's progressive politics. If we get out of here, I have about six months left to live—if they'll even qualify as living!"

"Even if all of that was true, would you really want to live the rest of your life like this—hating everyone, and making them hate you?"

"Why shouldn't I?" she cried. Her anger didn't faze Aleksei; it was a relief after the trenchant bitterness. "I've been sweet and gentle my whole life, and where has it left me? Unwanted by my mother, pawned to a dictator who's used me to do things I can't even bear to think about, in love with someone I couldn't have even if he did love me back! I'm seventeen years old, Aleksei, and instead of dreaming about all the things I might do with my life I'm wondering if I'll live five months or six!" Mila was trying for a cynical smile, but the tears streaming down her face precluded it. "Do you have any idea what it's like to know the scientific name—in five languages—for every inch of my body the disease eats, but not to be able to stop it? Getting out of here means something to you, because you have something to hope for. I can only hope the disease will destroy my mind before I have to watch myself disintegrate!"

"So you'll just give in?" Aleksei cried. "Do you think that if we make it out of here any of our lives will be any easier? But you don't think anymore, do you. You're already dead."

He had meant it figuratively, but as soon as Aleksei spoke the words, he saw their truth. The Mila he had grown up with was gone, and he couldn't even name what was left in her place. Something ancient and vengeful. A fury? A fiend? Her eyes were glittering slits, her wet cheeks flamed with poisoned blood, even the hairs that had escaped her long plait seemed to sing with tension, like live wires.

"Say what you want, you're not going to whip me into submission like the others!"

"And you're not going to talk them into giving up their last chance!"

"They don't have a chance," she said, her voice suddenly soft and persuasive. "You don't have a chance. You'll never see Sifte again. You might as well accept it."

Aleksei didn't like this new tone, or the way it beckoned to him. "Is that what this is about? Jealousy? You can't have me, so you want to make sure that I can't have her?"

"Yes!" Mila cried, then shook her head, her face contorted with conflicting emotions. As quickly as it had invaded, the insidious tone retreated. "No…I don't know!" Sobs engulfed her again. "What have I said, Lyosha? I don't know what's happening to me."

Aleksei looked at Mila for a moment, and then he gathered her into his arms. She sobbed into his shoulder. Up until that moment, Aleksei hadn't believed Mila's story. It was too much like the other things they had been told or led to believe to undermine their confidence, or turn them against each other. But when his arms closed around her, Aleksei realized how frail Mila had become, as if something really were eating her from the inside out. Her body burned against his, light and hot as an ember, but Aleksei was cold with the thought that everything she had said might be true. Only then did he realize how much he relied on her, and how shamelessly he had accepted her devotion while avoiding this confrontation, for fear of losing the parts of Mila's love that he wanted if he rejected those he didn't.

"Mila, look at me," he said. She raised her tear-stained face. For the moment it was gentle, though troubled and he rushed to say what he had to say before she could change again. "It's true," he said, "I do love Sifte, but I don't know if Sifte will ever love me." He paused, considering his next words, then said, "Right now I can't imagine a future beyond the next few hours…but one thing I'm sure of is that it would be a sad future without you. So please don't destroy the Mila I love because you think I'll never love her differently."

Mila looked at him a long time, as though memorizing his face. Finally she said, "I don't know if I can promise you that. It isn't in my control. But I do know that you won't ever love me differently—I wouldn't love you if you could, perverse as that may sound. And you're right. It's not over for us, yet."

"But you said—"

"That wasn't me. I know—the part of me that's really me knows—that it doesn't end for us here. Whatever else I've said and done since then, that's why I let you stop me in the white room. And whatever else I might still say and do, remember that."

Aleksei scrutinized her face for hidden motives or meanings, but he saw only her old, familiar sweetness, though the overlying sadness was terrible. He squeezed her tightly once more, then said, "Come on, then. I need you to help me while you're still in the mood." Hand in hand, they left the Dacha for the last time.

*

Four floors were inaccessible by the time Mila and Aleksei rejoined the others. They swept the rest of the building, but there wasn't anything like a boat. They considered the possibility of making furniture into a raft. Most of it was made of metal or plastic, and therefore useless. Though there were wooden tables and chairs, Misha pointed out that with the time it would take them to cut and tie these, and with only paddles for propulsion, they wouldn't make it far enough away to avoid being sucked down with the building when it sank.

"Plus, it's winter," Anastasia reminded them. "We'd die of hypothermia before we made it to land."

Aleksei sighed. "Might as well work on it anyway, until we come up with something better."

They retreated to the White Level common room, bringing as much of the wooden furniture with them as they could, and began breaking it up into viable pieces. The sun had risen now, and the room was bright with green light. As they worked, Aleksei thought of Mila's assurance that they would get out. Their options were dwindling, yet there had been such certainty in her words. He kept trying to catch her eye, but Mila had retreated into herself. She spoke little, and her clouded eyes looked slightly past them, as if she was lost in a memory or daydream. It was unnerving, but better than her previous rancor.

They worked diligently, but by the time they could hear water in the corridors below, they didn't have anything remotely big enough to keep them all out of the water. "And if we're wet," Anastasia concluded, "we won't last five minutes."

They abandoned the raft. For a long time they sat in silence, listening to fate steal up on them from the dark corridors that had been their world. The sea-mellowed light ran over and around them, dancing on the white walls and pale wood of their last refuge. Aleksei was watching the light, half-mesmerized, trying to think what it reminded him of, when Mila spoke the thought he had been searching for.

"Fire," she said abruptly, her eyes focusing with startling abruptness on his own.

They looked at each other for a moment, then Aleksei jumped to his feet. "Of course! Come on, take as much of this wood as you can. Go up to the top, I'll meet you there."

He didn't wait to see whether they went, but sprinted off along the corridor, thick with shadows thrown by the dying emergency lights and echoing with the groans of the building as the water began to take its toll. He reached the docking bay as the second-to-last window collapsed. He found what he was looking for: a half-filled can of gasoline. He didn't see any matches, but eventually he unearthed a blow torch.

He carried his tools up to the roof, where the others had piled the tables and chairs. He soaked them with the gasoline. The torch whipped and hissed in the strong wind, but finally, with all of them sheltering it, Aleksei managed to light the upholstery of one of the chairs, and soon the pile was blazing.

"They're burning fast," Anastasia said anxiously.

"We don't have long," Misha answered.

Aleksei looked at Mila, but she said nothing.

"It's not very smoky," Anastasia persisted doubtfully. "Do you think anyone will see it?"

"If there's anyone out there, they'll see it."

"What if the wrong people see it?" Anastasia asked.

"Am I the only one who's read the history of Institute 1?" Misha retorted. "The school's Solntse's, but these are international waters. There could be fishermen or research vessels or cruise ships or whatever out here."

"And they'll be thrilled to bits when this place turns into the biggest sink hole in the Gulf of Finland," Anastasia said. "Solntse will have more than Sifte to worry about, then. Time?"

Aleksei looked at his watch. "We've got an hour left, if we're lucky." As if in response, the building shuddered under them and pitched west, with a guttural report like cracking pond-ice.

The sun inched higher, but didn't move far off the southern horizon, as if afraid to stray too far from shelter. They fed the fire half-heartedly. By the time the final half-hour turned, even Aleksei's hope was almost gone, but Mila was standing apart from the others, her glasses in her hand and her shortsighted eyes glued to the horizon, as if she were watching something.

"What is it?" Aleksei asked, but she didn't answer.

"Mila?" Anastasia repeated tentatively.

Mila kept her silence, but the rest of them could see it now, too. They gathered around Mila at the high edge of the slumping roof, straining to make out the details of what was still only a black speck on the indigo horizon. It was coming closer every second, though, and soon they could make out the shape of the boat, then the shapes of people on its open deck. One of the stick-figures had white-blonde hair beating out behind her like a pennant. Aleksei's heart clutched. A small, cold hand slipped into his, and he looked down at Mila, who looked back at him with calm eyes and a touch of a smile. He wanted to ask her how she had known, but the boat was pulling up to the wall, and Sifte's white, wide-eyed face was turning up to them.

"Jump!" she cried.

Aleksei had a moment to register the other people in the boat with Sifte—a blond man with a bandaged arm who looked like her, and a small, dark one with a grim face, standing at the helm—before he was flattened against the seat he had stumbled into by the force of their acceleration.

"Hang on," Sifte cried into the fierce wind, "in a second—"

She didn't have the chance to finish. The sea rushed backward like a rug pulled from under them. For a moment it seemed that the hole in the ocean would catch them, and then it began to close up.

Andrei throttled back, and Stepan looked at the terrified children. He smiled. "I think I can safely say we got here just in the nick of time?"

They gaped at him for a moment. Then they looked at Sifte, who had dropped to her knees, her eyes streaming with tears that froze before they could fall and her arms spread wide, to embrace them all at once.

16

The sea was empty and eerily still, but the desolation of the docks when they reached them was still more profound. Sifte could hardly believe that it was the same place they had left that morning. The looting parties and desperate Pomoshchniki were gone, leaving only the frozen bodies of the dead and the blue smoke of the dying warehouse fires.

"These are the main shipping docks?" Aleksei asked.

"Yes," Andrei answered tersely, already striking out toward Myortvograd.

"Where is everybody?"

"If they haven't run away, they're preparing to fight." He closed his mouth and stepped up his pace, making it clear that he would not humor any more questions at the moment. Sifte had known him just long enough to realize that this was a sign of anxiety rather than anger, but the others looked perplexed by his rebuff.

She fell into stride between Aleksei and Mila. They had already exchanged boiled-down versions of their various stories on the trip back to shore, and now there was nothing neutral left to talk about. They had entered the slums before Sifte found the courage to break the silence.

"I know that it will never be enough," she said, "but I wanted you both to know how sorry I am—"

"We've all done what we had to do," Aleksei said, not gently, but without hostility.

Sifte was silent for a long time. She looked at Mila to see what she thought of this assessment, but Mila was looking intently at the ground. Finally, Sifte answered, "I think you're being too generous. But I don't know why I would expect anything else."

Her friends didn't answer. They were staring at the sub-race shanties, which were nearly deserted. Sifte didn't know where the people had gone, but the charged atmosphere that had hung over the city like the fires' coppery smoke had not dissipated. It made the desolation eerier still. The whole world seemed to be holding its breath. It was a feeling she remembered from the early levels of Cave, when the game had often forsaken them to the twilight of a deserted, ruined city: the sense that all human eyes had converged into an invisible omniscience, waiting for her to make the move that would release it from its inertia.

It was almost dark by the time they reached the Technological Institute. The guards admitted them with a furtive look around the street, and then barred the door behind them. Sifte's friends were now visibly shaking with cold and exhaustion, and Stepan sent them down into the bunker.

Anastasia was chattering excitedly to Misha, and Aleksei retained a circumspect silence, but Mila took Sifte's hand as they started down the stairs. It was trembling. Sifte understood the reasons for Mila's apprehension. She had felt them all herself, only the day before.

Sasha met them in the doorway and pressed cups of hot tea into their hands. Sifte's friends stared at Sasha as if she were an apparition, following her dazedly through the corridors to her own room, peeking into the open doorways they passed. The rooms that had been empty when Sifte left were now full of people, some of them Soviet, but mostly sub-race. Families huddled in groups on the floor, much as they had huddled in the streets.

"They've been pouring in all day," Sasha said. "We've agreed to it, on the condition that the able-bodied will help us fight."

"So we will be fighting?" Sifte asked.

Sasha paused. "Let's leave that until you've all had a rest." She ushered them into her room, where she had set out food for them. "I'm working on warm clothes," she said, "and heating water for baths."

"About time," Anastasia answered. They all laughed.

When they were finished eating, Sasha left them to their dreamy, sated silence, but the peace only lasted a few minutes. Stepan and Andrei returned, the one looking excited, the other grim.

"What's the news?" Sifte asked.

Stepan and Andrei looked at each other. Finally, Andrei said, "Well, the evacuation of Institute 1 has created quite a stir, not to mention the rumors of Sifte's escape. People are questioning Solntse and things are...beginning to falter."

"Dissolve, is more like it," Stepan interjected.

"At any rate, Solntse's not happy. He's sent out the first public announcement since he shut down Glaza—"

"More like a threat—"

"A promise. To restore order using 'any methods necessary'—"

"Which you can no doubt surmise."

"So we're really going to war?" Misha asked.

"No, actually, Solntse's inviting the Soviet to tea to exchange blueprints for a new-and-improved social system," Anastasia answered.

Andrei blinked at her, and she stared brazenly back at him. Then, to all their surprise, Andrei began to laugh.

"You have to excuse Nastya," Misha told him. "She was brought up by fascists." Anastasia slapped him.

Still smiling, Andrei said, "To answer your question, Misha, yes: it looks as if war is inevitable."

"What do you want us to do first?" Anastasia asked.

"Rest," Sasha said as she entered with an armful of clothing and towels. "No arguments, please. The bath water is warm. Girls first, come with me." None of them dared argue.

*

When they had washed, Sasha showed them to a bunkroom. It hadn't yet been wired for electricity, so she gave them a candle and a book of matches. "Use them sparingly," she said. Before leaving, she kissed each of them.

They lay awake for a long time talking. Sifte let the sounds of their voices wash over her, wondering how she had managed to persuade herself to leave without them. They chattered and giggled like the children they had never had the chance to be. She couldn't imagine what her life would be now if she hadn't been able to save them.

Don't leave me, she thought, wishing she had the courage to speak the words out loud.

Finally the deep, even breathing of sleep settled over the room. Sifte, still wide awake, felt utterly bereft. And then the bunk above her creaked, a sound as familiar as her own breathing. In a moment Mila was beside her. She put her arms around Sifte's neck and said, "It'll be all right."

Sifte wished she could believe it.

*

She awakened to a distant, rhythmic thudding, feeling as if she'd only just closed her eyes.

"Bombs," Stepan said, coming into the room a moment later.

They got up and dressed quickly, and then went back to Sasha's room, where plates of bread and cups of tea were waiting for them. Andrei and Sasha were crouched on the floor, studying a map of the city.

"Eat quickly," Andrei said, his eyes flickering over them and back to the map. "We don't have much time."

"What's going on?" Aleksei asked.

"The Soviet know you're here, and the rumor's spreading in Solntsegrad."

"So?" Anastasia asked, her eyes on Andrei's grim face.

"No news yet from inside," Stepan said. "But they've rallied a sub-race army, they're out for blood —"

"It's chaos," Andrei interrupted. "Nobody's in control, there's no clear plan."

"Tell us what to do," Sifte said, pushing aside her tea and bread.

"Eat," Andrei said. Like Stepan and Sasha, he was trying hard to mask his anxiety, and failing. "You need your strength for what's coming."

"We'll eat," Anastasia said, "if you talk."

Again, Andrei looked at her with bewildered humor. "Well then," he said. "They're going for the bridges and Metro tunnels." He pointed out positions on the map.

"Solntse's army will be waiting for them," Sifte observed.

"That's what they're hoping for."

"What do they think they are?" Anastasia asked. "Fucking kamikazes?"

Andrei half-smiled. "In a word. But they have no clear target. For the first time in their lives Solntse's faltered, they've felt freedom —"

"And they'd rather die than go back to what they were," Mila said quietly.

"Which is just what they're going to do, if someone doesn't take things into hand."

"How are they doing?" Aleksei asked.

"Not so badly, all things considered," Stepan answered. "Apparently we're holding our own, but we haven't gained much ground. I hate to admit this, but I don't know if our army can match theirs."

"So what will we do?" asked Misha.

Andrei, Sasha and Stepan looked at one another, but it was Sifte who answered, "Go inside. Face Solntse himself." From the look on Stepan's face, she knew that this was exactly what they had been planning.

"And how are we going to do that," asked Anastasia, "when a whole army can't?"

Sifte shrugged. "A single soldier is less conspicuous than an army."

"All things being equal," Andrei said. "But every one of us in this room is conspicuous to Solntse."

"Then we need to blend in," said Sifte. "Look like officials."

449

"We have the uniforms," Andrei said doubtfully, "but after that stunt in the prison, I doubt they'll be so easily fooled."

There was a long silence. Then Aleksei asked, "And if we do get inside, then what?"

"A bullet in Solntse's head would be a good start," Anastasia replied.

"Right—we'll just march into the Fortress and shoot him," Misha said.

"I never said it was plausible."

"It's not even possible. It's not called the Fortress for nothing."

"Every man has a weakness," Mila said softly.

Again, silence; but Sifte was scrutinizing Mila. After a moment she said, "Do you remember what I told you about those times I played Cave, and the game went wrong?"

"Yeah, and the voices in your head," Anastasia scoffed. Seeing Sifte's look, she said, "What—you think that was him?"

"It said it was…more or less."

"It was just part of the program," Misha said.

"Then how come none of you ever ran into it?" Sifte shook her head. "It reacted. It felt. It knew things, showed me things that only Solntse could have."

"What, exactly?" Sasha asked, with an odd, guarded look.

Sifte told them what had happened in both of the games. When Sifte had finished, Sasha said, "When I was in the Fortress, I had dreams. Nightmares. But they never seemed to be coming from my own mind. Like you said, Sifte, it seemed there was something else in my head with me, controlling what I saw and heard and felt." She paused. You have to plug into a neurological console to play the game. And this links you to Glaza, right?"

"Theoretically," Misha answered. "We were only meant to be hooked up to the school's system, but since that links with Glaza—"

"No doubt, the technology's advanced since I was at Institute 1." Sasha touched the jack at the nape of her neck. "Every time I awakened from a nightmare, this hurt."

"Are you suggesting that Solntse's communicating with Glaza on a neurological level?" asked Stepan.

Sasha shook her head. "I think he's *controlling* Glaza on a neurological level. He's found some way to make his own mind function as part of the network. And I think that's what you meant about his weakness, isn't it, Sifte. He's only as powerful as Glaza."

"Even if it's true," Misha said, "we'd have to be plugged in for him to have any control over us. So how does that really help him?"

"That's the part I can't figure out," said Sifte.

"I think I can." Andrei reached into a pocket of his jacket, and pulled something out. It was a small, black device, with a plug that matched the ones in the games and target practice consoles at Institute 1. "I pulled this out of the jack of a dead official in the Fortress prison. I haven't been able to make it work, but Svetlana insists that he was communicating through it."

"Techno-fascism," Anastasia muttered.

"No," Sifte said softly. "Utopia."

She watched their doubt turn to horror. Mila sighed with a desolation far deeper than sadness. Anastasia's eyes narrowed in fury, and Aleksei shut his for a moment. Stepan put an arm around Sasha. But Andrei's sharp stare was fixed on Sifte, and for the first time, she saw respect in it.

Mila asked in a small, tentative voice, "Does his whole army have those things?"

"I don't know," Andrei answered.

"If they do," Anastasia wailed, "then what chance do we have?"

"We have one," Sasha answered. "Probably the only one. We have to sever his link with Glaza."

"But we have no idea how to do that!"

"Which is why we're going to have to go to the Fortress and find out."

Misha broke the following fraught silence, saying, "There might be another way." They looked at him expectantly. He grinned. "Good old-fashioned hacking."

Andrei said, "How would you do that?"

"Well, a worm might work. You know, an I.D. program that runs through a network. I can use it to locate the source of the link, and with any luck, disable it."

"If you can even get into Glaza in the first place," Andrei said, but his tone was speculative. After a moment, he handed Misha the dead device, saying, "You have your assignment. But it's a long shot, so someone's still going to have to try to get into the Fortress."

"I will," Mila said.

"No," Sifte said.

"I have the least to lose," she said, looking pointedly back at Sifte.

"You're also as good as a doctor," Sifte answered. "They'll need you here. Besides, for whatever reason, he talks to me." She saw them forming protests, and said firmly, "I'm going."

Aleksei said, "Then I'm going, too."

"You're going to need backup," Stepan said. "Coming, Sasha?"

"Don't be an idiot, Stepan," Andrei retorted. "You'll never get into the Fortress as a group."

"We'll split up, then, and meet once we're inside. Look, this is the best we're going to do in the time we have left."

A man burst into the room, a radio in his hand and a look of crazed elation on his face. "It's Olga," he cried. "They've taken the Gorkovskaya tunnel. They're into Solntsegrad!"

Andrei's face was a mixture of wonder and panic. "All right, Stepan. Get them ready. Mila, the medical supplies are two doors down on the right. You can get the volunteers started there. Misha, come with me and I'll show you the computer. And Anastasia…"

"Don't even think about leaving me here! I'm going wherever the action is."

Andrei smiled. "You've got it."

17

First, Stepan gave them semi-automatic handguns bearing the sun insignia and two clips of bullets.

"We're trained in automatics," Aleksei said, eyeing the neat rows of German-made rifles on the wall.

"Too easy to get carried away with them," Stepan answered. "We have very little ammunition. You need to think before you fire."

Next, Stepan led them to a room hung with rows of officials' uniforms. This disembodied clothing of the dead was repugnant to Sifte, but she accepted the navy blue uniform her father handed her without protest, plus a bulletproof vest. He found uniforms for the others, then he said, "There's one more thing."

He took something from his pocket: four hexagonal white pills in bubble-wrap packets. "In case you're captured." His eyes flickered over Sasha. "There won't be any escape runs, this time."

The sight of the pills filled Sifte with inexplicable fury. She clenched her hands together when Stepan offered it.

"Take it," Sasha said.

"No."

"I'd shoot off your legs before I let you risk him doing to you what he did to me. *Take it*."

Sifte and Sasha stared each other down. Then, without a word, Sifte took the pill from her father's hand and stalked off toward the bunkroom. She didn't know why she had challenged Sasha, or why she was so angry now. But she was angry, and growing angrier by the minute.

She pushed past a group of refugees gathered in the corridor and into the bunkroom, then changed into the Pomoshchnik's uniform. It was too big, but she didn't think that anyone would be in much of a mind to notice. She pocketed the poison tablet and the clips of ammunition and pushed the gun into its pocket.

Aleksei was waiting outside the door. She tried to move past him, but he pushed her back into the room. She pulled free and made for the door again, but he slammed it and leaned against it, meeting her glare calmly. "You're not going back out there until you tell me what's going on."

She looked at Aleksei, aiming her anger, and then, all at once, it melted. It was the first time she had really looked at him since they were reunited. His face had changed, not just in its expression, but in its very fabric. It was as if the trials of the last week had burned away everything extraneous, leaving only passion and determination, muscle and bone. She could only shake her head.

He sighed. "Let it go, Sifte."

"I don't know what—"

"The guilt, the cross, the burning flag—whatever it is that's made you decide to martyr yourself!"

Sifte looked away. "You don't understand," she said.

"Then tell me."

"Why do you all believe in me when I've only ever failed you?" Her voice was small, bitter.

"How have you failed us, Sifte?" he asked.

"I left you there!" she cried. "I left you knowing exactly what would happen to you! And it was only the beginning. The things I've done since then, the suffering I've caused... Vanya, Masha, Dmitri—"

"Dmitri put a bullet in his own head," Aleksei said, his voice harsh now, "because he lost faith, and blamed himself for something that wasn't his fault." He moved toward her. "Sifte, I meant it yesterday when I said that we've all done what we had to. A lot of people expect a lot of you, but you're only human, and they know that. You can only do your best, try to make the right choices, and if you don't learn to forgive yourself for the things that fall short, you'll end up just like Dmitri." He took a deep breath. "And you can't die, Sifte. I can't live in a world you're not a part of."

Finally she looked at him, and then she flung her arms around him. When he kissed her, his own cheeks were as wet as hers.

*

They all parted silently on the street outside the Technological Institute. There was too much to say and no words to encompass it all. Mila stood on the steps watching them go. Her brow was already furrowed with anxiety, but she managed one more smile for Sifte, and called, "God go with you!" Sifte moved off into the hazy streets.

The trepidation she had felt since she first heard the bombs had evaporated. Even the sporadic artillery thuds didn't faze her. She was relieved not to have to anticipate this fight anymore, simply to face it.

She was heading for Troitsky Most. They'd had a report from Olga that Solntse's defense on the bridge was weakening. More and more troops were being recalled. No one knew why, but clearly Solntse was facing a bigger problem than Soviet infiltration.

As she neared the Dvortsovaya Embankment, it began to snow, but it wasn't heavy enough to block her view of the action. The Soviet had a handful of antiquated artillery launchers, and they were firing at Solntsegrad's walls with varying degrees of accuracy. Solntsegrad's only apparent retaliation was the occasional light missile volleyed from the embankments by the Fortress. To Sifte, this languor seemed ominous, like an exterminator swatting at flies.

Troitskiy Most was a roiling mass of sub-race soldiers trying to muscle their way into the action, and Soviet leaders, their faces stamped with exhaustion, trying to establish some kind of order.

"Sifte!" a woman screamed in her ear, above the roar of the battle-drunk masses. Sifte turned, and found herself face-to-face with Olga. She said, "You'll never get through this crowd. You've got to go down. Across the ice."

Sifte looked at the river. The snow-cover was mottled with bullet marks and blood and the crosshatched tracks of tanks, which were poised with their sights set on Myortvograd. Here and there shells had broken the ice, and water oozed out of the holes like blood from wounds. Worst of all, the ice was crawling with Pomoshchniki. One look at the locked masses on the bridge, though, told Sifte that Olga was right.

"Make sure your people don't fire on me," she yelled.

Olga smiled. "I'll do my best. And you do yours." Olga hugged her, then turned back to the fight.

Sifte made her way back to Dvortsovaya Embankment, then, with one last look at her uniform to make sure that it was in order, she walked down the stone steps and out onto the ice. Almost immediately, a high-ranking Pomoshchnik stopped her.

"What's your business?" he demanded.

"Reconnaissance," she answered, adjusting her tone to match the cool detachment of his own.

His face took on a tinge of cruel anticipation. "Name and rank, please."

Just as she began to fumble for an answer, his expression shifted, then proceeded through a series of rapid changes at the end of which he said, "You're cleared."

Sifte stood blinking at him in surprise.

"As you were," he said, with a sharpness that stung her to action again. She walked away from him through the crowd of Pomoshchniki, imagining his eyes on her back, waiting for a bullet to follow them. It was only when she was half way across the river that she began to accept that he'd actually let her pass.

The guards who let her through the gates and onto Ioannovskiy Most barely looked at her. When Sifte crossed the ornamental bridge onto Zayachiy Ostrov and the Fortress, she knew that it had been too easy. But somewhere in this suspended calm, her destiny waited. Taking a breath, she passed under the time-sanded bas-relief and through the Fortress' open gates.

*

The crowds on Dvortsoviy Most hadn't been as dense or as fraught as the ones on Troitskiy, and none of the officials Aleksei passed questioned him. He entered the Fortress grounds about ten minutes before Sifte did. He passed the Archives of the War Ministry, now an officials' barracks, then the Mint and Trubetskoy Bastion, where Dmitri had once been a prisoner. The detail of these old buildings leapt out at him in disjointed fragments: gold leaf, Baroque scrollwork, faded brick and pastel paint. It wasn't until he stood on the cobbles outside the Cathedral's main entrance that he realized it was snowing. He stared at its accumulation on the trees' winterbare skeletons, collecting himself.

The door was painted white, and against the gray sky and falling snow it took on an ultraviolet tinge. The yellow of the cathedral's outer walls seemed out of place on this somnolent morning. Aleksei stepped toward the door, and it opened in front of him. Before he entered, his eyes flickered up to the angel at the top of the steeple. It swung equivocally in opposing gusts of wind.

The door shut behind him as soon as he was inside, sealing him in the whispering twilight of the cathedral's interior. There seemed to be gold everywhere. It shone from the elaborate moldings of the ceiling and walls, the sides of the pulpit, the saints and angels of the iconostasis. There were other colors, too: the pink and green of the marbled Corinthian columns and the ceiling's overarching vaults, the muted white of the tsars' sarcophagi, the bronze bust of Peter. Aleksei looked around, but he quickly realized that for all its splendor, the cathedral was a mausoleum for his country's past glory. Solntse wouldn't be here.

Two Opyekuni were waiting at the door next to the iconostasis. They stood so still that they almost blended in with the other statuary. When Aleksei approached, they stepped forward in unison and they each took one of his arms. They held him so loosely it seemed he could easily have pulled away, but he knew that like the cathedral's serenity, this was an illusion.

They led him through the door and toward the Grand Ducal Vault, but turned before they reached it, descending a set of modern-looking stone steps, and into a white, windowless corridor. They wove through a series of subsidiary corridors to a set of double-doors that looked to be made of obsidian. Here they let go of him, standing at attention again on either side of the doorway. Aleksei stood there for a moment, uncertain of what he was meant to do. Then he reached out for one of the doors. It opened soundlessly onto a vast room, lit dimly with pinkish light. It was the inverse of the cathedral above, all dark stone and metal, as pretentious in its spareness as the Cathedral was in its Baroque overstatement.

But Aleksei wasn't looking at the opulent trappings. He was looking toward the end of the room, at a dais made of something black and metallic. What he saw there was so bizarre that his eye could not at first accept it. Then, finally, it began to make a terrible kind of sense. He began backing away, toward the doors, but they had shut seamlessly behind him.

"It's too late for that," said an old, old voice, which seemed to come from everywhere at once. "Step forward, boy. I've waited a long time to meet you."

*

Sifte circled the building, and finally, on the side facing the Grand Ducal Vault, she found a door that opened. Beyond it a set of steps led down to a red-lit corridor. Taking a deep breath, she stepped inside.

Even after her eyes adjusted, she could see little; a few meters ahead, the corridor disappeared into its own shadows. The floor throbbed with a deep, rhythmic pulse, too low to be a sound, more like the buried workings of a great machine. Taking out her gun, Sifte started moving.

She hadn't gone far before she arrived at a dead-end. Ahead of her was a wall with two full-length mirrors. She pushed on the right-hand one. She wasn't particularly surprised when it slid open, revealing another corridor beyond, as dim and narrow as the first, but this time lit green. Before following it, she tried the other mirror, but it didn't move. As she stepped into the green corridor, the mirror-door slid shut behind her.

For some time, she proceeded in this manner, becoming more and more frustrated. Whichever door she chose always opened, and then the other wouldn't. A few times she tried to push two at once, but then neither would open.

Then, at last, one of the mirror doors let her out into a room. It was about three meters square, painted white, brightly lit, and bare except for a neural device like the one Andrei had showed them, lying in the center of the floor. Sifte picked up the device. A light on the back flashed ice-blue.

Kneeling, Sifte laid her gun down, keeping the device in one hand. With the other, she took the white pill from her pocket, put the whole bubble-wrapped capsule in her mouth, and lodged it in her cheek. Then she jacked in.

She hovered over the city, softened to an Impressionist landscape by rising smoke and falling snow. For a second, she felt pure, euphoric wonder.

I thought you'd appreciate it, the familiar voice spoke, without speaking. *It's brand new technology, not even on the shelves yet. The invention of a tiny company in Scotland. I have to admit, the West still has the upper hand when it comes to these things. For the moment, anyway.*

You didn't bring me here to talk about technology.

No. I brought you here to give you one last chance.

As in the films of the bombings, the city flickered, darkened, and then vanished. Sifte was tumbling through the void, screaming without screaming as Solntse laughed. Then, abruptly, the laughter stopped, and his presence retreated. Sifte came up short in the black nothingness, but without the pain of impact, as if she'd jumped with rubber cables and suddenly reached their limit. She cast her mind outward, but Solntse was gone. And then a different voice spoke into her mind:

Sifte?

*

Aleksei had imagined many faces for Solntse, but never this. At the center of the dais, in a raised glass casket, a body curled like a desiccated spider. The web of mechanisms around him was more complex than anything Alexei had ever seen or imagined. The man, or what was left of him, was nearly hidden by the tangle of wires and screens, fiber optic cables and winking colored lights. The wires and lights ran around and through his body, winding like creepers along the fragile balusters of his limbs, threading away from his shriveled fingers, snaking from his head like the writhing hair of an electronic medusa. Most of his skin was covered by dark leather, but what was visible was termite-pale, wisping away from the bones with the dry translucency of rice paper. His eyes were hidden behind two black disks. It was clear that there had been no human life in that body for a long, long time.

When Aleksei finally looked away, his shock deepened. On Solntse's right Nikolai lay on a plain, dark table; to his left, Tanya lay on another. Both were silent and still, their paleness accentuated by their dark clothing. Tanya's skirt flowed down over the sides of the table, disappearing into the shadows so that she seemed to grow out of them. Identical black neural devices, more elaborate than the one Andrei had showed them, blossomed like fungi from their jacks. Fine wires curved down their arms, like the first shoots of new vines.

"Are they dead, too?" Aleksei asked

"I've killed men for making similar remarks," the voice answered. "But, as you've had no preparation, I will overlook it. They are not dead. They breathe, their hearts beat."

"What's wrong with them, then?" he asked.

"Nothing. They're learning."

"Learning what?"

Solntse paused, then said, "It would be easier to explain if you plugged in. There's a unit on the table to your left."

Aleksei glanced down, and indeed there was a table there, though there hadn't been previously. On it was a device like the one Andrei had showed them.

"I don't think so."

"The human mind, unaugmented, processes so slowly. The device saves me the trouble of trying to explain what can only truly be intuited."

"Which is…?"

"What you came for. You did come looking for me. And it seems that you have achieved your goal."

"I'm afraid not," Aleksei answered.

"What, because you can't kill me? Did you really think it would be so easy?"

Alexei turned his face away.

"Don't feel bad," Solntse cajoled. "As I said, you've achieved your goal. You came in alone; you've faced me; it was a valiant effort. Worthy even of her."

Aleksei's eyes flew back up to Solntse's.

"That's what all this is about, isn't it? Proving yourself worthy, winning her love?"

Aleksei clutched his gun instinctively, but it only reminded him of his powerlessness. He couldn't bear to look at Solntse's rag-and-bone face. As he turned away, his eyes caught on the pale splotch of an oxygen canister. This, and the weight of the gun in his hand, gave him the beginning of an idea; but it barely had time to form before Solntse was speaking again.

"I know what you're thinking. Maybe you could even do it." The chalkdust voice had lowered, condensed into something colder. "However, I would think carefully about your next move, before you make it. Your friend Misha might say, 'Philosophy should be wooed by true men, not bastards.'"

Something in the tone of the words made Aleksei raise his eyes to Solntse's again.

"Interesting word, 'bastard'. I've never understood why it should be derogatory. After all, the details of a man's conception have little bearing on his worth. Take Nikolai: for all his breeding, he is merely adequate. But you, Aleksei, are exceptional. You may be the bastard, but if you play this right, you stand to inherit the crown."

*

Misha? Sifte cried. *How are you here?*

I fixed that transceiver Andrei found. There's no time to explain the rest right now. The main thing is, I found the central computer, and there's something wrong. The way it functions… it's more complex than anything I've ever seen. In fact, the only thing I've seen that looks anything like it is a computerized readout of brain activity.

So what are you saying?

I think the computer is part of him… like an extension of his brain. And I think it might be able to function without him.

Sifte's mind whirled with horrible possibilities. She said:

So killing Solntse is useless. What do you suggest?

I'm going to try to write a virus that'll take out the whole network at once. But he's got a lot of defenses up around this A.I., or whatever it is. I've been trying to reach you for a while, but I only got through a minute ago.

When something distracted him.

Well, it'll be the same for a virus. Someone's going to need to keep him distracted long enough for me to get it inside.

I can do that.

Not jacked in. When the virus hits, it'll destroy anything—or anyone—connected to the network. You've got to get out as soon as you can. You can get out, right?

Of course, Sifte lied.

And then Misha was gone, and Solntse was back.

I'm sorry for the delay. My attention is pulled in many directions at the moment, thanks to you.

What did you mean? About the last chance?

You know what I meant. You have access to all of my thoughts here, just as I have access to yours.

He paused for a moment, then continued:

I felt that. You hate me...and you fear me, too. There is no need. This is no different from what has always been.

You've always been inside my head?

It's more a case of all of your heads always having been inside of mine. Perhaps an analogy will make it easier to understand.

Sifte was falling again, but before the terror had time to take hold, she jolted back into her body. She was in the library at Institute 1. When Solntse spoke, his voice had lost its ubiquitous quality. It sounded cool, pleasant, and vaguely familiar: the voice of a teacher.

"Think of me as a library," he said, "where the minds of all of my subjects are stored like books. But books continually being written. Everything you do or say or create, it's all in me, all the time."

"So..." Sifte began, then stopped, considering her words carefully. "So you always knew about us—my friends and me? About what we were doing?"

"The simple answer is, yes."

"Why simple?"

"Because I don't know things the way that you know things. You incorporate knowledge from external sources. That knowledge always remains something separate from you. But all of you live in me. Everything that happens to you, happens to me. It's like memory, except that it is always immediate."

Sifte's mind was racing. "You watch what all of us are doing, all the time?"

"Of course not!"

"So true omniscience isn't possible."

"It isn't necessary."

A leather-bound book flew off one of the shelves and landed at Sifte's feet. She picked it up, opened it. The page showed a hazy, violet-tinged evening sky, framed by a wall with a jagged hole torn out of it. All at once, Sifte was no longer standing in the library, but in a tiny, filthy room. The hole was not in a wall, but in the ceiling. A red-headed woman huddled, shivering, in a corner of the room. She clutched a screaming baby in birch-twig arms. Then she turned and looked up at the skylight, her face a twist of fear and despair. Sasha's face. Before Sifte could get a good look at it, she was back in the ticking quiet of the library, and the book was gone.

"How do you know that?" she demanded. "You can't have been there!"

"I wasn't. But you were. Sasha was. Both of you have jacked in since then, and once you jack in, everything in your minds is mine. What you know, what you feel…what you don't even realize you remember."

She paused for a moment. "So the games, the weapons practice—"

"Fishnets for your thoughts. Soon we won't need them. When we can mass produce the transceivers, all of you will wear them all the time, and then—"

"We'll be permanently jacked into Glaza, like you."

The voice laughed dryly, then answered, "You are both still so naïve."

"What do you mean, 'both'?" Sifte asked, all the hairs on her arms suddenly standing up.

"Never mind about that, yet. You are right to say that you will all soon be jacked into Glaza, but not that I am. Glaza is permanently jacked into me. You might say it *is* me. I am its governing computer."

"How is that possible?"

"Anything the human mind can conceive of is possible. Sadly, most of it doesn't happen. As a race, we are chronically apathetic. Which, to return to my original point, is what so impresses me about you. You reject apathy with your every fiber."

"You still haven't told me what you want with me."

"Your help in transforming Russia into Utopia."

"You really should know better than to ask for my help."

"No," the voice answered, abandoning its warmth and affability with a suddenness that chilled Sifte more than the Repino blizzard ever could have, "you should know that I don't have to ask."

"Because I'm already jacked in? Even if you can keep me here, you can't make me co-operate."

"I don't have to. You've always been mine."

Misha's words flashed through Sifte's mind: *I think it might be able to function without him.* Sifte felt suddenly weightless, as if her mind and heart had already been co-opted. The only thing anchoring her was her resolve to keep Solntse distracted long enough for the virus to work.

"What is it?" he asked, suddenly wary. "You're hiding something." He was silent for a long time, then he said, "You can't escape this. It's what you were born for. You have a gift for omniscience. You are naturally agile within the construct of the electronic telepathy. In fact, you are the only one who ever heard me inside that game, certainly the only one who ever spoke to me, or saw what I saw."

Sifte was trying to distance herself from him, but Solntse compensated. Once again, his voice seemed to come from all sides, so that she remained at its vortex, no matter which way she moved.

"What are you hiding?" he demanded again.

She didn't dare think about Misha's virus, but suddenly she remembered Stepan's pill. She reached for it as she had once reached for the feeling of her body inside of Cave, and the visualization began to solidify, until she could feel it between her teeth.

"So," Solntse said, his voice thinning to a hiss, "you really are determined to resist me." He paused for a moment, then said, "I want you, little girl. I've wanted you from the moment Apraksina wrestled you from your demented whore of a mother. Utopia's implementation will be far smoother with you, but don't think that it won't happen without you."

"It won't!" Sifte cried. "You think that by getting rid of the Soviet and the sub-race you'll get rid of all opposition, but you're wrong. The super-race are still individuals. You can't assume that they'll follow you in this."

She had half-expected him to laugh, but he answered with the utmost seriousness, stretching every word so that they became more than words, almost sensations. "I do not assume. I am 'the source not only of the intelligibility of the objects of knowledge, but also of their being and reality; yet I am not myself that reality, but beyond it, and superior to it in dignity and power.' I am the form of good."

Into Sifte's mind flashed an image of a line of women, each handing a baby to a waiting Opyekun; close on its heels came another, a nursery with rows and rows of cots, each baby wearing a neural transceiver. For a few long moments, Sifte deliberated whether to bite down on the pill before she ever had to witness these images made real. But she also knew that she had only one chance to stop them.

"The form of good," she repeated. "You aren't even worthy of speaking the words."

There was silence for a moment, and then she was spinning into the void. She heard a cry of frustration, like an echo of a nightmare, distant, not quite able to touch her. Then she was hovering above the city again, and the voice said, *Is this what you want to save?*

She hurtled downward, toward Myortvograd. The missile fire had stepped up, and whole sections of the ruin were burning. Frightened sub-race families were running in every direction. Many more lay dead or dying in the streets.

Yes! she cried into the vacuum of his mind. I want to save our individuality, the sanctity of our own minds, whatever it is in the people I love that's allowed them to cling to everything that's just and good despite all you've done to corrupt it!

It's too late to save them.

Now Sifte was rushing headlong through the streets of Myortvograd toward the river, a ghost made of speed and pain. The destruction around her faded to a blur, and then everything came into focus again. She was near the wall, in the midst of a crowd fighting to enter one of the gates. Anastasia was at their head, fighting hand-to-hand with an Opyekun twice her size. Then he had a knife at Anastasia's throat, and she stopped struggling, hung still in his arms as bright blood ran down her neck.

The scene switched to a Metro tunnel clogged with people—sub-race, Soviets and Pomoshchniki, all in a tangled mess of blood and smoke and gunfire. She caught sight of her mother's pallid face in the crowd, and her father's, and then the maddened, desperate face of a Pomoshchnik boy, pulling the pin from a grenade. She saw a hospital tent in flames, a child with long Kirghiz eyes glassy on either side of a bullet wound, a dark-skinned boy face-down on the river ice.

The images whirled and shattered, and she was above the city again. From every direction, Solntse's troops were closing in, tightening around the burning blotch of Myortvograd like a noose. Sifte felt their triumph, their ruthless need to kill. She felt their frenzy consuming her mind, felt the parts of herself that were still herself begin to disintegrate. But somewhere beyond it all, something was screaming at her to hold on, not to give in, to trust her heart and not her eyes.

She looked down at the tightening clusters of panicked people, felt the terror in every one of their hearts: a blind, animal fear. Yet she knew that Solntse did not own the minds of the sub-race. He could not know what they felt, so it was only a fabrication.

With a thrust of will similar to the one that had allowed her to rescind sight when Cave trapped her as a terrified child, Sifte shut her mind's eye to the nightmares Solntse was showing her. *These are lies,* she said. *You don't even have any real control over us.*

Gradually, the images faded. She found herself back in the numb darkness. For a moment, she thought that he had abandoned her again. But then he said, in a voice shrunk to a ghost's whisper, *If that's what you think, then look at this.*

471

18

"What are you saying?" Aleksei asked. He took a few, irresolute steps toward Solntse, then stopped.

"Nikolai was planned, his mother chosen carefully from the ranks of the Opyekuni. Your mother was sub-race, a moment of weakness when I was...not yet so committed. She was beautiful, but not particularly intelligent. Mute, too. Maybe that was part of it...she would look at me with such hatred, and yet she could say nothing. It just goes to show, you never can tell."

"Where is she now?"

"Dead, most likely. They never live long."

Aleksei was trembling with shock and rage. "You're lying."

"Do you really think that I would attempt to coerce you by telling you that you're the son of a degenerate and a man you despise? I've told you the truth, Aleksei. You're here because I need a living body, and Nikolai isn't up to the task."

"And you think you'll convince me to do it?"

"Right now, I am only interested in whether or not you are able."

Aleksei was having trouble keeping his mind off the oxygen canister, but he knew he needed to keep Solntse talking to even have a chance of his plan working.

"I think you're lying," he repeated. "I think I'm here because you made a mistake, and your plans are crumbling around you, and you'll do anything you can to salvage them." He moved closer to the dais. Now he could feel the edge of a magnetic shield pushing at him with gentle persistence; but, as he had suspected, Nikolai and Tanya were outside of its protection. "Even beg your worst enemies for help."

"What makes you think I see you as an enemy?"

"You tried to drown me two days ago!"

"That was a test of your resourcefulness."

Aleksei smiled ruefully. "Resourcefulness only goes so far. You and I both know that Sifte Pierson is the only reason I'm standing here now."

"And so we come to the point." Solntse's voice had finally taken on expression; it was almost gleeful. "What if you could have her, too? What if the only way you'll ever have her is to accept my offer?"

"What do you mean?" Aleksei asked ominously.

"Why don't you ask her?" There was a laugh buried somewhere in Solntse's voice.

"Where is she?" Aleksei cried.

"If you want to find out, you'll have to plug in…and forget about your plans for martyrdom."

"Where is she?"

"Right here," Solntse answered, one of his wire-threaded arms lifting ponderously to touch his forehead. "Or perhaps not. Perhaps she's dead. There's only one way to find out."

With a snarl, Aleksei raised his gun. But as he aimed at Nikolai's oxygen canister, Nikolai's eyes flew open. He sat up, a gun in his own hand, aimed at Aleksei. Aleksei paused, momentarily thrown. The second before Nikolai's bullet left the barrel, the door opened and Aleksei turned. The bullet meant for his heart hit him instead in the arm, shattering the bone into splinters of pain. Nikolai aimed again, but someone was moving out of the light toward Aleksei, pushing him aside as Nikolai fired.

For a moment Aleksei couldn't make sense of anything. Then the pieces fell into place like images in a broken mirror. Nikolai leaned against the black table, looking as if he wanted someone to explain what had just happened. Tanya stood smiling down on the devastation below. And at Aleksei's feet, framed by the dark gold of her hair like a terrible masterpiece, Mila lay with wide, unseeing eyes, a dark blossom of blood unfolding across her white nurse's smock.

*

Sifte screamed. Solntse's laughter shivered around her, engulfed her like icy water. She tried to remember the feeling of her body, to make it real as she had realized the pill, but outside her own mind she could feel only Solntse. She could see him now, too, or what she thought must be him: a thing made of metal and mummy's skin, caught in a web of wires. There were others with him. She was aware of their minds, small and distant within his vastness, and receding behind them, many more. She didn't listen to them, unable to think beyond the dark hand of blood gripping Mila's chest, the tips of its fingers already touching the floor.

It's all real, the voice said, now silky-smooth, almost wheedling. Tragic, too. Almost Shakespearean, don't you think?

474

The noble heart that would give its life to save another; brother turned against brother; the ironic pointlessness of the sacrifice. I would never have allowed my sons to kill one another.

Sifte barely had time to grasp the words before the tragedy folded in on itself again. As though awakening from a dream, Aleksei looked up at Nikolai, raised his gun, and fired. Pain tore through Solntse as Nikolai fell, and he jettisoned Sifte, turning toward the sudden blank that had been Nikolai's mind. While he was distracted, Aleksei aimed again at the oxygen canister.

Lyosha, don't! Sifte heard herself crying, though she knew that he couldn't hear. *It'll kill you!*

Simultaneously, something screamed into Sifte's mind. It took a moment to penetrate the fog of grief and terror, but finally she realized that it was Misha.

It's coming! he cried. *Get out!*

I can't.

But you said—

I lied!

I might be able to disconnect you.

I'm not leaving Aleksei.

There's nothing you can do from in there!

I can try to keep Solntse from killing him.

And die trying!

I don't care.

Sifte!

Sifte shut him out, looked down at Aleksei through Solntse's red haze of rage and pain. Two Opyekuni were holding his arms. Tanya had risen from her cradle of cable and light, and stepped onto the floor. She moved toward Aleksei through a pool of Mila's blood, with empty eyes and intractable menace.

Stop her! Sifte cried. *Please, don't take him too!*

Solntse flung the words back at her with the force of a physical blow. As Tanya's hand came down on Aleksei's shoulder, trailing wires like the tendrils of some trench-dwelling ocean creature. Sifte thought of Dmitri's cryptic solicitude and Stepan's persistent belief in her despite his friends' warnings and his own better judgment. She thought of Sasha's desperate knife at the throat of a child she loved more than life itself and the blood on Mila's shattered chest. But brightest of all was the love in Aleksei's eyes when he looked at her, untainted despite everything she had done to deny it.

In that moment, Sifte realized what Aleksei had meant that morning when he had told her that he couldn't live in a world without her in it. She wondered how she could have been so blind and stubborn, or how she could have assumed that there would always be time to choose differently. But the very best and the very worst things we do come out of these moments of clarity, a combustion of passion and transient lunacy, and in that moment when Sifte realized just how much she stood to lose, she also realized that there was a way to save it.

Tanya had taken the gun from Aleksei's hand, and was drawing it upward with unhurried certainty. Tearing her eyes away, Sifte cast her mind out into Solntse's omniscience.

You can have me! she cried. *Just let him go!*

Solntse didn't answer immediately. Then he said, with a shade of disbelief, *He means that much to you?*

The gun was against Aleksei's temple. He looked up at Tanya with all the courage he had always lived by.

Yes, she said.

476

Solntse was silent for a long time. Tanya's finger paused on the trigger.

No, he said.

There was a moment of hot-white pain, a noiseless flash, and the image of a pale bird flying against the sun. Then there was nothing.

*

When Sifte regained consciousness, she was lying in complete darkness, but it was not the darkness of Solntse's mind. There was a solid floor under her back, and the sense of an enclosed space around her. A computerized voice sounded, somewhere distant, "Detonation in nine minutes, thirty-two seconds." She leapt up, spitting out the bubble-wrapped pill and ripping the dead transceiver from her neural jack. She fumbled for the door, pushed it open.

The corridor outside was no longer dim red, but bright with the glare of emergency lights. When she reached the first set of mirrors, she found that neither would open. She shoved them, then kicked them, but even the glass remained solid. She stood thinking for a moment, as the smooth, computerized voice informed her that she had eight minutes left before whatever self-destruct Solntse had rigged was triggered.

Sifte ran back to the room she had just left. The door was still standing open. She turned to the one beside it, and pushed. It didn't move. She threw all her weight against it, and heard something deep within its mechanisms give. She shoved it open, and stumbled into the half-light of Solntse's room, not far from Nikolai's body.

Aleksei lay pale and still, surrounded by the sprawled bodies of Tanya and the Opyekuni. Sifte shoved them aside, pulled open his jacket and bulletproof vest, and put her head to his chest. His heart was still beating. The voice told her that she had six minutes left. She gripped Aleksei's shoulders and shook him.

"Wake up!" she cried. "Lyosha, wake up!" And then his eyes were open, looking up at her with the dazed terror of a child waking, disoriented, from a nightmare.

"Sifte," he said, "my arm…" He turned his gray face away from her, retching, and only then did she remember that Nikolai had shot him. The sleeve of his jacket was soaked with blood, and she thought she saw splinters of bone at the center of the wound.

"Lyosha," she said with a mixture of pity and brutal determination, "I'm sorry about this." Pulling the belt from her trousers, she looped it around the top of his arm, and pulled it tight. He groaned, but somehow managed to hang on to consciousness; even, apparently, to understand her purpose. "Can you walk by yourself?" He barely nodded. "Good. Because you're going to have to get us out of here."

"Wait," he said, "Solntse. Make sure he's—"

"He is." She picked up Mila's body, then joined Aleksei by the door Mila had left open.

Through a red-gray haze of pain, Aleksei led Sifte back up into the cathedral. All the officials they passed were dead. As they burst out into the grounds, now thick with snow, the computer informed them that there was one minute left to detonation. Sifte moved across the courtyard and pulled Aleksei under the shelter of a heavy façade.

"We've got to keep going," he said, looking at her with glazed eyes. "The whole island is probably wired."

"We'll never make it off in time. This is the best we can do—so pray." She pulled him against her, held him as the end of the countdown played inside her head. And then the world seemed to shatter, flinging shards of itself outward in every direction.

The city paused at that moment, turned, watched: Anastasia and Olga fighting back-to-back to hold onto the last few feet of Troitsky Most; Misha at the computer, tears streaming down his face because he thought that he had not pulled Sifte out in time; a handful of Soviet soldiers on the street outside the Technological Institute, where they faced rank upon rank of Pomoshchniki; Sasha and Stepan in the fetid dark of the Metro tunnels near the Gorkovskaya station. Sifte's mind filled with the image that had haunted her since childhood, of a city flung heavenward on a pillar of dust, consuming itself.

It was only gradually that she realized it hadn't happened, that she was still huddled in a doorway clutching Mila's cold body and Aleksei's warm one, and that the dust was raining down around her was not golden, but black intermingled with the white of the snow. All around the city the people breathed again, as the world gradually resumed its familiar shape.

Yet it was not quite the same. The nightmare that had haunted it had burned itself out, fallen with the ash. The snow was already burying it, and the people, released from their long imprisonment, had already begun to forget. When Anastasia and Olga turned back to the bridge, they saw not an army, but a retreating patch of gray and blue like a fading bruise; and when Misha looked back at the screen, the computer informed him that his task had been completed successfully; and the Pomoshchniki by the Technological

479

Institute who hadn't died with Solntse dropped their guns and raised their arms in surrender; and Sasha and Stepan, emerging from the tunnels, were deafened by the cry of triumph that came up from Myortvograd as their ragged army finally broke through the wall that had subjugated them.

EPILOGUE

"You must therefore each descend in turn and live with your fellows in the cave and get used to seeing in the dark; once you get used to it you will see a thousand times better than they do and will distinguish the various shadows, and know what they are shadows of, because you have seen the truth about things admirable and just and good. And so our state and yours will be really awake, and not merely dreaming..."

Socrates to Glaucon
On the Simile of the Cave
"The Republic"

1

The first days after the Soviet victory were the most terrible of Sifte's life. The elation of victory soon dispersed into the oily black smoke of the fires they'd lit to receive the bodies of the dead. She worked from dawn until dusk cutting and hauling wood and carts of bodies. At first she thought that the sheer scale of the carnage, compounded by the diabolical heat and smell of the fires, would drive her mad. Back in the bunker she sobbed for hours, fell asleep to appalling nightmares, then rose again to face their reality.

Stepan told her that she would get used to it, and he was right. After a week of the fires, she found that she could forget the faces of the dead. After another, she stopped seeing them at all.

Terrible as it was, Sifte was lucky to have the work to occupy her. She could fling her anger into the blows of the axe as she split the endless rows of wood, feed her desolation to the fires with the limp bodies. Aleksei wasn't so lucky. He was weakened by blood loss, and infection set in after the doctor operated on his arm. For a few days nobody knew whether he would live or die. Sifte wouldn't leave him until she was certain that the danger was past, and even then, she spent every moment she wasn't working with him. She slept on the floor beside his hospital cot, clutching his good hand as if to keep him from leaving her.

When he regained consciousness, he was silent and apathetic, and at first Sifte attributed it to weakness. But the pall didn't shift even when he began to get better, and then she knew that Mila's memory was poisoning him. She tried to talk him out of his despair, but nothing she said seemed to make any difference. He spent his days at the fires, watching them burn with hard, bitter eyes. Sifte in turn watched him, her anger growing steadily.

One afternoon, three weeks after he left the hospital, as Sifte was piling wood, she saw Aleksei watching her from the other side, his face twisted with self-contempt. Her anger finally broke its barriers. Flinging aside the wood, she hit him so hard that he stumbled backward. She caught him before he fell, pulled his averted face around so that he had to meet her eyes. He smiled at her, cold and acrid. Unaware of the tears streaming down her face, she hit him again, and again she caught him before he fell. The smile was gone, but not the bitterness. The third time she caught him, he was sobbing.

Sifte pulled him into her arms, held him as both of them cried. After a long time, tears spent, they sat down with their backs to the fire. Sifte held tightly to Aleksei's hand. "It isn't your fault she died, Lyosha," she said.

"Isn't it?".

"How could you have known she would come?"

He shook his head. "There's more than one way to kill someone, Sifte."

483

She waited. Aleksei wiped a hand across his face. "And then to shoot Nikolai, knowing he was my brother…I don't deserve what she did for me."

"I don't think it's for you to decide that."

"I know you mean well, Sifte," he answered, "but you can't understand this."

"Can't I?" she asked evenly, but with an undercurrent of the anger that had made her hit him. His eyes flickered away from hers and settled on the fire, which mirrored his own restlessness. "Do you remember what you said to me that morning, before we left for the cathedral?"

"Which part of it?"

"You know which part."

He smiled sadly. "I was pretending."

"Pretending what?"

"That you might choose me, someday." He shook his head. "But I don't deserve you."

"Why?" she cried. "Because you aren't perfect?" She saw that this was exactly what he thought. "Don't you realize that you're the only reason I'm standing here now?" She drew a shuddering breath. "When I saw you and Tanya there, when I knew she was really going to kill you, I realized what a stupid, blind idiot I'd been to not see how…how precious…" Sifte's eyes filled with tears, so she didn't see the darkness lifting from Aleksei's face, the hope beginning to take its place. She struggled for a moment, then pulled herself together enough to continue, "You think you're unworthy, yet you've loved me honestly, you've never been anything but true to me, while I've denied it…denied *you*. I'm the one who's unworthy, Lyosha."

"Do you still deny it, Sifte?" he asked softly, reaching out with his good hand to move the soot-stained hair from her cheek. At this, Sifte, who had nearly mastered herself, dissolved again.

"Don't you know?" she sobbed.

He sighed. "I don't think I'll ever quite know, with you."

"Okay, then…I love you, Aleksei. I love you more than anything and…and…if you don't love me, too—"

"Enough," he said, and it was with the voice she remembered, the voice that wove in and out of all she was and ever had been, as inextricably as her own. When he kissed her, she knew that she would die before she would ever deny him again.

2

They did not give Mila to the fires.

At first, Andrei argued that it wasn't fair to give preference to her, when so many others had died just as bravely. Misha and Aleksei argued back. Sifte yelled, and then she cried, and then was silent. Stepan shook his head; Sasha looked at her brother with savage eyes.

Then Anastasia said, "No one will ever really understand what happened in there that day, but I do know this: Mila loved us more than she loved herself, and as much as Sifte and Aleksei and Misha, she's the reason why we're all standing here now. If we're going to honor them, then she deserves equal honor." Andrei took one look at her intent, impassioned face, and then went in search of a pick-axe.

They chipped the grave out of the lawn in front of the pile of rubble that had been the cathedral. They all suspected that it was the proper place, and when Sifte uncovered the tarnished tip of the weathervane angel's wing, they knew it.

Aleksei carried Mila from her temporary resting place in Stepan and Sasha's old room on Dvortsovaya Square. Sasha went alone into Solntsegrad, saying something about a museum, and returned with a robe that had belonged to a seventeenth-century princess. It was made of red and white silk, embroidered with gold and brightly-colored thread in a pattern of birds and flowers and vines.

Within its folds, with her hair in two long braids on her breast, it seemed to Sifte that Mila had never really belonged to them at all. She pictured her as a child again, in some otherworld far beyond the scope of imagination, free of the misery that had haunted her in this one, reaching out to a new set of people who needed her.

Only her friends officially knew when Mila was to be buried, but somehow the news traveled. Like Solntse's demise, her death had taken on mythic proportions. On that morning the sun shone in a flawless sky, and people filled every available inch of Zayachiy Ostrov. They crowded its roofs and trees for a view of the child who symbolized all who had died for them, and all they hoped to become in the wake of those dead. There was no ceremony but the perfect silence as Anastasia and Misha, Aleksei and Sifte lowered the coffin into the icy ground. But when they stepped back from the grave, and the others began to pile earth into it, Sifte found the words of Mila's favorite poem running through her head:

"And if ever in this country they should want
To build me a monument
I consent to that honor,
But only on the condition that they…
Build it here …"

She looked up. A pale-gray pigeon had risen from the wreckage of the cathedral. It dipped and swooped across the sky, then pitched down toward the city, straight and still as a crucifix. For a moment it hung against the winter sun, then it beat upward again, and was lost in the brightness. Sifte laid the angel's wingtip on the mound of crumbly earth. There were plans to build a monument later on, when enough of the city had been rebuilt to afford time and materials for such things, but Sifte felt that no monument could ever speak better of what Mila had been and done for them all.

3

In the month after Mila's burial, all the able bodies threw themselves into the work of rebuilding, and the irony of this was not lost on Sifte. Here was the symbiotic society Solntse had dreamed of, yet it wasn't made up of the intelligentsia but of those he had scorned as incapable of understanding Utopia; it wasn't built on technology but hard labor. Once the funeral pyres had burned out, though, and the last residue of resistance had been eradicated, people began to worry about the future.

The day the U.N. sent its first message, Andrei, still the nominal leader of the Soviet, called a meeting. It was held in one of the roofless lecture halls of the Technological Institute, open to anyone who wanted to attend. The crowds swamped the room, perched on its jagged walls, clogged the streets outside.

"The world will be coming soon," Andrei said, looking out at the people, "and if we want to keep this country our own, then we need a plan in place before they arrive."

"Whatever we choose," Anastasia said, from her place by Andrei's side, "we have to be sure that nothing like him will ever happen again."

"We need a leader, though," Misha said, with an irritable glance at Andrei, who was looking at Anastasia with rapt attention.

"I think," Sasha suggested, "that a leader is just what we *don't* need."

There were murmurs of agreement from the crowd.

"A country can't run itself," Stepan said.

"Can't it?" Sasha asked.

There were a few moments of silence, or rather the silence of a crowd, which is really a low rumble, like a faraway train. Sifte looked up at the moon's ocular, which peered back at her over the jagged line of a crowd-covered wall. She said, "I think I see." What she didn't see was the way the eyes of the crowd suddenly fixed on her, nor did she hear the gradual subsidence of the murmuring, as everyone strained to hear her. "One leader can never represent a whole people. Maybe no representative ever can, really, but a group would come closer."

"A council," Anastasia said. "A soviet."

"But not this soviet. Something like it, but chosen by this Russia, for these people." She gestured to the crowd wavering in the torchlight.

"Even a council doesn't solve everything," Stepan said. "The first Noviy Soviet was a council, and they were as bad as any government we've ever had."

"So," said Aleksei, "we need a way to find the best candidates to rule, to make sure we have the least chance of the wrong person coming to power again."

"I can't believe I'm saying this," Sifte said, after a pause, "but maybe we shouldn't do away with *all* of Solntse's system."

"Do you want to keep the ethnic cleansing, or the mind control?" Anastasia asked.

"The schools," Sifte answered, with an assurance that told them she'd been thinking about this for some time. "Solntse's idea of Utopia may have been a travesty, but his ideas for implementing it weren't all bad. Plato said 'we should make it our business...to choose men with suitable natural aptitudes for the defense of our state.' What if we assesses all children at a certain age, along a set of guidelines set out and voted on by all members of our society, to decide which of them will make the best leaders. And then, those ones are educated into the role."

"That's great," said Anastasia, "except that everyone has a different idea of Utopia, so everyone will have a different idea of what makes a good leader. We might be able to agree on a set of guidelines, but each assessor will have his or her own bias. It will be meaningless."

"Do it by computer, then," Misha suggested. "Feed the data into a program, and let the truly unbiased decide." Anastasia, along with some of the others, looked dubious, but no one said it wouldn't work.

"What about families?" Sasha asked after a moment. "You'll never convince them to give up their children again."

Sifte shrugged. "Why should they have to? The Institutes were designed to shield us from the outside world. There was no reason beyond that why we had to live there. The new Institutes could be day-schools."

"I think they'd have to be," Aleksei added. "A leader needs to live among the people to understand them."

There was another pause, while everyone considered these ideas. Finally, Andrei said, with a half-smile, "Sifte, once again, my apologies for underestimating you." But he was looking at Anastasia, and she was smiling back at him. Misha rolled his eyes.

"We'll put it to a vote, then," Stepan said.

Andrei recollected himself, and turned back to the crowd. "The first set of points will be posted around the city next week. The first ballots will be taken the week after. Meeting adjourned."

4

Three weeks later, the first council of twelve was chosen. Andrei, Sasha, and Svetlana were all voted onto it. Stepan and Olga had both been nominated, but declined. They had begun drafting a plan for the new education system based on Sifte's original idea.

A week after the council was chosen, the first of the foreigners arrived: U.N. soldiers and aid workers of various nationalities. People lined up along Nevskiy to watch as they infiltrated the city with their tanks and jeeps and helicopters. The foreigners looked at the Russians with equal curiosity. Few of them had ever met one.

The Russians' initial wariness evaporated as the foreigners began to unload crates of food and clothing, medicine and building supplies and fuel, and the work began in earnest. Sifte joined a building team working on a hospital, along with a group of British soldiers. On their breaks, the British sat together, speaking in English and laughing more than Sifte had ever seen anyone laugh.

Sometimes they talked about Russia, about the city and the people and their work there. Often what they said wasn't flattering, but Sifte listened to their opinions with anthropological interest. She knew that Britain would look as strange to her as Russia did to them.

Gradually, she realized that one of them was different from the others. He was not much older than she was, with a round, good-natured face and wire-rimmed glasses. The nametag on his uniform read, "O'Connor." Sometimes during the breaks he would join in the conversation with the others, but more often he read from a screen. Finally, Sifte's inborn hunger for knowledge overcame her shyness. She approached him with her rehearsed introduction, but before she could begin, he said:

"I'll lend it to you, if you like." He hadn't even looked up from the text. He spoke perfect Russian, but different from Sifte's. It was the language of the oldest books, of Akhmatova's poem. He paused, apparently finishing a sentence, and then looked at her. "I have a translation program." He smiled with an openness that was as foreign as the name on his pocket.

"That won't be necessary," she answered in English, smiling hesitantly back.

His face showed both surprise and embarrassment. "I'm sorry," he said in English. Sifte thought she heard a lilt in his accent that wasn't in the others'. "I thought...I mean, I didn't think that someone like you..."

"Would be working here," she finished for him. "Do the educated in your country work only with their minds, and never with their hands?"

"I suppose so, generally."

"Then what is your business here?"

He laughed. The other soldiers were watching them now, and grinning. One of them said, "Looks like O'Connor's got himself a native girlfriend."

"Be careful," O'Connor said. "She speaks English."

Now they were looking at her with curiosity, and Sifte was beginning to wish she had kept to herself. But O'Connor turned back to her and said, "Don't worry about them. They don't understand a lot of things."

"Why not?"

"Well…for a lot of them, this is only a paycheck, and they aren't paid to understand."

"Are you paid to understand?"

O'Connor smiled again. "Point taken. Tell me, where in this country are people taught to speak English?"

Sifte shrugged. "It was obligatory at the Institutes."

"Solntse taught you English?"

"Among other things."

"Such as?"

Sifte sighed. "It is difficult to explain. We were taught to govern, I suppose. That's the answer that will make the most sense to you, anyway. And where did you learn to speak Russian?"

"Oxford," O'Connor answered. Sifte had heard of Oxford. To her it was a fairy tale: an institute where the learning was not restricted, where the paths to new knowledge were endless. Yet the look on O'Connor's face when he spoke the word was one of discomfort, even distaste.

"Did you not find the right learning there?" she asked.

"I suppose that would be one way of putting it. As you said, it's difficult to explain."

"I don't see how one could be unhappy in a place where there is so much knowledge waiting to be uncovered."

O'Connor studied her, then said, "Wasn't there 'knowledge waiting to be uncovered' at your Institute?"

"Of course, but all of it…how do you say it…took Solntse's bias?"

O'Connor shrugged. "Well, let's just say that Oxford has its biases, too, and street boys from Dublin are high on their blacklist."

"Is it Irish people they do not like, or poor people?"

O'Connor shook his head. "Neither? Both? I suppose they like the idea, but not the reality."

"And this is why you are working with your hands instead of your mind?"

"You could say that. Look, it's time for our hands to get back to work. But take this." He handed Sifte the screen. The title of the work ran across the top: *War and Peace*. The words intrigued her. "You can give it back to me when you're finished."

"But don't you want to finish it first?"

"I've read it five times. You read it and tell me what you think."

Sifte nodded, and turned to join her work group, but O'Connor called after her, "Oi!" She turned back. "What's your name?"

"Sifte," she answered, and once again his face changed.

"Not Sifte Pierson?"

"Yes, Sifte Pierson. Why do you look like that?"

"I guess I figured they'd have you…I don't know, giving press conferences. Meetings. Whatever."

"Why would anyone want to meet with me?"

His look of puzzlement deepened. "Don't you realize you're famous?"

"What for?"

"What for! Most of the world has been trying to oust Solntse for years."

"But why?"

"Don't you know about the technological monopoly?" Sifte shook her head. O'Connor sighed. "Your Solntse had the most advanced neural transmission technology in the world. A few more years and he would have had the power to control all of the world's computer systems. He was already sending out threats about some master plan called—"

"Utopia," Sifte finished, appalled. In all her years of hating Solntse, she had never considered that he might pose the threat to a world beyond Russia. For the first time in her life, Sifte felt like a child.

"—and all by yourself, you managed to do what the best minds in the world couldn't."

"All by myself?" Sifte asked, her eyes unreadable, now. "Is that what the world is saying?"

"Well, it's true, isn't it?"

Sifte looked at him for a long moment, then she said, "You might have gone to Oxford, O'Connor, but you still have much to learn." She turned and left him gaping after her.

5

Over the next few nights, Sifte read O'Connor's book, sleeping only a couple of hours before dawn and stumbling through her daily work. At first, Tolstoy's Russia fascinated her for its alien splendor, but soon this sense of foreignness fell away, and it was the very familiarity of the characters and their motivations that entranced her. Their lifestyle was foreign, but their passions were Russian. Sifte implicitly understood their joy and sorrow, their open-armed embrace of the passion of love and war. She read certain passages over and over again.

"'Where, how and when could this young countess, who had had a French *émigrée* for governess, have imbibed from the Russian air she breathed the spirit of that dance?'" she read to Aleksei, by the flickering light of a kerosene lamp in the bunkroom they still shared with Anastasia and Misha. "'Where had she picked up that manner which the *pas de chale*, one might have supposed, would have effaced long ago? But the spirit and the movements were the very ones—inimitable, unteachable, Russian—which 'Uncle' had expected of her. The moment she sprang to her feet and gaily smiled a confident, triumphant, knowing smile, the first tremor of fear which had seized Nikolai and the others—fear that she might not dance it well—passed, and they were already admiring her.

"'Her performance was so perfect, so absolutely perfect, that Anisya Feodorovna, who had at once handed her the 'kerchief she needed for the dance, had tears in her eyes, though she laughed as she watched the slender, graceful countess, reared in silks and velvets, in another world than hers, who was yet able to understand all that was in Anisya and in Anisya's father and mother and aunt, and in every Russian man and woman.'"

Aleksei smiled at the rapt joy on Sifte's face, but he prepared for devastation.

When Sifte gave the book back to O'Connor, she said coolly, "I liked it."

He gave her the half-puzzled, half-astonished look she was beginning to get used to, and said, "How could you possibly have finished it so quickly?" Sifte shrugged, puzzled herself by the question. He shook his head. "So, you liked it. Is that all you have to say?"

Sifte looked up at the skeletal ceiling of the hospital, at the builders suspended on it like spiders on a web, and on into the fragile blue of the sky beyond. She knew she could never say all she had to say about that book to O'Connor. Even if she had been able to find the words, he wouldn't have been able to understand them.

Finally, she answered, "I want to read more."

"You can borrow the screen for as long as you like."

"That's not what I meant. We have screens here, and books, too. But not 'War and Peace.' I want to read the books we've lost. And I want somebody to tell me what they mean."

His round face was serious when he answered, "You're going to have to leave Russia to find all that."

"I know," she said.

"I don't think there's a university in the world that wouldn't be honored to take you."

"Even Oxford?"

He smiled. "Even Oxford. But if I were you, I'd look around a bit before I made my decision." He paused, then said, "Are you sure about this?"

Sifte hesitated. "Well—there is somebody I have to talk to first."

He looked at her closely. "A boy?"

She smiled. "A man."

"Too bad," he said with gentle regret.

*

"I already knew," Aleksei answered, when she told him what she wanted to do. They were sitting in the space beneath the lower of the intact domes of the Church on the Spilled Blood . They had brought up their dinner and a few blankets, and now they sat, wrapped against the cold, watching the sun set over the city. It was clear from this vantage point that two halves of the city were already growing back together. Solntsegrad had dulled as real life began to wear at it, and Myortvograd brightened as ruins were rebuilt and rubble cleared. Soon, Sifte knew, the halves would be indistinguishable in the dirty, noisy, joyful rush of a city which is loved and lived in.

"Am I so predictable?" she asked.

"Yes," he answered, looking troubled. "And no."

"What's wrong?" she asked, taking his hand. "Don't you want to see other places?"

His look turned to one of confusion. "Of course, I'd been thinking of going abroad, too. But I didn't think you'd want me to come with you, now that…"

Her own look was equally confused. "Now that what?"

He sighed. "I've seen you talking to him, Sifte. That Irishman. He knows so much, he's seen so many things…I couldn't be half as interesting."

Sifte's laughter tumbled down into the street below. The people passing by didn't know where the sound was coming from, but it made them smile. "Are you telling me you're jealous, Lyosha?" she asked.

He scowled at her, his eyes reflecting the last of the golden light. "Why shouldn't I be?"

"How many times are you going to make me say it? Okay, fine. I like O'Connor, and I want to go abroad and learn all the things I never had the chance to learn here. But none of that will mean anything if you don't go with me. I love you, Alyoshka, only you, nobody else! If you don't come with me, then I won't go."

"How could I deny the world their newest celebrity?"

They sat in silence for a time, then Sifte said, "Remember the last time we played Cave? You never told me what happened in your game."

There was a pause, during which they listened to each other's breathing, and the whisper of ice floes brushing together as they moved down the thawing canal, toward the sea. "I think you know," he said, finally. Sifte couldn't look at him, and she felt the blood climbing to her face.

"Sifte—" he began, then stopped.

She looked at him. His face was luminous in the first light of the moon. His look was the same as the one he had given her before she turned down his gentle offer in Cave's dreamhouse. This time, though, she pulled him toward her, and before long she had forgotten her fear, forgotten everything but him. And then they slept deeply in each others' arms, cradled by the cornflower sky, while the pigeons muttered softly above them and their city of light and shadows slept below.

6

Neither Sifte nor Aleksei went back to Russia during their years in America. They talked about it when Sifte's sister Nadezhda was born half-way through their second year, but in the end they both decided that it would be too emotionally difficult, too distracting. Though neither of them said it, both also knew that when they went back to Russia, it would be for good.

During those years, Sifte kept abreast of Russia's news, but she consistently refused the politics classes everyone tried to convince her to take, and later, to teach. Everyone assumed that Solntse's system had killed her interest in government. In fact, she avoided these classes because she did intend to take up politics someday, and she knew that she couldn't do this until she fully understood her country—not just the dark times it had passed through since the holocaust, but also what it had been before that. She was looking for the source of Natasha's dance, and she buried herself in Russian history and literature with an intensity that even Aleksei could not match in his study of medicine.

They kept in close contact with their family and friends. Anastasia and Andrei had shocked everyone by marrying right before Sifte and Aleksei left, and their first child, Dmitri, was born a few months after Nadezhda. Misha had taken a programming residency at Edinburgh and was considering staying on afterward. Sasha was hard at work in the new councilors' chambers on Nevskiy Prospekt, and Stepan had devoted himself to the care of Nadezhda since her birth.

Nadya was still too young to be much of a correspondent, yet it was she who lived most vividly in Sifte's mind and heart. She had a recurring dream of her sister, in which the child looked up at her with Sasha's dark eyes, framed by Stepan's pale hair, reached out a hand to her, and then, just as Sifte was about to take it, shrieked with childish laughter and ran off. This never seemed sinister to Sifte. It only meant that she had to wait a little while longer.

At the end of five years, Aleksei was awarded his M.D. with honors, and Sifte a Ph.D. in Russian studies. After graduation, the medical school asked Aleksei to stay on in their teaching hospital for his residency, and Sifte was offered a professorship. They were still talking about it in the early hours of the morning before they needed to make their decision.

Finally Aleksei went to bed, leaving the discussion still unresolved, but Sifte was too restless to sleep. She picked up a book she had been given as a graduation gift by one of her favorite professors, a first edition of Anna Akhmatova's poetry. She opened the book at random, and four lines leapt out at her:

"No, not under a foreign sky,
not under the shelter of alien wings—

I was with my people then,
There where my people were doomed to be."

The words drove straight into her. Like loving Aleksei or losing Mila, she knew that the answer she sought had never really been in question. Sifte looked out at the dawn breaking over water-stained church spires and smoke-smudged tenements. With her heart rather than her eyes she looked past them, across the wide, cold sea and the patched plains of Europe, into the heart of her own country. It beat with the rhythm of Natasha's dance and the armies' march, with the passion that sometimes caused her country to overreach itself, but ensured that it would go on beating.

Sifte saw herself with a pen and a vast sheet of paper. From the pen flowed the words of all the people she had known and loved, who heard that heartbeat and believed it was worth dying for. She would be their scribe, and record all that they had been and done. She would record the war and the present peace and whatever was to come.

But first, she got up from her desk and climbed into bed. In the street below, the first of the schoolchildren began shouting to each other in English and Spanish as the sun crested the tenements.

"Lyosha," she said, as his arms closed around her, "I want to go home."

In his half-sleep, he smiled.

Permissions

Every effort has been made to contact copyright holders of material quoted in this book. However, the publishers would be delighted to receive corrections, clarifications or omissions and will acknowledge these in future editions of this work. Please email permissions@snowbooks.com with any correspondance.

The publishers acknowledge the use of an extract from:

Illuminations (*Theses on the Philosophy of History*) by Walter Benjamin (English translation by Harry Zohn) © 1969

Selected Poems, by Anna Akhmatova (English translation by Richard McKane Bloodaxe Books) © 1989